HART ATTACK

A TITAN NOVEL

CRISTIN HARBER

ISBN-10: 1942236093
ISBN-13: 978-1-942236-09-2

www.CristinHarber.com

Published in the United States of America.

THE TITAN SERIES

Book 1: Winters Heat
Book 1.5: Sweet Girl
Book 2: Garrison's Creed
Book 3: Westin's Chase
Book 4: Gambled
Book 5: Chased
Book 6: Savage Secrets
Book 7: Hart Attack
Book 8: Black Dawn

THE DELTA SERIES

Book 1: Delta: Retribution
Book 2: Delta: Revenge

Each book can be read as a standalone (except for the prequel) but readers will likely best enjoy the series in order.

CHAPTER 1

COVERED IN DIRT AND SQUINTING against the smoky debris that rained down, Roman Hart growled into his comm piece. "Get me out of here, Rocco."

"Working on it." His team leader barked in the background about a new extraction plan. "Hang tight, Roman. Cash, get a move on, man."

Cash remained radio silent as explosions blasted around Roman. The vibrations killed, his headache raged. Worry churned in his gut that Cash's target was still active, and Roman hadn't heard a word from—

"Would help if I had some eyes." Cash's words drifted through Roman's earpiece.

Good. Still alive. Still throwing digs, not that Roman could help the predicament. Seeing as he was Cash's spotter, this wasn't the greatest situation. Another blast exploded. Roman took a deep breath, not loving the tight spot he'd found himself in, but, even more, hating that they'd come up empty-handed. The ground shook, burning ash floating from the black sky courtesy of some weapons-stealing asshole with a grenade launcher. "Come on, dude. Take out this guy already."

"Gimme a minute…"

Whoever was sending grenades Roman's way was getting closer. Another round of shrapnel and fire rained down. He pinched his eyes closed, waiting.

There was a pause in the blasts, and Roman checked his surroundings. Detonation spots encircled him, basically forming small craters. A few yards right or left, he'd be in pieces. Nothing sounded for more than a minute. His confidence grew that it was almost time to roll.

"You're good," Cash said.

"Took long enough." Roman bolted from his makeshift cover and made his way back toward the team.

"What good is my spotter if he can't say where the hell my target is?"

Roman grumbled. He *had* told both Cash and Rocco where the dude with the bag of grenades was, but at the time, Cash had still been on the move, not ready to shoot, and their team leader was too busy with the flu, trying to keep down his lunch and not bothering to lose his mic. But when Rocco wasn't being sick, he was shouting orders. Dude was good like that.

"Get in, get safe," Rocco muttered.

They had acted on bad intel, gone after stolen codes that could arm an older-than-shit nuke *that had never existed in the first place.* That was, if you read the news reports and believed reporters. Widespread panic had ensued among several foreign governments. Over a weapon that *hadn't existed.* So Titan had been called in. Boss Man stayed at HQ and Rocco led their team on the ground because a stolen nuke and codes trumped the flu. Rocco hadn't balked. They'd hit hard, though they'd hit *wrong,* and were lucky to get out with their asses still intact.

If Roman had to guess, Boss Man was in his element tracking the sources of the intelligence screw-ups.

With the weight of a mission gone wrong on his shoulders, Roman arrived to rendezvous. Winters was already there, Cash seconds later. Silent, they shifted in their boots as though each had the ramifications of the day's fuck-up running through their minds.

Rocco appeared from wherever he'd been bunkered, shaking his head and looking pale, though that probably had less to do with a virus and more to do with a stolen older-than-shit nuke.

"Bad news," Parker's voice came through Roman's earpiece from Titan HQ.

"Don't wanna hear bad news." Rocco scrubbed his face.

"Alright, okay news for now. Tagged their phones with a tracker. Soon as one of 'em makes a call, we're back in business. Roc, Jared's patching through to you."

Rocco switched channels and turned away. Seconds later, his face looked darker. "We've done what can do here. Load up." He stopped, putting his hands on his knees and hanging his head.

Everyone took a step back just in case.

Cash squinted. "Maybe a little R and R is needed before the baby comes."

Rocco laughed harshly. "You think Caterina Savage has any intention of letting the flu in our house? It'd be all, '*ay, Dios mio.* Spray down with Lysol.'" He stood, looking like he was going to lose it again, but then recovered and checked his watch. "Chopper approaching from the southwest in less than one."

As if on cue, the eerily quiet stealth chopper hovered overhead, making ripples in the late-summer air and stirring the dust.

Roman itched to get home. He dug his hand into his pocket and toyed with a small slip of paper at the bottom. Who the hell knew why he kept it, but he did. His fingers had played with it for hours on end, making the thing soften and roll.

"Let's go, boys." Rocco stood back, waiting for the team to load first. He had that look in his eyes, wanting to get home, and that had nothing to do with the flu. Winters and Cash hustled too. They were heading home to their women. It'd been a subtle shift as each of them went down that road. But Roman had noticed.

He thought about the woman who'd shoved the paper into his hand, promising it was only one of the many reasons he'd never get her naked. Thinking about that hissy fit over Chinese takeout, he couldn't help but smile. Beth was something else, and damn if he didn't want her naked and in his hands.

But for now, all he had was a stupid cookie fortune that said *Beware of short life lines*. It made no sense. Especially didn't make sense that Beth was using it as an excuse. Then again, when had she ever had an excuse that wasn't ridiculous? Each one was more absurd than the last, but that was likely because each excuse came with a slew of almosts.

Almost a touch. Almost a kiss. Almost a moment where neither could stop. But they always did.

The girl had a serious set of brakes when it came to him, and man, he loved a challenge. Swallowing her memory, he pulled himself into the chopper. Rocco boarded behind, and then they swayed, lifted, and moved closer to home, closer to her.

Yeah, he wanted her as a distraction from everything nasty that the world had to offer. He looked around, then noticed his serious lack of participation in the general post-mission bullshit as they all stripped gear.

Rocco groaned. "I need my bed."

"Probably what's in your bed," Parker offered from the safety of an earpiece.

"Ass." But then Rocco rubbed his temples. "You all haven't seen shit till you've seen pregnancy hormones."

Winters nodded. "Second that craziness."

"You two and domestic, parental bliss…" Cash grinned as he unholstered his backup M9 Beretta. "I taught Clara a few counterattack tactics she can throw down in her next game of hide-n-seek."

"Nothing she doesn't already know." Winters smirked at Cash. "Little girl is the queen of the playground. And that has more to do with the defensive maneuvers I taught her than your triangulation tips."

Cash opened his mouth, but Winters shut him down.

"You guys realize how you sound, right?" Roman shook his head. "Little Clara starting a kindergarten militia won't go over well with your wife. Tell me someone knows that besides me."

"I hear ya," Parker muttered. "Mia would kill his ass."

Roman eyed each of them. "Christ. Tell me someone realizes that you're talking about *hopscotch* or whatever instead of how RPGs were flying, Rocco's puking, or Cash taking a tight kill shot. Someone has to think of *something* besides getting home."

For a long moment, no one said a word. Not only was Roman a single guy not whining about missing the same-old day in, day out, but now he'd pointed out that they had lost their damn minds. All of them except Parker. Hell, if those guys weren't careful, they'd all lose their edge.

"Seriously, if you weren't reminded, you'd all get soft."

Winters cleared his throat. "Roman, man?"

"Yeah?" He loosened the straps to his body armor.

"One word."

"And what's that?" He leaned forward, planting his forearms on his knees and shaking his head at the team. "You, my friends, are whipped."

Cash started laughing. Then Rocco.

"What?" Roman narrowed his eyes.

"You can't name that one little word?" Winters leaned back, laughing alongside them. "Ready?"

Cash doubled over. Parker and even Jared chuckled in Roman's earpiece.

"*What?*"

"Beth," Winters said, slapping his leg.

Beth. Roman toyed with the fortune that said he would die early and not get lucky any time soon. She was a headache for him even when he was on mission a continent away. "Nice try, assholes."

But the truth was, soon as he had a chance to see her, Roman would be there, willing and ready to play their game, because it might not be today, might not be tomorrow, but he never lost.

CHAPTER 2

BURROWED DEEP IN HER BED with a down blanket tucked in to ward off her blasting AC, Beth fought off a nightmare. She didn't see anything. Couldn't touch anything. Just that noise. The same one that haunted her. The sound of rope stretching, spinning, creaking. She wanted away from it. Wanted to pretend she couldn't place the sound. But she always could.

Buzz, buzz, buzz.

Wait. That wasn't her dream. *Buzz* again. Familiar. Pulling her further awake. Oh! A buzz in the middle of the night meant only one thing. Her cell was ringing, and Roman was home. Not that she cared. Ha. At least he warded off the nightmare.

Beth threw herself out of bed and grabbed the phone. *Not* ringing anymore. Which was fine. Because she didn't care.

Buzz, buzz, buzz. She smiled, watching her phone blow up with Roman on a text message roll. So maybe she cared...

Roman: *You awake?*
Roman: *I'm back. Too exhausted to go to sleep.*
Roman: *Tell me ur not sleeping.*

She rubbed sleep out of her eyes and tried to focus on the screen. Not easy since the brightness was burning her corneas out. She didn't think. Just typed.

Beth: *hey!! awake.*

This was like high school—if they'd had cell phones when she was in high school—but really, it was like passing notes in the hall. The same feeling at least, and she was basically grinning in the dark of her bedroom like the most popular kid in class had noticed her. Though Roman probably *had been* the most popular kid back in high school and college, judging from the stories his sister, Nicola, had told.

He didn't write back, and waiting for him made her stomach twist. Seriously, she was a grown woman. A CIA spy. Not a girl pining for the cool kid to pay attention to her. Which he wasn't doing anyway. Whatever, it didn't matter, because even if he did, he only wanted one smokin' hot, wham-bam thing, and that was such a bad idea. *Buzz.*

Roman: *Let me up*

Her stomach dropped. Hard. Her mind went a million places. This was so bad, so good. She was excited to see him and completely distrustful of herself. But that didn't stop her from falling out of bed, adding shorts to her T-shirt-and-underwear pajama combo. Grabbing a ponytail clip to wrangle her pillow-teased curls, she ran to the bathroom, threw on deodorant, lip gloss, and lotion, then stared at her phone.

Beth: *Alright. But I'm rolling out of bed. No judgment.*

Why was he there? And why hadn't she asked that before she'd let him up? It didn't matter. No matter what his answer was, he would be in her condo in moments.

Wrapping a throw blanket around her and keeping most of the lights off, she wandered out of her bedroom, listening to the quiet padding of her feet on the blond hardwood floor. She could barely breathe. Her skin tingled, and her blood rushed in all the wrong—or maybe very right—places. Roman Hart did terribly delicious things to her, and she had never even touched him.

Knock.

Just one knock from the cocky bastard who showed up at her place in the middle of the night for no reason at all. She bit her lip. There was actually a very good reason she could guess. One day, she would lose the battle of ignoring their fire. Then she'd get burned. It would be disastrous, but not before it would be awesome.

Her throat knotted as she opened the door. He loomed huge, sexier than any man to ever walk the earth, crossed arms making his muscles pop, and he was staring at her. She tried to swallow and couldn't. Just stared back...

"Hey, party girl." His low voice rumbled over her skin. "Surprised you were sleeping."

"Oh, you know, a girl needs her beauty sleep."

Roman walked past her. "Guess it works."

Beth's cheeks heated. Even her neck felt hot. Using the blanket as a shield against his charm, she tightened it and hoped she didn't look as flushed as she felt. But it was dark. Another layer of protection.

Roman switched on a hall light as if he owned the place, left most the others off, then turned on one lamp next to the couch. He plopped down and studied her. So much for her lights-off line of defense.

"Did you need something?" She twisted side to side slowly, holding the blanket even tighter.

"Do I need anything?" he semi-repeated slowly, leaning back, a dark, sinful presence on her perfect white couch. "Sit down."

"M-kay." As though navigating a minefield, Beth took careful steps and sat on the opposite side of the couch, legs tucked underneath her, and wondered how his massive hands would feel running up them. "You guys got home tonight? Aren't you exhausted?"

"Ever been too tired to sleep?" he asked.

"No."

"How about too much on your mind?"

"To sleep?" She knew that feeling all too well.

"Yeah."

"So… rough job?"

Roman shrugged. "Other than some dude trying to blow me to pieces and the whole thing falling apart, not bad."

"Doesn't sound good."

"It's much worse than it sounds, but that's… not what's on my mind." His eyes held hers, and the look could've melted the Arctic shelf on a winter day.

"What is?" she asked, though she knew the answer.

"Games."

Maybe she didn't. "Excuse me?"

He laughed quietly. "Doesn't matter."

Disappointment bled through her veins. She wanted to hear, *You, Beth. You've been on my mind.* Shit. No, she didn't want that… Actually, yeah she did. Beth bit her lip, confused and frustrated and angry. "Why are you here?"

"You want me to go?" Again, the rumble of his words drifted over her.

"No."

His eyes narrowed in the semi-dark. "I don't want to go, either."

The one lamp didn't shed that much light. But it gave enough that she could see something indescribable on his face. Whatever it was, it made her hands ache to touch him. She inched closer, her heart screaming to close the distance, her head telling her to keep her ass in place.

"Why are you buried in a blanket?" he asked.

"I was cold," she lied.

"Better answer would've been because that's all you have on."

Now it was her turn to laugh quietly, but she said zip. This was their dance.

"I know, I know." He casually tossed up his hands.

"I still don't know why you're here, Roman."

"Like I said, I don't either." A half-grin hung on his face. "Just thought I'd swing by."

"At two in the morning?"

He leaned forward. "Why'd you let me in?"

"I don't know." As well as she'd been trained by the Agency, she couldn't look at him while she said it.

Roman caught her chin. Using the tips of his fingers, he turned her head to face him. Everything slowed. The room went warm, her body jumped to life. All she could feel was his touch. Espresso-brown eyes looked black in the dim light. His perfect, full lips were waiting for her. All she had to do was give him the go.

Beth let go of the blanket. It loosened but didn't fall away. His fingers slipped down the slope of her neck, to the blanket, pulling it down farther. She shivered. Her nipples tightened, and she wondered how the stubble on his cheeks would feel against her skin.

"Pajamas. You weren't lying." His hand abandoned the blanket, moving to her thigh. The same fingers that had caught her chin now walked along her leg, toward her knee, then slowly glided back up. "I'm here because I like our game."

"What's our game?" she asked too wispy for her liking, but it was out of her control.

His palm slid down again, and she repositioned, giving him free roam. She was such a slut, and a total sucker for strong, rough hands that could make her nerve endings sizzle.

"Party girl…"

She nodded as his hands went up, crossing the boundary of her shorts line, then squeezing his fingers and pausing. The touch, the pause, it stilled her heart.

"So fuckin' soft. Acting sweet, but I know you have a bite." He stole his hand away. "And you know… me. Our game."

He had her so close to saying yes to any- and everything without realizing it. She'd been lost in the gravel of his words, the heat of his hold. Want swirled deep within her belly. She knew him. *Knew* him. Cocky. Arrogant. And her best friend's older brother to go with every other reason to avoid Roman Hart at all costs.

He shifted, and her eyes traveled down to the bulge in his pants. Sweet mother...

Her mouth watered as her mind wandered. She needed him, maybe worse than she ever had before—

The scratchy, creaking sound of the spinning rope broke into her dirty thoughts. It haunted her ears, reminding her exactly why she wanted Roman to hold her tight and keep the nightmares away, as well as exactly why he couldn't. The sexy mood was immediately killed.

She looked down and away, hating herself, and decided it was best to stare at the collection of bland, abstract paintings across the room. They meant nothing to her, which was perfect. Yes, she could recite what an art collector should see in them. But she saw absolutely nothing, and it helped her shut down.

Seconds before, she had been pliable and probably panting. Now she was rigid as the obnoxious marble columns in her entry foyer.

"I should go." Roman must've read her all wrong.

"Okay." Because what else was there to say? Certainly not the truth.

He stood, wrapping her back into her blanket, then stared down. She didn't look up. Wouldn't look up. But then she did, and they were stuck, eyes glued together in the semi-darkness. She wanted to find the right words. Then any words. God, she wished she had the strength to pull him down. But she bit her lip and gazed away instead.

"Eyes up here, party girl."

Without thought, she obeyed, and guilt overwhelmed her.

"Beth... I'm here because if I didn't have another round of us, I wouldn't make it through the night."

Her mouth fell open. Finally, she whispered, "Don't say that to me. I can't..."

His eyes narrowed. "Don't want to play our game anymore?"

"I..." She sighed, feeling uncried tears burning her throat. Why was tonight so heavy? That stupid nightmare, that was why. "I need a truce."

He crossed his arms over his chest and studied her. If she could've moved, could've buried herself in the blanket and not had to see his concerned scrutiny, she would have.

"A truce it is, party girl." He leaned over, kissed her cheek, turned out the light, and left her alone to suffer.

CHAPTER 3

THE LIGHTS IN TITAN'S WAR room were low. The wall of flat screens was blank. The massive table where life-and-death plans had been scripted to the most minute detail was empty. Roman rubbed his temples, warding away a headache. Not enough sleep and too much Dr Pepper. Maybe too many thoughts of Beth. *A truce?* What was up with that? And her eyes... how they went from soft and hungry to dead. No matter how many times he replayed the night, he didn't know what had happened.

A snore from the end of the table interrupted his thoughts. Rocco, half-asleep with his head pressed to his arms, groggily looked around. "Where's everyone?"

"Parker's in his lair. Jared's somewhere."

"Right. Fuck me. I feel like crap." Rocco's head went back down. "We need to get this shit show on the move already."

"Why'd you bunk here last night?"

"Just wanted to make sure I made it to this meeting. Headed to Cash and Nic's tonight."

"Unless we go wheels up." Nothing would keep Rocco down.

The man groaned. "Which would suck. But the job would get done."

"Yeah," Roman agreed.

Jared's call for the meeting this morning had caught them off guard. It happened faster than Roman had expected. But that was good. They all wanted details. Needed them, really. Whatever it took to keep general world destruction from happening. No pressure. But as serious as the situation was, these types of deals *never* happened quickly. So a morning meeting was a surprise.

"Get up, sunshine." Jared walked in the door trailed by Thelma, his bulldog.

Thelma bee-lined for Rocco with a maternal instinct that Roman could never wrap his head around. Seconds later, Cash and Nicola walked in, followed by Brock, Winters, and Parker. If Brock was in the room, then the Delta team would be involved. That said something about the complexity and need for more boots on the ground. It also said that they were way, *way* off the books on this job—which tended to happen when foreign countries came to his country and said they'd lost nonexistent weapons of mass destruction.

Rocco mumbled a hey from his forearm pillow. Winters shook his head like Jared had. Parker and Cash laughed. Nicola walked over to Rocco and dropped down, mother-henning the big guy until he swatted her away to a seat at the table.

She squirted hand sanitizer on her palms. "I might be nice, but I'm not going down with that."

"Dude." Roman pushed Rocco's chair away, which earned him a middle finger. "Cat's not that mean. She'd let you go home."

Rocco glared. "I'm not bringing this anywhere near my pregnant woman. How many times do I have to explain that?"

Cash's eyebrows furrowed. "So you bring it to my place? Nice, man. Hope you aren't expecting Nic to cook for you. *We're* on a raw diet."

"Lifestyle," she corrected. "I need you to live forever, buddy. Food is fuel. Learn that, and we'll be all good."

"If I wanted food, I'd head to Winters." Rocco's forehead pinched. "But food's the enemy. So shut your faces."

Roman looked around the war room, thinking that Mia Winters cooked a hell of a meal. "Am I the only one who hasn't offered you safe harbor? Didn't know that was a thing."

"It's not." Rocco waved his arm limply. "They have wives that do the offering. No one here has manners for shit."

"Polite," Jared grumbled, "would be not puking for the next thirty minutes."

He walked to the door, opened it, and let in a guy Roman had never seen before. Wasn't Delta but was cut out for it. He had a Special Forces look to him.

"Two things. First, this is Montana. Montana, the team." Jared picked them off by name. "He's here from our Battalion buddies at Ft. Benning."

So dude was a Ranger. Solid.

Jared continued, "Montana knows the players. Uncle Sam wants his hands clean, but if we need anything we don't have, Montana's our go-to. While he's here, he'll pick up some Titan. Cash, Roman, he's with you."

They nodded.

"Hell, you may know his older brother—"

Roman's eyes narrowed, trying to place the possible new recruit. The familiarity hit him. "Bryce Richmond your brother?"

"That's right," Montana said.

"Damn." Cash leaned forward. "Look a lot like him."

Bryce came from good stock. Fuckin' good soldier. Having his little bro on the team had to be a good thing.

Boss Man cut back in. "Glad you all have met. Keep him close. Roman, you in particular. I want him thinking like you think. Got me?"

Roman nodded.

Jared pivoted to Montana. "Sit." Then he turned to the rest of the room, glaring. "And for the next item on my agenda, the cluster that was our nuke job." He stood at the head of the table, palms flat on the surface. His head dropped, then, when he faced them again, an angry sneer had replaced his normal glower. "Bad intelligence could've killed one of you, and I'm not fuckin' happy."

He pushed off the table and paced. "But you survived. Would've been pissed if you hadn't. You wrapped that defunct job, and now we're building off of *nothing*. Fresh start. Everything we had, we tossed. Parker and the rest of the fuckin' intelligence community has a new idea. Decent one. Who's selling, who's buying. After the shit storm yesterday, everything's gone dark. So we wait. We watch. We inch in. Then we attack and intercept."

The mood in the room became tense. A nuke was in the wind, and they were operating on a *decent idea*. Shit...

Winters leaned toward Parker, saying something that earned a head shake. The lack of expression on Parker's face said their odds weren't the best. Roman's stomach felt a touch flu-ish, though he doubted it was a bug. Potential terrorist attacks would do that to a guy.

Jared turned his glare to Winters. "You two have something you want to share?"

Winters emptied a container of Dots into his hand. "Nope."

"Share anyway."

He downed the candy. "Just wanted to know if this was a best guess or a wild-ass goose chase."

Jared kept eyes on Winters. "Parker?"

Parker worked his jaw back and forth, then leaned forward with his elbows on the table. "Complicated situation. Reeling from yesterday. We're not working with a lot, but we have assumptions that lean heavy in our favor. The more we work our new angle, the better the outlook becomes."

So a non-answer.

Jared slapped the table. "A location and a point of contact are all we need. Parker will get it. After yesterday, the intel we're using is our own or what we can vet."

Nods came from around the table, not that Jared was looking for approval.

"When the time comes, I don't care who or where it goes down, this is the team that will end this shit." He glared at each face. "Anyone disagree?"

The room stayed silent.

"Rocco, your team's good to move?"

Rocco swallowed away any hint of the flu. "Absolutely."

"Brock, Delta good to go?"

"Affirmative."

"Good."

Before Brock had gone to lead the Delta guys, Roman couldn't remember a time Jared had both teams ready for business. If both of them were involved, it meant they needed deniability. Delta operated behind the scenes in almost all operations. They were ghosts.

There was a time when Roman could've appreciated living off the grid. Back when Nicola was *dead*, during her jaunt in witness protection, or in the CIA, when he *still* hadn't known his sister was alive. How many times had Titan and the CIA crossed paths? How many times had he almost run into her? Until he did. Never should've gone down like that.

He tamped down a growl, that automatic reaction he couldn't control when it came to time lost and heartache. Roman rubbed his biceps, thinking how he would've eaten up Delta if it had existed back then... though it didn't really exist now. That team was completely, one hundred percent untraceable.

"Now, to the inching in part." Jared glowered down the long table. "There might be an angle that Nicola can work. We're already weaving in backstory through our contacts. Her cover's simple, if this pans out. She'll be a code authenticator for the nukes."

Because what was the point of buying stolen nuclear weapon codes if they weren't able to wipe out a small country?

"Nic, if this works out, once we get you in there, you'll set eyes on our goods, give us a way to trace the weapon, and we'll be positioned for a grab."

They all took in what Jared had said. The tension and stakes had grown thicker almost instantaneously.

"Wait." Winters looked ready to voice what was rumbling in

Roman's head. "We're going to let them walk out with the authenticated codes before we grab them?"

"No choice," Jared said. "If we position too close and they make us, the codes are gone."

Very risky move.

He zeroed in on Nicola. "You good being the eyes on the inside, princess?"

She nodded. "Of course."

Boss Man turned to Roman and Cash. "Brother or husband have a problem with that, speak up now so she can tell you to cut the crap."

From across the room, Nicola smiled. Roman wasn't sure he'd ever get used to her walking into danger zones, but for the most part, he'd adjusted his attitude. Mostly. Still didn't keep the worry away. He rubbed his arm, lost in thought about how life changed when he least expected it. Maybe one day he'd get the opportunity to make things right, to prove to her he was the protector and she was his little sister, but not likely. The woman was a badass, and apparently, badasses didn't need big brothers overseeing their every step or making up for lost time.

"Nicola." Jared walked down the room to stand in front of her. "As with every job, if either of these boys give you hell—" Someone who didn't know her might have expected Jared to say *just tell me, and I'll handle it*, but that wasn't going to happen. "Try not to tear them apart too badly. I need Cash on the trigger and Roman on eyes."

"Don't worry about them." She smiled way too sweetly.

"Good," Boss Man grumbled. "Alright. Off job until I call, then be ready to go. Roman, Montana's with you on all projects. Parker, find us what we need. Princess has an arms dealer to befriend."

CHAPTER 4

THE CIA SECTION CHIEF'S OFFICE was decorated with awards and commendations that no one outside the Agency would ever know about. Just like those plaques, everything about the building was draped in secrecy. Beth related to the professional decorations. Inside the confines of the CIA's overarching structure, she was an intelligence desk jockey, chained to an office job that required her to be calculating, covert, and calibrated. Outside the building, she fit perfectly into their designed role of DC socialite and consultant to the likes of the Smithsonian.

But Beth wanted more. She always had. Though when she'd been working as Nicola's handler, it'd been somewhat fulfilling, if not just plain fun, to play spy games with her best friend. Now that Nic was gone, time had stalled, and the job sucked. More than anything, Beth wanted out in the field, what she had been initially recruited for. She had more than a pretty face and an ability to schmooze with the DC elite.

An assistant popped his head in. "Just another minute. Sorry for the delay."

"No problem." She sat in the formal office and waited as the air conditioning chilled the room. If there was one thing she knew, nothing in Langley happened by chance. If she was sitting cold and alone in the office of someone way above her pay grade, then there was a reason.

The door opened, revealing the section chief that she vaguely knew and didn't care for.

Beth stood. "Hello."

"Miss Tourne." Everything on the man looked persuasive and powerful. Expensive suit, toothy white smile. No wonder he was the face the CIA put in front of scandal-hungry reporters.

Joseph Jasper was a public relations guru with a background in Cold War spycraft. So he knew how to play games. He was also someone who could take any headline the Agency found itself in hot water over and bring it down to a simple simmer—leaving just enough of an issue that no one looked for bigger problems, which there always were.

That brought Beth back to the most pressing question: Why was she here? He didn't oversee her division. Not even close. But Beth was ready to jump head first into whatever lay ahead. She put on her most professional, even-keeled smile. "Mr. Jasper."

He walked the long way around his office, making sure to pass all of his commendations, then dropped into an overbearing, pretentious executive leather chair behind his desk. "Guess you're wondering why I've asked you here."

"Yes."

He swiveled in his seat, watching her. "You want out in the field, and I have a spot that would fit you well. Interested?"

Beth's pulse jumped. This was the conversation she'd wanted from the first day she'd walked into a recruiting class full of wannabe Farm boys. "Yes. I'm interested."

Jasper leaned back, his fingers steepled under his chin. Their staring showdown lasted several seconds before he scooted forward, opened a desk drawer, and extracted a folder. With one smooth move, he slid it to her.

She didn't touch it. "What's this?"

"Project Gilgamesh."

This was really happening. Screw the party girl image, someone had finally agreed that her expert-level marksmanship and her ability to change disguises with chameleon-like precision was worth something more than traipsing around the boring political-party scene and listening for intoxicated diplomats sharing their secrets to an overly interested set of boobs. She knew her job and wasn't kidding herself. It was important, but it was also a waste of her talents.

Jasper cleared his throat. "You've done an exceptional job over the last few years. Infiltrating inner circles while still keeping your man in the field safe and well-situated. Now, I'd like to see how you'd do in their place."

More of a smile than she wanted to show appeared without Beth's permission. This was the day she'd been waiting for after a half-dozen official requests and more than double that in unofficial favors called in. "Thank you. I think I'd do well, given the opportunity."

"Then open the folder and let's talk."

Fingertips tingling in anticipation, she paged open the folder—and it was someone she knew of. Local. DC snobbery, aristocracy in full effect. "What's this?"

"Gregori Naydenov."

"I know who he is. I thought we were talking about a field position."

"We are."

"He's here in DC."

"Yes—"

"I was hoping for something different. Another focus. Where I could use my professional know-how."

"You do that now."

"I smile. I party. And I listen." She reined in any further response.

"All of which make you an exceptionally talented agent. Sometimes we find that women have the finesse needed to establish relationships. Men and women think in different ways."

The male–female argument? What was this assignment going to be? All her excitement dried up, and an uneasy trepidation took its place. Beth dropped her chin, swallowed away all the pointless complaints she had, and tried to regroup without calling the jackass a chauvinist prick.

"Mr. Jasper, if you've read my file, you'll see I'm an expert marksman, fluent in several languages, and have proven more than once I can slip in and out of cover without fail."

"And I think you are perfectly suited to use those talents, plus the years we've spent cultivating your background, to help with the Gregori Naydenov problem."

"And what is that problem?" she asked, biting her tongue.

"What do you know about him?"

She knew he liked the scene. And that the scene loved him. Attractive. Wealthy. Well connected. "He likes a girl on his arm and makes the rounds of the who's who events."

Jasper agreed. "He's a money launderer, money-wiring expert. His clientele are the illicit upper crust. He handles the cash flow for several of the most notorious cartel leaders, terrorists, and arms traffickers."

"Interesting." She'd heard that Gregori Naydenov also had an accent that made clothes fall off beautiful woman. "Where's he from?"

"He calls Georgetown home, but he's from the Eastern Bloc by way of Monaco."

Beth pulled one of her curls, trying to make the connection between very unrelated regions. "How did that transcontinental transition happen?"

"Naydenov's dynamic. He talked his way right out of Kosovo as a child and worked his way through Monaco."

Kosovo to Monaco. She'd heard his accent was hard to place, French sounding but not quite. Now she knew why.

Jasper steepled his fingers again, tucking them under his chin as though he had profound musings to share. "And you're also aware of his interests in rare art?"

"No." She shook her head. He'd never been on her radar. "But that'd fit his profile." Georgetown, society-page interests, working with big money. Rare art sounded like a hobby a man like that would be into. Boring but expected.

Jasper leaned back in his chair. "In 2003, during the Iraqi occupation, several thousand rare historic pieces were looted from the National Museum of Iraq. Items that dated back to 2300 BC. Some of the greatest artifacts ever discovered. We took heat for the looting, and I'm in the business of fixing our reputation."

Beth chewed on the inside of her cheek, trying to see where the CIA could be involved. She knew that the FBI and the military had worked on the looting problem, but not the CIA. "I don't understand your jump from—"

"For years, the US has helped in the retrieval of stolen relics."

"Okay. That I know." Given that the Smithsonian was her cover job, she had a working knowledge of the issues stemming from the museum looting.

"Naydenov not only knows where one of those pieces of art is, but he's buying it in an underground auction in two weeks. He wants a piece called the Sun Bowl. We want to know where it's been and where it's going before we get it and give it back."

"The Sun Bowl?" She tried to process Jasper's explanation. The CIA was involved in art theft? That wasn't right.

"It's a sixty-five-hundred-year-old Sumerian bowl. Apparently, it's the hottest thing on the stolen fine arts market at the moment."

"And you want me to...?"

Jasper smirked. "Be on his arm when the auction happens. If not his arm, his hotel room. Find where the other players are, provide intelligence to intercept—"

His hotel room? Indignation swirled with bile in her stomach. Her molars ground together. "I've worked on counterterrorism *for years*. If you could, please explain to me, Mr. Jasper, how years of studying the ins and outs of national security–worthy play makers equates itself to being a piece of arm candy to an art snob who washes money."

His smirk deepened. "Miss Tourne..."

She'd said too much, but it had all come out. Not that it mattered anyway. Years of filling the role they had wanted and it was all for jokes. The only way into a man's trust in that time frame was to let him between her legs. That wasn't her style. Not once had she gone that route. Nicola never had either, and Beth admired that about her. They'd always found a way around the inevitable.

But two weeks? To get invited to tight-knit meeting and navigate the obvious assumptions of a man inviting a woman to accompany him on an international trip? Shit, this wasn't what she wanted.

Eyebrows raised, Jasper cleared his throat. "If this isn't for you, say so. There's plenty of work to keep you busy. But if you do take this one and the job goes well, then maybe our next discussion will be about how accurate your shot is or how useful your working knowledge of Arabic would be."

She stared numbly.

"You'll be placed in the capable hands of one of my best handlers, and you'll be allotted security from the pool of operatives familiar with the scene. Given your socialite status, it would raise eyebrows if you were to travel to the Middle East without a bodyguard. Naydenov wouldn't suspect a thing."

A handler she didn't know and a bodyguard who would know if she wandered off to Naydenov's bedroom. Humiliating.

"Think it over, Miss Tourne."

Beth squared her shoulders and choked down the bile in her throat. "I'll have an answer for you by this time tomorrow."

Not waiting to hear any more, Beth rushed out before frustrated tears made her look like a fool in the section chief's office.

CHAPTER 5

EARLY EVENING—ACTUALLY LATE AFTERNOON—and the crowd of warm bodies surrounded Beth as she pushed her way to the bar. Nicola guarded an empty barstool, ignoring the drunken advance of some jerk who must've had a death wish as he breathed down her neck.

"Hey." Beth took her seat and gave an evil eye to the guy.

The neck-breather's smile lit. "*Two* gorgeous girls. My lucky night."

With one stupid move, he tossed his arm over Nicola's shoulder and leaned for Beth. Before Beth could warn the dude of the danger, Nicola elbowed him with that special touch of hers. His cheeks puffed out, his brow dropped down, and he doubled over.

Not turning her head, she gave Beth a roll of her eyes. "I tried to say 'go away' politely."

"Jeez. Alright already." The guy stumbled away. "Bitches."

Beth evil eyed him again. "God, I've had enough of cocky, assuming jerks."

Nicola shook her head. "I warned him while you were gone. Oh, and I ordered you a little somethin'-somethin'."

The bartender placed a shot glass in front of Beth and filled it up.

"Just you tonight." Nicola nursed the soda in front of her. "I'm on call. Nothing too hard for me."

"Tequila? A beer would've been fine, hon."

Nicola turned on her barstool. "Prepare yourself."

One eyebrow up, she asked, "For?"

"Cash and Roman will be here any second. A little liquid courage always helps you two."

"*Helps?*" Beth's stomach flipped. She hadn't found a way to mention Roman dropping by last night and how things had ended. Well, they'd ended like they always did. That wouldn't be newsworthy. But she didn't normally act so affected, and he didn't normally act so bold. Never, *never* before had a truce been called.

Shot in hand, Beth clinked glasses with Nicola and tossed back the tequila.

"Whoa!" She shook her head and grabbed the lime. "That burned."

Nicola's phone buzzed as she sipped her soda. A second later, she lit the screen. "Cash. They're in here somewhere."

A shiver ran down Beth's spine. While it was lucky for the neck-breather who had escaped with only an elbow to the groin, their arrival was bad for Beth. She had that buzzy, warm, swimming feeling that only Roman could give her. And she bit her lip, knowing she'd violated the only major life rule she had at the moment: *Don't drink around Roman, especially just hours after he'd slid his hands up her leg in the middle of the night.*

"Why'd Cash have to bring Roman? That wasn't the plan."

Nicola laughed. "Where there's one, there's the other."

"I know…" Beth toyed with the lime she'd finished.

"Oh, I forgot." Nicola scanned the room. "There's a new guy. Strict instructions from Boss Man for him to stay close to Roman."

"Good guy?"

"Think so. They've got some uber-military connection that has them all bro-ing out. They went through boot camp with the guy's older brother. I don't know. It's a guy thing."

Beth nodded as if she wasn't excited and apprehensive that Roman was nearby. Maybe his little buddy would allow for a distraction.

She saw Cash and Roman out of the corner of her eye. They moved through the sea of bodies. Both were big guys. Cash was taller, Roman wider. Beth would've bet that almost every woman that saw them stuttered in conversation as they passed. Some guys just got all the looks, and her one shot of Señor Patron was reminding her of that right now.

Shit. One shot of tequila wouldn't do that to her. Noticing his mussed, dark-blond, almost-brown hair or the intense espresso brown of his eyes that swept a room or even the simple way his shirt melted over his muscles, Beth could only blame herself.

She tried to center. Failed immaculately. Then looked around for something, anything, to use as a distraction.

Behind Roman was a guy who had to be their friend. Nice looking. Younger. But damn if she wasn't drawn back to Roman and his chiseled jaw. He even had a little dimple in his chin that, some nights, she might've sworn was her sole reason for living. Just to see that little indentation deepen when he smiled at her.

Nicola bumped her shoulder, breaking Beth out of her trance.

"I hate you, Nic. You know that, right? Hate. Hate. Hate."

Nicola laughed.

"Don't leave me alone with him."

She giggled harder. "I know."

"No. You have no idea." Because Beth hadn't gossiped yet about last night or her job offer. She hadn't expected Cash would arrive so early, and definitely not with Roman.

Roman's eyes caught her, and her body reacted. As much as she wanted to blame too much tequila, that excuse wouldn't fly. Not when her stomach somersaulted when he gave her the slightest hint of a knowing smile.

Nicola spun on her barstool, happy-squeeing into her husband's embrace. Slowly, Beth turned fully around on her stool and couldn't have felt more obvious if she'd had a sign above her, blinking in neon lights, that Roman Hart was her rock star.

Cash wrapped an arm around Nicola. "You two look like you're having fun." He pointed to the third guy. "Montana, this is Beth. Beth, the new guy on loan."

She shook Montana's extended hand. "Nice to meet you."

Montana made polite small talk, but it took him two seconds to head his own direction, and for that, Beth was grateful. Not that she wanted alone time with Roman. Ugh, maybe she did. No. Most certainly not. It would be easier if Montana walked his military butt back here. *He* could talk to Roman.

Roman pushed to the bar, leaning in next to her but not saying a single word. Not even turning to her. So this was Roman on a truce. She hated it. Until his arm brushed her back and she couldn't move. Each time he touched her, she was doomed to the same fate. Stupid, spectacular shivers where they connected.

Instead of embracing the rush of him across her skin, Beth needed to have a conversation with Nicola. Because, forget Roman stopping by in the middle of the night, how could she figure out this CIA job without Nicola's advice?

Nicola was still laughing because she didn't know the nightmares were back. Didn't know how Beth craved and feared Roman's touch. Nicola, without the reminder being shoved in her face, forgot about Beth's history and really wanted her best friend and her older brother to get together. Beth couldn't blame her. So much time had passed.

Cash pulled Nicola against his chest. "What's with you, sweet girl?"

Beth ignored Nicola's giggles and grumbled an answer for her. "She's up to no good."

"Ah." Cash shook his head, knowing what Beth meant. "Leave them alone."

Finally, Nicola stopped laughing and deadpanned. "I have no idea what you're talking about."

But from the way she said it, she knew her little plan had worked. Operation Get Beth and Roman in the Same Room was always a go where Nicola was concerned.

Beer in hand, Roman nudged into the conversation. "What's with the giggle box?"

"Take a guess." Beth rolled her eyes.

Because it wasn't even a secret. Nicola had made her intentions loud and clear to them both.

"I'm down if you're down." Roman winked at Beth, laughing a deep rumble because what he read into the situation was no-attachment sex. Not that there was any possible way for anything else to happen. Truth was, that was how he knew her—emotionless when it came to relationships—so she couldn't blame him. Then he teased and whispered, "Oh, I forgot. We're on a truce."

"Oh my God." She spun back to the bar and waved down the bartender. "Can I get a Sprite?" Next, she turned to Nicola. "I thought we were due for a girl's night. I'm calling that in. *Now.*"

As if Nicola and Cash had a secret mind-melding, wife-husband connection, they smiled in unison, making Beth roll her eyes.

"We are." Nicola leaned against Cash. "But how can I say no to a face like that?"

Beth sat up straight in her chair. "Easy. No. *No.* No."

"She's really good at saying…" Roman took a sip of his beer "…no."

Cash laughed, tossing back his head and spinning Nicola off her barstool. "Come on. Leave Miss Grumpy Pants to her Patron."

Sprite. No alcohol for her. One shot on an empty stomach was survivable. More than one would do some damage.

Montana walked back over. "Hey, guys. I'm out. Catch up with you tomorrow."

They all did their goodbyes. Montana hadn't said much to her, but he had a good vibe. Beth liked him. Roman and Cash obviously got on well with him.

"I really like that kid." Roman leaned back against the bar, reading her mind. "His brother's a tank. Think the whole family comes from military."

"Hooah." Cash raised his beer then downed it.

The bartender arrived with Beth's soda. It was a freakin' Sprite, her last-ditch defense mechanism. Tonight wasn't going the way she had in mind. She hadn't talked to Nicola about work, hadn't decided what she was going to do about the job offer, and couldn't stop leaning into Roman.

Focus on work.

Since day one, she'd wanted out of the confines of the CIA office and into the field. Now the opportunity was available... but it sucked.

Could she sleep with a guy for the job? Her stomach sank. Lots of people did, and what Beth claimed to want—what she *did* want—was a good-looking man she could be with and know that she'd *never* fall for. Well, she wasn't going to fall for a money launderer.

Her eyes found Roman. She couldn't fall for him either.

The guy was muscle built on muscle, corded and carved. Sinewy in the right spots. Even the veins that traced down his cut arms were sexy. And the way his smoldering voice, with that low gravel to it, carried over her...

Everything warmed too much when he looked at her. Then there was that deep twinge of guilt in her chest, reminding her of the scars torn jagged across her soul. Add in the fact they were friends, sorta.

Crap. That was the problem. She wanted Roman until she realized she *liked* him, and liking a man wasn't fair, much less allowed.

Beth rubbed her temples and sighed, snagging the lonesome straw in her Sprite and taking a sip. It was a little flat, and the straw must've had a crack in it, giving her lots of air. It made the soda feel funny on her tongue. One disappointment after another.

"Thought you were in it to win it." Roman settled onto Nicola's abandoned barstool. "What is that?"

She spun the defective straw around the glass. "A lemon-lime fail."

"What?"

She shook her head. "Nothing."

"I don't think I've ever seen you frown. Hey!" Roman hollered as the bartender passed, and pointed to her shot glass. "Two shots of whatever she was drinking."

"Sure thing, buddy." The bartender cleared Nicola's half-empty glass and left them alone.

"I don't need another shot. But thanks." She tried another sip of the Sprite. Blah. It wasn't working for her.

The bartender arrived with the tequila, placing both glasses in front of Roman. Roman slid one in front of her. "No one *needs* a shot. But don't leave me hanging."

"It's, like, four in the afternoon."

"Better than four in the morning. Least while we're on truce."

She glared at him then at the shot, hoping maybe it might jump back into the bottle. "No, I'm not in the mood."

"Oh, come on. When have you ever said no to a little drinking fun?"

True. And all that stupid work she'd done to make her cover believable was her downfall. "M-kay."

Without waiting for him, she threw it down, loving the burn. Maybe too much, but it made her giggle, made her arms feel warm instantaneously, and her fingertips tingled. She relaxed for the first time since he'd walked in. But she was just drinking away her problems, and that wouldn't do crap to help her figure out if she should sleep with a mark—

"Beth?"

His low rumble did something wicked to her, and when she looked up, she couldn't ignore the pull of his deep eyes. He didn't want a truce. "Hmm?"

His head tilted for a moment, then he sipped his beer. "Joking aside, you doing okay?"

How was she always so obvious to him? "Work stuff I wanted to run by Nic. Nothing really."

Roman took another sip, studying her. "If you say so."

She grabbed her purse from the hook under the bar. "I'm going to run to the bathroom. Make sure no one roofies my Sprite, okay?"

"No roofies. Got it." Roman helped her off the barstool with a confident hand around her waist.

He was too much to be around. The idea of feeling sorry for herself while sitting next to him was worse than the prospect of a hangover if she kept throwing back shots.

"Careful, alright?" His hand lingered on the small of her back for a second too long.

"Always."

The farther she walked from the main bar, the darker it became. Neon signs were the only lights in the back hall, making the area half lit. She wandered into the ladies room, stared at the mirror, and dialed Nicola. No answer. Of course.

Beth leaned against the counter, staring at a wrinkle that might not be so imaginary, and cursed *everything*. What she wanted. What she missed. What she could never have again. Plus the job. That deserved a lot of cursing.

Then she closed her eyes and ordered herself to get over it.

This was the deal. The job. She'd committed herself to doing what it took for the sake of her country. Patriotic duty. If she could take a bullet for the country she loved, surely she could get close with a handsome guy.

Maybe... Her stomach turned. Maybe not. No. She could do this job. She could...

She put on her lip gloss, threw back her shoulders, and decided to ask Roman to drop her off at home. She'd make herself dinner, do a little Googling on Gregori Naydenov and the Sun Bowl, and she'd take on the job. Easy.

"You've got this," she said to herself, looking like an idiot. Talking to the mirror in the bathroom wasn't her smoothest move, but it was the needed pep talk. She pushed open the bathroom door, powered out, and slammed into a towering hulk of muscle.

"Party girl. You okay?"

Well, the bathroom pep talk had been a good one until she had run into Roman. His eyes held her, and the back hall seemed too narrow, like the ceiling was dropping and the walls were closing. Her cheeks and neck flushed. Thick anticipation hung over them. And fuck it all, she couldn't take a deep breath. There was no hiding from him tonight. Maybe ever.

"Hey," she whispered before swallowing the remnants of her pity party. "What's up?"

"You wobbled away, thought I should check on you."

"I didn't wobble." She turned, but his hand caught her shoulder. The electric air around them stopped moving. Just him and her, and she couldn't break away. "It doesn't matter."

"Beth..."

She melted at her name on his tongue. He closed the space between them, and the warmth from his hard abs pressed against hers.

His thumb grazed her ear when he pushed back her hair. His lips tickled as he whispered, "Cash and Nic left."

She knew that would happen. Hoped it would, too, maybe. But that hope was pressed far back in her mind. Because she could never be with Roman...

He bent closer. His lips teased. Strong hands glanced off her shoulders, sliding down her arms. Everything about him was overwhelming. Broad. Rugged. Sexy. Just too much.

Shivers shot down her back because, except for the desperate need for self-preservation, she wanted Roman. Badly. And he knew it. Damn.

"You want to go?" he asked. His expressive eyes tested her boundaries. Their flirting in front of everyone was fine, almost expected.

Last night had been different, but she'd shut that down. Now, alone again, they were still walking a fine line of why the hell not?

Seriously. Why the hell not?

The inches between them were fast disappearing. Tequila had been a bad idea. Beth wanted to go with him, anywhere so long as it was private. Her chin tilted up as if it had a mission of its own. Heart beating faster, she wanted to hold onto Roman and he wasn't backing away.

"You are making our truce very hard to stick to." He pushed a piece of hair off her cheek and inched back. "I'll drop you off at home. Your booty-call embargo will remain intact."

"I'm not a party girl. You know that, right?" Having a good time was one thing. Titan knew who she was, who she worked for. They were supposed to know the real deal except maybe that she took her cover too seriously. Maybe she'd used it for more than one reason. A party girl life was much better than being a young widow who should've seen it coming. The memory made her sick, especially thinking of it with Roman wrapped around her.

Fuck. There was too much to think about, and none of it she wanted to remember.

"So we're outta here?" he asked.

"Sounds good." She nodded. Her lips tingled for wanting to feel his against hers. When he stepped away, she couldn't stand losing him. Her fingers grabbed his thick arm before she could think better of it.

Roman looked at her hand then at her. "Don't tempt me, Beth."

None of the reasons to stay away mattered when she needed to forget everything. "But—"

Roman backed her against the wall, hands crawling up her arms, down her back. His body was too cut, too big. Too much to want to say no to. She arched into him, on him, her body far too stilted.

His fingers traced her jaw, his lips so close to hers. "You've changed your mind?"

No. Maybe. "Yes." Thick air filled her lungs, rabid hunger made her lust drunk. The promise of his almost-there kiss teased her without touching. "I changed my mind."

He took a step back and bumped his fist against the wall over her shoulder as his head dropped back. "Fuck me." He took a shaky breath. "You've been drinking. Let's go before I become the asshole prick you think I am."

CHAPTER 6

ROMAN HELD BETH UNDER THE crook of his arm, guiding her through the parking lot on the way to his truck. She leaned against him, and the woman smelled sweet, which was something that he'd never wanted... until now. That made him smile because she didn't show a soft side. Sure as hell didn't own it. The attitude she had could go for days. But underneath her CIA cover, her makeup and fancy-ass dresses, underneath it all was fuckin' sweetness.

He didn't understand their dynamic, the give and take, but he did appreciate a good game. Still... knowing all that, today wasn't their normal. Last night hadn't been their normal. And for as much as he wanted her naked, legs spread and waiting, he paused on his asshole tendencies, tried to blame the tequila—knowing that she'd had next to nothing to drink—and decided that whatever was bothering her was his to fix.

He gave her a squeeze before opening the passenger door and lifting her in. "Twenty minutes to get you home. Might as well fess up."

She shrugged and scooted in. "Nothing. Just girly stuff."

"Bullshit, gorgeous." He shut the door and wandered to his side. If he wanted, he could find a few extra minutes, make the drive longer. *If* she wanted to talk, which wasn't promising. Roman took his seat, tried again. "Talk, babe."

She shook her curly brown hair and played with one soft spiral. She pulled it down, it popped back into shape. That wasn't how she always did her hair. When she didn't have her whole act on—the party dresses, freckle-covering makeup, and curls wrangled into a bun—she looked real, like she wouldn't break.

"Seriously, Roman. I appreciate you looking out for me, but really, I'm fine. Nothing more than a little drama to figure out with Nic."

He shoved the keys into the ignition, shaking his head. "Try again, party girl."

Her head snapped to the side. "Gorgeous. Babe. Party girl. That's not all I am, ya know."

But it pretty much described her. "Easy. I wasn't trying to hurt your feelings."

"My feelings don't get hurt."

Oh yes, they did. On the defensive and in denial. Yeah, he was more curious with each snarky-ass snap. "Something's up with you." He pulled out of the parking lot.

She chewed on her lip then laughed sadly. "How about this? You're right, but it's nothing I can share."

"Progress," he grumbled, partly happy he was right, partly bugged she wouldn't tell. "So work shit?"

Nodding, Beth stole a glance his way then stared at her hands in her lap. For all the acts that she played, for everything he knew about the real girl and the working girl, Beth wasn't shy or quiet. He slowed, rolling down the street, and decided to take the long way to her condo.

"It's faster to take the interstate."

"Yeah, I know." He pegged the cruise control near the speed limit and ignored his proclivity to floor it.

"What are you doing, Roman?" Her eyes flicked to him, then away, making unease settle in his mind.

"Waiting." The seat belt across his chest pulled too tight, and the tension in the air had nothing to do with sex and everything to do with stress.

"For?"

"You to spill."

Beth sighed in a wounded-puppy way, and another round of tightness pushed at his nerves. Stress and… what? Sadness?

"Can I ask you a question and have it just be… a question? Nothing to lecture me over or whatever. I'm just looking for advice or something. You game?"

He looked at her, chest still tight. Whatever was going to come out of her mouth was going to be problematic. He could feel it. "Yeah."

"Have you ever slept with someone for the job?"

He swerved into another lane. Honks blew around them. *What. The. Fuck.* His seatbelt had to have crawled up his chest and wrapped around his neck. Because that question wasn't what he'd expected. Or wanted to hear. The words reverberated in his head, making him jealous and angry and… fuckin' jealous, ready to kill people.

"What?" he growled.

She clutched at the oh-shit bar above her window. "Jeez, dude. I wouldn't have asked if I thought it'd get us killed." But then another sad-puppy sigh. "But have you?"

"Fuck me, Beth. You can't be seriously asking that." Palms sweating and white-hot *vicious* anger pouring through him, his fingers flexed around the steering wheel as Roman forced himself to keep driving. "*Cannot* be asking."

She shrugged. "Okay, so you have."

"I didn't say that." He nearly spit through his teeth. He wouldn't answer the question. Hell, he wouldn't participate in this discussion because no way, no how, would she need an answer or advice on anything like that. Absolutely not. Just fuck no.

"So you haven't?"

"Shit, Beth." He scrubbed a hand over his face, pinched between his eyes, and went back to his stranglehold on the wheel. "What the actual fuck? *That's* the thing you wanted to talk with Nic about? No go, babe."

Who did the CIA want her to screw anyway? He shook his head. Nope. Not gonna happen. No way some cartel-leading, terrorist-training, kingpin motherfucker was gonna stick his dick in anything sweet like her. Fuck no.

"You're supposed to be my friend, Roman, and I asked you not to lecture me."

He worked to slow his jackrabbit heart. "Let's just back up a second." Because if she didn't correct why he thought she was asking, Roman was going to go ballistic. "Why? The Agency asking you to... do that?"

"Just curious."

He slowed for a red light and nailed her with a glance. "Bullshit, Beth. What's going on?"

And if she said that she had to for the job, he was going to go rip-shit mad. Screw those Farm boys. He'd tell them for her how it was going to go, and it wouldn't be her riding anyone's cock for national fuckin' security.

"It's just work stuff that I have to figure out." Her hands fidgeted in her lap. "I don't even know why I asked. Ignore me. I need to talk to your sister, not you."

"You asked me because we're friends." His teeth sawed silently together.

"We are?" she asked, pulling at a curl. "We're kind of like almost friends."

"Christ." Roman growled. "Fucking friends. Yes. Write it down. Remember it. Whatever you have to do."

"I don't know."

His eyes were gonna pop out of his damn head. He tried to calm down. "Yes, Beth, we're friends. No matter this back-and-forth thing we have going on. Alright?"

She tugged the curl straight and let it pop free. "Alright."

The light changed, and he maneuvered through traffic. "You don't sound convinced."

"I'm not." Beth let her head fall back against the headrest.

"At least you're telling the truth. So try again. Why are you asking about sleeping with someone for the job?"

"Because I have a job opportunity, but I can't think of how to accomplish what I need to without, ya know, doing that."

It all came out in a blur of words, but he understood each one with crystal clarity. There was a strong chance the steering wheel would crack under his grip. He sawed his jaw back and forth, looking for sage advice but came up with nothing.

"Don't do it." That was all he had. But it was the right answer. "Do *not* do it."

"I—"

"I'm serious, Beth. Don't do it. You're better than that."

"You're taking the long way home."

"Yeah, I am. Deal with it. Someone has to talk some sense into you."

She didn't say anything for at least a mile while his anger dropped a couple notches. "How'd you know something was wrong with me tonight?"

He laughed, shaking his head slowly. Finally, an easy question. "Because I've been trying to get you naked for at least a year. And you suddenly just say game on?" He looked over as she bit her lip. "Not that I didn't want to. I'm going to live to regret walking away."

She released her lip, and damn if he didn't want his mouth on hers.

"I'm not just a party girl."

"I know. CIA isn't going to hire some bubble-head Barbie."

"Barbie's a blonde." She twisted her fingers in her lap. "I miss my friend. This would be easier to figure out with her."

"Who? Nic?"

Beth nodded.

Every red-hot feeling that'd been building in him flatlined and turned into something dark. "I know the feeling. You spent years with her that I never had."

"What?" She turned her head, looking up through thick eyelashes. "Are you mad at me?"

"No." He was just angry in general at a situation that never should have happened, and knowing that Beth had had time with Nicola when he hadn't… well, he didn't like it.

"Yeah, okay."

Roman ran a hand through his hair. "Just sucks, you know. You're complaining about not having her at work, or maybe that she's spending more time with Cash than you. But I lost her for a decade." He crossed an arm over his chest, keeping one hand on the steering wheel. "So I'm not the guy you complain to about a lack of Nicola time. Okay?"

He was all over the place, going from one extreme to the other. Changing lanes, he glanced at Beth. Her eyes were wide, but she was quiet. Silence was not a Beth-like quality. All because he'd jumped all over her. *Nice, dude.*

"Look." Roman blew out an exasperated breath as he pulled into Beth's super-deluxe condo high-rise. "I didn't mean it like that. I mean, I did. But you're not to blame. No one is. I just… overreact about Nicola sometimes."

Beth shrugged. Still silent. Not good. Seconds that stretched for years passed as he moved around a waiting black town car and parked in the horseshoe driveway.

"Beth…"

Her head titled when she looked over. "Hmm?"

"What are you going to do?"

"About the job?" she asked.

"Yeah, babe."

"What I have to, I guess." Beth opened the door and hopped out. With a quick wave, she mouthed, "Bye," and left Roman gaping in the drive.

Wrong. Answer.

All over again, red rage boiled violently in his veins. No way. No fucking way was Beth spreading her legs. He threw the truck in park and jumped out. "Beth."

Already halfway through the glass doors, surprise marred her face as he stormed up. "What?"

"No."

"Roman, seriously." She looked around, backing into the lobby with him following close. "We *really* can't talk about this."

National security issues be damned, he grabbed her arm. "And you *really* can't do that." They were so close he could smell her shampoo and a hint of tequila. It made him growl. "I don't want you to. *Me.* I don't want you making a move like that."

Her eyes went wide. "Don't say that."

In the middle of a deserted high-rise lobby, he ran a hand around her back, pulling in, her chest against his. He cupped her chin, thumb caressing her cheek.

"Please..." Her heavy eyelids drifted shut, and her lips parted. "Don't do that, Roman. Please."

"Why the fuck would I want to stop?" Her skin was silky smooth, perfect.

Eyes still closed, she offered no argument. Just a silent go-ahead with her lips parting farther. There was a reason he'd said no to her earlier. There was, but he couldn't remember it.

"Roman..." She clung to his shirt, fingers biting into his chest, sighing as his mouth lowered to hers. Such sweet lips, the softness of them was shocking as she melted in his arms, and a hunger that he hadn't expected came to life, from both of them.

His tongue chased hers, his mouth devouring every kiss. Her arms locked around his neck, and the curve of her full breasts pushed against him. Everything that he thought kissing her could be was a waste of a dream. Because kissing this woman was perfect fucking temptation.

"Wait." Beth tore out of his arms, pushing back. Surprise and want painted her face a sexy shade of blush. Lips kiss swollen, she looked like his fantasy. "I'm..." Her fingers pressed against her lips. "I have to..."

He said the only thing he could think of besides *give me your mouth*. "Don't sleep with someone for the job." He shook his head. "Just don't."

She took a step back. His eyes roamed her killer body, and in the background, the elevator dinged in the lobby. A couple walked by, but still, she didn't look away from him. She took a step back.

He took a step forward. "I don't want you to, Beth."

Her fiery green eyes welled with tears. Of the million possible things she could do, that hadn't been on the list of reactions to kissing him. One fat tear fell, and she turned, leaving him confused and standing like a moron with a boner in the lobby.

A doorman walked out from a back room. "Can I help you, buddy?"

Roman turned on him, wanting to put his fist through a wall. The doorman shrank back. Smart. But he needed an outlet. Fast. Roman's gaze tracked to the elevators, but she was gone.

Screw it. He had places to go, with chicks that wouldn't fuckin' react that way. Whatever *that* was. "No worries, dude. Just leaving."

CHAPTER 7

THE ELEVATOR RIDE TOOK TOO long. Beth would rather have climbed the walls than trap herself in a tiny box, but it'd been the fastest escape plan. Roman's kiss lingered on her lips. She could smell him on her, could still remember how he towered over her, pressed against her... How could she forget after she'd clung to his body like a woman starved for a man's touch?

And what had she been thinking? Flirting was fine. She'd decided that long ago because completely ignoring him was impossible. But kissing him? No, no, no. So bad.

A conversation with Nicola was needed ASAP. She wasn't going to answer, probably too busy ditching Beth and hanging out with her husband, but Beth still pulled out her phone and dialed. It was just as she thought. No answer. The elevator doors opened, and she stepped out, dialing again.

Come on. Answer.

Nothing.

Okay. New plan: stop the crazy redials and confess everything via voicemail.

Beth let it ring once more, ready to enact her new tactic. "Nic. DEFCON five. Red alert. Serious trouble and I'm sending out an SOS. Stop whatever it is you're doing with that sexy beast of a husband and call me back. Now. Please and thank you."

Beth threw the cell back into her purse and walked down the long hall. Why wasn't Nic calling back? They could go somewhere to meet up. They could grab dinner, hash it out. Everything would be fine.

Seriously, DEFCON five and a promise of gossip deserved an immediate call back after multiple calls. No dice. Instead of continuing to her condo down the hall, Beth pulled her phone out again and texted Nic.

Mayday. SOS. I kissed Roman.

Nothing. Beth growled and continued walking. Normally, the building didn't bother her. She could ignore the caged-animal-in-a-museum feeling. But nights like tonight, the place was too stuffy, too prim and proper. Too not her. She dropped her head, feeling like a fool, hanging out in the hall alone, and—

The phone rang. *Thank you, Jesus.* Nic's smiling face danced on the screen under "incoming call."

"What took you so long?" Beth all but screeched into the phone. "I'm in a full-fledged panic."

Nicola was laughing. "Oh, my God."

"Nic. Seriously. This is so bad."

More laughing. Even a little snort-laugh. "*Finally.* That's all I'm saying. Hang on." Nicola whispered off the phone—Beth's guess—to Cash. "Okay. I'm back. So that's good. You guys are finally over—"

"No! He kissed me. Like seriously kissed. With fireworks and sparklers and stars." She groaned, leaning against the hallway wall. Her cheeks heated just thinking about it. *Lots* of things heated when she recounted that hard hunger of his kiss. "But then I ran from him. Like fell back, stuttering, and *ran* from Roman."

Nicola's laughter never stopped. "Oh no, you didn't."

"I swear I did, and you better stop laughing. You know *exactly* why this is a bad idea."

Nicola giggle-whispered off the phone again.

"Nic, stop talking to Cash. This is an emergency." Beth resumed walking down the hallway. The more she thought about it, the clearer her stupidity became. "I've ruined everything."

"Don't create drama where there isn't any. Roman probably didn't notice."

"Didn't notice me sprinting away? After I climbed his chest like he was Mt. Everest? I am *so* embarrassed. Seriously, dying."

"Maybe this is, ya know, a go-ahead to start moving forward with life again."

"No," Beth snapped, annoyed that Nicola *did* remember the root cause of all of Beth's fucked-up shit. Not just concern about Roman having a once-and-done attitude.

"Seems like all the stars aligned. This was bound to happen. You have to move—"

"Let's not talk about that. Please…" Beth shut her eyes and remembered the stare Roman had levied on her, demanding she not touch Naydenov. She slowed to a near crawl before she turned down the last corner in her hall and leaned on the edge. "Plus it was a little more complicated than that."

"Yeah? How so?"

"This would be a ton better in person."

"Beth, c'mon."

"I got a job offer. But it requires... a little *something-something*. I told Roman. He freaked out and demanded that I not."

Beth stopped at her apartment door. A small package leaned against the door jamb. That only happened when a job had been set into motion. But she hadn't agreed to Naydenov yet. Was the CIA moving forward as if she had agreed? Or was this another event, another party where she had to smile and listen? God, she hated surprises. Unless she was the one surprising people.

"Beth? You there?"

Dreading what she would find, Beth picked up the package, unlocked her door, and walked into a polished, perfected, designer explosion of white. White marble, white walls, white granite, white in a million shades. All stupid white. "Yeah. Sorry."

"Did you hear anything I just said?" Nicola was dead serious. "Do you want me to come over?"

Beth crashed onto the couch and tore open the package. A red ribbon. A violent contrast to everything in the room. But it held meaning. Fancy dress and hobnobbing somewhere. There was a single printed word. *Now.*

Shit. How long had this been here? Whoever her damn handler was on this project could've arranged for a heads up. She thought about the black town car waiting in front of her building and knew there was a game already in play. She sighed. "Not right now. I think we're a go, whether I'm ready or not."

"So what are you going to do?" Nicola asked quietly.

Beth bit her lip. "My job."

CHAPTER 8

RED RIBBON IN HAND AND hopping into her blush-nude silk peep-toe slingbacks, Beth let the door slam behind her. She rushed down the hall, wishing to hell she'd had a little warning. Downing half a pot of black coffee and getting into an evening gown at warp speed wasn't good for her mood.

With no idea who she was to meet or who the handler was on the project, Beth took a calming second as the elevator opened into the lobby. The town car was still waiting. She guessed she'd find out the answers to all her questions soon. Maybe she should call Jasper and say something about his assumption that her answer would be yes.

She jumped into the car, and without a word, the driver pulled away from her complex. At least she recognized him. Looking around, she saw no folders. No reports. Not a single clue. They hopped on the interstate. Black tie and headed toward DC? There was the first lady's birthday soiree that people would kill for an invite to. Beth hummed. That was a stretch and had probably started hours ago. Maybe an after-party?

But they passed every hotel and after-party spot she could think of and headed straight toward the White House. Well, shit. Go big or go home.

They slowed at the gate for the Eisenhower Executive Office Building, far from the gate guests used to enter. The driver parked, left the car, and opened her door. She didn't have a clue what was going on and didn't see anyone in the late-summer falling night.

"Thanks for the lift." She gave a wave to her driver and walked toward the dark wrought-iron gate.

A tuxedoed man came from the shadows and took her arm. "Miss Tourne."

"Hello…" She didn't know or recognize him.

"Come with me." The gate clanged open then closed behind them as they moved quickly through the guard shack with a minor already-arranged hello.

They ducked into the staff entrance of the White House and continued silently through dark, narrow, low-ceilinged hallway. Scared to death her heels would slide on the floor, Beth tried to keep up while holding the navy floor-length sheath dress away from her feet.

The guy who had said a total of five words gave her a look and pushed open a hidden door. "Here we go."

They went through and walked out of an alcove. Suddenly, they were milling about in the White House and heading toward what sounded like party central. Laughter filtered through the closed doors.

Beth leveled a stare at the man who had nearly made her run while wearing haute couture. "Care to explain what we're doing here?"

The man pivoted, trailing his eyes around the empty hallway. "Naydenov's date for the evening quietly left due to a personal issue."

Yeah, Beth bet she did. Poor girl. What did they do? Threaten her friends, family, and loved ones? Poison her? That would be easy enough. The threats and actions that were lawfully issued, under the dirty disguise of justice, never ceased to amaze Beth.

But back to the tuxedoed man in front of her; she focused on what he was explaining. Gregori's date was out, so she was in. Got it.

He motioned to a Secret Service agent as they got ready to enter the room. "I'm a *close friend* of Naydenov and plan to make introductions as the event lets out. We've got about two minutes." He glared at her. "He hates—"

"To be without a girl on his arm." Beth wanted to spit back that had anyone told her she would be on the clock tonight, she definitely wouldn't have been making out with Roman. "I know enough about him to—"

"No." The condescending scowl on the man's face pinched even more, aggravated. "Naydenov hates to be without a *pretty* girl on his arm who plays the part well. He loves to catch time in front of the cameras and will surely have plans to hit several of the after-parties. Build that relationship. Work your contact."

Her eyes shifted, but he was right, whoever he was. Tonight was a job, and she'd do what it took to complete her mission. "Understood."

The man's lips flattened into a telling frown. "Look, Jasper mentioned you weren't officially on board yet. But we had an opening. I took it. I hope you're good with that."

"Jasper was right to move forward." Even though the decision had been made for her, it was still the same one she would have come to in the morning after a good night's sleep and a reassessment of her long-term goals. "I'm glad we're a go. Are you my point of contact?"

He nodded. "Evan Nathaniel."

"Nice to meet you, Evan."

That time he gave her a real smile. "It's nice to meet you too, Elizabeth."

The guy didn't even know what to call her. "Beth," she corrected.

"Beth." He tilted his head. "I understand you didn't have much time to get ready."

Understatement of the day. Actually, the understatement of the day was Roman saying that he'd changed his mind, saying no when she almost begged him to bed her. Then he'd kissed her. Her stomach bottomed out. Everything about tonight confused her, so she focused on Evan. "Not a lot of time at all, but I'm glad to hear I pulled it off."

His eyes flicked to the doors as applause boomed. "Ready?"

People filtered out. Immediately, Beth and Evan were surrounded by the who's who of the first lady's friends. Evan took her by the arm, leading her upstream into the crowd. Dead ahead was Naydenov. Pictures didn't lie. The guy had a definite GQ look to him. Strong jaw and great hair. Probably the kind that felt thick between fingers. Funny how, with all those perfect attributes, when he caught sight of Evan approaching, Naydenov had a crooked, boyish smile that was almost endearing.

"Greg," Evan called over like this was a chance meeting. "I want to introduce you to Elizabeth Tourne."

"Beth." She stepped forward, extending her hand and adding a little bit of sex to her smile. "Nice to meet you."

"Beth," Naydenov repeated in the beautiful accent of which she'd recently learned the roots. Her name sounded like a sweet caress as it rolled off his tongue. "How very beautiful."

Evan continued, "She's an attaché for the Smithsonian, and it occurred to me you'd have interests in common."

"Really?" His eyebrows rose. His large hand took hers and shook it with confidence. "Lovely to meet you. What's your specialty?"

Well, shit. This is where a well-planned operation would come in handy. The CIA had moved her on paper throughout the Smithsonian enough that she could claim just about any job, and she knew enough to cover her butt in most situations. But what would she focus on for Naydenov? She gave a look to Evan, who should've given her more information than he had. "A little bit of everything."

Evan stepped up. "Don't play your talents down, Beth. She

specializes in Mesopotamian relics. Amazing, really, to hear her stories."

If Naydenov had looked interested five seconds ago, he looked positively ready to explode now. His cute smile now beamed. "Is that so?"

And there was a smoothness to his accent. It made her sway under its power. "Not a very exciting job to most, but it's important."

Now that she registered all the attributes that made him a talking, walking piece of man-candy, she tamped down her reactions and got her head in gear. What the hell did she know about flippin' Mesopotamia, other than what Jasper had mentioned in his office? Something about it being the beginning of time, where civilization had started. Iraq, Iran, Kuwait, Syria. That part of the world.

His enthusiasm radiated. "Important, yes. But on the contrary, I find it riveting. The creation of man, the forming of the world's first cities. It's fascinating."

At that moment, she realized there was a *very* real chance she could work him over and *not* sleep with him. Gregori Naydenov might've been a money launderer for the worst of the worst, but the guy had a hard-on for history or maybe art. That was her closed-legged way in. It was far more important to be an asset to his interests and hobbies than it was to be a warm body he could screw before moving on. Time to own the history—art connection.

"Beth." Greg stepped closer to her, and she could feel a dozen eyes on her back—curious people wondering who he would walk out with. "Not often I find someone with the same interests."

No kidding. It sounded boring. But then again, not a lot of folks would understand her fascination with shooting guns or collecting shoes. But she did it. So to each his own. Gregori Naydenov wanted to have a boring hobby. It could be worse. Like a kinky hobby.

She sent a quick glance at Evan, and his quiet smile said more than she expected. Did he realize as well that she might have the ability to gain access without sleeping with Naydenov? Maybe Evan would be a good handler.

He put out his hand to shake Greg's. "I need to catch up with a colleague." They clasped hands, and Evan turned to her. "Elizabeth, will you be okay if I leave you with your new friend? I hate to run…"

Why did he insist on using her full name? "Of course."

Greg laughed. "I'll take good care of her. Might even pick her brain. I have a very specific project coming soon that I could use expert insight on."

"Thank you, Evan." She waved goodbye then focused on her mark. "Mr. Naydenov."

Evan patted her mark on the back like they were boys, then he walked away.

"Greg," he corrected her. "Mr. Naydenov is for my staff, not someone like you."

"Me?"

He leaned forward, a boyish smile hanging on a face that was used to getting his way with women. "Gorgeous and intelligent who I can share my inner history buff with." Again, the crooked grin broke across his perfect face. Crystal-blue eyes twinkled at her. "I like ancient pottery." Then the guy winked. "Don't tell anyone."

Oh, he was good. She could see why his reputation preceded him.

Greg guided her through the near-empty ballroom as the last remaining guests from the party left. They stepped around the scattered chairs and abandoned tables, then Greg cleared his throat with an impossible cool that Beth thought only Roman had. "Beth, I have invitations to every after-party there is."

"Popular guy."

His hand found the small of her back. "I'd love for you to join me, if you'd like to continue this discussion."

Imaginary fist pump because she... was... *in*. "I'd love to."

"Excellent. Shall we?" He took her by the arm.

She was familiar enough with how these things worked that she knew their next move. It was time to exit the main gate and walk by the paparazzi and news cameras who were waiting to cover the event.

Greg kept his hand on her back. They wove in and out of the milling crowd and headed for the red-carpet exit. More than a few jealous glances were cast her way as they hit the first step. Onlookers didn't know how he made his money. He didn't have a nasty vibe, nothing that made him seem like a dick. He came off as a catch, and if Beth hadn't known better, she'd easily see how someone could become smitten with the massive wealth and boyish good looks. Add on the accent and, yeah, she understood his effect on ladies.

"Did I say *gorgeous* before?" he crooned in her ear as they breezed down a walkway. His arm cupped around her waist as they hit the first round of reporters and DC paparazzi. Greg paused, posed, then headed for the next round.

She thought about his "gorgeous" comment and didn't happy-sigh from the purr of his words. There were no tingles. No tummy flips. Nothing when it came to him, and that might've been the most attractive thing about the guy.

After the last round of cameras, he motioned to one of many limos waiting for their pickups. "Ready?"

"Get me out of here."

He tilted his head, helping her into the backseat. "Don't like the lights and cameras?"

"What I really like is a chance to talk about something interesting with an interesting person. You, Gregori Naydenov, are an anomaly."

His blue eyes danced. "I could say the same thing about you."

"You seem real. Honest." She almost choked on her lie. "Not every day a girl meets someone like you."

"Thanks for joining me tonight. I'm…" He pulled back, studied her, and grinned. "Real and honest?"

"Am I wrong?"

Greg shook his head. "Not at all."

"Prove it," she challenged him. "Tell me something that shows that."

His grin hitched. "Something honest? I've never, not in my entire life, had a woman ask me to be real with them. They don't want that. They only want to scratch the surface."

Or maybe she could work the angle that, if he wanted her, she wasn't going to be a piece of ass he could do on the way to a party and drop off at the end of the night. Either way, she wasn't spreading her lips or her legs for him. "Who are the women you've been hanging out with? Lord."

He laughed, his eyes tightening on her. "Vapid girls offering blow jobs in place of a real conversation."

She laughed. "That's about as real of a thing as I've heard all night." And it probably was. A woman knew when a man was interested. *Really* interested. Gregori Naydenov was. "What's your angle with me?"

"No angle. Never an angle." He leaned back in his seat. "Just after tonight, and lately… it just gets old. That's all. I plan to call Evan and thank him for introducing us."

"You've known me for thirty minutes, Greg. I should warn you, despite your being absurdly handsome and disgustingly wealthy, that kind of candor sets off warning bells for a girl. *Wanting to thank someone for introducing us?* You're going to make me blush."

"Wow. With each passing second and every oddly negative compliment, I'm enjoying myself more than I have in a long time."

The driver said something to Greg and the partition rose. They pulled into traffic. For several seconds, Beth wondered if, despite his words, he'd get her in closed quarters and reevaluate how much more enjoyable a blow job would be than discussing ancient relics.

But he didn't. Instead, he pulled out his cell and swiped the screen several times. A moment later, he held it for her. "Egypt."

There was Greg with two men she didn't recognize.

"My brothers."

His brothers? What? This guy was opening up in a major way, and they barely knew each other. He sure as hell wasn't acting like an international terrorist money launderer. "Vacation?"

"Yes." He grinned. "Though I didn't use that word. Vacation sounds dirty, lazy to me. I'm an entrepreneur. So, if I'm not working, I must be dying. But… this was a fun time. With my brothers who I hadn't seen in years."

Why was he passing on such personal information? "Have you been drinking?" She raised an eyebrow. "Or maybe lost your mind?"

"Why?" His brow pinched.

"You don't know me. I could sell all these tidbits to some stock tips company—*Gregori Naydenov retiring from wherever it is you work*—and make some serious dough off of it."

"Are you going to?"

She shook her head. "No."

"I didn't think so."

"But you don't know me."

"True. But I like you. And I have no idea why other than we have a hobby in common. Doesn't happen too often."

"Why not?" she asked.

He shrugged, scrolling through the pictures and showing her various behind-the-scenes, big-money access to museums in Egypt. "People always want something from me. And you? I can't see that you want anything."

Her stomach turned. She wanted a whole lot from him. His network. His accounts. Knowledge on how he laundered funds and hid wire transactions. But it was the first time she'd ever noticed a twinge of guilt, knowing that she was going to play him. "I'm very needy, just so you've been warned."

His eyes shone. "You're also very beautiful. I bet you get whatever you need."

Her mouth gaped. "I…"

He held her gaze then dropped his eyes to the phone. "And look at this one…"

He told stories on the rest of the pictures in his phone, and for the first time ever, she questioned whether the Agency had gotten it wrong. This was a nice guy. Charming, well spoken, talked openly about his family, his job running what looked like a very legitimate, extraordinarily profitable company. This was not what she'd expected.

Unable to explain the urge, she had no interest in hitting the after-parties and had a wild idea that could keep her mind occupied while maybe learning more than she would from party small talk. "I have an idea, but this is going to sound far more forward than it is."

His crooked smile flashed. "Interesting... an offer that's not what it seems. Shoot."

"We skip the after-parties, and I show you something that you will love."

"Keep talking," he encouraged, but she knew she had him. "At the Smithsonian?"

She shook her head. "At my condo."

Beth watched his face react slightly. Surprise with a hint of... what? Something else.

"See, Greg? You want to read into it. But I promise this has to do with work, not anything else." Then she whispered, laughing and teasing, "Like blow jobs."

His laughter mingled with hers. "Definitely the most real person I've met in DC."

Ha, ha. Maybe the Agency had trained her well and it was just Roman she couldn't get one over on.

CHAPTER 9

GREG POCKETED HIS PHONE AND gave the driver the change in plans. It was refreshing to skip the stodgy after-parties where he behaved the same way, did the same thing, and saw the same people every time. The humdrum was killing him.

Then there was Beth. He couldn't take his eyes off her. She was nothing like his normal, and everything that could disarm him. Sweet, smart, and with curves that made him itch to get out of his tux.

She was different. The women he knew swirled around DC, trying to find their next husband or land a photo in the *Post*'s Style section. Truth was, he thought he'd seen Beth at other events. Now he regretted not being introduced before.

He could be himself, talk about interests without her eyes glazing over, and she made him laugh. A real, honest belly laugh. He hadn't known he had it in him anymore.

Maybe life had been too easy. That was certainly the case with women. He could joke about a blow job and his date-for-the-night would drop to her knees, almost instantaneously. But not Beth. She made fun of it. Almost making fun of *him* and that was… fun.

"How'd you get started?" he asked.

"At my job?"

He was more interested in her answer than he should be.

She hummed and bit her lip, maybe lost in thought. It didn't seem she meant the move to be provocative, but hell…

"Family tragedy. I lost someone who meant a lot. I worked for a company that took care of their own, and I was passionate about what I did. When life turned to shit, I threw my heart into it. Learned everything I could. Looked for every opportunity to excel. Then there was an opening, and I took it—"

"The opening for what?"

Her gaze drifted over him. "A project I wasn't sure I could do at first. Didn't know how to handle it. But… I figured out a way, I think." She shrugged. "What about you?" She asked as if she cared about the answer.

He smiled. "I'm boring. I like numbers the way I like history. It all tells a story; you just have to know where to look for it."

"And what kind of story are you looking for?"

He leaned back, rubbing a hand over his chin. "Good question."

"Whatever story it is, it seems like you've done well."

He nodded. "It's nice to be compensated for what you enjoy."

"So you… like what you do?"

Wasn't that the question he'd been struggling with for months? The answer was no. It had been no for a while. When he thought about where he'd come from, how he'd clawed his way to the top, it seemed to make sense—working with the dirtiest pigs on earth also meant earning the best paycheck possible. Coming from where he did, sharing stale loaves of bread for a week with his family just to survive, it hadn't seemed morally repugnant to launder money. But now it made his skin crawl. He was literally helping the world meet its demise, holding the hands of terrorists, kingpins, and traffickers. But maybe his skin was crawling because he needed a little bump. His mouth watered for a little bit of blow.

Greg eyed Beth. She didn't seem the type who liked cocaine. He normally had a good eye for these things. Maybe he'd keep that pastime to himself for now.

So he focused his mind. Did he like his job? No, he was a sellout to the highest buyer. But it had taken him years to realize that, and that realization meant he had evolved. A poor, third-world street kid who had become a financial king, attending presidential parties and earning the trust of gorgeous, well-off women who trusted him enough to be with privately.

He could retire tomorrow and be better than fine. Greg rubbed his nose, bouncing back and forth between hating himself and wanting nothing more than to bury his head in beautiful distractions. Art, relics, history.

And maybe even Beth.

The night was still young, and Roman didn't have to report to Titan HQ in the morning. Good, because he couldn't get Beth, or her stupid job, out of his mind. Seriously, the girl was going to spread her legs because the Agency said so? Screw that. Just fuck that. No way would he care about her stupid-ass mistakes. His blood boiled. Frustration wrapped its ugly hand around his neck and squeezed until he couldn't breathe.

Forget that kiss. And the tears.

Forget the damn girl.

Didn't work, and his truck had a mind of its own, because Roman looked up and the sign for the Pour House hung across the street. That bar was his comfort blanket. He could drink some beer, shoot some pool, and forget about Beth.

A quick glance through the parking lot showed zero cars he recognized. Pressure still built in his chest. Going home wasn't going to happen. He gritted his teeth. Drinking some beers it was. He parked and headed in through the brisk night. Wind swirled around him as he pulled the heavy door open.

Neon lights and barroom noise soothed his soul. The familiarity comforted him even though the only recognizable face was the regular guy behind the counter. He maneuvered to a barstool and appreciated the simple fuckin' fact that no one he talked to, no one he brought home, nothing in this damn bar would *cry* on him.

"Hey. What's your poison?" The bartender threw a napkin onto the well-worn bar. He glanced over Roman's shoulder. "That was fast. Good-lookin' trouble heading for you. On your six."

Roman raised his eyebrows. "Yeah?" Trouble, good looking or not, wasn't on the agenda. Drinks and attitude problems were. "Give me a bourbon."

The barkeep tilted his head. "The brunette with fake tits from last week."

The woman who'd spent most the night trying to milk him for free drinks. Well, that wasn't all she'd been trying for, but Roman hadn't taken the bait. No reason, really. A tight body and a pretty face. She screamed no strings and was exactly what he wanted, but he hadn't done anything about it. Tonight wouldn't be different. As worked up as he was over Beth, the idea of another woman's lips where hers had just been? He gnashed his molars.

Not worth the aggravation. Or worth ruining the kiss he could still feel all the way to his groin. "Better make it a double."

"Roman." Hands rested on his shoulders, and the brunette's voice said she wanted to pick up where they'd left off.

He turned around. Yeah, Fake Tits was still very attractive, very much looking for a good time. Her hands ran the width of his shoulders and back to his neck. He shrugged away. "Hey, you…"

Shit, what was her name?

"Ashleigh."

Right. Ashleigh. "Yeah, I know."

She laughed, shaking out her hair. "Okay."

Hovering, waiting for an invitation, he almost wanted this to be harder. If he had to work for it, maybe he'd want someone besides Beth—who made him work his ass off, then ignored him. He growled to himself and patted the empty barstool next to him. "Want a beer?"

"I'll take an appletini."

Of course. "Sure thing."

Beaming and shoving her tits up, she sat down. Their friendly, nosy bartender headed off with their order.

Ashleigh made endless chatter while Roman's mind was stuck on Beth. When he wasn't reliving the seconds—and feeling like a pussy for doing so—he stared numbly at a television hanging over the bar. Every few minutes he'd nod, agree, whatever, and Fake Tits would continue. She took it as a thumbs-up for her to run her hands over every part of his chest and arms. The more she did it, the less he liked her, and that wasn't saying much. Roman's phone rang on the bar, Nicola's picture popping up on the screen. Ashleigh unabashedly eyed it, and that just bugged the shit out of him.

"My sister," he said, not that he cared what Ashleigh thought.

The visible irritation washed away. "No problem."

Right. He accepted the call. "What's up, Nic?"

"You kissed her! You *kissed* her!" Nicola squealed. "Seriously, Roman. You have got to tell me—"

"Come on now. If you want the gossip, call your girl."

"I'm not trying to gossip. Just... I don't know. I'm excited. *Finally.*"

He laughed more at the irony than at her reaction. "Nothing to get excited over. You know Beth and me. Just a little bit of fun that got out of control. But no joke, I'm not talking to you about her."

Ashleigh cleared her throat, the irritation back and upped a few pissed-off points.

"Where are you?" Nic asked.

"Pour House."

She groaned. "Why?"

"Needed to clear my mind."

"Don't be a piece of shit, Roman. Come on."

"Hey, nothing going on here. Just grabbing a beer."

Ashleigh smiled, putting her hand on his forearm. "Can we get out of here?"

"Hey!" Nicola apparently had heard. "Who was that?"

He glared at Ashleigh. "Nothing. No one—"

Women were manipulative. Well, sometimes. All the times? Well, not Nicola. Maybe not Beth. A vivid flashback of her fingers clawing into him, then her teary eyes. If that wasn't manipulation, who knew what it was.

"Roman Hart, I swear if you are grabbing some piece of strange hours after you kissed Beth, I will personally find you *tonight* and punch you in the throat."

He rubbed his eyes. "Easy there, killer."

"I'm serious. Don't hurt her."

"Her? Beth?" He cackled. "Maybe you better get the whole story from your girl before you go around threatening throat punches."

Nicola stayed quiet long enough for Ashleigh to take two long sips off her light-green martini. Then Nic sighed. "Between you, the Agency, and her past, she has a lot going on."

That made him laugh again. "I think you're wrong. Well, at least with me."

"You like her."

"Of course I do. She's a good girl. She's your friend, always around. Doesn't mean anything more than that."

Ashleigh rolled her eyes. "Are you almost done?"

Nicola growled. "Tell whoever that is to hit the road."

"Calm down, Nic."

"Look, Roman. There's a lot you don't know about Beth."

"Doubt that. Everything I've seen has been straightforward." Except that wasn't true at all, and if there was more beneath the surface, not only did he believe that, but he wanted to dig and find out what.

"Think what you want, big brother. You don't know all."

"I know enough." Not even close. He sipped his beer, ignored Ashleigh, and focused on the television. The eleven o'clock news was more interesting than both Ashleigh and Nicola. At least less work than them.

"Cocky, cocky," Nicola chided. She had to be shaking her head. "Alright, look. I just wanted to say I think you two are a good thing."

The television cut to footage from the White House, some big political shindig. If they could skip that crap and get to the sports—

Wait. What did he just see?

Blood rushed in his ears, and his pulse pounded in his neck. He put the phone down, narrowing his eyes. Beth? In a fancy dress on some dick's arm? Roman had dropped her off at her condo a couple of hours ago. So that was… impossible.

Absolutely fuckin' impossible.

"Hey!" He flagged the bartender. "You got DVR in this joint? Back that up fifteen, thirty seconds."

The bartender looked at the television, picked up the remote, and rewound. "You want the news?"

"Yeah, man. Do it now. Back it up a minute or whatever, until you see—stop, stop. Hit play."

Sure enough, Beth was on a douchebag's arm, smiling as she exited the White House. Roman pushed off his barstool, leaning toward the television as though maybe he was hallucinating. Nope. That was Beth, and the dude screamed piece of shit, money-coated dick.

And the way she smiled? Fuck. That. Roman wanted to tear her off of him.

Nicola called out. "Roman? Hello?"

He picked the phone back up. "She's at the goddamn White House? And who the hell is that guy?"

"What?" Nicola asked.

"Who. Is. He?" Roman growled into the phone. Screw that. He'd find out on his own. "Never mind. Talk to you later."

"What are you—?"

Roman hung up and glared at the screen. Anger wasn't even the way to describe this. He could toss cars. Throw punches. He was ready to heave a bolted-down barstool off the floor and fling the thing out the door.

"You good now, buddy? I think sports is on." The bartender brought the screen back to the live feed.

Ashleigh stood. "I think I should go."

"See ya." His teeth were clenched. Never in a million years did Roman expect Beth to do a job where she'd have to screw her way through a mission. Heart pounding in his chest, he didn't looked at Ashleigh. Just continued to stare straight ahead.

"Ass," the woman scoffed as she took her drink and bailed. Thankfully.

He picked up the phone and dialed Beth.

No answer.

He threw some bills on the bar and left the Pour House. Not even thinking about where he was going or what he was doing, he red-lined his truck back to Beth's high-rise. She wouldn't be there because she was dolled up and hanging on an asshole's arm. But maybe he'd seen the whole thing wrong. Maybe Beth had a doppelganger and the real Beth wasn't answering because she was asleep.

Minutes later, he left his truck in front of her building, ignored and bypassed the doorman, and headed to her unit.

He banged on her door with a balled-up fist. "Beth, open up."

No answer.

He banged more, paced, tried to knock but ended up banging it again. No answer again. He called Beth *again* and got goddamn voicemail.

"Open up, Beth."

Still nothing, and he was cracking up. Was she fucking the job as he knocked on her door? Fury built in his chest. The possessiveness almost knocked him over. If he ever got his hands on that man—he tried the door again. "Open the fuck up."

A neighbor poked his head out into the hall then ducked back in. Someone was going to call the cops if Roman didn't tone it down. But he couldn't. Whatever was raging through him at that moment had knocked sense away.

The neighbor's door opened again, and this time the man walked out. "Hey, buddy, I think you need to leave."

Goddamn it. "Mind your business. This is between me and her." Roman banged on the door again and thought about the merits of tearing it off the hinges.

The neighbor took a step closer. "She's a friend, and I don't know you. I'd like you to leave, or I'll have to call the police."

First, Roman laughed. Then he appreciated that Beth had a neighbor who would be willing to walk out into the hall and risk a tangle with him. He stared at the ceiling and shook his head. "Right, man."

Because why was he there anyway? Beth was at work. On the job. Wouldn't be the first time or the last time that either one of them was put into a position of having to do something they didn't want to for the sake of their op.

His stomach tumbled again, thinking of her in his arms earlier. Violence surged in his blood all over again, and he slammed his fist against the door then walked away, cursing as he maneuvered the halls. Stupid, swanky condo building with its doormen and nosy-albeit-protective neighbors—

The elevator opened, and out walked Beth and her motherfucking *date.*

Her face paled, and her frown reached into his soul, shredding it to pieces. "Roman. What are you doing here?"

"Can we talk?"

Her eyes went wide, and she shook her head. "No, I'm sorry. I'm—this is work. I'm—"

Work? She was actually bringing him back to her place, even if the condo was just a CIA cover that she lived in like it was her own. God, he wanted to beat that man within an inch of his life. Maybe more.

The dude stepped forward, confident, hand extended. "What my lovely colleague is trying to say is we have a project to discuss. Gregori Naydenov. Nice to meet you..."

Roman glared, meeting the man's hand with a shake that would crumble cement. Gregori Naydenov matched the grasp. "Roman Hart, and I need to speak with Beth privately."

"Roman, now's not a great time," Beth said.

Now might've been the best time he could think of, and why did the name Gregori Naydenov sound familiar? "Thirty seconds, Beth, then you can deal with this guy. I'll be out of your hair."

Dude stepped back, a smug smile on his face. "Beth, if you feel safe with this man, I have no problem giving you a moment."

Safe? Roman ground his teeth, and Beth glared.

"Come on, Roman." She strode past him in a dress that curved over her body in a way that made him stupid. "What are you doing?"

Same question he just asked himself. He bent forward and whispered, "You do not have to sleep with him. Do. Not."

"I know." Her emerald-green eyes shot daggers.

"But you're going to anyway? Poor form, Beth."

"Would you stop? You have no idea what's happening. Just back off."

Roman coughed a harsh laugh. "Trust me, I know enough."

"He wants to talk."

Shaking his head, Roman nearly refused to believe she was that stupid. "Forget it."

He left her and walked past Naydenov, unable to rationalize the evening. Roman hit the call button for the elevator and looked back. Beth stared at him, sadness radiating where a smile had just been. She never should have told him. She could've told Nic or Cash.

And Roman never should've kissed her.

His phone vibrated, and he looked at it. *Jared Westin.* Good, because he needed to kill off the part of his brain that thought Beth was a great idea. "What's up, Boss Man?"

"We've got a job. Get to the office."

Thank fuck, because working a *real* gig, not screwing an asset, would keep his mind away from her *and* the question of "Since when did he care?"

CHAPTER 10

BETH UNLOCKED HER DOOR AND slid the key back into her purse. Her hands were shaking, and that had nothing to do with Greg walking in behind her. She would kill Roman. Just wring his thick neck and shake until he understood that he could *never* act that way again. Cocky, overreacting, alpha jerk.

She took a breath and tried to calm her indignation. She needed to forget about Roman and focus on the surprisingly normal, nice guy in front of her.

Greg had a cool-guy elegance as he walked past her, surveying her apartment. His was a completely different kind of cocky than Roman's. Roman was brash and harsh and *knew* he made women weak in the knees. Greg had Bond-like qualities. He killed it in a tux, and he appreciated things in a more refined way.

Damn it. Why was she comparing the two men?

Regrouping, she focused on the job at hand, and more importantly, the condo that the CIA had expertly furnished for her cover. It was appropriately nice, decorated to fit her public persona.

"Where's this incredible piece—" But he spotted it before he finished his question and abandoned her, almost running toward the display of ancient pottery that was to be featured in *National Geographic*. They'd done the photo shoot and an interview at her condo the day before, but the pieces weren't scheduled to go back until tomorrow.

After raving on and on, Greg moved from one piece of art to the next, taking it in quietly. He'd yet to say anything about Roman, despite her deluge of apologies, which spanned "I don't know how he made it past the doorman" to "I'm so sorry his attitude rained on our evening."

Nothing Roman had said seemed to faze Greg, and none of her apologies were accepted as needed. She took his profile in as he inspected her bookshelves lined with everything she'd never read. But she could answer a half dozen questions about each title. Maybe one day she'd find it in her to pick up some first-edition literary fiction, but what she really wanted was her e-reader stocked full of super-steamy romance novels.

Greg was meticulous and careful as he moved about her apartment, far more interested in what lined her walls than in how easily—or not—her clothes would come off. That made her nerves settle slightly.

She studied him. He probably had his hair cut once a week and paid someone to give him a shave. The thought of Roman in a barber's chair, letting a man with a straight razor work on his face, was absurd.

"What's funny?" Greg asked, letting just the hint of a French accent decorate his question.

"Nothing. Just… didn't expect the night to go like this."

He checked the Rolex on his wrist. "Do you want me to go?"

"No." She shook her head. "Absolutely not."

Though she'd die to get out of these heels. That would be the only good thing to come from Greg leaving now. Her feet would be free of her killer, albeit spectacular, Louboutins.

He nodded, and somehow that movement accentuated how his broad shoulders filled out the jacket. Add in those eyes that someone—*not her*—could get lost in, and Gregori Naydenov was a package deal. How had he seemed so arrogant before she'd met him, when now he was just… comfortable to be around?

So the issue at hand was how would they move forward? How would she secure an invitation to the auction? And did he truly want a business relationship? Maybe, maybe not. He was an expert-level friend of the enemy, so he wasn't trustworthy. No matter how he acted in front of her, he had a reputation, and she'd seen him in action from afar. So did he have expectations that went along with traveling to the auction?

"Beth? Where'd you go?" he asked, turning to face her. "How did you want the night to go?"

"Spaced out. Sorry." Beth chewed the inside of her cheek. "How did I *want* it to go or *expect* it to go?"

He took a step closer, and the comfortable casualness somehow morphed into a sexy, predatory gaze. She had no idea how he did it. Was it the walk? The way he carried himself?

"Whichever has the better answer," he said.

Her stomach dropped. Yes, Greg knew how to change simple words into panty-dropping commands. Whatever had enticed her to ask want-need questions had disappeared, and she backtracked to work topics.

He paused her. "Excuse me a minute, bathroom?"

She pointed him to the hallway door and wandered around her

condo, casually looking at all the art that he enjoyed so much. It bored the hell out of her.

The door swung open and a livelier Greg reappeared. "Alright, I really love that piece." He chattered faster than before while his eyes darted.

She took in his quick personality change, wondering how deep in his head he'd gone. Some people *really* got into history. She didn't get it, but she could work it. "Some people say that a man on the search for the start of creation, who's looking for answers about the formation of the world, might hold God-like worldviews. Maybe even Godlike opinions... of himself."

His crooked smile popped into place. "You're asking if I can act Godlike?"

"Maybe." One eyebrow raised, she tilted her head.

"I do have a pretty hefty dose of self-esteem. But I'd say it's well earned." Greg abandoned the wall of books, ignored an expensive piece of pottery that he should have found interesting, and stepped close to her. "You've known me for—" he checked the Rolex again — "a couple hours, and you've already made comparisons to something akin to the alpha and the omega. What does that say about you?"

"I'm curious."

"You're confident." He took another step forward.

"I'm wary."

"You're smart."

She agreed. "Very."

He'd closed the space between them, leaving only a foot or so. This was not the Greg from thirty minutes ago. "I like you."

And what did he mean by that? "I'm easy to like. It could be either a personality plus or flaw." She shrugged. "Depending on who you ask."

"It's a plus."

"Well, good." Her nerves were getting the better of her. Greg was her mark to work over, but suddenly she felt like the one being scrutinized, being poked to see how she would react. It didn't seem malicious. Though he wasn't acting innocent, either.

"I've seen you at functions before, Beth. Why have we never talked?"

She smiled. "I don't believe you, but you're sweet for saying you've noticed."

"Most people, sweetheart, don't tell me they don't believe me."

"Aren't most people on your payroll or vapid, smiling blow job givers?"

Disarmed for the moment, he laughed. "Touché."

Roman would never say *touché*. "But I do like you, too." *Bring it back to work.* "And I want to know more about your collections. Do you prefer sculpted pieces over carved?"

She tried in vain to remember something so particular that it wouldn't matter to anyone but a collector. An auction invite wasn't going to happen if she didn't prove herself worthy. If only Jasper had given a heads up, or even if Evan had talked to her before throwing her into the assignment with zero prep work.

"Sculpted." He took a casual step in retreat. Maybe he got the message, or maybe he was staving off his approach. Really, he confused her.

Beth tried for pseudo-honesty to keep him focused. "I'm glad you want to talk about work."

His head tilted. "Yes? Why?"

"I could give you a line about wanting you to respect me, but really, I get very excited about what I do."

He could read into that whatever he wanted. What she really was excited about was an opportunity to prove herself in the field and move on from a stupid arts-and-crafts assignment.

He smiled. "I'm not lying about liking you."

"Do you lie to girls often?"

"Gorgeous girls wrapped around me, asking for the world and my bed? Maybe."

"That doesn't make you very likeable, Mr. Naydenov."

He laughed. "But it does make me truthful. Which is interesting. I *really* like you, my new friend, Beth. You are... refreshing."

"I'll ignore the likeability issue." She let her lips upturn. "This time."

He threw his head back and laughed a little too loudly. "Thank you, Miss Tourne."

"You're welcome."

"I wanted to feel you out more—I'm not this spontaneous—but you are too much fun. I'm traveling to Abu Dhabi for a private auction. Would you care to join me?"

She held in her victory dance and played coy. "Are you luring me to a faraway country with the promise of dirty pieces of rock?"

"Absolutely." The crooked smile beamed.

"Then you've sold me, yes."

For all the crimes and evils the man had reportedly perpetrated in his life, something happy and innocent washed over his face. "I'll have my people work it out with your people. I'm sure the Smithsonian would love to get their fingers on this."

"Probably so."

Greg paced the length of the bookshelf again. "Are you going to tell me about your angry… boyfriend?"

Laughing, she shook her head. "He's most definitely not a boyfriend."

"An ex?"

"Nope. Just an overprotective coworker. He works security. It's in his nature to act like a brute."

"Hmm, I know people, can read them well." His eyes danced. "It seemed like there was more there."

Apparently, Greg did know people. She shook her head and toyed with a curl that had escaped onto her face. "Nope. Not with a guy like that. I'm sorry he was rude earlier."

"You've apologized for him enough. Besides, I've seen much ruder in my line of work."

"And how is that? You're at the peak of your career, crème de la crème of parties, you seem to have sway. You know art, travel, and your accent is… what is it?"

"I'm from Monaco."

She sighed. "I've always wanted to go."

"Really? Why?"

"Doesn't James Bond swing by it for something? Or maybe that was Iron Man? Maybe both? Seems like a place that rains champagne and the finer things." That would resonate with Greg. Truth was, she hated champagne.

"You're intrigued by movies about spies and action heroes?" A dangerous flare lit his eyes, catching her off guard. "Fascinating."

"No." She spun, heading for the kitchen. "But I do like heroes that win at the end of the day."

He followed close behind. "You're an idealist?"

She shrugged, turning, and found herself nearly nose to nose with him. She wasn't sure enough about his character profile to commit to one answer over another. An idealist probably wasn't a good thing to him, which was good because she'd long ago lost her sense of an ideal life. But why take the chance on the wrong answer?

Before she could change topics, he did. "Let's play a game." Inches away, his eyes were wide, pupils fluctuating, and his words carried a whisper of mint.

What was it with men and their games? She turned to the cabinet and grabbed two glasses and a bottle of wine. "I'm good with a game."

He took the bottle from her hand, opened the right drawer to find the corkscrew, and went to work, nodding to his first drawer choice. "I'm a good guesser."

"I've got my eye on you." She took the offered glass of wine. "Does that mean I'm predictable?"

"Not at all. But that's why we have the game." He winked, surprising her. "Pepsi or Coke?"

"Pepsi."

He scrunched his nose. "Beer or bourbon?"

"Bourbon."

That, he nodded to. "Hero who saves the day or villain proves himself right in the end?"

She put her hands on her hips, shaking her head. "That's a trick question."

"But your answer is very important."

She sipped her wine. "Some things a girl has to keep to herself."

"That sounds like a challenge to me."

The words, coming from six feet of tuxedo-dressed stud, dripping sex, should've had an effect on her. Just like always, she enjoyed the attention but nothing else. There wasn't even a stir within her. She was one hundred percent, absolutely, completely broken.

She glanced up and saw Greg watching her. Shit. She took a step back and set her glass down. "Tell me about the auction."

He took the carefully placed hint and backed away without so much as a faltering step. He really could read people well. She'd have to remember that. Not much would get by him.

"The auction." He cleared his throat. "Simple. We go. I schmooze. You give me a thumbs up or down on appraisal price. I bid. End of story."

"That's it?"

His backstep from seconds ago reversed. "Do you want there to be more, Beth?"

Such a loaded question. She tried not to fidget and picked her glass up again. "I wouldn't mind schmoozing a little myself."

"How about this? We'll get out, meet some players..." He studied her. "I have something even bigger coming up. We'll see how this trip goes, and maybe we'll work together again. I will need a strong right-hand man when it comes time for this job."

"I'd like that."

He clinked his glass to hers. "Funny. I think I'd like that too."

CHAPTER 11

ROMAN BURROWED FURTHER INTO HIS layer of debris. Under the night's blanket of safety, he'd been sitting for hours since he, Cash, and Montana had received their go-orders from Titan HQ. This was a non-sanctioned, US-funded job to take out a sex-trade cartel kingpin. Their job was easy. One shot, one kill. The fallout from the fucker's death would cause a shift in power, allowing Mexican and US deep-cover agents to move further up the food chain. In the long run, one assassination would save further women from rape, slavery, and murder, so it would be a job well done in Roman's mind when the guy fell over dead.

Now that he'd been awake for more than twenty-four hours—during which he'd kissed Beth, watched her on TV, and almost beat her asset to a pulp—the almost-daybreak-night surrounded him. He stared into the horizon through the green tint of night vision, ready to wrap up any time now.

A set of headlights sped forward several clicks down the only road leading to the compound. Roman signaled Cash on the radio. "Vehicle heading in on avenue of approach."

A half-click away, Cash was perched and angled to shoot. "Roger that."

Montana signaled to Roman. Something else was in the distance. Another set of headlights appeared.

"Hang tight." Roman studied them. "Two vehicles. One's a decoy."

"Let me know," Cash whispered.

Roman zeroed in on the vehicles, trading information with Montana. One rode lower to the ground, both identical makes. "Half a click and approaching the gate. Wind from the northeast, ten miles per hour."

Keeping his eye on both vehicles, Roman watched them maneuver, hitting the divots and bumps on their route, the lower-hanging one hitting them harder. That was their target; the vehicle had to be armored. "Target's in the second one."

"Second vehicle. Got it."

Roman watched them enter the gate. "I'm blind. Wind shifting, north, five miles per hour."

"Give me five, four, three…" Cash went silent. Seconds ticked by. "Bull's eye. Let's go."

Roman rolled over and jumped up from his burrowed hole then booked it to meet at the rendezvous location. They had two vehicles hidden away, one he and Cash had taken, the second Montana had for back up.

He was there first and hit the driver's seat. Forty-five seconds later, Cash jumped into the passenger seat. Roman slammed the gas, bumping onto the road through a thick wall of brush. Montana would likely be about a minute or two behind them. They all knew where to go. The job had gone long, but in the grand scheme, it was a cake walk.

"Well done, dude." Roman pulled off his equipment as he drove with his knees. "Working with the kid ain't bad." He picked up his comm piece. "You hear that, Montana? Great eyes, buddy. Nicely done."

"I hear ya, buddy." Montana downplayed his contribution, which made Roman like the kid even more. Everything happened for a reason, and with Cash off playing husband all the time, it would be good to have another guy around to shoot the shit with.

"Agree. Kid did well." Cash rummaged through a bag on the floor, grabbing granola bars and throwing one at Roman.

Roman dropped his comm piece into the console and relaxed. Starving, he and Cash raided the box of granola bars and drove several miles down a broken road in silence.

Cash balled up his wrappers and tossed them in bag. "I'm not going to meddle, but—"

Meddling could only mean Beth.

"Christ." Roman shook his head and pushed the gas pedal down as though driving faster would keep this conversation from happening. "Leave it alone."

"Beth called Nicola."

The speed didn't help. "You sound like a freakin' chick playing telephone."

"And Nic said you nearly started a fight with the asset Beth's working over."

Roman grumbled. "*Asset* she's working over. Nicely worded."

"What has you so damn worked up, man?" Cash turned his head. "I mean, you and Beth have been dancing around whatever it is you two have, but, seriously. Storming her building, getting in her guy's face when you know she's working a job? I don't get it."

If Roman tried hard enough, he'd be able to rip the wheel off the steering column with his grip. "Dude's name is Gregori Naydenov. Why's the name ring a bell?"

"That's the dude's name?" Cash asked.

"Yeah. What do you know?"

"Not much. Guy's a money launderer for a couple big-name terrorists."

Roman groaned. "Fucking spectacular."

"What the hell happened the other night?" Cash chuckled.

"Nothing you don't know already."

"Kissing Beth wouldn't make you lose your mind like that. I don't care if her lips taste like sugar or some shit."

"Yeah, yeah." Roman grumbled, remembering that they did taste exactly like sugar and were addictive as hell. Not that he wanted to kiss them ever again. And crying? Then another guy? Nope.

"Roman, man. What gives?"

"Nothing worth getting into."

"I don't believe that," Cash said.

"Truth…" Roman's grip on the wheel made his knuckles ache. "She's gotta bed Naydenov for the job."

"Huh." Cash whistled low. "Didn't expect that."

"Tell me about it."

They drove for miles in silence before Cash shook his head and started in again. "Fine. Beth does a little dirty for the gig. Not unheard of. But what's the whole situation with—"

"The other night, when we were at that bar, before I kissed her, she said *alright*."

"Alright, like alright-alright? You two…"

Roman nodded. "And I backed down. Because she'd been drinking and I was sober as a minister on Sunday."

Cash threw back his head and laughed. "Man alive, I'm enjoying this side of the show."

"What?" he scowled.

"The crap you guys gave me when Nic popped back up. Now I can see why. This is great." Cash gasped in laughter, slapping his leg and howling. "Fucking awesome. Hilarious."

"Dude, shut up. It's not like that."

"The hell it isn't."

Roman ran off the road, making the tires rumbled in protest. Cash stopped laughing long enough to see they weren't crashing, but as Roman pulled back on to the road, his buddy fell apart worse than before.

"Not funny, asshole."

"Beth is your Nic. Everyone knows it, but I think maybe you're just realizing it."

Roman rubbed his forehead, sliding his fingers down to pinch the bridge of his nose. Then cold dread grabbed his stomach. "No." He shook his head. "No woman of mine would spread her legs for the job. Beth's sweet, hot. I bet she'd fuck like a porn star. But nope, none of that Beth-is-my-Nicola shit. The only thing Beth *is* is a permanent headache."

"Eh, maybe. Maybe not. Think you just need to wake up and see what's in front of you."

Shaking his head, Roman couldn't—wouldn't—do that. "How about we radio in Montana and talk some of Titan's strategic—"

A loud explosion echoed in Roman's ears before he registered a flash of light. White. Red. Yellow. It came out of nowhere, wrapping around the windshields. The vibrations shattered his eardrums. Pinching his eyes shut, his hands lost the steering wheel as their armored vehicle flipped. They went sideways, its heavy tonnage slamming the road. Roman growled through the blast, the crash.

They flipped again. The impact so jarring his teeth slammed together, the metallic taste of blood coating his tongue. The seatbelt tore into his neck, the impact giving him whiplash.

Finally, their trajectory stopped, stuck at an angle, and his head dropped forward. He tried like hell to regain his bearings, to hear something besides the ringing in his ears. The scent of blood and fuel burned in his nostrils. He wanted to sit up, to move his arms and legs that ached in a thousand ways, making his head spin to the point of nausea.

His head rolled to the side. His eyes loosely focused. He took in the cracked windshield, the shatters window, and—Cash slumped in the passenger seat.

"Cash?" But Roman wasn't sure if the word came out. He tried to move. The ringing in his ears continued, and his surroundings looked like a stilted movie, almost as if he were slowly clicking through a slideshow.

He lifted his arm to wipe the blood out of his eyes. Hurt like a motherfuckin' bear. Then the sulfur smell of smoke made him twitch. React. Realize that somewhere, something was sparking. Who knew what they'd been hit with, but they had to get out of their vehicle.

"Cash," he coughed out, reaching for his own seatbelt.

No answer.

"Cash, wake the fuck up." Roman couldn't even hear his own voice. Damn it.

He unbuckled the belt and fell to the side. Right, they were at an angle. He seriously needed to get his thoughts together. No telling who was after them, how close, or what they wanted.

"We gotta go, man." Roman checked Cash's pulse but couldn't make sense of anything.

So help him God, if anyone took Cash away from him, he'd lose his mind. Years of not having his sister? Now Cash wasn't moving? Not responding? "Dude. Come on."

Roman groaned through the pain. His eyes watered from whatever was smoking and sparking, from the leaking fuel, and from his blood mixed with sweat seeping down his face.

Cash was still out. But alive? Seemed that way. *Had* to be that way. They had to get out or neither one would be for long. Roman turned to his door, kicking to open it. It remained shut. He tried the handle, but no use. He turned to Cash's, same routine, same result.

"Wake up." Fuck, he felt weak. Helpless.

His hands clawed for the satellite phone, not finding it as black smoke filtered into the cab. He unbuckled Cash, who fell sideways, and Roman heard a low moan. Good. Cash was alive and Roman's hearing was coming back in pieces. But shit, they were still stuck, and Cash was still out.

"Come on, man." Pulling his leg up, Roman saw it was blood coated. His eyelids tried to sink shut. Moving both his legs was almost too much. But he kicked and kicked, growling and shouting at the goddamn window that was already partially shattered from impact.

Stupid. Safety. Glass.

Another kick and finally the window spider-webbed. It clunked out with a final kick, giving them enough room to make an exit. Roman pulled Cash toward the opening, then pushed himself through it.

The world spun as he fell and hit the fuel-soaked ground. His eyes ran over the vehicle. Definitely hit by an RPG or an IED, and how often did folks survive rocket-propelled grenades or improvised explosives? Not often. Hell, he didn't want to go like this, especially when the hard part seemed over.

He stood, staggering and swaying as the world swirled at Mach One. Nope, the hard part wasn't over yet. He summoned enough strength to pull Cash through the window, hoping to God the dude didn't have a broken spine.

Roman focused, gritting his teeth, and leaned against the door. A small fire broke out under the hood. More smoke plumed out. As soon as it hit anything fuel covered, they were dead.

"Cash." Roman held him. "Dude, come on." Because he couldn't do this on his own. "Wake up."

Roman gripped Cash's arm, tugging as white-hot pain ripped into his muscles and a pounding headache threatened to knock him out. Sweat poured off of him, and he was so dizzy. Too dizzy. He couldn't comprehend. Couldn't think about survival. Just that he had to get them away.

One more horrible blast of pain, and Cash's limp, moaning body fell down on top of him. Fumes, smoke, and gasoline surrounded them. Roman rolled over and crawled on his stomach, dragging Cash along with him. They had to escape faster. But he couldn't. Inch by inch, he pushed away from the vehicle. Maybe they'd make it.

Dirt caked his skin and pushed into his mouth. Muscles aching, unknown wounds tearing him apart with each move, Roman couldn't do it. His chest heaved. The pain was intolerable. Roman looked at Cash next to him, the vehicle not that far away, the sky—

Another giant explosion ripped into the night. The force rattled him. The heat and rippling vibrations flattened him to the ground. Again his ears bled in pain, his eyes burning from the onslaught.

He wrapped an arm around Cash again, covering his friend's head and fighting for survival, to stay conscious. And… just… couldn't.

CHAPTER 12

ROMAN'S EYES CRACKED OPEN AS he awakened with a headache to trump all headaches. Dim lights surrounded him, and the hum of machinery beeped in his ear, forcing his headache to epic pain levels. He did a mental roll call of body parts. All hurt like hell but were accounted for.

Slowly, he tried to take in his surroundings. IV bag. Vitals monitor. Yup, hospital room. He was unsure where in the world he was or how he'd gotten there, though. His memory reached into nothing, drawing a blank for why he was on his back and aching like he'd gone to blows with a bull.

"You're not dead. Wake the hell up." Jared leaned over Roman and growled. "I have no patience for my favorite sniper-spotter team finding the easy way into an R & R request."

Rest and relaxation? Surely he was dead. Being unable to move and having Boss Man bark orders into his face. Yeah, absolutely dead and hanging out in hell.

He jolted. Cash. Montana. "What happened? Where's—"

"Take it easy."

"Where's—" He coughed, igniting another round of pain.

"Cash is laid up, like you. Montana came upon you and called in for the troops. You owe him."

Montana got them home. Roman owed the kid. That was doable.

As Roman processed the information, his mind went fuzzy. Heavy and sore, he let his eyes slide shut, slipping back into the peaceful bliss of what he hoped were painkillers. Otherwise, if he really were dead, this was going to suck.

Swirling coffee in her cup, Beth numbly trailed Nicola down the hall, watching in fascination as the strongest woman Beth knew became as weak as a feather, unable to function and focus. Nicola had called her right after Jared had called with bad news. The details were sketchy at best. Roman and Cash had been hit by a cartel-launched RPG after they had assassinated a cartel kingpin.

The new guy, Montana, had been in another ride. When Roman and Cash were attacked, barely escaping, Jared received a quick go-save-your-guy heads up from Montana. Titan Group went in hard and fast, pulling their own out and moving them back to the US. Everyone owed Montana a thanks.

The rescue mission had happened with such fine-tuned finesse that Beth wanted to tell Jared that he ran a tight ship. But the guy scared the crap out of her. And if she admitted it, the idea of Roman not making it back...

She shook her head, not willing to think about Roman. That second, she centered in on her numbness and thanked God she'd given up the ability to feel anything for anyone. Anything for Roman.

Beth was here for Nicola.

Roman was just a friend.

Yes, he was Nicola's brother, and they had checked on him. Well, Nicola had checked on him. Beth remained glued to the wall, thankfully slipping into Cash's room later. Cash was Beth's comfort zone. Roman was nothing but dangerous, making her question everything she'd come to relish with her numbness. She couldn't go into Roman's room. Couldn't take a peek or listen to the doctor's rehash of what had happened. The idea of knowing how close he could've come to dying made her dizzy, and there was no need to be a shaking, quivering duplicate of Nicola. Except now, when Beth tried to take a sip of her coffee, her hand shook.

She scowled at the cup and placed it on the small table in Cash's hospital room. Nicola was on his bed, curled around him as though the wires and doctors who poked and prodded him weren't there.

In one giant swoosh, the door opened and the hanging curtain was swept to the side. There, lo and behold, was Jared Westin, looking ready to strangle someone.

His eyes ran over Cash and Nicola. Nicola didn't say hello. Then his gaze swept Beth's way, and that dangerously hard look landed on her as though it was *her* he wanted to strangle. She'd known him long enough that he shouldn't scare her with a nasty glare, but his look right now was one for the record books. The guy was angry.

"Hi."

"Beth." His eyes narrowed. "Why the hell are you in *here*?"

Okay, yes, angry at her. But why? "Oh, um. Nic brought me. Well, I brought her."

Jared's scowl intensified. "Beth."

"The girl got a phone call about her husband and her brother. She wasn't in a good place to drive."

He shook his head.

Nicola sat up, pushing off the bed to walk to the chair next to Beth. "Boss Man."

"Princess," he said with his version of a smile.

Beth glowered at Jared. "She's Princess? And all I get is snarls and—"

"You're a stubborn pain in the ass. Just like Roman."

Beth's mouth dropped. "Excuse me?"

"You're sitting in here, sipping coffee, while he's practically unconscious next door."

Nothing wrong with that or the fact that she didn't dote over Roman. Except for the inner war waging within herself. Hold him. Stay away from him. Care about him. Never care for anyone. "Nicola checked on him."

"I assumed she did."

Beth's eyebrows pinched together. "What do you expect from me?"

"They're friends. That's all, Jared," Nicola volunteered.

Yeah, what Nicola said. Except Beth's throat was in knots, and she couldn't say anything at all.

Jared glared. "Get your ass up and in there, so he doesn't wake up alone."

"He's not alone. He's got you, Nic, and the team of guys that have been running in and out of this hospital scaring the crap out of every nurse and doctor here."

Jared shook his head slowly. "Didn't take you for the dense type. It's not my face that the guy wants to see."

What? It wasn't hers either. "Jared—"

"Get in there and stay. Simple."

She rolled her lips together to keep the "yes, sir" response to herself. But still, she stood and whispered, "Fine."

What would she even say if he woke up while she was in there? Their last less-than-friendly encounter hadn't gone well, and she didn't know if it should be addressed or ignored.

Beth dragged her feet on the way to Roman's room. Around her, nurses shuffled by, and other visitors checked on family and friends without a tenth of the dread she could feel painted on her face. But it wasn't just their last run-in. It wasn't even the kiss that she'd run from. It was so much more, which had always been her problem with Roman. More with him wasn't fair with her past. It wasn't even... *possible.*

"Beth," Nicola called from behind her as Beth opened the door to Roman's room.

The curtain was still drawn, and most of the lights were off. She didn't want to go in. *Couldn't* go in. Thrilled for an excuse to turn around, Beth pivoted, trying for a casual look.

Nicola's scrutinizing face said that Beth failed.

"What's up?"

"If you..." Nicola stepped through the door with Beth and let the sentence linger as though Nicola reached for a something that couldn't be put into words. They stood awkwardly in the tiny space between the door and the curtain until Nicola sighed. "If this is too much, Beth, then you really don't have to. Jared's a jerk. You know that."

It *was* too much. Beth crossed her arms over her chest and waited for Nicola to come closer. She did, then threw an arm around Beth. They stayed there for a minute. None of this made sense. The dread. The cold fear at Roman lying unconscious. Even at Nicola comforting *her* when it should be Beth comforting Nicola. It wasn't Beth's husband or brother.

Nicola hugged her tighter. "I really shouldn't have asked you to bring me here."

Beth's brow furrowed, then she stepped back. "Of course you should have."

"I mean... like it or not, Roman in your head is on caliber with—"

Beth's heart stopped. Confirmation that Nicola never forgot, even when they hadn't talked about it in years. "Don't say that."

"You two have a connection."

Beth shook her head. "No way. No."

"Don't be like that. You never, *ever* have a thing for anyone. That's part of your charm. Part of why you do your job well. And part of the reason I'm always pushing you two together. I want that for you."

It was that second when Beth grasped what had been happening. If she was ever going to replace Logan—Logan who'd left a gaping hole in her very existence—it wouldn't be terrible if Roman filled that spot and soothed that ache. And thinking that made her a traitorous, abandoning wife. Or... widow. Whatever she was called. "You're wrong."

"You care about him," Nicola prodded.

No, this conversation really couldn't be happening. "He's a friend by default because he's your brother. He's... around. That's it."

"He makes you smile."

Beth couldn't look at her. "Everyone makes me smile."

"He makes you *run*, and no one makes you run."

"Shut up, Nic."

Nicola stepped closer, whispering, "When's the last time you really cared for someone... besides—"

"Don't you dare." Beth grounded her molars together. "Stop, Nic. You're wrong." But she wasn't. Shit. *Shit!* Tears welled just like they had when had Roman kissed her and Beth's heart stopped, in shock that her dried-up, turned-to-stone heart beat wildly, announcing the heat, desire, and a lusty longing that ricocheted from limb to limb.

"You know, you can like another guy. Logan won't fault you—"

The tears spilled from Beth's eyes. "Of course he wouldn't. That's not it. None of this is it. Just back off."

But yes, Logan would fault her. He wouldn't have died if she had just opened her eyes, tried harder, loved better, been a better wife.

Damn it. Her throat felt like it was bleeding. Her stomach ached at all the lost possibilities that their life could've been. A family and babies and the PTA and bake sales. Whatever normal people with perfect husbands did with their all-American lives. Fuck. Fuck, she couldn't think about the loss. Focusing on the future, the CIA, and living only in the present moment were the only things she could do.

"Beth, then what is it—"

Too late. Memories and regret were the worst. Way past the nightmares. Once she thought about them, they wouldn't stop. Beth broke free of Nicola's inquisition. She rushed down the hall, ignoring Nicola calling after her and people's stares as she ended up running the last few feet and slapping the elevator call button over and over again.

CHAPTER 13

EYES STILL CLOSED, ROMAN FELT like an eavesdropper in his own room. This time when he'd awakened, two crystal-clear voices pulled him from the fog and confirmed he wasn't dead or in hell. If he really had been dead, his aching body would've continued to ache when he heard Beth. But it didn't. An absurd amount of energy, maybe even anticipation, coursed through him, knowing that Beth would be in there soon. But then that conversation he'd partially overheard? And Beth leaving again? Running away from him again? *That* he felt in his gut, and it sucked. It also raised a couple major red flags. Maybe he didn't know everything there was about the girl who made him wish he could let someone in.

Nicola pushed past the curtain and walked in. Her eyes widened and her cheeks flushed when she saw him awake. "Hi. How are you?" Her fingers twisted together. "Been up long?"

He sighed, not wanting to answer, and instead shifted, looking for the remote that would raise his bed. "Got a headache that'd rival a mortar hit to the dome. But nothing that won't heal." The doc had been in and made Roman swear up and down that he'd take it easy. That brain trauma was like a bruise. Some worse than others, but it still had to heal.

She sat on the edge of his bed. "Glad you're okay."

"What just happened there?" he asked. "With Beth."

"Hmm? Nothing." She reached for the remote and turned on the television. Roman put his hand on his sister's forearm, and she started furiously flipping through channels as soon as the screen lit.

"Nic?"

"Are you feeling a movie? Or something—"

"Nicola?"

She looked at him, all her guilt hidden from the world, except he knew his sister down to the tiniest micro-emotion.

"What was that conversation with Beth?"

Nic fidgeted, eyes darting around the room. "She was here but had to go."

"I heard."

She winced. "It's not—"

Montana popped his head in the room. "Roman?"

Roman squeezed her arm then let go. "Don't worry about it." Because he wouldn't. Beth was too much work to figure out, and he didn't want a woman that would kiss him, then sleep with another guy. If that made him an asshole, so be it. No one would be shocked. It wasn't like he wanted to care for another person. He had the team, his family. That was all he was capable of.

"Hey." He angled his head toward Montana. "Nic was just about to tell me how Cash is."

The guy grabbed a chair and hung back. Roman needed to say thanks for getting him and Cash the hell home. That was legendary stuff, the kind that made a debt owed forever.

Nicola sighed. "He's in, he's out. Concussion. Mostly just resting, sleeping it off. Strict orders for recovery after he's checked out. So a little worse than you, but not by much. I hate that you were both hurt."

"Nothing that won't heal, like I said."

"You two aren't invincible." She scowled. "Neither are you, Montana."

The kid grinned. "Didn't say I was. Just hanging out."

Roman scoffed, which made him cough, confirming that his ribs were bruised. "But we are the closest thing to it."

Nicola shook her head, mumbling, "Cocky."

"But he's been up?"

She nodded. "A little bit. You both slept through all kinds of tests. The doc will update you, but you're probably benched for a while."

He laughed, already having had the speech from Titan's doc in addition to the rotating hospital doctors. But why tell that to Nicola? She'd only try to keep him there longer, just in case. "We'll see."

A knock, then a nurse walked in. She checked his vitals. "Dr. Tuska will be back this afternoon if you need to talk to him again."

"Again?" Nicola asked.

The nurse looked sideways then went back to Roman. "If you need to speak with him sooner, let me know."

He shrugged, and his muscles complained. "Whenever is fine. So long as he gives me a hall pass to go home."

The nurse laughed and looked at Nicola. "You called it."

"Yeah." She turned to Roman. "Much to the concern of Mom. Dad didn't seem too fazed by my prediction, but Mom…" She shook her head. "You know her rule."

Mom's rule: He and Nicola could do whatever they wanted, as long as no one got hurt.

Damn. He didn't want his folks to see him like this, most certainly not his mom. She'd dealt with too much stress over the years. Not that she was weak, but why add on more when she'd suffered so much over Nicola? "You know better than to let Mom show up at hospitals."

Nicola shrugged. "Not much I could do."

Inside, Roman grumbled, majorly irritated that Nicola didn't see how inconsiderate it was to loop their mom into his injuries. He didn't want Mom worried, especially if he was knocked out and couldn't comfort her. "Next time, leave Mom out of it."

"Next time? No next time, Roman. You guys can't keep tempting fate. Don't assume there's a next time."

His irritation was growing. First Beth talked crazy and ran out when he really wanted to at least see her. Then it was Nicola's turn to talk crazy. *Shit.*

The nurse tinkered with the machinery, reading his vitals. "Are you doing okay?"

He looked at her. "What?"

"Your blood pressure is rising."

Of course it was. He took a deep breath. But no, he wasn't okay. He was annoyed and irrational and ready to tear into Nicola for being so cavalier with other people's feelings. Didn't she understand that having loved ones love them was… complicated? "Mom should be kept in the dark."

Nicola rolled her eyes. "Right."

"I'm—"

Jared walked through the door. "Princess, your lesser half is waking again. Go say hello. Montana, keep our boy company. He can think of ways to say thanks for saving his life."

Nicola's smile could've made sunshine look gloomy. She turned with a quick wave goodbye. For all the apprehension Roman had ever had about her and Cash, his best bud was the right guy for her. How he'd missed it for so long, Roman had no idea. But they worked. Yin and yang and all that crap.

Nicola looked over her shoulder at the door. "Just call her, Roman. Whatever you two have, it's special."

Nothing he'd ever had was special. The word made him

uncomfortable. Jared rolled his eyes and made a noise from his perch against the wall.

Nicola ignored both of their grumblings. "Call her."

"If for no other reason than to get you off my back, I might."

She smiled over her shoulder and took off, leaving Boss Man to glare at him.

"What?"

Jared rubbed his chin. "Doc Tuska said you can get out of here if you want. He'll want to talk to you this afternoon, but expect to be cut loose."

"Yeah? Nice."

"Your discharge instructions say something like don't base jump or head into rapid-fire target practice for a few days."

"Do they now?" Roman chuckled.

"Think you can handle that?"

He nodded, feeling there was an unspoken catch. "Think so."

Just call Beth. Nicola's request wouldn't leave him alone. He could leave, then he'd get a good 'script out of it and could veg on the couch with the TV on. That way he wouldn't have to think about the girl who had moved into his brain without permission.

Nicola's words infiltrated also. What was that piece of advice she'd just given Beth? *You can like another guy. No one would fault you.*

Another guy? Faulting her? What was that? Whatever it was, Beth was upset, and that had something to do with him.

His gut churned, and he scrubbed his face, wanting out of the hospital and to take a hot shower. Then a dose of painkillers and to go sleep in front of the television. Not his bed. That way, he wouldn't have delusional thoughts about her warm body to hold close. Maybe he'd take Nicola's advice and call Beth. Or maybe not.

"You need a ride out of here?" Montana asked.

"Sure as hell do." And decision made. He wouldn't call Beth. Or maybe he would.

CHAPTER 14

GREG SNIFFED TWICE, EMBRACING THE racing, rushing blast as the coke hit his system. He loved high-quality blow. Evan had a great hook-up, straight from a cartel friend they both did business with.

A butter-soft leather chair held him as he rocked back and forth. He needed a little more, so he ran his thumb over the mirrored tray then rubbed his bottom gum, letting his mouth water over the powder remnants he hadn't inhaled.

"Good?" Evan asked, sitting across Greg's massive desk.

He rolled his shoulders back. "Very nice."

"Smooth."

"Absolutely." Greg sucked in his bottom lip, wanting a hint more, then thought of another something he wanted. Maybe just as badly. "Let's talk about Beth Tourne."

Evan smiled. "Elizabeth."

"Probably does not partake?"

"I think she'd do just about whatever you want her to."

Greg scowled. "I hope not. That's part of her appeal. She doesn't seem to care what I want. She's... very much an individual. Smart. I like her."

Evan pulled back the tray and diced out a line. A quick bend, snort, and an eyes-closed cocaine smile pulled tight on his lips. After a few seconds, his eyes opened with a head shudder. "Then I'm glad I introduced you."

"It seems you have the hook-up on everything I have a desire for. What's it going to take for more access to this?" *And maybe more information on Beth.* But even in his hopped-up euphoria, Greg held back his interest.

She might not like him, or maybe just a little. But he liked that. She was a challenge. So real and of such a high caliber.

Evan cleared his throat. "I need in on another deal. You'll get more of this, plus your standard percentage. But I have to make more."

Greg kept his knowing response to himself. Evan was having a much harder time keeping up with his nose candy habit than he wanted to let on. But Greg did Evan's books. He knew exactly how much money was coming in and going out. The man was snorting a couple hundred thousand dollars' worth of high-end product on an annual basis.

Greg tapped his fingers on the desk, embracing the jittery need for just one more line. "I have clients who have something very big in the pipeline."

"I want very big." Evan nodded greedily.

"It's about as big as it comes. Might stain your moral turpitude."

"I have no moral turpitude. Like you."

How true that was. Greg loved his money and investments. He also thoroughly enjoyed women, particularly the likes of Beth. He pushed the tray back, declining another hit as Evan offered. Maybe he'd tamp down some things—like blow—and see if Beth was a good fit as a new... hobby.

The tingle in his chest was more than drugs. It was the excitement of her accompanying him to Abu Dhabi. Knowing he'd have to slow the drugs was fine if that meant he could keep her around, almost like a pet. Yes, Beth was something he wanted to call his, if nothing else because his addiction to collecting things was stronger than his addiction to cocaine.

It'd been a week since Beth had run out of the hospital after Nicola had gotten into her head. It'd also been a week of texting and chatting with Greg. He was exactly what she needed, a meaningless person to work over, someone she could focus on, learn about, and extract information from.

Evan, her handler, had been thrilled at her quickly building closeness with Greg, and truth be told, Greg was an all-right guy. His file said he was a piece of shit, but nothing Beth had come across suggested that.

The last few days of predictable normalcy had been exactly what she wanted. What she needed.

It was Saturday morning, and she lounged in bed, pillow over her head and phone in hand. Greg had texted good morning and said he had news for later. Later was a great idea because now she could drift in and out of sleep, relaxing. Her phone buzzed, and she answered the call, putting Greg to her ear without opening her eyes.

"Your definition of later is skewed. I'd call that five minutes." Her voice was sleep drenched, but knowing what she did about him, that probably worked in her favor. He might've developed an interesting crush on her, but it was more her indifference to his money and power that he liked. She just didn't think he realized it yet.

"What are you talking about?" Roman's voice rushed over her senses, making her ache before he had two words out.

"Roman, what—hi. I wasn't expecting you."

"I got that," he growled.

"You're home?" Even though she'd known he had been for a few days now. She had wanted to check on him, but what was the point? Nicola had pointed out exactly why Beth shouldn't, and staying away was the right thing to do, even if it hurt.

"Yeah, home."

"Are you... okay?"

"Yeah."

The right thing wasn't the easy thing. "Roman, maybe we should talk."

"Nothing to talk about."

She laughed, aggravated and turned on, and surprised by how she felt him *everywhere*. "What's your problem? *You* called me."

He remained quiet.

"Seriously, Roman. Can we move on? You're mad at me. I'm sorry, okay?"

"What do you have to be sorry for?"

"Because I messed us up. We're fun. We're a joke. We're nothing, and it worked."

"I heard you talking to Nic."

She cringed. "About that..." But she didn't know how to explain. The only thing she could say was something she'd never admit.

"And the tears?"

She cussed silently. "I wish everything would go back to how it was."

He said nothing. Again. Her silent, overly emotional, overwhelming tears were back and burning her eyelids.

"Look, Beth." He paused. "I don't want to."

The words were so low she almost thought she had imagined them. "What?"

"I don't want everything to go back to how it was. I've sat here for days, fighting the urge to call you. And what's the point?"

"What's the point?" she repeated.

"Babe, what I'm saying is I want to talk to you. I want *you.*"

A full-body shiver erupted and ran down her back, sliding along her nerves. Roman wanted sex. That was all, and it should've been fine. But it wasn't, and because of that, she needed to say no.

"Babe?"

Ugh! She wanted to *hate* him. Her chin dropped, and she ran a hand into her mess of hair. She was completely messed up in the head. "No, Roman, you don't want me. I'm doing you a favor, ending this now."

"Say it to my face."

She bit her lip. "You're asking me to come over?" The invitation made her heart rip through the barbed-wire stranglehold. All kinds of emotions bled together: nervousness, excitement, and the always-present guilt.

"I want to see you. Wherever. However."

"Why?" she asked.

"Does it matter?"

Yes. "No." She closed her eyes. "I'll head your way after I take a shower."

"Good." Then the line went dead.

Thank God he'd hung up, because now she couldn't back out.

Beth took too long in the shower, shaving her legs even though she didn't have to, and letting the water run down her body. She thought about touching herself, imagining it was him running his hands over her breasts. Her nipples beaded so tightly they hurt. And between her legs... God, she ached. But for what? Nothing worked. No relief. Only complete frustration.

Instead, she turned the water to scalding and let it burn her skin until she couldn't take it anymore and had to abandon the shower. The want hadn't gone away, and she was so confused that she decided it wasn't arousal at all. It was aggravation at a level she'd never experienced before.

Freakin' aggravation.

That was the only option, because if it was arousal, and if there was the chance that she could have an orgasm while thinking of Roman, than she was fucked.

"Stop it." She stared at the steamy mirror. "The past is the past, and Roman is not an answer."

He'd never shown an ounce of interest in having a *relationship* with her, or with anyone, for that matter. She was a conquest. A fun to-do.

With that understanding, she calmed her wildly beating heart, got dressed, and jumped in the eco-friendly Lexus that the Agency thought fit her cover.

Instead of obsessing over him, Beth listed the reasons she hated that car as she drove to his place. It was pretentious. It was the wrong color. It was not her. Though it did have a glass roof that allowed for a killer view if she ever took the time to lean back and relax, which she never did.

Focusing on how much she hated her car helped her keep cool. She was a seasoned operative who knew how to hide her feelings. She could do that. Easy. But her stomach knotted as she arrived at Roman's. This was absurd. As long as she didn't acknowledge wayward feelings, they didn't exist. It would be as though she'd boxed her innermost thoughts and walked away.

Beth parked in the driveway of his nice house, which sat on a huge piece of property. After a quick knock on the door, it opened. Roman was bruised and battered and shirtless, and the shelved box of feelings came screaming open. Whatever his agenda was, the shirtless hello wasn't fair.

"No, no, no." She closed her eyes and pointed blindly. "Turn around, get dressed, and we can try this again."

She stood her ground and wouldn't cross the threshold. There was no possible way to remain detached when a wall of perfectly sculpted muscle stood a few feet away. "Roman." She shook her head. "I'm not a booty call, go find a shirt."

"Babe."

She peeked through one eye. Holy shit! He was perfect. Her mouth watered. Definitely dangerous, he was a man who could leave her without a sane thought left.

"I didn't say you were a booty call, Beth." He left the door open and walked down the hall. "Come in or leave. Either way, shut the door."

Freakin' attitude problem. "You're a jerk."

"Surprise."

"The asshole routine isn't a good look for you, just so you know." Though the shirtless look was. Carefully, she stepped into his house and prayed that he'd put on a shirt. Well, kinda.

She went down the hall to where it opened into an expansive living room. It'd been a while since she'd been to his place, and she'd never seen the inside. She had visited for a backyard beers-and-brats-type thing. Somehow, she'd thought it would be sparsely furnished, but it wasn't. Had Nicola done this? Dark colors and thick leather couches. Comfortable but somehow refined. "Nice place."

"Thanks." He collapsed onto an overstuffed leather couch. "Took a while to make it look like the place was lived in, but it's done."

"You did all this?"

He shrugged a yes as she walked along the wall, eying pictures. It occurred to her that Greg had just done this in her place the other day, studying what made her tick. Now she was doing the same thing. The difference was, she hadn't decorated her place—the Agency had. Everything fit her profile, the person she was supposed to be. Roman's house was very much his, and she liked everything she saw. It was oddly familiar.

She picked up a picture from Nicola and Cash's wedding. It was the four of them on the dance floor, scrunched together for the photographer. Cash and Roman were in tuxes, Nicola looked gorgeous, and Beth smiled from under Roman's arm. They had been the best man and maid of honor and acted as a tag team that night, giving a little hell to the bride and groom and helping them celebrate.

"That was a fun night." Roman pushed off the couch, went to a wet bar, and came back holding two bottles of water. "Want one?"

She took the water as if it were a peace offering for his shirtless hello, though he was still shirtless. "Thanks."

He flopped back on the couch. "I can't knock the bride, but you were the best-looking girl there."

Beth sat on the other side. She blushed. "Nic will have your butt for that. Careful."

"Do you ever not downplay a compliment?"

She turned to face him, slipping off her shoes and tucking her feet underneath her. "No. Not really."

"Why?"

"I don't know. Why do you act like the world revolves around you?"

"You mean it doesn't?" He gave her a wink, stretched, and groaned. Roman kneaded his shoulder muscle. "You left the hospital in a hurry the other day. You want to talk about that?"

She bit her lip. "Sorry you overheard any part of that conversation. It wasn't meant for you."

Still working on his neck and shoulder, he shifted. "Heard bits. Wasn't trying to."

She was mesmerized by his hands kneading muscle. His skin was tan but looked suspiciously soft. Her mind drifted, her hands wanting to replace his.

Roman stopped, oblivious to her staring, and cracked the water. "For all the pain pills the doc gave me, they don't do shit for knots."

"Turn around." It came out before she thought better of the offer. "I can help."

"What?" His eyebrows rose as he stopped with the water bottle midway to his mouth.

"One-time offer for a backrub that expires in three, two—"

He squinted as though he still hadn't realized what he'd been doing, then gave her his back. "Alright."

He sounded as tense as she thought his back and neck might be. Beth scooted closer and put her hands on him. For a long second, her palms rested at the base of his neck, and her heart pounded. Shallow breaths screamed in her ears, and Roman's body, though lax on his couch, reacted under her touch. Without moving her hands, her thumbs lightly stroked his neck. A rush of chill bumps erupted, decorating his skin.

"You good?"

He nodded wordlessly.

Her hands floated down the cords of his back, fingers feathery over sinewy muscle. When she got to the base, her hands smoothed up, stronger, surer, and again clasped over his shoulders. As she massaged him, Roman didn't relax so much as he bent to her will.

Minutes passed as she ran her hands over every inch from his neck, down his back, and across his arms. Finally, she settled against him, daring to rest her chin on his shoulder. She let her palms come to a stop on his biceps, knowing it was a bad idea to be that close but unable to stay away. "Better?"

A large, male hand covered over one of hers. Her lungs stopped, ignoring the fireworks sparking in her blood and rushing through her veins. Now was her turn for the goose bumps. They ran along her arm, up her neck, and down her spine.

Roman turned around, his hand staying with hers too long. He finally let it go. "Much."

He tucked a stray curl behind her ear, letting his fingers slide across her cheek on their retreat. She needed to feel their touch again, and her eyes shut. The rise and fall of her chest mocked all her years of CIA training.

"What do you want from me?" Her throat ached. "Because seriously, I have nothing to give." Or nothing that she wanted to give. It would be cruel to fall for another man. To feel so deeply that a look from him would curl her toes. And… to be so scared of losing someone that she couldn't live. That'd been her, not that long ago, when she couldn't function or see through the tears in her eyes. Love had ruined her life.

Not that she loved Roman. But that very second, she couldn't move away from him, and if he didn't kiss her soon, she would cry.

"What do I want from you?" he repeated. A confident but somehow simple, sweet grin grew on the face that still showed the scratches and cuts from the explosion. "I want your mouth again."

Her lips parted, and she wasn't sure why. It wasn't shock. Maybe want. All of this was arousal, and that was just impossible. His fingers traced her jawline, and with the careful touch of a hard hand, Roman brought her back from her hopeless past.

"And you want that, too." Roman moved over her, closing the already tight space between them.

Her stomach tightened. He had good lines. The guy knew exactly what to say to make a woman swoon. That was all this was. He wanted her in bed, and now that they were both sober and in the same spot, he was making his move. Casual sex, nothing that should make her panic. That was all it was. Sex.

Nothing emotional.

Nothing that should make her warm and fuzzy on the inside.

Nothing like what was happening between them now.

Shit.

His fingers touched her cheeks again, pushing her hair behind her ears. Warm palms cupped her face, sliding down to her chin, her neck, then he took his hands away. She wanted them back as much as she wished she'd never felt his touch.

She closed her eyes and still saw his chiseled face. "Don't be sweet to me, Roman."

"I'm not."

Beth opened her eyes and focused on his lips then his eyes, wishing that he would act like a belligerent ass, not this guy whose words held such gravity. "Then don't do whatever that was."

"What? Touch you?" His fingers found a curl of hair, and he rubbed the strands. "Why not when it's so much fun?"

Ah, fun. That was the problem. Holding herself up much longer would require significant and obvious assistance. Everything he did turned her into a puddle of goo. And here he was having a great time. La dee flippin' da.

"I think I should go." She jumped off the couch without looking at him. Her legs decided to work at the last second, saving her from a moronic tumble as she tripped while trying get away. "I don't want to be here."

"Liar." Standing behind her, he closed the distance until his stomach pressed against her back. She could feel the length of his erection as he held her to him.

She *was* a liar. He spun her around, and she nearly apologized for doing so. Her stomach swirled. Arousal betrayed her with just the tickle and tease of his few words.

But she had no follow through. Her heartbroken body would be an embarrassment. Even if she wanted him, there was no way anything would happen. She'd fake it and then disappointment would eat her alive. God, she wanted him to be different, and she *seriously* hated herself for admitting that. Because...

No one had made her feel alive since Logan died.

Certainly, no one could make her come.

When it came down to it, she was defective. Maybe faulty wiring both upstairs and down because she hadn't had an orgasm since her husband—her *dead husband*—

Except... Roman gave her butterflies, and that hadn't happened in years. He made her *feel*, all the way deep down in her soul.

Fuck him for that.

CHAPTER 15

UNTIL DEATH DO US PART.

Well, she'd been parted by death. Far, far too early. Her husband had left her. He'd killed himself, and goddamn, that hurt as she dealt with life alone.

There had been circumstances. Some people never really came home from war. She should forgive Logan and move on, but she couldn't. He'd abandoned their future, severing the connection that she was only supposed to feel with him.

"Babe?"

She stared blankly, needing to run but stuck in place.

"Beth?"

Turning her head, she whispered, "I am a liar. And I'm a mess. Just forget me."

"Not in the mood."

That was said with a growl. She heard it. Felt it.

"I don't get you," he whispered into her ear, grazing her skin as he pulled back.

"I don't get me, either," she said. "I'm screwed up. Completely, categorically crazy."

His eyes narrowed, but he didn't back away from her. He actually brought her closer. "Everyone's got a little crazy."

"Roman…" She tried to look elsewhere, but he caught her chin. If he only knew how messed up she was, he would run. He *should* run.

"Yeah?"

"This is the worst idea you've ever had."

He shook his head then rested his strong hands on her shoulders. They were chest to chest. His *bare* chest. He was huge and overpowering and had a hard-on pushing in his jeans that begged for her to drop to her knees. A fine scattering of hair decorated his well-defined pecs, and when she looked away, her eyes were drawn to his Nicola tattoo. It had his sister's name, the date she was born and died, then the date she'd come to life again. The ink was dark, the designs beautiful. The whole thing wrapped around his bicep. Mixed within the barbed wire, the block letters, and scrolled numbers was an angel that looked like a warrior.

He followed her gaze. "Something to say?"

"It's gorgeous. I always meant to tell you that."

His jaw flexed. "She deserved it. Though its meaning changed. Obviously."

"What is it now?"

"A reminder."

"Of?"

"Of loss. I will never open myself up to hurt like that again."

Her mouth gaped.

"Babe..." He'd read her all wrong.

She wasn't hurt. She knew where they stood, and that gave her a solid dose of relief.

"Beth, that's not to say—"

"Shut up. You couldn't have said anything more perfect."

She put her hands on his bare, flat stomach. His abs flexed, making her palms itch for more. She slid her fingers up his torso, his chest, the light hairs scratching deliciously under her touch, standing there for her to explore. She did. Ripped muscles, perfect skin marred by the occasional healing bruise.

"You are so..." Her fingertips trailed along the hard swell of muscle, tracing the line of his breastbone as it disappeared into a six-pack.

"Don't say cocky. You should know better by now."

She caressed a nearly gone bruise on the side of his ribs then took her fingers to a healing scab on his cheek. "Such a warrior."

Roman's hand threaded into her hair. His mouth took hers, biting her bottom lip and kissing her with the strength of that word. One lift, and he had her wrapped to him. Her legs gripped his hips.

"The things you do to me," he growled while kissing her. "It's fuckin' fierce."

Hard and fast, he backed to the wall. The impact made her moan, drop her head, begging for more.

"That's what you want, babe?" Roman flexed against her, rubbing his cock between them.

"Yes..." Her hands knotted in his hair.

Roman, dry fucking her against the wall, silenced her gasps with tongue-whipping kisses. He moved them down the hall and up the stairs.

It'd been too long since she'd felt alive. She wouldn't lose the feeling. Couldn't. It was just too much, too good, and—

"We're good?" he asked.

"No, no, no. Don't slow down."

"Beth?"

Shut up. Please just shut up. He could make this physical, make this happen for her. All she had to do was survive her own guilt. "Take me to bed. Right now. *Please.*" She tried to kiss him, but he pulled his head back.

"Roman?"

"Are. We. Good."

"I don't even know what means!"

His eyes narrowed. "Fuck, sweetheart. This works for me. But you've said no. A lot." The deep rumble from his chest made her shiver. "Look at me, Beth."

Shit, nothing, *nothing* he'd said was *please ruin this moment, please open up to me.* But that was what she heard. She cringed. "I have to tell you a secret."

His jaw flexed. "Am I going to get pissed?"

"I don't think so."

"Is it going to make me want you any less?"

Her throat tightened. *Probably.* If she said that sad, pathetic truth out loud, he'd set her down, pat her head, and run like hell. "Maybe." Without her permission, her eyelids burned as her eyes went watery.

"Unless you want to stop, keep your secret your secret, party girl." Two-hundred-plus pounds of muscle surrounded her as Roman bent close and whispered against her skin. His lips tickled her neck, her ear, making her heart stutter. "Tell me later, and I promise I won't tell a soul."

She melted when his tongue traced down her neck. Full lips slowly caressed its slope. Strong arms held her, and she tilted her head, existing in the undeniable tension and letting it flood her senses.

Guilt warred with excitement, and then she lost control of reason. "The only thing I want to say is I need you so badly I can't breathe."

And to hell with the emotional fallout.

CHAPTER 16

PINNED TO THE WALL, BETH was light in his arms. He liked her in his home, feet from his bedroom. This wasn't a place he brought women. It was his sanctuary. Everything here meant something to him, and Beth, whether he admitted it or not, was included in that. And Beth proclaiming she couldn't breathe because of him. Now *that* meant something.

"Stop fighting me for a second, and you'll feel what I feel."

She nodded.

Every layer he peeled back, he wanted more. Somewhere, there was an invisible wound. That was his thing. He was a fixer. A protector. And whatever her secret was, he wanted to be in the know. But not right now. Thank Christ, she'd wised up and kept quiet.

"Then let's go, party girl." He held her to him, arms and legs still locked tight, and made his way to his bedroom.

A massive bed had housed his recovery. A thick wooden frame and heavenly sheets surrounded him. Each time he'd woken, his mind would slide to her. How sweet she'd taste, how good it'd feel to sink deep into her pussy, pounding until they were sated beyond what he knew possible. His pulse thumped in his neck. Big expectations to live up to. Because...

She meant something.

He worked his jaw back and forth and thought about blaming the pain pills for accepting crap that should've pissed him off—playing coy, hinting with whispers of secrets—but didn't. Fucking painkillers. Except he hadn't taken them all day, trying to clear the fuzz from his head.

He placed her on the bed. The more he ran his hands into her hair, the wilder her curls got. "Good look on you."

She rolled her eyes, trying to stop his screwing up her hair. "It's messy."

"We're messy."

She smiled, and her green eyes fired. "You say that like you don't care."

His fingers traced her jaw then the collar of her shirt. "I care, babe."

"I like that."

"I care about how you sound." He leaned into her, ignoring the soreness in his arms. "And how I can make it happen again."

"Lots of caring…"

"True."

She watched him watch her, and he slid his hands over the full swell of her breasts to the bottom of her shirt. He tugged it over her head, displaying a green satin bra as vibrant as the color in her eyes. "And I care that you're here, with me, ignoring whatever is scaring you so that we can just be."

Her eyes went watery. He'd gone too deep.

Feeling her in his chest, he desperately fought to keep it superficial. "Careful." He smiled quietly until his lips found hers, then he dumped them over together and pinned her to the bed. "I'm injured."

Beth laughed as he kissed her. "Shut up, Roman." Her hips flexed, purposefully rolling the V between her legs against his dick.

"Christ, party girl. You do something bad to me."

She put a hand on the side of her pants. For as simple as pants were, they didn't look like they came off easily. "Hidden zipper. Come on, let's go."

He heard the invisible zipper start to lower. "I swear to God, woman, if you take all the fun out of getting you undressed, I will be pissed."

"Have at it."

Have at it? "You're killing me."

She had wild hair spread around her head, and her breasts overfilled their silky cups. He took charge of the hard-to-remove pants, found the camouflaged zipper, and slid it down, baring her as he explored the smoothness of her legs. He was lost in the girl before him. Wow, was he lost.

"Roman…?"

Hot didn't describe her. He didn't know the right word. "What's better than gorgeous?"

Her pink lips silently fell open. He dropped her pants off the side of the bed. Matching green panties. Not a thong, which might've been the sexiest surprise he'd never expected. Somehow they did something to him that a scrap of lace could never achieve. Her body was tight, strong but soft, and that made perfect sense. Beth's eyes slowly fell from his face to his chest and stomach then to his erection bulging in his jeans.

"What?" he asked, unsure of her searching glance.

"How long have I known you?"

He shrugged.

A smile curved her cheeks. "I've been missing out, huh?"

"Yeah you have." He crawled over her, whispering words against her skin. "Coulda, woulda, shoulda, baby."

"Cocky ass." Her words hitched as his lips skimmed across her.

Not a kiss. Just a touch. "Yeah."

They'd gone from laughing and teasing to whispering, far more intimate than he ever intended. His lips found hers, and he kissed her mouth, testing her tongue with his. With a slow move, he had them on their sides, and his palm ran the length of her back, rounding over the curve of her ass.

He stayed on his side and let her fall flat on her back. His fingers traced the jut of hip bone, rubbing over her stomach. As slowly as he could stand it, he moved his hand back down the inches of bare skin until he could slide his fingers under the boy shorts and between her legs.

His heart slammed in his chest. "Christ, Beth."

She was aroused and moving under his fingers. Her face flushed as her eyes closed. She couldn't have been more of a temptation. Until she tilted her head and opened her eyes. Then he was done for. She had no idea what she did to him, because fuck it all, he wasn't even sure he knew.

"Roman." Her quiet voice sounded near pain. "I want…"

The tip of his finger ran along her bare seam. "I got you."

Beth's eyes melted closed, her swollen breasts heaved, and her legs inched apart as she mewed for his touch. One of her hands cupped her breast, squeezing and making *him* groan. His cock nearly exploded as her massage intensified. But he'd wait for that tight pussy to hug him.

"Two hands, sweetheart."

Both her hands worked her chest. He slipped off her absurdly sexy panties and spread her legs to him.

"Eyes open, Beth."

She complied but stilled her hands, cupping them over herself.

Roman pushed her hand away, leaned down, and sucked on one bra-clad nipple. His fingers teased her open, slipping across her clit and making her arch.

He bit her nipple through the fabric. "More?"

Her nod barely registered, but her gasp said definitely.

"More of this?" He bit again.

"Yes," she moaned.

"Or more of this?" He slid two fingers into her.

"That!"

"Maybe we'll just stick with both."

"Yes. Both." Beth writhed as he went back and forth.

Abandoning her breast, he moved to kiss her lips, still working his hand between her legs. Her eyes locked on him, and they touched something deep in his chest. Something played on her face. Desperate want and absolute terror. He slowed his roll.

"Beth—"

"I swear to God..." she gasped. "If you stop, we won't even be friends."

He laughed but focused back on her. "Not trying to be your friend right now."

"Keep the jokes to yourself." She covered her face with her forearms then dropped them to the bed as he homed in on her clit. "Oh God."

He worked her, watching her, and wanted her to come more than he'd ever cared about anything in bed before. Eyes squeezed tight, lips pursed, and cheeks richly pinked, she rocked against him, giving him little *oh*s that worked like a kiss to his cock.

"Come for me, pretty girl." The transition from party girl to pretty girl didn't do her justice.

Her head went side to side. Wild, thick curls splayed on the pillow. "I don't... I can't..."

God, yes, she could. She would if it killed him. Beth looked one deep kiss from falling apart. Mouth open, little gasp, and—

"No." She shifted away, stilling as though she'd seen a ghost. Her pink cheeks paled.

No?

There was a word he'd never heard before, but he knew what to do. As if he'd been trained for it, one little two-letter word made him stop and back up. He almost threw up his arms in surrender. But *no* didn't keep confusion from knocking him stupid.

What had just happened? He could barely handle wanting her, and she had to have been a microsecond away from a climax. "Beth?"

The blush on her cheeks had morphed into more embarrassed or angry than aroused, and he had no idea what to do.

"Beth? What... the hell?" Was he angry? Was she okay? Yeah, all of the above. What the fuckin' hell?

"I just can't." She wouldn't look up.

"Can't what?"

"Just can't." She winced, scooting away and curling to cover up. "Nothing. Never mind. Look, I need to—"

"So help me God…" He shook his head. "If you say anything about leaving this bed, I will make you explain yourself and your secrets and anything else you feel the need to torture me with."

Beth pushed up, acting as though she had on way more clothes than she did. "I shouldn't be in your bed. I just wanted to check on you. Not jump you." She rolled her bottom lip into her mouth. "I'm sure you have some doctor's note to rest." She tried to slide away.

He caught her arm. "What the hell is going on with you?"

"Nothing." She shook her head, chin up and cool collectedness in her eyes, then turned.

None of this made sense. "You can't possibly hate me that much."

She spun to face him, jaw dropped. "*Hate* you?"

"I always thought that one day we'd end up in bed. We had a game. But damn you, I liked it."

Her mouth shut. "Not a game. Sorry to bust your bubble."

"No, Beth. I'm not saying you're a game. Fuck." He pulled her back to the middle of the bed. "What I'm saying is that—fuck. I don't know what I'm saying." There was a reason no woman ever made it into his home. *His bedroom.* He jumped off the mattress, throwing her clothes at her and grabbing his.

Clothes pressed to her stomach, she seemed to shrink in on herself. "Fine."

"Who the hell would rather give the finger to someone than get off? That's what I mean. That makes no sense unless you hate me, and while I might be a son of a bitch, I've never been that way to you."

"You think I hate you?"

"If not hate, then what?" Because she was driving him crazy, and now it was like she'd snatched her orgasm away from him. It was his. He owned it, and the primal asshole inside was pissed. "I don't even know why I care." More head shaking. "Actually, I don't care at all." Except he did. Damn her.

"Roman—"

"See ya. Don't let the door hit your ass on the way out." He tugged on a shirt, heading anywhere in his house to avoid her and the mess of bed-head curls. But he turned back, unable to leave without one more look. "What was this, some fun way to teach the cocky SOB a lesson?"

She bit her lip silently.

"A tease ain't a good look on you, party girl." Though looking at her holding herself on his bed, he ached to tell her she was the prettiest thing he'd ever touched. "I might be a cocky fuckin' prick, but that makes you—" He balled his fists, shoving them in his pockets. His mind raced. This mix of hurt and possessiveness was about to make him completely lose his cool. More than he already had.

"Stop it," she whispered.

"Just go."

Her eyes welled up with tears as she pulled on her shirt, and he paced the length of the bedroom wall because, try as hard as he could, he couldn't walk away.

"It's not like that," she pleaded as she abandoned his bed. "Just stop."

"Then what the fuck is it like?" Without thinking, he slammed his palm against the wall. He stopped, staring at his fingers, ready to rip into the drywall then dropped his head, completely mind-fucked. It was like he needed her to come more than he needed to come himself. Or maybe it was how he needed to *make* her come.

"I can't." Standing in her shirt and panties, she wouldn't look in his direction, and her tiniest, saddest whisper was a sucker punch.

"You can do whatever the hell you want."

"No, I can't... come."

Incredulous, he felt his anger and frustration quickly begin to cool. "What? Like... an orgasm?"

She nodded, still not looking at him.

"*What?*" He tried to remember everything he'd just said to her but blanked. "Look. Okay." He couldn't register what had just happened. It didn't matter; her admission was a lie because the girl had been about to buck on his fingers. "Maybe no one ever told you, but you pretty much almost nailed it."

For a second, their eyes connected, but she stole hers away and stared at the wall.

Finally, she shook her head. "I know."

"But you... you *can*." This would've been seriously awkward if he wasn't pissed and confused.

"I know." She wouldn't bring her gaze back up even when he stepped closer.

"I don't get it. I don't get *you*." Or himself, at the moment. He moved within arm's reach, needing to touch her face, her curls, to lay her back down on his bed, spreading her hair on his pillow. "But you just did."

"Not quite," she said.

"Because... you stopped it."

Beth finally looked up. "Guess we all have a little crazy, huh?"

He sat on his bed, still keeping an eye on her. The tension in the room was enough that he wanted to leave. That would've been the easy route, but he didn't want anything easy. Not with her. For a long while, they stayed in heavy silence. Neither dressed or talked or moved until he came up with a plan.

"I'll make you a deal."

A shy smile painted her face. "A deal, huh?"

"I'll make it happen for you, then you won't have this hang-up anymore."

"That simple?" She laughed, rolling her eyes but still looking embarrassed.

"Yeah."

"Cocky." She toyed with a strand of hair. "To think you can just fuck my problems away."

"You wouldn't have it any other way."

Her green eyes rose, holding his. "And what do you get out of this arrangement, other than the obvious?"

Good question... "Don't worry about me. Deal?"

Her eyelashes fluttered. A possessive protectiveness surged in his veins. He wanted this as badly as he wanted her. This was a problem he could fix.

Beth bit her lip. "It's complicated."

"So make it simple."

"I'm scared."

His eyes narrowed. "Why?"

"Because then I'll forget. And because I don't deserve it." Her eyes darted. "Like I said. I should go."

She snaked her pants up her legs, leaving him speechless on the bed.

CHAPTER 17

BETH'S STINKIN' KEYS HAD TO be in her purse. She'd gotten there, hadn't she? If she had to go back into Roman's house and ask to look for her keys, she would die. No super-special-spy star on the wall for her at the Agency. Death by devastating embarrassment didn't carry any award-winning honor.

Beth dumped everything in her purse on the trunk of her Lexus but still came up short. This couldn't be happening. Just *couldn't*.

She looked up and down the large lots in his neighborhood and at the quiet street. Not exactly the kind of place to expect a bus stop, not that she even knew where to go if she boarded one. Calling a taxi would be an okay solution, except she'd eventually have to get her car. *Or* Nicola could do it. The girl owed Beth a favor or two, and when Beth promised to deliver on the details of this SNAFU, Nicola wouldn't be able to resist.

Out of the corner of her eye, Beth saw his front door open. Furiously, she searched harder for her car keys until she could stare no longer into her purse.

"What are you doing?" Roman stood on his front porch, cotton T-shirt painted on. And wow, was it a mind-numbing display of the guy's physique. He crossed his thick arms over his broad chest, making his muscles bulge in a way that wasn't fair.

She tore her gaze away. "Nothing."

"Just hanging?" he teased.

Her cheeks went red hot. "Something like that."

"Guess you're not looking for these?"

She peeked over, and her car keys dangled in his hand. Shit. Slowly, she shoved everything back into her purse and trudged back toward him. "Yes. Those are mine."

He held them out, and as she reached for them, he grabbed her hand, not releasing the keys. "Did you sleep with Naydenov?"

"What?" Indignation rose.

"You heard me."

"*No*. I didn't sleep with him, not that it's any of your damn business." She tugged her hand back but he didn't let go. "Don't be an ass."

"Why not?"

"Seriously, Roman."

"'Cause you can't come? That's your—"

"No, you stubborn jerk. If I had slept with him, I would've faked it. God!" She growled at him. "*And* I wouldn't have to humiliate myself and dredge up the hell of bad memories." She used her free hand and poked him in the chest. "So if you'd give me my damn arm and my keys, I can leave."

He let go, and she stumbled back.

"Why the bad memories?"

"Go to hell." She ignored him, rushing back to her car.

Footsteps followed. "Why not fake it ten minutes ago?"

That stopped her in place. Slowly, she turned, glaring at him. "I changed my mind. I do hate you."

He stepped closer, arms still crossed, and had the audacity to glare back. "Get back inside, Beth."

"Excuse me?"

"Stop trying to be such a challenge."

"Yes, that's what I'm doing. I'm trying to challenge you." She should've run to her car, but she couldn't move. This was the worst escape ever, like a walk of shame times a thousand.

He continued walking in the most smoldering, deliberating way possible. "You're confusing."

"Nope." Her voice wavered.

When he was a foot away, he finally uncrossed his arms and let the glare soften. "And you're the most goddamn gorgeous girl I've ever seen."

Her stomach flipped, and her bottom lip quivered, and she hated that. Rushing sadness overpowered her. "Please don't say that."

"How long have you known me now? A year? Two? You think I'm letting you off the hook that easy?"

She couldn't speak.

"Guess the better question is, do you want me to?"

"To what?" she whispered.

"Let you leave."

Yes! But really no, because she wanted his arms holding her until she couldn't remember the past. Beth shook her head. "No."

"Good." He wrapped her to him then ran his hands into her hair. "So I won't leave."

His hands fell away, and he took her hand in his, turning them back toward his front door. But it wasn't that easy. She couldn't get past all of... *this* without laying out what was on her mind. "Wait—"

His grip tightened. "Not gonna happen."

"Before—"

"Certainly not going to happen in my front yard."

"I can't go inside there."

"Fuck. I don't want to hear about anything *before*. Before what, I don't know. I—it's selfish. I get that. But you're going to tell me a reason that we can't... whatever, and I'm a selfish, fuckin' prick that doesn't want to hear it."

"Then just know why."

He turned from her, scrubbing a hand into his hair. "Seriously, Beth."

"I'm begging you. If I can't say what I need to say, we'll agree to forget today."

He paced, eyebrows pinched. "Fine."

Relief and unease battled for top contention. "Fine? Okay..." She wouldn't have thought it was in him to agree.

"Inside you go." Roman scooped her up and carried her across the threshold. Once the door was kicked shut and they were in the middle of his living room, he set her down. "Say whatever you have to say."

"I was married."

Surprise washed across his face. "Alright."

"But he died." God, how long had it been since she'd said that out loud? Years. And even then, it'd only been to Nicola when Beth had strayed from her promise to ignore the hole Logan left in her heart.

"Died..." Roman's jaw worked back and forth. "M-kay."

Died... she could hear the spinning rope in her head and tried to block it out. Tried, failed. Tried again and gave up. So she sucked a deep breath.

"Yes, he died, and *I* died right along with him. Inside... I turned to stone, just became gray, until I decided to close that chapter of my life and move forward, focusing on work."

His head tilted. "I had something similar to that, as you know."

Nicola. She bit her lip. "Working at the CIA was the only thing I'd ever done, and it was perfect. You know my cover. Party, have a good time... fake it all."

His hand rubbed his bicep. "Okay."

"But you." She shook her head. "You fucking jerk." Saying that made her laugh quietly. "You pop up, looking how you look, acting like the world is your flippin' oyster or whatever. I met you once, and it was fun. Met you twice, and I realized I wasn't pretending to have a blast when you were around. And the third time, it became crystal clear. When you were near, I felt different, and earlier, when we were... I guess I'm not as dead inside as I thought." She looked down, biting her lip. "So that's the gist."

Roman ran his hand through his hair then shoved both into his pockets. "Look, I'm a bastard. You know that."

She shrugged.

"If you want to leave, I get it."

Beth twisted a curl around her finger, unsure if he even wanted her to stay after her morbid, mortifying confession. The guy wanted fun and easy, and she personified complicated.

"Is that what you want?" she whispered.

"Hell no," he answered quickly, lust burning dark in his eyes. His voice was lower than it had been, rough, scratchy sounding, making her tummy flip. He stepped closer, fingers on her chin, tilting her face up to him. "But what do you want?"

There were so many things she wanted from him. The shocking realization was simple. She wanted *him*, in any way he'd offer. If the only way was in bed, she'd take it. To hell with the heartbreak that was a given.

Beth swallowed past the terrified lump in her throat. "I want to finish what we started."

He leaned down, his lips brushing her cheek, softly teasing her ear. They dropped below the lobe, pressing against a sensitive spot. It wasn't a kiss, but it made every nerve fire to life, giving her weak legs. His hands worked up her arms, sinful and slow. Cascades of goose bumps rolled down her back. She looked up as she shivered, seeing trust that she hadn't asked for but craved.

She lifted her arms above her head, and Roman slipped her shirt away before she let her hands drift into his thick hair. He walked them backward, retracing their steps upstairs to his bedroom, and her heart slammed in her chest.

Still, he hadn't kissed her. He just stared down, backing up until they met the bed. Roman found her pants zipper, slid it down, and took them off with her panties, then her shoes. His fingers ran up her legs, her hips, inching along her spine to the clasp of her bra. A quick snap, and he had it off, leaving her naked under his scrutiny.

"Why are you looking at me like that?" she asked.

"There's no other way to look at you. You're the definition of beauty."

"Oh." Heat rose up her neck.

He chuckled. "Oh?"

She couldn't remember ever feeling like she was about to be ravished. "You look predatory, Roman."

"Exactly." Hooking his arms under hers, he crawled onto the bed, taking her with him. He placed her within reach, tore off his shirt, then went back to work, drawing circles around her belly button.

"We should just, ya know." Beth shifted. "Get back to it."

"I will." Slowly, he traced her collarbone. "All you have to do is relax."

"I'm relaxed."

His mouth found her shoulder, biting, sucking, licking. "Relax more."

"I don't think relaxing will help with my end goal."

His hand fell between her legs, and she moaned. "Why don't you let me be in charge of that, pretty girl?"

She nodded. "Okay. You win."

"Thought so," he said as he stroked her.

As though he'd memorized his moves from before then upped the ante, Roman made her world spin. Every touch, whispering what she did to him… she was at his mercy.

"Pretty girl." Two thick fingers entered her. "Pretty everywhere."

She had no words. Lying on his side, Roman speared her again. Her hips pushed off the bed, and her body angled to take more of him deeper inside her.

"Tight."

She tossed her head.

"Mine," he continued.

His.

"You think you want this, sweetheart?"

Focusing on anything but him was impossible. Roman towered over her, breathing hard, making her die to come.

"My girl… I want to see it, feel it."

His girl? She moaned in agreement.

"I want you knowing that only I can make this happen."

Screw him for saying the goddamn truth. But he was right. So very right…

The build was coming, tightening, making her ready, and like an explosion lit, she detonated, bucking and throwing her head back, crying for more. Crying for him.

"Goddamn, beautiful," he growled into her ear, hand still working, slowing, between her legs.

God, she came. She had an orgasm after years—*years*—of not. "Roman..."

Eyes watering, she pictured his face and couldn't believe it. Then she could, because Roman was the only one who could do that for her. That she knew.

And as fast and hard as she had come, she went limp in sated shock, arms splayed loosely. Her cheeks and neck were hot. Blood thundered in her veins, deep within her. She absorbed the tsunami that overtook her body and found a Zen peace that had unexpectedly arrived.

Roman pulled her close. "You never do what I think you will."

Finally, she opened her eyes wide. "Wow."

"Yeah, well." He lay down next to her, their cheeks both on the mattress and their eyes locked.

She didn't blink. He didn't either.

Neither moved until she crawled into his arms and kissed him. "I can't imagine ever having enough of you."

He groaned into their kiss, his jeans-covered erection thick and hard between them. Her body ached all over again, and her imagination did an amazingly good job of anticipating how it would feel to have him thrust inside her.

Roman was a brick wall of warmth, and she clung to him as he moved against the headboard, pulling her to straddle his lap.

"You survive?" He messed with her hair.

"There's nothing I can't survive." *Except maybe you.*

CHAPTER 18

FROM FAR AWAY, DOWN THE hall and in his living room, Beth's phone rang, stealing her attention from Roman and her acceptance that surviving him was impossible, as was walking away.

He angled toward the door. "It's done that a few times."

Her phone had been ringing, and she hadn't heard it? A true testament to how under the influence of Roman she was. She hadn't heard anything except for the dirty awesomeness of his words.

"Shit, sounds like work…"

"Stay here." He hopped up, tucked her in, then left her alone to drown in thick sheets that smelled like man and sex.

She burrowed into the pillow, and his scent rushed over her, making her imagine falling asleep against his chest, listening to his heart, and feeling the weight of his arms holding her naked body to his. She sighed. Even if he broke her heart later, at least she would've earned a nice consolation prize.

Roman padded back into the room, jeans hanging dangerously low on his hips. "Getting comfy?"

"Don't judge. You have surprisingly soft sheets."

He laughed. "Pretty decent pillows, too. When I'm home, it's nice to sleep like that."

"Versus?"

"Sleeping wherever and whenever I can find a couple minutes on the job."

Logan used to say things like that. He used to sleep in ditches he dug in the desert or under the protective barrier of a mountain boulder. Roman and Logan had a scary amount of similarities. Army. Operatives. Killers in bed who made her heart swell.

She closed her eyes, burying her head into the pillow. Why did she have to compare the two men? They were different. *She* was different.

Roman sat on the bed. "One big-ass bag that won't stop ringing."

She opened her eyes, forcing a smile, and pretended Logan hadn't tried for headspace while she daydreamed about Roman. "Thanks."

"I can tell the difference."

"Hmm?" She dug through her purse until she found her cell, phony grin still in place.

"Fake cheesin' it won't fool me, pretty girl."

Busted! Her stomach jumped. "I—"

"You probably have a lot on your mind." His eyes roamed her body. "But I'm not finished with you yet."

She tried for a strong coating of fake confidence. "Good, because I'm not finished with you, either."

He folded his arms across his chest. "Good news, Miss Tourne. I found my decoder ring. This happy-go-lucky smile you've got going on? And the you're-going-to-screw-me attitude? I'm starting to figure out what's for show and what's for Beth."

As high as her stomach had jumped, it free fell down to the ground. Pride kept her from agreeing. Stubbornness kept her from refusing. Instead, she scrolled through her phone, checking the missed call. *Gregori Naydenov.* She held up her phone, wiggling it back and forth. "Work."

"Work?"

"Gregori Naydenov."

"Ah, that guy." Roman scowled. "Ditch him. Stay here."

"Done."

He chuckled, lying back on the bed. "That was easy. Too easy."

"You know I can't." But it'd be nice if life were sweet and carefree like bubblegum and cotton candy. "Are you going to be all moody every time his name comes up?"

"Yup."

"Prepare yourself, big boy." She shifted in the covers, burrowing closer to the mountain of Roman. "If all goes according to plan, I'm traveling with him in about a week."

"I hate that dude."

"He's an oddball, that's for sure."

"That's all? An oddball? Dude washes money for terrorists."

"I wasn't trying to absolve him of his sins. Just saying he's not a normal mark."

Roman grumbled. "Where you going?"

"Abu Dhabi."

He turned to her, brow pinched and eyes shooting angry daggers. "The fuck you say?"

"Oh, don't tell me you have a problem with that."

"Of course I do."

"Why?"

"I hate when Nicola takes the garbage out after dark. You think I won't have a problem with you heading to the fuckin' UAE?"

"There are worse locations to go."

"And much, much better ones."

She shook her head. "Don't be like that."

"Beth, I don't care if you wear a Kevlar-covered burka—"

"Come on, I know you're super overprotective. I've known that about you since before I met you."

He grumbled, easing an inch back. "Lotta good that ever did me."

"See. Right there. Don't be like that."

He lounged back, tucking his hands behind his head and making his chest widen, if that was possible. "Answer me this, Beth."

She laid her head on his chest and trailed her fingers over his smooth stomach. "Okay."

"All this hard-to-get act, it was over a memory?"

Her fingers froze mid-caress. "Yes."

"I've seen you date other guys."

God, but Roman was different. Didn't he know that? He'd been different for so long, and that was what messed with her head. But telling him that was a no-go because his Titan-sized ego would inflate even more. "You have."

"And you haven't…"

"Jeez, Roman. Personal boundaries."

"You're naked in my bed. We're past personal boundaries. Plus, I'm curious."

"You're looking for a trophy is what you are."

"Am I really that much of a dick to you?"

She bit her lip. "No. Defense mechanism. Sorry."

"So? What's different?"

"So… I feel something inside when you look at me. And I hate it. Except… I don't."

Roman studied her, and with each passing second, her lungs tightened. He took one big arm and wrapped it around her. "I'm sorry you were hurt. Life never goes the way you think it should."

She nodded, buried in his heavy hug. "Life just… happens."

"But for someone who smiles at it the way you do, I don't know… it seems wrong."

"Felt wrong." She pressed against Roman. The memory of her

husband didn't make her sad or angry. But the guilt was still there. "There's more."

Roman remained silent, but his other arm wrapped around her so that he bear-hugged her to his chest. "Alright, more. Tell me."

"He killed himself, and I should've seen it coming." Tears wanted to fall, but she wasn't about to cry over Logan while Roman held her.

His fingers stroked her hair. "Oh, pretty girl. Those things aren't predictable."

"He went overseas and came back a different person."

Roman hummed. "Army?"

"How'd you know?"

"You seem like an Army girl."

A quiet laugh escaped her lips without her permission. "You were Army."

"Hooah." But his voice was low, and his chest rumbled against her ear.

Repositioning his arm, he loosened his hold, and she set her chin on his chest. "All the signs were there. I just didn't see them."

"How'd he do it?"

She could hear the creak and spin of the rope, an instant auditory recall whenever she least expected it. When would it stop haunting her? Probably never. "He hung himself in the garage when I went to the grocery store."

Roman blew out a long sigh. "Fuck, Beth. That's rough."

"Yeah." Unshed tears burned again as her voice cracked. The terror from that day bloomed in her chest. And the panic. What was she supposed to do? Help him? Lift him? Hurt him? She wanted to beat him senseless, but he'd been dead, and she could do nothing more than collapse to her knees screaming.

"I'm sorry life shit on you. But if anyone's going to make it through that, it's going to be you."

She sniffled. "Me?"

"Hell yeah, look at you. Smart. Lucked out in the looks department. A *spy*." He made his voice drop like he was telling a secret. "You've got it going on. And you're strong. A survivor. You can take on anything. I have a knack for shit like this. I know."

Her mouth opened to rebut him, but her phone rang.

"Swear to Christ, if that's Naydenov..."

Instead of recounting the thousands of ways Roman was wrong, she rolled out of his arms and grabbed her phone. *Gregori Naydenov.* "Save your threats. He's not worth it."

But she let it go to voicemail. Roman stared, and the way he looked at her, she was safe and hunted all at once.

"What?" she asked.

"Now that you're fixed or whatever, you going to run out and screw every guy senseless? I mean, I might if I were you."

Disappointment rushed through her veins, and a sudden, sad heaviness hung in her arms. She painted on her practiced casual smile and shook her head. She wasn't "fixed." It was the guy, not the act. Only Roman. "Nah, too much *work* to do."

He chucked a pillow at her. "Don't sleep with him."

She laughed, but her heart hurt.

"I'm serious. Don't do it." His jaw muscles flexed.

Still wearing the smile he'd never see through, she climbed out of bed and started to dress. "Why?"

A minute passed, no answer. Roman stood and walked to her. He tucked her under his arm, squeezing her close to his bare chest. "Come on. I'm starved. All kinds of stuff in my freezer. Take your pick, and I'll microwave it just for you."

He leaned over and kissed the top of her head as they wandered down the hall, and somehow she knew this was something that would never happen again. She'd shared too much. There was no sex after a confession like that. As long as it didn't affect their hanging out as pseudo-friends, it wouldn't totally destroy her.

But... what if...?

She bit her lip. What if they worked together?

Pieces of a plan clicked into place. She was supposed to have security on her trip. Jasper had said someone from the CIA's pool of able bodies would fill in, but Roman could do it. He was built for the role, knew how to act the part. Plus, if she had to bet, Roman would want to insert himself into that job. The guy's overprotective nature wouldn't say no.

"Hey, Roman." She pulled him to a stop. "I have a proposition for you. All you need is an open mind and a little time away from Titan."

CHAPTER 19

GREG'S BODY ITCHED. HE'D HIT redial what felt like a dozen times, and his pet project was ignoring him. Which made him want her all the more. In planning his strategy to put Beth on his arm, he realized that he had to slow down his cocaine consumption. Easy. He was a man of willpower. But right now, his skin itched, and his muscles twitched. His mouth watered, and his anxiety was high as the fucking sky, especially when what he really wanted wasn't answering the damn phone.

Switching tactics, he scrolled through his contacts and found Evan's name. Evan had the hookup on the two things Greg craved. He hit Send and waited.

"Greg?" Evan answered on the first ring.

Thank God. "How often do you talk to Beth?"

Evan laughed. "Hello to you, too."

"Beth," he snapped.

"Okay. We know each other, but I wouldn't say we're friends."

Unacceptable. "Get to be friends with her."

"Get to be? Greg, if—"

"I don't ask a lot from you." He shifted back and forth, jonesing for a hit of something, ideally Beth. "We each have our… needs. I have a need now."

Evan laughed casually. "Say no more, friend. I'll get you what you need."

The line went dead. By the time he dropped the phone, Greg didn't care if it was stolen art, cocaine, Beth, or a whore. He needed something to dull his cravings.

⊙━━◈━━⊙

Maybe Beth should've thought out her plan of attack when

extending this offer to Roman. She probably only had one shot, and standing in his hallway, when they were pulled from bed by her work phone calls, he might not have been in the best mindset.

Still shirtless and wearing jeans she'd decided were made for his perfect backside, Roman hitched half a grin and nodded. "Alright, what's the deal?"

What was the worst thing he could do? Laugh in her face? He could shake his head and see through her pathetic let's-work-together scheme as a sad excuse to stay around him.

She followed him into his kitchen. "CIA's having someone around to assist with my Naydenov project when we travel."

Roman pulled several boxes out of his freezer and started opening them. "Someone around? Meaning?"

"Meaning I get to have a helper bee."

He chuckled, using both his microwave and a toaster oven to heat several thousand deep-fried and frozen calories masquerading as legitimate food options. "Helper bee, huh? And what does that person do?"

"Travel with me to Abu Dhabi."

His eyebrows rose. "All I have to do is not beat the piss out of Naydenov?"

"You'd have to act like you're a bodyguard or private security. Which wouldn't be a stretch. Evan would have to sign off, but it shouldn't be a problem."

"And who the hell is Evan?"

"My handler."

He growled.

"Are you going to be moody any time another man is mentioned?"

He looked at her sideways. "Pretty much."

"Why?"

He shrugged, swapping out microwaved food for another plate full of microwavable munchies. "Plates are behind you. Grab us some." He snagged a stack of napkins and sat at the table. "You're telling me that you want me around the guy you're going to sleep with for work."

Instant heat crawled up her neck. "Roman!"

"I'm just clarifying what your expectations of me are. Don't kill the guy? No fucking his world up until you accomplish whatever your objective is? Then it's game on?"

She put the plates down on the table then her hands on her hips. "You don't want me spending time with another guy?"

"Ha. *Spending time?*" He tossed a couple mozzarella sticks onto their plates before standing and backing her up until she pressed against the wall.

As fast as that happened, her heart pounded, and she couldn't swallow past the lump in her throat. "Roman?"

His eyes narrowed as though he were analyzing her. Tracing her jawline with his fingers, he slid his hand down the slope of her neck then down her arm until his fingers tangled with hers. They didn't interlock, just touched. Fingertips kissing fingertips, and she wanted those fingers to run over her whole body.

"What are we doing?" he asked.

"Snacking." She looked away, playing down everything she wanted and failing to make a joke through the thick tension hanging between them. "Wasting the afternoon away."

"Bull, pretty girl." He kissed her throat.

She couldn't keep her eyes open. They drifted to the side when his tongue touched her skin. She wanted to say something, but no words came. Only sounds of suffering. Prisoner against the wall, she realized it wasn't just how she craved his kiss. But rather, Roman could compete with the memory of Logan, and she liked it.

Maybe even more than liked it.

His teeth scraped where his tongue had just been. "Whatever this is, I like it."

"Whatever you're doing..." She groaned when his teeth did it again. "That's not fair. Can't think when you're biting me."

"Fair isn't fun," he whispered.

Roman's arousal pressed against her. His breaths were hot on her skin, mirroring her cadence. His hands ran into her hair, down her sides, and she wrapped her hands around his neck. He pushed against her, somehow rubbing her breasts and between her legs, and she was throbbing.

Now that she could feel *alive*, her body was instantly addicted and every sensation, screamed at her to make up for lost time.

In the background, a buzzing started, and she tore away from this embrace. Her phone.

"Ignore it." He bit her neck.

She nodded, mouth agape. It stopped ringing anyway. That was a sign that they should abandoned their frozen food smorgasbord and go back to bed.

Until the phone started again. Shit.

His skilled hands moved to her pants zipper with such smoothness that she wanted to smack him. Practice made perfect, and she didn't want to be some stupid plaything. But his fingers loosened the waist enough to grab her ass—rough calloused hands and all. Her complaint that he was too skilled was stupid.

"You are such bad news."

"The worst." He tugged her pants down just an inch. Maybe two. The fabric scraped across her skin, creating white, delicious lightning that made her see stars.

Her phone started up again. What the deuce?

Roman stilled. She had to step back from him. Maybe walk away, take a breather, something. Because that had to be work calling. It was the only option really, and she had *never* not jumped when they said to. Except when they suggested she sleep with Gregori Naydenov. Damn it. Choosing herself over the job had never happened before, and now it seemed that was all she was doing.

Still keeping her pinned against the wall, Roman grabbed her purse and handed it to her. "Hating this job."

"Right about now, me too." She dug until the culprit was found. Cell phone with missed calls. Again, her phone started to ring. It was Evan. Hoping she didn't sound like the man of her dreams had her against the wall, she answered, "Hey, Evan."

"Where the hell have you been? Gregori Naydenov is looking for you. *Looking for you.* Do you understand what that means?"

She did. There was a lot to do, and she had a very close relationship to build with Greg in a very short amount of time. "Yes, I—"

"Get your act together, Beth."

"Are you kidding me?" She shrugged out of Roman's hold and headed to the hallway. "I miss a couple of phone calls and you—"

"Unless you're on your knees in front of the guy, you answer the damn phone."

Red rage blinded her. "Watch yourself."

"I should say the same for you. You have no idea what you've gotten yourself into."

"This is an art project. A waste of time, of money, and my damn talent."

"Find Naydenov. Be his friend. Be his fuck. Do whatever it is that you have to do, but keep that invitation to that auction."

The line went dead. What the hell kind of handler was Evan? She glared at the phone, fighting the urge to throw it. She should've called Greg. But instead, she spun, wanting to find respite in Roman's arms. She slammed into a wall of angry muscle.

"That's your handler?" He held her by the shoulders in a grip that was rigid and would have been scary if it weren't for the unnamable quality burning in his eyes. "Prick has an attitude problem."

She painted on her picture-perfect party-girl smile. "All those Farm boys do. Used to it."

He rested his chin on her head, and she could feel his heartbeat. His arms wrapped around her. "You said I made you feel something inside. That you hated it, but you didn't."

Well, shit. He was a listener. Heart in her throat, she partly wished her bout of honestly had never surfaced. "Yeah, yeah."

"Beth?" He forced her to look at him. "I didn't want to like you. You knew my sister when I thought she was dead. You were all smiles and sunshine while I'd suffered through some of the darkest years of my life."

Her mouth opened. "I'm sorry—"

"But I get a kick out of you."

"Sweet," she joked and rolled her eyes. That still semi-protected her heart, too.

"I'm inherently distrustful. You"—he shook his head—"aren't what you seem. Every time I get past a layer of you, it makes me wish…" He released her from their hug and ran his hands through his hair. She stayed there until his arms dropped back down and held her. "It makes me wish I were something more than I am."

"What?" she whispered. "I don't know what that means…"

"You don't know how amazing you are, do you?"

She gave him a placating grin, avoiding wherever he was going. "I know enough to get by."

"Don't play it down, babe."

Beth hated the truth in his eyes, hated how she liked that he saw past her walls. "I get a kick out of you too, Roman."

Deep, dark eyes brooded, and the dimple in his chin appeared. "Good. Glad we've reached an understanding."

"That we amuse each other?"

"That I don't want you to sleep with Naydenov."

"Ah," Beth said. "We're back to that. Full circle."

He kissed the top of her head. "I like your freckles."

"What?" Her self-defense protection mode wasn't set to avoid sincere, off-the-wall compliments about the real her. Besides, she worked way too hard at hiding those.

"You have a couple on your shoulders and your nose."

He'd noticed? Her cheeks flushed, and she wished he'd focus on something that wasn't considered a flaw. "Not my most flattering feature."

Roman laughed. "I like them."

Beth bit her lip. She had no comeback for that one.

"Call Evan the asshole back, and tell him you've got your bodyguard."

"We're going to work together?" A rush of excitement flooded her. She wanted this for all the wrong reasons. But she also wanted him to know she was more than arm candy on the party scene. "I'm going to nail this assignment, ya know."

"Yeah, pretty girl. Wouldn't miss it. Or a chance to make sure everyone's friendly money launderer keeps his hands off you."

CHAPTER 20

AN HOUR LATER, ROMAN SAT alone at his kitchen table, rolling a beer bottle back and forth in his hand. Given what was in his freezer, he'd made the best meal he could think of—which wasn't much—then spilled his guts.

Inherently distrustful?

That losing Nicola was the darkest thing that'd ever happened to him?

His life had been ideal before Nicola had died. His baby sister gone, he had filled the days with war, with sex, bleeding for his country, fighting for what was right. It all came down to not wanting to look back. He'd joined the Army to survive and to keep his thoughts disciplined.

What he'd found had been a lifesaver, giving him the ability to cope. Structure. Repetition. A band of brothers. Then his home for life with Titan Group.

And then when Nicola came back? He had learned she'd been living away from their family. It wasn't right, even though he understood her motives. There were dark days after she was home. And Beth had had those years with Nicola. If anything, Beth should be the poster child for why he couldn't get close to anyone. Look at what had happened to him, to her...

But he could fall for Beth. Maybe he had already. Maybe not. She was a challenge, and he didn't lose. But when he was with her, he wasn't *just* coping.

He was living.

Roman scrubbed his face. What did it matter? Frozen food summarized his life. The only certain thing was his uncertainty. Jared would call him, say they had a job, then Roman would walk away from whatever he was doing—whoever he was doing—and head to who-the-hell-knew where, staying for however long it took to get the job done.

So life wasn't conducive to fresh produce. Or a steady woman.

But fuck, man. The girl who had just walked out of his house had left with a piece of him.

Add on that she was working over a dude Roman didn't trust or particularly want her around, and his gut churned. The whole thing was indigestion inducing.

Sometime today, he'd have to tell Jared he'd volunteered to work on a CIA job without running it by Boss Man first. That would be a great conversation. Roman rubbed his temples.

This was a serious case of hormone-driven overprotectiveness, and he ticked off the reasons Beth should walk away from her operation. Naydenov would kiss her. Fuck her. Hurt her. She'd like him too much. She'd be too impressed with the high-roller world. She'd get sucked in. Her cover could be compromised.

Yeah, he needed to stop thinking about what could go wrong. Draining his beer, Roman tossed it in the trash and wandered to the window. His phone rang and, as he answered it, Nicola was already talking.

"Slow down, Double Oh-Seven."

She huffed in his ear. "Would you please tell Cash to come home? That's an order, not a question."

"He's not—" He heard what he assumed was Cash's Wrangler pulling into the driveway. "What? You two get into a fight?"

"No. Just send his butt home."

"Maybe."

Nicola growled, "The doctor said he shouldn't drive."

"Well, he's not driving. He's parked. Sending him home would be the wrong thing to do if that's what the doc said."

"Roman, I swear to God, you listen to me."

"He's at the door. He's fine. Call you back. Love ya, girl."

"You both drive me insane."

He laughed as she hung up. Opening the door, he shook the phone at Cash. "A little warning before the Mrs. calls looking for you."

Cash's brow furrowed as he passed Roman and headed to the kitchen. He slammed to a standstill, taking in the whole freezer-food explosion. "What, did you have a Stouffers-DiGiorno buffet all to yourself? Man alive, why did you nuke all that stuff?" Cash grabbed a now-cold slice of pizza. "And why the crap do you eat pizza with pineapple on it? Though it's a lot better than *raw* food."

After a second bite, Cash tossed the pizza in the trash and started on leftover mozzarella sticks. He grabbed a napkin then studied the sink.

"What?" Roman asked.

Cash popped another mozzarella stick into his mouth. "Two plates?"

"Sniper boy can count."

"Was this some try at a romantic dinner, courtesy of Paul Newman?"

"Go to hell, my friend."

Cash moved through the rest of the food on the table. "These are good, though." He popped a couple of Tostitos in his mouth.

"Doesn't your wife feed you?"

Cash ignored him. "So who was the lucky lady?"

"It's not like that."

"Man, you broke out the crescent rolls. Of course it's like that." Cash pivoted, head tilted. "Is this a Beth thing?"

"No."

"Not a thing? Or not Beth?"

Roman stared at the rolls. "If you choked and died this minute, I'd be okay with it."

"Well, hell. Now I owe Nic fifty bucks. Fuck you very much."

Roman's mouth dropped. "Excuse me?"

"She said you'd sleep with her. I said you'd sooner cut your balls off."

Roman scowled. "And why would I do that?"

"Because Mr. Overprotective can't do shit about her CIA jobs, so you'd sooner cut off your nuts than admit to falling for a girl you can't control."

Roman shoved his balled fists into his pockets and glared. "There are so many things wrong with what you just said. If I cared, I'd correct your sorry ass, but I don't."

Cash laughed and went back to the pizza, picking off the pineapple on another slice. "Alright."

"Alright?"

"Well, if you don't want to talk about Beth—"

"Go home."

"Nah, Nic's on a raw-food kick. None of it tastes good."

"Careful—"

"Wasn't knocking my girl." Cash threw his hands up. "Just sayin'. You try raw kale for dinner and see if you don't head where there's something deep fried."

"Like there's anything you wouldn't agree to when it comes to her."

"Trust me, if I weren't starving, I wouldn't indulge in your post-Beth feeding extravaganza. But I'm withering."

Roman ignored the Beth mention. "What more do you know about Gregori Naydenov?"

Cash popped another handful of food into his mouth. "Why?"

"Beth's still working him over. They're headed overseas."

Cash threw back his head, laughing. "You're jealous. Fucking hysterical."

"Not jealous. Dick."

"She plans to travel around the world with the guy and suddenly you're freakin' Betty Crocker? Something's going on there."

Roman ignored the dig and considered the merits of asking what Cash knew about Beth, mainly what Nicola might've spilled. "How well do you know Beth?"

"Know enough to say she's a good one." Cash took another bite of pizza. "Great catch."

Roman scowled. "That's not what I'm asking. What do you *know* about her?"

"Are you asking about…?" Cash helped himself to a beer and leaned against the fridge. "I know more than I probably should. Marital privilege and all that."

Roman rubbed the scruff on his chin, lost in thought about Beth's dead husband and how much Cash might know but never said. "Huh."

"Huh," Cash agreed.

Minutes ticked by, and Cash drained his beer and tossed the bottle into the trash. The glass clattered in the can, and they both stared at it until he cleared his throat. "So you two… spent time together?"

Roman cracked his knuckles. "That's one way to describe it."

"And she…" He raised his eyebrows.

So Cash had known the girl had some issues. Roman didn't like that for several reasons. It was personal. It was Beth. It was Beth with Roman. That about summed it up. Still, Roman said, "Yup."

"Think she faked it?" Cash asked.

"Nope."

"Huh." He crossed his arms over his chest.

Roman leaned back in his chair, still rubbing the scruff on his face, remembering the red scratches he'd left on her neck. "What the shit does that mean?"

"I couldn't tell you." Cash paused. "But I think it's something besides knowing what you're doing in the bedroom. Not to get too personal."

"Yeah, dude, I think we've crossed that line."

Cash nodded. "So it's a *you* thing."

"I was afraid of that." In the pit of his stomach, Roman wanted that to be true. To know that he and Beth had something… damn cool, and the way he made her feel, made her come, that was unique to him. *Only* him. But that also meant way more than he wanted with anyone. He didn't do relationships. Ever. When he looked over, Cash was mean-mugging it. "What?"

"Man, Nicola's going to string you up if you fucked her best friend for fun."

But he hadn't—fucked her or done anything just for the fun of it. "Dude, what do you want from me?"

"Nothing. Other than to keep you alive. You're a good spotter. I'd hate to have to try to keep Montana." Cash blew out a slow sigh. "Plus, Beth's sorta become like a sister to me."

"Great. Now you know how it feels to have your best friend screw your sister." Though he hadn't slept with Beth.

Cash shook his head. "What I'm saying is, she's a good one. You've known that for a while."

"No." Roman tore apart a roll, not eating it. "What I've known is I've wanted Beth in my bed for a while."

"Say what you want, man. I've seen you chasing her since day one."

Roman shook his head. "Just have a hard time walking away from a challenge. A feisty, irritating challenge."

"Roman, man, think about what you're saying."

"What?"

"Beth's not a challenge. Shit."

"I don't have it in me."

Cash's jaw worked back and forth. "You ever going to forgive Nicola?"

"Already have."

"Bullshit, man. She still feels the angry vibe. You get that, right?"

Roman ignored him.

"It hurts her." Cash crossed his arms.

"No—"

"Here it is, Roman, since maybe your head's too far up your ass to know. She did what she had to do. And no one in the goddamn world was more devastated than me. You got that? *No one.* You're her brother. But she was *mine.* And I couldn't say a fuckin' thing. I was angry, so lost you can't imagine. But she's back, and she had her reasons, which included keeping your ass alive. Gotta forgive her. Gotta just let it go."

Silence. Roman rubbed his chin, not sure he'd ever heard the situation put in terms like that before, and sure as hell not thinking about it from Cash's perspective.

"Don't ignore Beth because you're angry at Nic."

"I'm not."

"Never mind." Cash laughed. "Sometimes you have to figure stuff out on your own."

"It's not like that."

"Right."

Roman groaned, needing to change the subject. "Hell, I have to call Jared."

"Why?"

"I volunteered to be her bodyguard on the Naydenov project."

Cash walked over and slapped Roman on the back "You, my friend, are so far gone. And watching you deal with this?" Cash waved a hand over their frozen dinner remnants. "Makes me pretty damn happy for raw kale and a woman I can go home to." He grabbed a mozzarella stick, took a bite, then pointed it at Roman. "Something to think about."

Roman stared at the table long after Cash had left. Finally, the trance broke, and he shoved everything from the table into the trash can. "I haven't even slept with her yet."

CHAPTER 21

BETH BALANCED IN HER KILLER spiked heels that made her butt look spectacular though her pencil skirt was a deep breath away from being too tight around the waist. She spun to the mirror. The look worked—expensive with a solid dose of book nerd. She fluffed a couple of curls, sprayed the hell out of them so they would stay put in DC's humidity, and headed for the door, ready to take on Evan and then Greg. Two men who needed equal amounts of coddling in their own ways.

She scrolled through her phone after stepping into the elevator and pressing the button for the lobby. It stopped mid-descent.

A woman about Beth's age boarded. "Hey."

Beth smiled, going back to her phone.

"Do I know you?"

Beth glanced back up. "No, I'm not sure we've met."

An awkward silence continued on the way to the lobby.

"It's just that you look familiar."

"Recognizable face, maybe." Beth shrugged. "Sorry."

"Oh! You were on TV. The first lady's dinner last week, gorgeous dress. Was that Chanel Couture?"

Only in this building would someone remember the news because of a designer dress. Suddenly, Beth realized why Roman had stormed her apartment after her night out with Greg. "Oh, right. That was me. One of those once-in-a-lifetime moments."

"Are you in politics?"

"No, just a lucky date with a politician's friend, I guess."

"That's so cool." The elevator doors opened. "Nice meeting you."

Well, they hadn't exactly met. But Beth had had a revelation and wasn't nearly as confused about Roman's outburst from that night, even if the thought hadn't been plaguing her. The more she figured out about him, the more she—

"Evan?"

Polished and poised with an annoyed scowl on his face, her handler held two cups of coffee. "Beth. I need to apologize."

"I was on my way to meet you. You didn't have to come here."

He grimaced. "Yeah, I did. I was out of line earlier on the phone. You deserve more respect than that."

She didn't know him very well, but this seemed out of character. "Um, okay."

"Coffee? Lots of cream and sugar."

He was right on the money on that one, and she'd kill for a little caffeine. "Unneeded apology accepted." She took the coffee and smelled hazelnut. "Thanks for this. I didn't have time and was dying."

He turned to leave the lobby. "The town car is waiting outside if you're ready."

Balancing on the heels of her shoes, she felt something tingle at the back of her neck. It wasn't danger. More like unease. "Let's go."

The swanky black ride idled, and Beth slid into the backseat. A driver she recognized from the Agency greeted her as Evan got in the opposite side. An unneeded apology? A ride to Naydenov? What on earth was going on? Anxiety raced through her, making her hyperaware for something big, something major.

"So you have friends at Titan Group?" Evan asked too casually.

Something Titan. She swallowed an aggravated sigh. What had they done now? "I do."

Evan nodded. "We have lots to learn about each other."

"I'd agree with that." But she wasn't going to be the first to volunteer anything.

"My boss got a call from Roman Hart."

And there it was.

"Then *I* got a call from Roman Hart."

She was going to kill Roman. Though she had no idea what had been said, it couldn't have been cordial. Roman was a little rough around the edges, and given the parts of her conversation with Evan in front of Roman... well, there was no telling. "He's a bit protective of me."

"I'd say." Evan sipped his coffee. "In no uncertain terms, he told me he's working Naydenov with you. You know about that?"

"I think that'd be a good idea." That was a non-answer to his question, but it was also true. "So we're good?"

"I didn't have much say."

"He's good at what he does."

"If he's Titan, he'd have to be. But..." Evan rolled his coffee cup between his hands. "If there's something more there, I need to know."

She bit her lip. "I've known him for a while."

"You're sleeping with him?"

"No." Not a lie. Maybe it was a good thing she wasn't, because she could still pass a poly if needed.

"Want to sleep with him?" he pressed.

"If you don't want the truth, don't ask the question, Evan."

"Shit." He grumbled. "Don't complicate this job."

"Right. Don't mess up the CIA's fancy art project. Got it."

He rubbed his nose, sniffing. "Alright, let's read you in. Roman Hart is on loan from Titan for an undetermined amount of time. Due to his... bulk and *good-natured attitude*, acting as an archaeological assistant won't fly."

"His bulk?"

"The guy looks like he could deadlift this town car, so he isn't going to fit in any cover but one."

"And that is?"

"Body guy, bodyguard, whatever you want to call it."

That was exactly the role she thought Roman should play.

He continued, "Naydenov will understand that you are extremely valuable to the Smithsonian, and between his pseudo-grade-school crush on you and your specialized archeology background, he won't be able to say no to your security requirements. Besides, look at some of the women that man dates. Private security for that class of woman is expected."

Out of everything Evan had said, the pseudo-grade-school crush stayed with her. She got that vibe from Greg too, but she was ninety percent sure that he wouldn't act on it. It seemed like he didn't come across many well-versed women that he considered equals. Speaking of which...

"I have enough of a working knowledge to BS my way through a few conversations. But—"

"Have no fear. Here's everything you need to know about that time period, their artifacts, relics, et cetera, et cetera. I'll warn you, boring crap."

She nodded, agreeing with Evan for maybe the first time. "Yeah, I've got the most riveting jobs the Farm has to offer."

"Don't let the benign nature of this fool you."

She sipped her coffee, deliberately choosing to embrace the hazelnut scent and ignore the eye roll that she was dying to give. "Not fooled."

He handed her a thick folder. "Memorize everything in here."

This was like being in college all over again. Memorizing useless facts. Logan had drilled her when they studied for finals. God, had it been that long? Almost ten years since they'd graduated together. She'd spent most of her senior year clipping out pictures of wedding dresses and assuming—correctly—that he'd propose after graduation. They'd had a fabulous storybook wedding, almost to the point of being clichéd, right before the Army whisked him off to war. Huge church, big dress, tons and tons of tulle, bridesmaids, and pictures.

She inwardly groaned. Why had she been thinking about him so much recently? She'd gone weeks, months maybe, without thinking about him like this. What was the point? He was gone. She'd tried to move on but couldn't. That told her it was wrong to try, that she should never forget, that Logan deserved better than a forgotten memory. Hell, he certainly deserved a wife that should have seen what was going to happen and saved him.

"Beth?"

"Hmm?" Her eyes darted to Evan. She had totally been caught in a daze. "Sorry, what?"

"You'll learn everything in there?"

Of course she would. "Yes."

"Good, because believe it or not, this op is the real deal."

Her phone rang and she silenced it. It started again. Silence. Then a text came through. She looked at it this time. *Nicola*. What in the heck? She opened it.

Nicola: *There's been an accident. Can't find Roman.*

Roman bent over, sweating in his home gym. Weights had been hell, but they'd been needed. He'd gone too many days without pushing himself. The treadmill had been another necessity that had damn well nearly brought him to his knees. But it was done. Hurt like he couldn't believe, but felt good all the same. Sometimes embracing the pain was needed. Especially if it helped clear his mind.

"Roman?"

He shot off the bench, every muscle aching, and spun to face Beth. "What are you doing here?"

"You weren't answering after I'd been knocking, so… I picked the lock."

He clenched his jaw. Something was wrong. "Why?"

"You weren't answering your phone. Jared and Nic tried to get a hold of—"

"Where is she?"

"Tracking down Cash."

"Why?" he growled, stepping forward. "What's wrong?"

Beth shrank back a step then steeled herself. Chin up, shoulders back. "There was an accident."

His blood froze, icicles crawling in his paralyzed veins. Who was out on a job? They'd lost a chopper filled with men weeks ago, and that had been terrible. But it had to be someone closer if this deserved a drop-by. "Who?"

"Montana." Her lips pressed flat. "Someone jumped the median. Hit him head on. It was instant. I'm sorry."

What? Roman had just seen him. Just... the guy was too young. Too promising. Anger burned deep inside, just like it always did when someone he knew died. He'd been that way ever since Nicola had died, and it became even worse after he found out that she hadn't actually. Some people were sad at death. Roman's reaction was always anger and aching. He'd barely known Montana. But the man had been fierce. Respectable. Shit. *This* was why he let no one in. Ever.

"Roman?"

He thought of Montana's older brother. Roman knew that kind of hell. He wanted to shake his head, to tell the guy anything that would soothe that awful kind of loss. But there were no words. That, he knew all too well.

"Alright, good to know." He turned and looked at the heavy bag. It would hurt, and that was perfect. "Fine. Thanks for dropping by, babe."

He decided to ignore anything more that Beth said. All he could do was focus on methodically binding his fists.

She stepped in front of him.

"Move aside, Beth."

Her mouth was moving, but he didn't want to listen. Or couldn't listen. Hell, he didn't hear a damn word because of the blood pounding in his ears. They rang, dulling the surrounding world, reigniting the injuries from that accident in Mexico where Montana had saved his ass. Saved his motherfucking life, and Roman hadn't been able to repay the favor. Shit, he hadn't even—

Beth put her hands on his chest. "Stop it!"

That, he heard. The woman had bellied up a primal growl, stopping Roman dead in his tracks and bringing him back to the present.

He stepped around her. "Out of my way. I'm working out."

"No. You're—"

He worked his jaw, hoping to break through the echoing roar

burning in his ears. "Doesn't matter what I'm doing, does it? He's dead. That sucks. Life goes on."

She scowled at him, stepping back into his line of fire. "You don't mean that."

No shit. "Doesn't matter."

"Can you please say something?"

"I already did."

"Can you please say something that makes me think you're not going to explode?"

He narrowed his eyes on her. "No," he said then picked her up and set her to the side.

"Roman!" Beth wrapped her arms around his chest.

"What?" He spun, backing them the few feet to the wall. "What the hell do you want me to say?"

Her lips were flat, her eyes sad. "I just wanted to make sure you're okay."

"I'm okay because I don't care."

"That's a lie."

"No, this—him, you, Nicola, everyone—is the reason I don't have a place in me for anything other than Titan. Other than being an operative. I'm cold. Heartless. It makes me good at my job. It lets me survive. So no, Beth, it's not a lie. It's a way of life."

"Liar." She ducked from under his arms. "Call me when you get your act together. Or if you want help. Either way, get it done."

Long after she was gone, Roman continued to lean against the wall. His heart was heavy, and she was right. He wheeled around and beat the bag without thought to his form or injuries, just hitting until he couldn't lift his arms. Nothing to do but collapse on the ground and stare at the ceiling, chanting that he didn't care and hurting because he did.

CHAPTER 22

JARED AND SUGAR'S HOUSE WAS like them—big, bold, and loud. The walls were bright. Their guns were on display, almost like an ode to art and gun collectors everywhere. Beth sat on the couch, feeling slightly out of place. Titan surrounded her. The group did things a certain way, and apparently, if there was a funeral, they arrived in force. They were an overwhelming presence, unified.

She watched the guys she knew, the men she didn't, and tried to ignore the obvious. No Roman.

Sugar wandered over, looking somehow respectful in skintight black leather and boots. "Where's your boy?"

"Not mine. But I don't know."

Mia Winters left Colby's side and joined Beth and Sugar. Beth got the feeling that this was a planned attack as the women sat on either side of her, readying their inquisition.

"He's not going to handle this well," Mia said instead of hello.

Not at all... but that wasn't Beth's to share. "The bit I saw..." Beth shrugged. "I'd say you're right."

Sugar picked at a painted nail. "Jared said Roman was taking Montana under his wing. First time he'd shown any interest in anyone new... since you."

Beth rolled her eyes at Sugar's fishing. She didn't know what Jared had said, but Beth had her concerns. Was Roman really not going to come? "He said he didn't care."

Mia shook her head. "He does have a hard time with letting folks in. Then this?" More head shaking. "He's hurting."

Sugar leaned in front of Beth to ask Mia, "So, Miss Head Doctor, what do we do?"

"Nothing. He needs to figure it out on his own."

Beth bit her lip. Roman would regret missing this, especially if what they said was true. "He's too stubborn to do that."

"Maybe," Mia said. "Tough exterior but a little broken inside."

"Exactly." Sugar's bright lips pursed. "Beth needs to go get him. And fix him."

"Uh?" Beth looked between them. "One, I don't think anyone can just *go get* Roman. Two, I'm not the one who should. Maybe Nic? And three, I don't think he's broken. Nothing to fix."

Sugar and Mia hummed.

Then Mia shook her head again. "Nic, God love her, is the reason why he likes to close out the world, as much as he won't admit it."

Nicola and Roman seemed fine to Beth, all healed up and memories rightfully stowed in place. "You might be wrong."

"Just because they're in a good place doesn't mean he's not haunted by the past," Mia said.

"I agree," Sugar added.

Of course they agreed. Beth knew this conversation wasn't a first for them. Their back-and-forth was too coordinated, too scripted.

Jared walked over and crossed his arms. "Where's Roman?"

Beth glared at him. "God, I'm not his keeper. Why does everyone keep acting like I am?"

He ran a hand over his jaw. "It'll take you twenty minutes to get to his place. Get him and meet us at the cemetery. The bastard will regret this, and you're the only thing that can make him go. Don't disappoint me, Beth."

Her jaw fell open.

"Go," he ordered then turned away.

"You heard my man. Go." Sugar's bright red lips smiled. "And he's right."

"I have no idea how to get him to do anything. Have you met him?" Frustration built in Beth's chest. She wanted to get him. Being around him made everything better, and funerals were the worst. "He ignores me most times, anyway."

"Roman is intense," Mia said. "He might not do what you think he should, but he's listening. Maybe to you more than anyone else."

Beth bit her lip. "So I should say… what?"

"It'll come to you." Mia stood, and Sugar did the same. "See you there."

Beth had no clue what words could get him to a funeral he would barely acknowledge, but God did she want to ease his hurt. She nodded and headed for her car. Operation Get His Ass to the Graveyard had no strategic plan, no operational guidelines. But it did have a mission objective. She'd never been one to fail before, and she wouldn't fail him now. Even if he wanted her to. Roman was going to that funeral if it killed them both.

⚓

A soft knock on Roman's door interrupted his time spacing out on the couch. Staring at the white ceiling was the only thing he wanted to do today. Not answer the door when Beth came calling.

And it was Beth, he knew it before he could see her. Knowing that and having her there irritated him to no end. There was only one reason she'd be at his place right now. At least she could've called. That way, he could have stayed on the couch to tell her to go away, stared at the ceiling, and, if he found a burst of energy, gone to his liquor cabinet and downed something with a smooth burn.

A harder knock taunted him this time. "Open up, Roman."

He sat up then leaned over, putting his elbows on his knees, head in his hands. He'd showered, shaved, and dressed for the service. But damn if he could walk out the door.

Roman cracked his neck and weighed the pros and cons of leaving Beth outside his door. The woman could pick a lock. She wouldn't stay on the outside too long. He shook his head, amused in the midst of all this crap. She made him smile even when she didn't know it.

A hollow, slapping noise sounded on the door. "Now. Or I'm coming in."

He'd called it. It made him laugh then immediately scowl because nothing about today deserved laughter. "Coming."

He opened the door. Beth wore a dress as black as the dark days he'd suffered through in his Nicola-spurred depression. Her wild hair was pulled into a tight knot on top of her head. The polished-princess look worked for her in a major way. Then he remembered why she was dressed like that. She pushed her way in, seemingly unfazed that it took threats of breaking and entering for him to relent.

"Well, make yourself at home." He swept his arm around, sarcasm dripping from his voice.

She spun on a heel and shook her head. "You get thirty seconds more of that, then we get in my car and head out."

"Not a chance," he grumbled. "But you get an A for effort, party girl."

"Mia said I'd know what to say, but I don't. I have no clue how to move a mountain that would just as soon sit on his ass, in his suit, ready to go but not leaving."

"That's because there's nothing to say."

"Montana was a good guy."

"You didn't know him."

Beth fidgeted. "Alright, fine. But you did, and you respected him, so obviously, he was a good guy. You need to go say goodbye."

"I don't know why you're making a big deal out of this."

"Look at you. You're dressed, Roman. You wanted to go. You just didn't."

Because he couldn't. "And that's why the CIA pays you the big bucks. Great analysis."

"God, you're a dick."

"At least you know what you're working with."

Beth stormed by him, and without thinking, Roman snaked an arm around her, grabbing her to him. Face to face, their eyes locked together, she kissed him. Hard. Aggressive and sanity saving. She bit his lip, lashing her tongue and making him come completely unglued. The pain in his chest stopped. If he hadn't been knotting his hands into her dress, grabbing her like a ragdoll, he would've finally been able to take a breath.

She pulled back, ragged gasps escaping swollen cherry lips. "Get your head out of your ass and get in my car."

"Why do you care? I don't."

"Because you *do* care, and if you can't realize it, then I will for you." Her lips tickled against his, and fuck him, that was a tender touch that soothed away the darkness.

"Why would you do that?" His voice was harsh, gravelly.

"Because hurting while you're alone is the worst kind of pain. You don't have to admit it. Just—" She paused, then her eyes forced back to his, vibrant and determined. "No one deserves to feel like that. Certainly not you."

She slipped her hand into his and pulled him toward the door. Against his plans, against the promise he had made to not leave the house today, he followed as though she were the Pied Piper.

Each step toward the car beat him into the ground. Then he dropped into the passenger seat, a complete mindfuck if there ever was one, but he wouldn't drive there. Couldn't. Because he was a pussy-ass bitch.

The ride was a slow hell, but then they were there. He wouldn't look out the window to what he knew was across the rolling green grass and field of marker stones. A funeral with all the military trappings stood at the ready.

They were five minutes from the start. His stomach knotted along with his throat. For as strong as he was, he wasn't sure if he could push out of the seat. Funerals. Final endings... he couldn't stand them.

Beth didn't look at him. "Out."

Then she left him sitting in her car as she stalked toward the rows of people ready to pay their respects. The farther she got from him, the tighter Roman's chest felt. He wanted her touch. Hell, he wanted that kiss. The one that had almost drawn blood. That cried for pain and release.

Roman dropped his head back and stared through the moon roof of her fancy little eco-car. He had to go, and he didn't see another ride he could hitch. So... hotwiring her car was the only escape. She'd kick his ass, but he could deal with that. Decision made, he pushed out the door, heading toward the driver's seat. The woman should've left the keys. Or left him at home.

Rounding the hood, he startled when the lights flashed and a quiet thump sounded from inside the vehicle.

What. The. Hell.

The car doors were locked. She'd *locked* him out of her car. He looked over and couldn't see her. Rage built in his chest. She would give him those keys. No time for games. Not when he'd been suckered and the funeral was starting any second. Damn it, man.

He spun toward the crowd and powered over, searching for her among all the people cloaked in black. *Beth.* There she was, next to an empty seat. Like hell, what was she trying to prove?

"Excuse me. Excuse me." He scooted down the row, ready to grab her keys and demand—

"Thanks for joining me." She looked at her phone. "It never occurred to me there was an app that could get Roman Hart to behave himself."

"Have you lost your fuckin' mind?" he growled.

"Sit, Roman. Try to keep it down."

"You have no idea..." His molars gnashed when he caught sight of Bryce and knew the pain of an older brother mourning that kind of death. "...what you are asking of me."

"You weren't going to join me. I'm not stupid. And you'd regret leaving."

He glared at her.

"Maybe I know you better than you think. What was the plan?

Hotwire my car?" Her eyes drifted down the winding driveway. "Home's too far to walk. No one would give you a ride."

He boiled on the inside. Around them, a few people glanced their way. "You're making a scene."

She ignored him.

"Beth."

A hush fell over the intimate crowd, and Roman closed his eyes, knowing what was next. A chaplain and the casket. An American flag and the family. His dry throat ached. Damn Beth to the level of hell he was in right this fuckin' second.

Minutes passed. A eulogy was said. The chaplain was done, and Roman's chest squeezed. Then, the bugler started. The sound of "Taps" carried across the cemetery. If he were less of a man, he'd leave. Walk away and tune it out.

Beth's knuckles touched his, and he realized his fists were balled. She didn't take his hand, just pressed hers against his. Her slight touch reached into his soul. He took a breath. Then another. Slowly, his fingers relaxed, loosening until they were limp. She locked her pinky around his, and he shut his eyes.

She didn't say a word, didn't try to take his hand to soothe him beyond what he was capable of. But she had given him a life vest, without him knowing that he needed saving. With the strength of one finger, she helped him live through the last painful notes of a song that embodied everything that hurt on the inside.

CHAPTER 23

BACON AND EGGS SIZZLED IN the background. The air smelled like grease and dishwater. Chatter churned around them as Roman stabbed the waffle on his plate. The last hour had been spent in near silence, but he looked less like a homicidal maniac, so there had been progress.

Some. Not a ton. Beth had decided the Waffle House waitress didn't know what to do with him. He was too attractive to ignore, but he emanated attitude. Plus, they were both dressed in black, clearly on the way home from a funeral. So the whole scene had to be confusing.

The poor waitress ventured back. "Want some more coffee, honey?"

He ignored her.

"I think we're good," Beth offered. "Just the check."

The woman popped a piece of gum, tore off their ticket, and smiled. "Pay up front when you're ready. No rush."

Other than ordering waffles, Roman hadn't said two words since the funeral. He hadn't stuck around to talk to anyone, just bee-lined for the car. And when Beth had parked in the Waffle House's lot, he had gotten out silently and headed into the restaurant.

He could stay quiet, as long as he stayed. When their fingers had found each other, it was a solace. He couldn't say it, and she would never ask about it. But she'd somehow known that he needed her. The undeniable, unflappable man who she needed more and more had a weakness, and she'd helped him survive. That made her heart swell. Not that she'd ever admit it.

"You ready?" she asked.

He stood, his non-answer giving enough of one that she followed. Roman grabbed the check, pulled out his wallet, and tossed a hundred-dollar bill with the slip of paper at the register.

Grabbing Beth's hand, he tugged her into the parking lot. "Give me your keys."

Her forehead pinched as she stared at him.

"*Please.* Give me your keys."

Beth dug them out of her purse and put them in his large hand. He walked them to her obnoxious car, put her in the confines of her passenger seat, and headed around the front. His face was drawn as he studied the pocked asphalt, and she wished he would say... anything.

The slam of his door echoed in her ear, then Roman revved the Lexus's engine, spinning tires out of the parking lot.

"Whoa." *Look at her little eco-Lexus go.* It wasn't the right time to smile, but she couldn't help herself.

Roman floored it, redlining it, and probably sending an alert somewhere that she was in a car chase. The CIA didn't give you a car if they weren't going to monitor it.

After a dozen hairpin turns that knocked a few years off her life, Roman went from not-so-populated roads to deep-woods back roads. Before Beth knew it, they were screeching around wooded corners as if in a Formula One event, spitting gravel as they summited hills and tummy flipping down hollows. If this was how he needed to release tension, then she could allow him to let it out. There was nothing like a practice round of escape-and-evade training to blow off steam.

Finally, he pulled onto an old country-road overlook. It was maintained, but by who knew who, since they'd been off state roads for miles. Roman dropped his head to the steering wheel. The sun was starting to set, the fall leaves turning the trees a deep red-orange. The sky changed pinkish-purple, and there wasn't a sound except for the occasional gust of wind. Fall was here, and it was the first time Beth had noticed the change of the seasons.

Roman took her hand in his, locked their fingers together, and closed his eyes as he repositioned.

Beth bit her lip. She'd been silent for at least an hour, which must've been a record, but she couldn't do it anymore. "You know, when Nicola called me to find you, I was working. I ignored her calls. Then she sent me a text message. *There's an accident. Can't find Roman.* She didn't mean to terrify me. But I started shaking. All I could think was that something had happened to you. I made them turn the car around, and I walked away from a meeting."

He cleared his throat. "Sorry."

"No, there's no reason to apologize. You just need to know that."

He turned his head. "Why?"

Good question. "I don't know."

He pressed her knuckles to his lips, sighing over her skin. How much tension had he bottled up? At least it seemed somewhat alleviated.

"Are you better?" she asked.

"Yeah. I just couldn't breathe before."

"And now?"

"And now..." He turned his head, and his dark eyes flared. Something intense and beautiful moved in where clouds had been. "I can."

CHAPTER 24

IT WAS A NEW DAY, bright and chilly, and the fresh air gave Roman a new perspective. At least his mind tried as best it could to let go of the funeral that had taken place days ago. The truth was, that was mostly due to Beth, not to the weather or sunlight or sheer willpower. Admitting she had that kind of sway over him was an eye opener. Coping through the darkness hadn't been so bad when she was there to hold.

As good as that news seemed on the surface, it had the potential for disaster. It meant he was letting her in. He should've backed off the Naydenov job, or at the very least met her at the private airport to head overseas in Naydenov's fancy-schmancy jet. But they needed a few minutes to iron out the last-minute details.

Whatever. Roman couldn't fool himself. If Beth was going to play arm candy to a dickhead for God only knew how long, then Roman wanted alone time with her now.

The doorman to Beth's building had apparently been given the green light to let him in. A casual wave and Roman headed toward the elevators. He needed to go through their Naydenov plans one more time if he was going to be comfortable with Beth working the guy over in front of him. As of right now, he just wanted to kill the dude.

"Beth." Her door had been left ajar, and he was going to have to talk to her about that. Forget the fact that the girl lived in a pricey museum; she was vulnerable without a lock in place. That wasn't going to work for him. "Babe?"

"Still packing," she called from somewhere deeper in the apartment.

He wandered into the living room, wishing this job required tactical pants and Kevlar instead of khakis and a button down. Sticking his hands in his pockets, he glanced around the place. Pretty nice stuff, though none of it was Beth. He found it interesting how far the Agency went to make sure everything looked its part, and also that the more he got to know her, the less Beth seemed like her cover. He looked up as she rolled a suitcase into the living room.

She parked it beside one already standing by the door. Next to them was a purse the size of his ammo bags.

He eyed all the luggage. "You know we'll be there about a week, right?"

"Yup."

God, the woman hit the looks lotto. He shifted in his shoes, wishing they were boots, and tried to keep his urges to himself. "How much longer is this going to take you?"

"Not much. Have a seat or look around."

He shrugged. "Where's the remote?"

Laughing, she shook her head. "Over there."

"What's so funny?"

"You."

"What?"

"There's gotta be a million dollars' worth of history lining the walls— art, books, whatever—and you're going to try to find *Duck Dynasty* or something?"

"First, there's nothing wrong with *Duck Dynasty*. Second, I'm not Rocco. So if you've confused me with my reality-TV-watching teammate, we're gonna have problems."

"Suit yourself, big boy." She rocked back on her heels but didn't leave. "You look very nice, by the way."

He shrugged again. *Get a compliment, return a compliment.* But as his eyes took her in, nothing polite came to mind. He could hike that skirt up and be in heaven. They'd never get out of her condo.

"Roman?"

Busted. "Nice..." *Tits. Face. Pussy. Mouth.* "...dress."

"What were you going to say?"

"Nothing that'd get us out of here on time."

She raised an eyebrow. "M-kay."

Seriously, he'd have that white dress over her ass, her bent over her fancy white couch, or up against the snow-white wall. Maybe on her too-white carpet. Christ, he wanted the real Beth to come out and play, not this CIA–sculpted version, all whitewashed and controlled. Everything was blasé except for the art and books and crap that someone else decided needed to stand out in a boring mecca to a colorless color.

"You want something to drink?" She headed toward the open *white* kitchen.

"Let me guess, white wine?"

"What?" She tilted her head.

He narrowed his eyes at her then at all the old crap that was set up to act as a pristine showboat. "Say you had a million dollars to decorate your place…"

"I did—"

"Nope, you didn't choose this stuff."

"Of course—"

"Stop it, party girl. Don't bullshit a bullshitter."

"I'm not."

He walked over to a muddy, dirty-lookin' piece of a bowl—not even a whole bowl—sitting on an immaculate perch. "You picked this?"

"It's a—"

"Nope. Did you pick it?"

She raised an eyebrow. "No."

Then he walked over and selected a random old brown book from the annoyingly white shelf. "And this one?"

"First edition—"

"Don't care. Did you specifically ask for it?"

The raised eyebrow fell. "What's your point?"

"That none of this is you." He spun in a circle, gesturing to all the things and ignoring the start of a raging boner. "It's all for show."

She crossed her arms, and, teetering in ridiculous heels that made her ass look like God's gift, she strode to the couch. "Alright, Roman. Surprise me."

Now it was his turn to raise an eyebrow. "Meaning?"

"I have a million dollars and no constraints. How do I decorate?"

"I don't know." He shrugged.

"You seemed so sure."

Because he was.

"Roman? Impress me."

"Already have."

The corners of her mouth ticked up. "Then prove your point. How would I decorate?"

How would she…? "Pictures. Of real people. Your friends. Real life, not this meaningless history."

"Some of this *meaningless history* is from the beginning of recorded time, the birth of humanity. Pretty significant, if you ask me." She pivoted on a heel that made his eyes crawl up her legs and skim over her curves. Even if it was white, her dress was unlike everything else in her apartment. There was something spectacular about the way it made her look. That, and she'd likely chosen the dress herself. Very Beth, even when she was in hiding.

Then his gaze landed on her face. Green eyes popped like emeralds.

"None of you is in here, Beth. And the more I learn about you, the more I know you have a history that's way more interesting and significant than a dirty piece of a bowl."

Her lips parted, but she stayed silent then looked away. "Other people do pictures, I… don't."

He crossed his arms and watched her wander around her condo as if there were something she was trying to do. There was nothing personal there. The more he looked around, the more he resented her place. She could get away with a few personal items. But it was all so clean.

He took out his phone, walked over, and pulled her close. "Smile, party girl."

The phone clicked with the picture, and he checked it. Beth was annoyed, glaring, and smiling all at the same time.

She gave an uncomfortable laugh. "What was that all about?"

"You need something that's not so contrived." He handed her the phone. "That's a great fucking picture."

She looked at the screen then handed back the phone. "We're not even looking in the same direction."

"Man, you've got your skirt too tight or something." His hand laid over hers as he went for the camera.

"Meaning?" She pulled her hand from his, but her cheeks were tinged pink.

"Putting a little bit of yourself on the job isn't the worst thing."

"I think we both know that I've volunteered to put *more* than a little bit of myself into this job."

His forehead bunched. "Don't be like that."

"Then leave it be."

"Why are you acting like—"

"Never mind," she huffed.

"You do have pictures somewhere." He went room to room with her following him. Each one looked like the last, all canned and very well thought out and befitting whoever the CIA wanted her to be. "Show me."

"Give it a rest, Roman."

Roman flipped the lights on and off, covering a lot of ground in the surprisingly large place. "I want to see your secret stash of Bethness."

"There's no secret stash of anything." Her gaze lasered on him, and in that second, he knew it was a lie.

He stopped his bull-in-the-china-shop approach, crossing his arms over his chest and leaning against her perfect wall. "I won't get rid of my tattoo. 'Cause I don't want to forget."

Her mouth dropped open. "Wh-what?"

"I could easily change it. Fix it. Nicola's alive. Little sister was a spy. I get it, and when I had this done, I needed the sting. I had more and more added on because I wanted to feel it. And when there was nothing more to add, I looked at it more than I should. Because it hurt. Because it was a reminder. And now... Nicola's been back for a while. I still use it as a reminder of what I went through and how deep I hurt." He had no idea why he'd shared any of that. Really, he hadn't verbalized any of that to anyone, ever.

Beth rolled her bottom lip into her mouth and stared at his biceps as if she could see his ink through his shirt. Finally, she turned and walked away, heels clicking down the blond hardwood floor. She walked into a room, and he followed her.

Her bedroom.

The room was expansive, the majority of the walls covered with floor-to-ceiling windows behind gauzy white curtains. He passed the meticulous furniture, the perfectly made bed, to the walk-in closet where Beth had kicked off her shoes, hiked up her skirt, and was *climbing* the built-in shelving. She jumped down with a box in hand and walked by without saying a word.

"So..." She sat on the floor, using her bed as a backrest, and Roman did the same, dropping to the floor and staring at her.

"This is my tattoo, I guess." She opened the top, and inside were pictures, a ton of them. She started to shuffle through them, and he caught a glimpse of a couple. They were of Beth. Younger. Freckles not so hidden by makeup, curly hair wild and loose.

She handed some to Roman. "Here. That's him. Logan."

That might've been her husband, but that was absolutely her —the real her he was certain must still be buried deep inside. For a second, Roman was jealous of a dead man who had taken his own life. That guy had been with Beth in all her glory, nothing held back. But then Roman's gut twisted at the darkness the guy had to have been struggling with to walk away from her and give up.

Beth took the stack, skipped through a few more pictures, then stopped again. Roman shifted closer to her, for the first time connecting how similar their pasts, and maybe their problems, were.

"It wasn't a million dollars, not even a thousand," she whispered. "Maybe a hundred if I was lucky, but you want to know how I'd decorate if it were just me deciding? Well, this was me. My first house with my husband. No picket fence, but it was as close as we could pull off."

Roman took the picture and studied it. In her old house, there *were* pictures on the walls and on the shelves. He *knew* she was a picture person. And whoa, there were bright colors. The room matched her eyes, and above all, Beth stood in the forefront, glowing.

Roman had no words to offer, nothing that could make her picture stack come back to life. Compared to what he held in his hand, her current place was... cold and emotionless. His heart hurt for her, and, unable to conjure up an appropriate word, he put his arm around her and kissed the top of her head.

They stayed there until he stood, pulled her up, and patted her on the butt. "When we get back, tell the Smithsonian you're sending their shit back. You and Sugar have similar tastes. She will bitch and complain and love to go shopping."

CHAPTER 25

HEART THUMPING SADLY, BETH STOOD, replaced her box, and stared at Roman. "My pictures. Your tattoo. We're even. Right?"

His jaw flexed. "Babe, I wasn't trying to—"

"I know." She scrunched her face. "I just didn't know what to say after a moment like that." And it had been a moment, heavy and expectant.

He covered the ground in a way only Roman could—super alpha, very manly—and pulled her into his arms.

Sometimes it was nice just to be held. "Thank you."

His lips danced over hers. "I'll give you a few minutes."

Because maybe he thought she needed to cry? Collect herself?

Odd, but now that their sharing session was in the open, she wanted to stay in his arms and call in to work, *not* run away from him and bawl. So, shoes in hand, Beth walked into her bathroom, hopping into each heel.

Roman had been right, and she'd seen Sugar's style in action. Maybe they would go shopping. Or maybe she could dump this condo if she could change gigs at the Agency. She wouldn't have to pretend to be a party girl.

Her cell buzzed, and Greg's name appeared on the screen. He was late, which was unlike him, but she couldn't complain. It had given her and Roman time to share something not even Nicola had seen.

She answered the call. "Hello?"

"Beth, dear."

"Hi, Greg." She leaned against the wall, wanting to get Roman and hide away from the world.

"There's been a change of plans. I'm running late, so I wanted to apologize."

"Not a problem."

"The jet is still waiting for you, though. I thought you might like to continue without me and start the evaluation, plus I promised you schmoozing time."

"You're not coming with me?"

"I'm right behind you. Go ahead—wait. You were set up with security, correct?"

"Yes, you met Roman."

He laughed. "Ah, you're bringing an attack dog. Interesting."

She grinned. "I believe the term is 'colleague.'"

"Beth…" He let seconds drift by. "Are you scared of me?"

Not a chance. But his ego probably wouldn't mind her cowering before his money and power. Plus, there was something more to his question. A hidden meaning behind his voice. Like maybe he questioned if she knew anything about the real Gregori Naydenov. "Should I be?"

"No."

"Do you do scary things?" she teased. "Have hidden, scary secrets?"

"No," he repeated playfully.

"Then I guess you're not scary, and I'm not scared. We can continue to call Roman my colleague. And if there's nothing to be concerned about, he'll have to suffer through a boring few days with us."

"Very well." Greg laughed. "I'll be there soon, at most half a day behind you. You'll have a driver meet you in Abu Dhabi. Enjoy your time until I see you."

She didn't trust Greg at all, but she did trust Roman completely. If plans were going to go rogue, she was glad he was by her side. She checked her reflection in the mirror one last time, and a sudden bubble of excitement grew. She'd be kicking it G4-style with Roman. Holy butterflies…

"Roman?" She went in search of him and found him on the couch, kicked back in the middle and surfing through her television channels. "Guess what?"

He muted the TV. "Tell me."

"Just you and me on the way over. Flying high for hours."

"No Naydenov?" His eyebrows rose, a sly smile playing on his face that made the dimple on his chin deepen.

"He can't make it until late tomorrow."

"I think I can handle that. So no rush…" His eyes dropped to her heels and slowly moved up her legs, her dress, lingering over her chest, finally landing on her face. "C'mere."

God, he didn't say a seductive word, but all of her bubbly excitement changed into something hot and bothered. "M-kay."

His eyes hadn't left hers, but her heart thumped harder with each step.

"Closer."

Finally, she stood in front of him, his gaze drinking her like she was a sight on display. His button-down shirt was loosened at the neck and wrists. His thighs looked powerful, even hidden beneath khaki pants. She loved the Titan badass garb, but this was another side of him, all clean shaven and perfectly mussed hair, and it was sexier than she ever could've guessed.

His body greedily took up most of the couch. The air had charged, turned intense. And every sexual fiber of her body was aware of the growing bulge in his lap.

"That dress, those shoes..." Roman leaned forward and put his hands above her butt, then tugged her to stand between his thighs. Slowly, his hands ran over her backside, letting his fingers flex. "They've made my dick hard since the second I walked in."

Her mouth fell open.

"And those pretty little lips. Perfect fuckin' tongue." His right hand rose from her ass and cupped her chin, thumb running along her bottom lip and pulling it down. "What I wouldn't do..."

For what? For her? For a blow job? How would Roman taste? Or feel when he came for her?

Beth let her tongue lick his thumb as he let go. Whatever he wanted, she was ready. The memory of coming with him made her sway between his knees. The anticipation hardened her nipples and dampened her panties. All she wanted was his touch, their friction. "Roman..."

Her head fell to the side, the visual of her luggage reminding her they had places to go. But as his palms ran to her shoulder blades then crept down her dress, skimming onto the back of her legs, she couldn't keep from moaning quietly.

"What are you thinking, pretty girl?"

She locked eyes with him. "That I want to make you come."

"Good fuckin' Lord."

She reached behind her and pulled the dress zipper down, then let her clothing fall to the floor. "They can't leave without us," she whispered, letting her gaze roam over him. "Are you going to let me have what I want?"

He gave a sharp nod, his chest rising under his crisp white shirt. He drank her in, making her feel sexier than she thought possible as she stood under his fierce study in only heels and scraps of nude-colored silk.

"Beth, baby. Do you have any idea what a body you have?"

No, she didn't. Far from perfect, she was a little small where she wanted more, a little rounded where she wanted less. But as he licked his lips, it didn't matter.

His fingers skimmed over her stomach, leaving a trail of goose bumps. She shivered under his deliberate, delicious, slow caress. Roman was calculating, and the juncture between her thighs pulsed, wanting his attention.

"Roman," she murmured. "You're making it impossible to stand."

His chuckle was subtle. It consumed her senses, making her nipples pebble harder. She wanted his tongue, his teeth, for them to rasp against her sensitive spots. But truth was, she'd moan for him if he so much as blew her a kiss.

He pulled the silk thong to the side, letting his fingers slip along her. "Can't have that."

Beth's eyes rolled shut, and her mind went blank. "That's…"

"Such a good girl." He stroked her, parting her folds and sliding one thick finger inside her.

Her hips rocked as she stood before him, wanting the heel of his palm to press against her clit. Beth couldn't think as one finger became two.

"Wet for me."

She nodded, her lips burning for their kiss. She inched closer, stepped wider, and he continued his onslaught, one hand squeezing her ass cheek until it hurt, the other rhythmically working her.

"Pretty girl."

"God…" Her body basked in the climb. "Roman."

"Only me," he growled. "Come for me."

Unable to hold herself up, she grasped his shoulders.

"That's right, baby. Hold on."

It was all she could do. Beth bit his shirt as he finger fucked her harder. Her back arched, his palm and fingers working her to the brink.

"God. Roman." She clung to him, embracing the violent ripple of her climax.

He pumped, she flexed, crying his name again. Beth gasped to fill her lungs but couldn't. She fell into his arms, and he wrapped her to him hard with her legs straddling his thighs.

"You sound"—he nipped at her ear—"fuckin' beautiful."

She summoned enough strength to push up and touch her lips to his. His hand that had made her come stroked her cheek, cupping her chin and outlining her lips with his fingers. They were damp with her arousal, the scent of sex between both of their lips. They didn't kiss. Just existed.

"Maybe you do taste like sugar." Then he kissed her until she melted against him.

Roman stood, holding her to him. He kicked off his shoes and walked down the hall. He stopped short of her bedroom, slamming her back against the wall. She gasped and moaned and reveled in his force.

He pulled back, dark-brown eyes studying her. "Tell me right now this has nothing to do with that box."

She shook her head, her curly hair now loose and flying around her face. "Nothing."

"Nothing to do with memories and pictures?"

"No," she whispered, but it sounded like she begged. "Please, Roman. Don't stop."

Roman flexed his hips and rubbed the hard length of his erection between her legs, reigniting rapid-fire sensations. "Beth, give me a promise."

"I promise. I swear. Nothing." She gasped again as the friction and strength increased. "Just you and me."

"Good." The word came out in a growl.

Still pressing her hard against the perfect walls in her perfect condo, he kissed and bit and made her mouth beg for more. God, she hoped they scuffed the wall. It would be a memory that she could call up when she was all alone.

He carried her into her room and tossed her on the perfectly made bed. White down comforter and white silk sheets. All expensively flawless and everything she hated. She'd never realized how they drove her crazy until Roman had thrown her in the middle of the mattress, messing up their impeccable design and her well-orchestrated, well-designed life. The sheets scrunched and bunched when he followed her onto the bed.

Nothing about him was gentle, and she couldn't wait for him to fuck her until she came on his cock, destroying the walls that she'd built to protect an old memory. She prayed that this time would be worth the hurt.

CHAPTER 26

ROMAN ACHED, WANTING TO DRIVE balls-deep inside her. He hurt with needing release. How had he not taken her against the wall? On her couch? On the goddamn floor? It was the wild hair and vivid eyes. He wanted to see them in a sea of white, softness surrounding her while he made her scream.

Her smile waned. "What'd I do?"

"When?" He tilted his head.

"Just now."

"No idea what you're talking about, babe." Because all she'd done was lie there, looking like everything he'd ever want to pound until they passed out.

"You've got this angry, intense look going on." Her cheeks took on a pink tint. "And I thought…"

Not sure about angry, but intense. Maybe. His chest felt filled to capacity. His mind raced as he craved more of everything—her skin, her kiss, her taste, the wetness between her legs, and the sighs and gasps that were hard earned.

Temptation existed, and it was sprawled in heels and a thong in front of him. His dick had never been so hard, his expectations never so high.

He focused on her bra. If he could make a list of mission objectives, he'd be golden. Bra, thong, shoes. Nah, keep the shoes on. Easy enough plan. First objective, the bra was to be a goner.

With Beth beneath him, he bent over her and toyed with her dark, curly hair. Such a vivid contrast to her pretentious bed. Her breathing was shallow, audible… and mirrored his. Wasn't that hell of a revelation?

Her hands cupped him through his pants, and he shook his head. "Don't distract me. Once you start, I may not let you stop."

Roman removed her bra. The tight tips of her nipples were cherry-colored perfection. They matched the color of her lips.

On display for him, she ran her hands up his arms. "Intense works on you."

He laughed, getting closer and letting his mouth and tongue trail down her neck. "Everything works on you."

Perfect round breasts filled his hands. Never before had he been a tits guy, but never before had he been subject to Beth's.

"I want you naked, Roman," she whispered. "I want all of you."

He wasn't sure why that sounded as though it took courage to say, but bravery danced on her face. He'd comply. Hell, he'd do anything she said.

"Damn, woman…" He hooked her wayward thong, sliding it off and leaving her naked. "You are perfect." Her eyes shut, but he wanted them on him. "Beth?"

"Yes."

"Don't you dare use me in place of someone who's not here anymore."

"What!" Her eyelids flipped open as she scooted away. "Don't be a prick. You're gonna ruin everything."

Maybe he was. But he needed to know it was him. No ghosts from the past. "You know what kind of man I am."

"Tell me."

He moved toward her. "The selfish kind, but you know that."

She parted her lips.

"The demanding kind and you love that." He leaned over her, caging her with his arms. "The kind of man that makes your pussy wet."

"I—"

"That makes you come." He gave her his weight, lying between her bare legs. "Hard. And long."

Her eyes widened. "You're using what I told you against me."

"Wrong, babe." He shook his head. "I'm making sure you know who you're in bed with."

"Of course I know. You ass."

"Say it."

"What…?" Her little nose wrinkled, and he wished her freckles weren't hidden.

"Say it, Beth."

"Don't ruin a good thing, *Roman*."

Smart little mouth he'd put to work soon enough. "Keep those gorgeous eyes open."

"They were." The rise and fall of her breasts came faster.

"Nope. They're one of my favorite things about you. I would've known if I'd seen green fire lighting in your eyes."

Her smile faltered.

"You want to keep going, pretty girl?"

She looked ready to protest because she was Beth and because she couldn't help but fight against them, even when he knew if his hand went between her legs there would be no argument about what she wanted.

"Tell me. I want to hear it."

"Yes," she whispered.

"With me? Not some memory."

She inched back again. "Roman, don't say—"

"I want all of you. Not some perfect tits and a sweet cunt looking for a great ride."

"Roman!" She tossed her head to the side.

"I want Beth. Everything that's there to give."

She glared then stole her eyes from him.

He leaned away and started on the buttons of his shirt, slowly working his way down. "And I like that you know what you want."

She watched him sideways in silence.

"But you have to give it to me." He shrugged out of his button down and ripped his undershirt over his head. He took her hands, pressing them to his stomach. Her fingers flexed. "That's my girl."

Still, she didn't speak. He rubbed her palms up the hard ridges of his stomach, leaning over to feel her palms savor his pectorals. "I want you too damn much to not get all of you. Face up, eyes on me."

She did.

Their eyes locked.

Then she nodded. "I'm with you, Roman. Only you. Eyes open. Promise."

Time ticked by slowly. Her eyes followed his hands as he rested them on his belt and unbuckled, dropping his pants. He moved off the bed, tossing away the last of his clothes, and palmed his throbbing erection.

Her eyes took him in, mouth agape. "You are... spectacular."

For the first time, maybe ever, he blushed. His neck and cheeks warmed. A half-grin tugged on his lips, her reaction made him harder than he could imagine. Slowly, he worked his length. "Think we're finally on the same page."

"What page is that?"

His thumb rounded the crown, wishing it was her tongue. "Dying for you, baby."

Beth nodded.

If he didn't feel her tight sweetness hug him soon, he'd be useless. "Lie back down." He pulled a condom out of his wallet and tore it open with his teeth as she obeyed. "Closer."

She scooted toward the edge of the bed, still in her fuck-me heels. "Cocky and bossy." But she smiled and bit her lip. "My eyes are open... because I need it to be you. I need... you."

However she'd said those words, the sound had changed his plan. Instead of sinking deep into her, he needed just a sweet kiss first. Roman pulled her to the edge and bent her legs, placing her heels on the mattress and putting her smooth pussy on display. His hands slid from her ankles to her knees then descended slowly down her thighs. Standing over her, he gripped her hips and dropped to his knees. His head dipped, enjoying how her thighs hugged him tightly, then he kissed her, long and wet.

"Roman." She jerked as his tongue swirled then gasped when his fingers took hold of her again.

Just a little taste. That was all. He looked up when she peered down. Her face was the stuff angels were made of, and he couldn't get to her fast enough. His body covered her, and when their lips touched, she sighed.

"I want all new memories, Roman, and I need to see your face."

His cock nestled between her legs, and she moved her hips despite his weight pinning her down.

"We can do new memories." His forehead touched hers, his shaft inching into her tight, hugging entrance.

She locked her arms around him and moaned until her vocal vibrations struck his soul.

"Yes," she whispered, kissing him softly.

He mimicked the kiss with his hips, rocking into her gently. However hot they'd started in the living room, things had changed. This was deep.

"God..." Again, she whispered against his lips, "You..."

They were good together, nothing like the fast and hard orgasms he knew. He could feel her tighten as she got closer. Her gasps needed more of him, and now he rode her slowly until she fell.

Beth's head dropped back. She arched and pulsed, and he'd never been so intent to watch and feel someone come. The show was all-consuming, and he came, gasping for her until they were a tangled mess.

His heart hammered. A light sheen of sweat covered his body. The exertion had been just as mental as it'd been physical, and he didn't know what to do other than hold her.

Minutes ticked by, and neither of them moved. Words wouldn't come to him, and she wasn't volunteering any conversation. The still silence made a decision for them. They weren't leaving any time soon. He'd keep her pinned to avoid the rest of the day. Abu Dhabi, Gregori Naydenov, Titan, and the CIA—they could all wait.

Carefully, he rolled them under the covers after he had removed the condom and trashed it.

Roman kissed her cheek. "They can't leave without you, so we stay here until we're ready." And now that he'd all but made love to the woman, he'd never be ready. "Just a little longer."

She didn't answer.

Pulling back, he looked down into her face. Her closed eyes and even breathing nearly killed him. Somehow, she'd fallen asleep in the time it'd taken for him to question his what-the-hell moment. Instead of running from her bed or fighting the apprehensions in his head, he leaned back and wondered if this was what it was like to let another person in again.

CHAPTER 27

BETH CURLED AROUND LOGAN IN that happy half-awake, half-asleep fog that made any morning when he was home better than perfect. He was home from war. He was safe. In their bed, relaxed and holding her. None of the demons that haunted him from overseas had had time to sink their nasty claws into him yet.

Morning, with that soft sunlight flooding through their bedroom, was her favorite time of day. She took a deep breath, but the air didn't smell like him. Beth closed her eyes, still loving the smell and trying to figure out what was so deliciously unfamiliar.

Logan sighed, shifting in the dark sheets and rumpled covers, and held her close. His lips brushed her temple, his voice murmuring something she couldn't make out. He sat up as she closed her eyes tighter, trying not to lose those precious minutes before the day started.

"Beth?"

That wasn't Logan's voice.

She couldn't open her eyes. But when she did, there was a tattooed bicep in her face. The words "TRAITOROUS BITCH" scrawled across tight muscle. Her stomach shifted and sank. Unnamable dread began to choke her. She pushed away from the words, the man, and stole a glance at his face.

Roman.

"Beth!" Roman had both his hands on her shoulders. "Wake up!"

Kicking and screaming to get away, she couldn't escape. Tears ran down her face as her legs tangled in the sheets.

"Beth!" He grabbed her, turning her, one hand on her chin, the other hand holding her place.

Her eyes focused. *Roman.* Roman was in front of her, holding her. Her gaze dropped to the tattoo from her dream. Her stomach turned. "I'm going to be sick."

Naked and tripping over the covers, she bolted for her bathroom. She tried to slam the door behind her, but her train of sheets wouldn't allow it. Beth dropped to her knees, hugged the bowl, and hated herself in a way that she couldn't explain.

Guilt made her nauseated. She wanted to heave, wanted anything to make this awful feeling go away. Nothing changed. Begging for relief to a God that sometimes abandoned her did little good, and she fell to the floor, taking the sheet and curling into it. On the white marble, curled in a silk sheet, she bawled at the overwhelming sense of loss and guilt.

A quiet knock sounded far, far away. She buried her face in her arms, pulling into a fetal position as she hiccup-cried, knotting her hands in her hair. Strong hands wrapped around her, pulling her from the hazy, depressing realization that Logan had left her on purpose.

Roman lifted her up and, holding her like a baby, carried her to the bed. He sat down next to her, not asking her to uncover her face.

She lost the concept of time. Even wrapped in the sheets, she could feel how strong and warm he was, could feel inside her how they'd just had sex and could smell his familiar scent marking her body. If her world hadn't been guilt drenched, she would've sighed, relaxing into the understanding that he held her without question. But it was.

Beth tried to swallow. Her throat was desert dry after the ugly cry on her bathroom floor. Still, Roman held her. Time passed. Minutes, hours, she had no idea.

Finally, it felt safe to unbury her head. "I'm sorry for that."

Roman studied her, pushing away a curl that was stuck to her tear-soaked cheek. "Nightmare?"

She stared at his chest, letting the silence answer.

He bobbed his head. "I get those sometimes."

"I haven't had one like that… in a long, long time."

He remained quiet for a few minutes.

"Are you mad at me?" she asked.

"What? No." A tight line appeared across his forehead. "I shouldn't have let us fall asleep."

Beth shrugged. "The nightmare probably would've happened anyway."

"Maybe."

"I feel like an ass. Probably look like it, too."

"If that's as close as you get to looking like an ass, you're doing alright." He pressed his lips to her hair then set her to the side. They both leaned against the headboard. "I've done a few things in my time that would earn the asshole designation, so count me as an expert. You shouldn't feel bad."

"M-kay."

"What… happened there?"

She shrugged again because there wasn't any way she'd go into details. "Oh, God. We need to get on that damn jet."

He chuckled humorlessly. "One-track mind: the Agency."

Kinda true. She used her job to block out life and avoid discussing her full-out panic attack in the nude while the man who caused it watched.

"Do you think I'm insane?" she asked.

He crossed his arms over his chest. The tattoo glared at her, mocking and urging her to confess the nightmare to Roman. Why, she had no idea. Maybe her subconscious was a sadist.

"No. Not insane, crazy girl."

"Then what?"

His tattoo flexed when he moved his arms—definitely mocking her.

"How about…?" Roman rubbed his arm. "Look. I get it. It's the same reason why I won't get close to anyone. We've both lost people."

For the fiftieth time that day, Beth's stomach churned and sank. This time *not* because she was remembering Logan, but at the reminder that Roman wouldn't get close to anyone. That hurt. Which it should. Because just like her dream had pointed out, falling for someone else was wrong.

"Okay, how about this?" He turned to her. "You put your fancy clothes back on. I'll do the same. We hop on your ride to Abu Dhabi and get this show on the road."

"Is it that simple?" Because it didn't feel that way.

"I think it has to be."

She had no idea what that meant. "Agreed."

Roman threw an arm around her and gave her a kiss on top of her head. "Get your cute butt up, my friend. We have a private jet waiting for us."

My friend. He'd called her his friend. Not that she was looking for a title, but she didn't want any subtle confirmation that she was meaningless sex. Though that might make her nightmares go away. At least there was that.

CHAPTER 28

THE DAYS WERE NOTICEABLY SHORTER. Cool air swirled. Roman took Beth's arm and guided her onto the private airstrip. She'd finally called to let the flight crew know they were on their way, only about six or so hours late. The jet was waiting, the lights in the cockpit and cabin door shining in the darkening night. Her throat tightened. The crew must've been watching because a flight attendant greeted them with a cool smile at the top of the stairs. They also must hate Beth for the obnoxious delay.

But as Beth and Roman boarded, the flight crew said their cheery hellos, and no one scowled at their rudeness. Nor could anyone apparently see what felt like a neon sign blinking over Beth's head— *Skanky, Traitorous Bitch.* So they were either closet haters or they were paid handsomely regardless of when the flight took off. Once Beth thought about it, the latter was the more likely option.

If only the flight crew's chipper attitudes were contagious. She and Roman had been skirting serious tension. Way for her to ruin a decent thing.

Beth shook her head, wishing there were a way to rewind the day and edit out the bad parts. She'd keep the screaming-hot sex and falling asleep under his bulky body. Maybe even keep the part where he held her after her little incident in the bathroom. But the nightmare and crying-heaving fit had to go.

Roman's hand touched the small of her back. "Ready?"

Such an innocent touch, except that was not how her libido took it. Every girly part she owned jumped to life, chanting, "Roman! Roman! Roman!"

She did *not* want to be *just* his friend.

Then she felt like shit.

Logic and emotion battled. Logan was dead. *He* had abandoned her. She knew suicide was so much more than that, but that was how she felt.

He'd never clued her in, never had asked her for help. Nothing. And since the day she'd found him hanging lifeless, she'd recounted every conversation, fight, homecoming, and redeployment, wondering how she could have fixed what he'd been hiding.

But besides all that, she'd stood in front of God and family and given him her heart, promising it for eternity. Eternity sucked now that she was all alone.

Except she wasn't.

Her eyes met Roman's, and it was like he knew what turmoil she battled.

"Miss Tourne," an attendant said, stealing her attention.

Roman moved away from her, acting his part as hired security.

"Hi," she responded, but she kept her eyes on Roman.

He stowed her carry-on bag and stepped over to another crew person. He motioned at a window, most likely mentioning her obnoxious amount of luggage in the town car, and then disappeared from sight.

"Did you want to come in?" the attendant asked, maybe for a second time, as Beth remained near the cockpit, staring numbly.

"Sure," she said.

The attendant followed her, readying for a flight that would take twelve hours, plus or minus. Given the late hour, Beth could sleep on the ride there. In a seat far, far away from Roman, because now that they were on the job and her feelings were hurt about his friend-status clarification...

She rounded a door and came face to face with Gregori Naydenov. An obviously pissed-off Roman stood beside him.

"You are stunning." Greg's voice boomed through the small space as he walked toward Beth, hand extended. "When I heard that you weren't flying until late tonight and my schedule had unexpectedly cleared, I thought a surprise might be in order."

"Surprise." She painted a grin onto her face. Stupid surprises. Life had dealt her too many in the forms of Logan and Roman. In no way did she want one from Greg.

He clasped her hand and leaned forward with bright eyes that looked a little too excited. Or maybe the look was knowing? They were a little red and a bit glassy, but still very beautiful.

Knowing what? she wondered. That she'd just been with Roman? That she was CIA? That her entire purpose for traveling with him was to use him and, eventually, take him out? Several possibilities crossed her mind, but none mattered if she didn't get her ass in gear and work over her asset.

"This is a great crew," he said, still holding her hand.

"Awesome." As if she cared about the crew. As long as they flew safe, they were cool with her.

Finally, she dropped his hand, and he bantered about whatever, playing the innocent card well. The guy didn't look as though he associated with the likes of world terrorists. Maybe he didn't. Maybe they were wrong, and his work was legitimate transactions.

"I took the liberty of opening a bottle of champagne when I saw your car arrive." He turned and looked toward the back, where a flight attendant with a perma-smile on her face teetered, holding a flute for Beth. The attendant passed Roman, who rocked a perma-frown.

"Would you like anything else before we take off?" he asked.

Beth shook her head. "No, I'm fine. Really."

"And your… coworker?"

She glanced at Roman as Greg walked her down the aisle with his hand on her back. The touch was placed higher than Roman's had been, but she felt nothing. That nothingness was wonderful because numbness was her normal. An attractive guy who smiled, touched, flirted, but who she never felt a thing for was her typical type, minus the friend-of-terrorists issue.

Her eyes searched for Roman's against her will. The beautiful, massive hulk of a man who was brooding in a jet, readying to kill everyone. For her. Oh God. Her stomach turned again, threatening to pull a dry-heaving show again. Her pulse quickened in her neck. She wanted that Greg-like numbness more than ever.

"He's fine, but I'm exhausted. I'll just pick a seat—" *far away from both of you* "—and cuddle up for the night, if you don't mind."

"You can cuddle all you like." Greg winked.

Roman hadn't seen the wink; otherwise, he would've come barreling over. Maybe everyone needed time in their corners. She certainly did.

Greg took a long drink from the champagne flute, and Beth eased past him, feeling Roman's stare. She couldn't—wouldn't—look over again. She found a seat that would recline and took the proffered blanket and pillow from the attendant. If she could sleep through the overnight flight, maybe she'd be stronger tomorrow.

Her phone buzzed in her purse as her eyes drifted closed. Probably work, but maybe it was Nicola. The phone buzzed again, and resigned to answering it, Beth dug it out. *Roman.* Excitement surged, and she hated how fast she opened the message screen.

Roman: *Lots of smiling over there. A plane and champagne make him interesting all of a sudden?*

Oh my God. Roman was jealous. Excitement morphed to aggravation.

Beth: *Just doing my job.*

A buzz announced his reply. After the last one, she didn't want to read it, but she couldn't ignore him.

Roman: *He's a prick.*

Predictable and irritating. Maybe bringing him had been a terrible idea.

Beth: *This again?*
Roman: *Just pointing out the obvious.*
Beth: *That you're acting jealous over something you want no part of? That's on you, buddy.*

She could pull the friends card too. *Buddy.* Nothing sexy about that.

Roman: *There's a difference b/w being overprotective and jealous. No news that I'm overprotective.*
Beth: *Fine.*
Roman: *I want no part of what?*

Well, shit. She should've thought that through before sending it. Reminding him that he wanted nothing to do with her, other than handing out orgasms, wasn't conducive to texting.

Roman: *Beth? No part of what?*

She stared at the screen for a long time, refusing to look up, though his gaze burned across the belly of the plane. *Fuck it.* What did she have to lose?

Beth: *Me.*

Send. But now that it was out there, the text looking back at her and his lack of response meant only one thing. That revelation was the wrong thing to share. She should've just ignored him, even though she could feel him staring. She wouldn't look at him. Nuh-uh, no way. He pitied her... or even worse, regretted her.

Eyes pinched closed, she tried to sleep as the plane began to move toward a runway. She repositioned in the seat, pushed off the blanket, tugged her pillow into a ball, then redid her blanket-pillow combo.

Her phone buzzed, and as much as she didn't want to see what he had to say, she had to. *Nicola.* She sighed. Not Roman.

Nicola: *Hey*
Beth: *You feeling better?*
Nicola: *Yeah about that...*
Beth: *hmm?*
Nicola: *I don't have the flu*
Beth: *Then get your cute ass back to work.*
Nicola: *I can't*

What? Nothing stopped Nicola. Ever. Beth had seen firsthand, the girl was unstoppable.

Beth: *? I don't get it.*
Nicola: *I *can't*... Like CANNOT go back to work. I do NOT have the flu.*

Beth stared at the phone, her mind turning the text messages over. Was she...? No. Couldn't be. Surely that wasn't shared via text message. But it was Nicola. Nothing was conventional. What else could it be?

Beth: *? Um... ?*
Nicola: *Pls figure this out. I can't tell you. Not until I talk to Cash.*
Beth: *oh...! Are we talking about the same thing...?*
Nicola: *Yeah, think so*
Beth: *Really? Are you sure we're on the same page?*
Nicola: *Hoping so (SQUUEEEE)*
Beth: *OMFG*
Nicola: *Surprise*

Maybe she didn't hate surprises.

Beth: *I thought you all weren't trying*
Nicola: *Yeah, we weren't*
Beth: *......*

Nicola: .... *yeah*
Beth: *Holy. Shit.*
Nicola: *No one knows yet. Just had to tell someone. Gotta go.* <3

Okay.
Okay? Okay. Whoa. Okay.
Nicola was pregnant? A baby? Beth couldn't wrap her head around it. But then again, a little Cash-Nicola baby? *Oh my God.* Beth was going to explode at the thought of all that blond hair and cuteness. Probably dressed in little pink-camo onesies. Or if it was a boy? Following his daddy around? This was almost too much to handle. She *had* to talk to Nicola. Like that second.

The captain came over the PA system. "Sorry about the wait, Mr. Naydenov. Looks like we're next in line to take off."

Beth saw Greg watching her while he was on a phone call, and she realized she was stupid-grinning, the kind of smile that made her cheeks hurt and let the world know that something crazy-awesome was happening. She tried to tamp down the smile, which only made Greg narrow his eyes and tilt his head.

And Roman. She absolutely could not tell Roman. Even if he figured it out on his own, Nicola might never forgive her. Okay. So she needed to redirect her mind to something else.

The only other thing that popped in her head was Roman. *Well, shit.* She should go to sleep. *Go to sleep.* She burrowed again, looking for the correct blanket-pillow combination. Frustrated, she counted to one hundred, named the capital cities of various countries, and reviewed every place she'd handled a CIA job. As soon as they were airborne, the lights would go down and the white noise would knock her out. Until then, nothing worked. She wasn't comfortable.

She heard him before she opened her eyes. Roman loomed over her. "You and me, party girl. Time to talk."

Party girl. Not pretty girl. Noteworthy, given their text messages. She hugged her phone close for some absurd reason, as if he'd somehow read her texts. Then her eyes darted around to find Greg. He was still in a far corner, ignoring them, phone pressed to his ear and magazine propped on his knee.

A growl came from Roman. "I don't give a fuck about him, and I won't say a word that messes up your shit. But you and me in that bathroom. Now."

CHAPTER 29

FRUSTRATED, ROMAN DIDN'T KNOW WHAT the fuckballs he was doing. Whatever ground rules they had established, they hadn't accounted for Beth having a nervous breakdown in her bathroom and deciding that he, along with Naydenov, was the enemy. They needed to touch base, get new ground rules, and figure out what the hell had gone wrong before they were wheels up.

She turned her head. "Go away."

"Not a chance in the world, babe. Ass up and in the head. Now."

Her smirk did little to quell the urge to rake his fingers into her hair. Restraint was nearly impossible. "Not playing."

She came out of her blanket cocoon and led the way into the teeny-tiny lavatory without a single verbal complaint. But the attitude radiated in waves.

He shut the door. "Beth—"

"What do you want?"

There was barely any room, and as the plane gained speed, they both shifted on their feet.

"I don't know what's going on with your sudden attitude problem, but you're gonna get us fucking killed."

"I—"

Knock, knock.

"Excuse me, but we're about to take off." The poor flight attendant had seen them both go in and probably assumed the worst, but Roman had no interest in explaining what they were doing to anyone and definitely not through a door, especially when he had no fucking clue himself.

Knock, knock. "Sir?"

"Back off," he growled. Given his frustration level, taking Beth hard and fast against the wall would at least calm him down. It was worth thinking about. "Beth."

"*What?*"

"What is your deal?"

Tart lips pursed together. There it was. She was thinking it over, knowing she'd fucked up. It was written on her face. "Fine. I got in my head. I'm not going to get us killed."

"So you're good?"

She nodded. "Good."

"Now explain your text."

Her brows pinched. "That was nothing. Like I said, I got in my head, but—"

"*I want no part of you?* Explain that." Because right that second, he wanted every part of her. Preferably naked. On her knees. With his dick resting on her tongue.

"Oh. That." Shaky laughter punctuated her irritating avoidance.

"What's going on with you, Beth?"

She shook her head. "Forget what I said before."

"Why?" His chest rumbled as he leaned over her, one hand above her shoulder, caging her in.

"Well, shit, Roman. *Why not?* Isn't that what you want? Friends? It works for me, obviously. I'm a bit of a whore. I get it."

What? His mind reeled. *Whore?*

Her eyes didn't house their trademark fire as she kept going. "You want simple. You want—"

"Stop." He inched closer, making the small bathroom feel even smaller. "Say that again, and you're gonna have bigger problems than worrying that Gregori Naydenov thinks you're fucking your security in the bathroom."

Her gaze shot to his. "I'm—"

"Careful. Say something unkind about the girl in my arms…"

They both shifted again as the wheels went up, angling them. He braced them by holding her against the wall—stomach to stomach, chest to chest. He could smell her shampoo and the light scent of perfume. The force of their ascent pressed them even closer, and he needed to hold her. Stop her. Fix her. Whatever was running through her head, if it could just pause while he held her.

"Say something like that again, Beth, and I swear to Christ, I'm going to lose my shit."

"But—"

"Whatever led you to think what you're thinking, you've got it wrong."

"Wrong?"

"Fuck yes."

"But—"

"I'm serious. I get that you have a lot going on, a lot to think about. Whatever happened in your condo, and now, with Naydenov making moves, but I'm telling you—"

"You set boundaries, Roman. I have boundaries, too. You want to stay friends. And I want..."

"You want what, Beth?"

She paused. Blinked. "You."

He took a breath. "Good. No one else has me, babe. Clue in."

"No one... else?"

He put a hand on her cheek, letting his thumb brush her skin. "I don't know what you think I did or said, but you read it wrong."

"Um..."

"I don't know what we are or what we're not, but you've got to pinch off the crazy." Because he didn't want to die on the job. Didn't want her to die on the job. And he sure as fuck didn't want to fight over something when he had no freakin' clue what the problem was. "Tell me you get this."

Beth's head tilted up, just enough that her lips touched his neck. It wasn't a kiss, but it felt like more. A need she wouldn't give in to, a want she'd decided to torture herself with. Hours ago, he'd been buried inside her, feeling her, seeing the real her, and loving it. And now this bullshit.

"Beth?"

"I got it. But..."

The jet started to level out, and he stepped back, aware that his cock was swollen. Roman brushed her cheek with his fingers. Her lips parted, her eyes fluttering shut. He traced the outline of her lips and watched the rise and fall of her breasts. For no reason, he ducked his head and gave in to one soft, sweet kiss that made his body sing.

Her lips turned down, and she whispered, "Please go away, Roman."

The words sliced him. Even if he hadn't wanted more between them, it hurt that she wanted a memory. Her husband. The guy she loved and lost. Whatever Roman had done in bed earlier hadn't been enough. His molars ground together. He'd failed to protect her, to give her the one thing that might stave away her nightmares or make her free from self-imposed hell. Acid burned his gut. Damn if he was adding another name to the list of people who could devastate him right this motherfuckin' second.

"Done." He did exactly as she asked. He turned and pushed open the tiny door, leaving her alone inside.

Cool air immediately surrounded him. Without the tiny space and party girl's lips on his neck, he could function. He checked his watch. Just another twelve hours until they landed and he could get space between them. Working a job would be good, even if it was watching her almost constantly. He took a seat, ready to relax.

"Your name is Roman?" Naydenov stood and walked toward the area Roman had staked out for himself. "We got off on the wrong foot. May I have a seat?"

Would this night never end? "Your plane."

"Very true." Naydenov sat across from Roman, rubbing his hands together. "Beth says you're a friend and a colleague."

"Yup."

"You don't look the type to handle... the finer things."

Asshole. That was a dig about him and Beth, Roman knew it. "But I am the type to keep them safe."

"Very smart, your friend Beth."

"We agree on something."

"I'm a businessman." Naydenov flicked an imaginary piece of lint off an eye-rollingly expensive suit.

"I'm not."

"What are you then, Mr....?"

"Roman works just fine."

"Roman." Naydenov leaned back in his seat. "You don't like me?"

"I have no opinion about you one way or the other."

"But you do like Miss Tourne?"

Roman leaned forward, mustering as much menace as possible. "Professionally speaking, there's not a thing in the world I would let harm her."

"Professionally speaking?"

"She's the job." Roman inched closer, letting his voice rumble low. "You got a problem with that, buddy?"

"You'd lay down your life for her?"

"Without question."

In the background, Roman heard the lavatory door slam open and shut. She was nearby, and he knew that his answer had less to do with the job than he would ever admit.

"Interesting."

Roman gave Naydenov a tight smile. "I'm not here to make friends or to look at dusty pieces of old Middle Eastern crap. I'm on this flight to make sure the woman back there does her job safely and gets her ass back on US soil. You might as well pretend I'm not here."

"I already do."

Dick. "So we have an understanding."

Naydenov stood but didn't walk away. "One more question."

"Shoot." Roman thought of several ways to kill the prick without moving more than three feet from his seat.

"We covered professionally speaking; now, personally speaking?"

Roman's jaw muscles ached as his molars clamped together. "Personally speaking, we work together, and she's under my protection. Should anything step between her and what I perceive as her happiness and safety, then I will *personally* destroy it. Does that make sense?" Roman stood, going toe to toe with Naydenov. "I will attack. Viciously and without concern for consequences."

Naydenov's lips flattened. He didn't back down, but he certainly paled. "No need for barbaric threats." He turned for his seat, walking a few steps before looking back. "Beth and I have both a professional *and* personal relationship. I expect you to respect that. Tone down the thug attitude, and we'll survive this trip."

It wasn't true. Roman knew the fucker had lied to his face, but it didn't keep Roman's rage in check. This was a job. Naydenov was a target. Everything was a charade, and nothing was what it seemed.

Roman kept that on repeat at he took his seat again, ignoring Naydenov, who headed for Beth. Her sweet laughter filled the cabin seconds later. The sound was salt in the wound of her "Please go away," and Roman balled his fists, trying not to plot the death of the asshole flirting with his girl feet behind him.

CHAPTER 30

THREE MAJOR THINGS WERE ON Beth's priority list. None were work, which was a problem because they'd landed, and their uncomfortable threesome was swept away by a driver to a hotel where the auction was to be held. The hotel was also one that Roman had all but demanded they stay at prior to finding out they were actually staying there.

But her list was her distraction. Nicola was pregnant, and that was apparently a secret. Beth and Roman were friends—so he said—that had sucked, leaving her with a major case of roller-coaster emotions. And finally, Greg was off. He flirted like a pro, but his eye-bouncing agitation became more prevalent, and every single time he had the chance, the man had uber-expensive alcohol in hand.

She shelved the list and spun in the hotel lobby as they checked in. Gold-gilded everything. Ornate tapestries. And money, money, money hung from everywhere. The people. The people's people. The cars, the rooms, the staff. She expected dollar bills to rain from the sky just because. Saying the hotel was the very definition of opulent wouldn't do it justice.

Greg had murmured his approval when they'd arrived.

But it was Roman who made the place even more interesting. Once they'd walked through the grand doors, he'd acted like he'd been there a hundred times before. She had watched the staff with a close eye. She swore they knew, or at least recognized, Roman. Their looks weren't the standard reaction to a massive dude with an unnerving, killer smile. Not a single person was affected by him. No double takes. Nothing.

Another thing: Roman didn't so much as question where the rooms were or how they were assigned. He didn't evil-eye Greg when Greg requested Beth's room be next to his and Roman could be wherever, preferably a different floor. Roman just acted as though he didn't care, which could only mean that Roman *more* than cared.

Or... whatever she'd seen happen between Roman and Greg on the plane had permanently changed Roman's opinion of her. What had happened there? And what had happened to her and Roman in the lavatory? She'd had way too much time wide awake while wearing a mocking eye mask to think about his words, his actions, how very close they were... and everything that had happened between them in her bedroom. Both the very good and the embarrassingly bad.

She'd had the audacity to try for new memories? Stupid, stupid, stupid. Except the more she thought about it, the more she wondered. Logan had loved her, really, truly loved her, no matter what he'd done. If he'd been able to stop the post-deployment darkness, he would have.

God, no matter how much she'd loved him, she'd had no idea how he was suffering. Had he faulted her blindness? Maybe. Maybe not.

She stood in the middle, Greg on one side, Roman on the other. They made their way to an elevator for an uncomfortable ride. A bellboy took their luggage, and she continued to watch Roman. He was the first one out when the gold doors opened. He walked to her room, swung the door open, and ran through a basic security check. Very basic. Very un-Roman.

"You good?" he asked.

"Yes."

Roman turned to Greg. "If the itinerary changes, I need notice."

"Of course."

Then Roman turned to her, and she felt his gaze sweep across her body. "And whatever you need, let me know."

Her cheeks heated instantaneously. "Absolutely. Thank you."

He nodded to her, glared at Greg, and left them alone.

Greg laughed. "Quite the bulldog they've sent you with."

"He's good."

"So he says."

She wanted to slap the uppitiness out of him. "Actually, he's the best."

Greg studied her with amused eyes. "Then excellent. I like having the best."

There was a connotation hanging in his words, but she ignored it. "So, the itinerary. We have a few hours before we leave for the auction?"

He inclined his head. "Would you like to join me for breakfast? Though here it would be dinner."

She was starved but shook her head. "I need to catch up on work and research, one or two more things."

"But—"

"Greg." She really didn't have the energy to play friend-not-lover games with him. "You want me to be the best. Let me do my job." She subtly batted her eyelashes. "We have to have you in the best position. Right? Best of the best."

That was his weak point. As nice as he was, he seemed addicted to the finer things—maybe even the finest things. That would be his downfall.

<hr />

"Yes, best of the best." Greg checked his Rolex, adjusting it for the correct time zone.

Someone knocked. Beth answered the door and let the bellboy in. The man stacked her luggage and exchanged pleasantries before he left. If her bags were there, Greg's were probably also in his room, and he was crawling out of his skin. Something had to give. He needed companionship or cocaine. This dance with her was moving much more slowly than he felt the urge for, yet he didn't want to ruin his play. She was quickly becoming more than an interest.

He was a collector of fine things, and Beth was his next commodity— a refreshing, challenging girl who might encourage him to consider retirement. This auction could mean big things for the future if what he hoped for was there.

He eyed her. She wasn't ready. Companionship wasn't going to happen. That meant he had a bigger problem. He'd been flying high when he'd foolishly decided he didn't need any product to help make it through his days around her. And now he had a taste for cocaine but none with him. Just like he wanted sex and had no one. A workout was in order. Or a blow job from a professional. That could be arranged. Whatever. Any kind of release would work temporarily.

He stepped toward Beth. "I'm going to head for a swim. Join me?"

"Maybe next time."

The urges quadrupled when she sucked her bottom lip into her mouth. Maybe it was a mistake to have brought her and not one of his favorite sluts with a dirty, sucking mouth. He gave Beth a once-over. "I'm across the hall if you need anything."

Her genuine smile made him feel good, dampening the urge for a fix a degree. The back and forth would give him hives if he weren't careful. *Fuck.* His thoughts were all over the place. He couldn't be reacting to a lack of high. He'd gone longer without blow.

Right?

Of course. So what was his problem? The issue was Beth. She was worth working for. Worth changing for. He'd been looking for a catalyst. An answer as to when it was time to retire. She was the answer to that question.

He didn't need a high. He needed Beth. There was little he was not successful at, and convincing her to be his would be entertainment enough. No need for drugs of any kind. He wasn't that weak. He knew better.

He took another step toward her. "A friend of mine has a private relics collection from Eridu. An ancient—"

"Sumerian city in what is now Iraq," she cut in with expert finesse, shutting down his explanation.

He blinked, nearly unable to hold back how impressed, and turned on, he was. "Correct. I'd love to show you. Just the two of us."

She looked at him through thick eyelashes that shaded brilliant eyes. "Are you trying to change the itinerary already?" Her laugh was gentle. "Because—"

"No, I'm asking you on a date. Something I've not done much of, and something, frankly, I can't stop myself from doing." He closed the remaining gap between them.

"Greg, I don't know."

"Easy answer. Yes?"

Beth closed her mouth, tucking in her bottom lip before her smile beamed. "Yes."

"Good." He turned back toward the door, more smitten with her than wanting sex or coke. He grinned. "I'll handle your security."

"But—"

Greg shook his head. "I insist, and I will guarantee your safety."

Her head tilted. "Have a good swim."

And that was another reason why he wanted to keep her around. No woman he'd ever spent time with would enjoy looking at antiquities, and none would be so patient as to wait for a date. They were all needy and insecure, maybe as they should be, because he had no long-term interests. They always gave up the goods in a misguided attempt to keep his attention.

He walked out her door, checking his phone and emails. *Perfect.* The email he'd been waiting on. The Sun Bowl and its hidden microscopic file were on their way to the hotel under tight security. The relic might have been priceless to some, but that file and its codes were what he wanted even if its price flew into the eight-figure-plus range.

Greg scrolled through his emails, knowing more than one buyer he could move the product to with minimal effort and an extraordinary profit.

He pulled out his room keycard, let himself in, and signaled his approval of the bags' arrival and unpacking. He looked out the window at the stretch of road leading to the hotel. Ferraris, Lamborghinis. The United Arab Emirates was a wonderful place to be, its wealth reminding him of everything he enjoyed in life.

He pulled up a new email, finding a contact with access to money and a depraved lack of morals, then shot off a message: *I have what you've been looking for. Take whatever your offer is and double it.* Greg read it twice then hit Send. He'd take the Sun Bowl and its file and buy his retirement.

CHAPTER 31

BETH LISTENED AT THE DOOR after Greg left. His room was diagonal from hers, letting her hear him open and shut his door. Then she went to work. Roman had been far too casual about this room for her liking. Time to sweep the place and confirm her assumptions—he had people working at this hotel. Or if the CIA rumor about Titan's palatial investments was correct, this was one of the places Titan Group had strategically placed around the world. They played it close to the vest, but she had a couple of clues they weren't as small as they seemed.

She went to her luggage, extracted the makeup bag, and found her screwdriver and the little gizmo that monitored radio frequencies. Meticulously, Beth unscrewed each light switch and electrical outlet cover, searching for bugs.

Nothing.

She checked the lampshades, the phone, the desk, and the drawers. Again, nothing.

Beth chewed on her lip. She inspected the vent covers. Those hadn't looked recently opened. Then she ran her hands along the bottom of the bed, the chairs, and every surface she could find with a lip suitable for placing a listening device. Even the channel changer was free of spy gear.

What the hell? Somewhere in this room there had to be something—

A knock sounded on her door, and damn if she didn't wish she had a gun with her. But it wouldn't fit her cover. She growled and peeked through the hole. *Greg.*

Shit. Quickly, she tucked the screwdriver between her breasts and glanced around the room. Nothing out of place.

She opened the door with a smile. "Hi."

"Last chance to ditch the research and go for a swim."

She leaned against the door. "I didn't bring my bathing suit."

"Even better."

"Oh my God." Her cheeks went hot.

Winking, Greg grinned. "Well, you know where to find me should you change your mind."

She waved goodbye and shut the door. Leaning against it, she slid down to the floor. There was something absurdly comforting about how he could make her blush without her having a single twinge of sexual interest. Unlike fucking Roman. God. That man made her fume, so damn mad she couldn't see straight, particularly because her room had to be wired and Roman hadn't mentioned it.

Beth kicked off her shoes, and for the next thirty minutes, she slammed around, looking for bugs and running her high-frequency reader, coming up empty handed. What the bloody hell? She threw the pillows on the floor and stripped the bed.

Arms crossed, she paced the room. Not a single thing had turned up. *Nothing!* And he wasn't checking on her. Very un-Roman-like. She clenched her teeth. No way was she wrong on this one.

Without thinking, she headed out and slammed her door, storming, *raging*, toward Roman's room. It didn't make sense. Her thoughts. Reactions. How she was acting insane. But she couldn't control the absolute need to scream in his face. To shake his ass stupid.

She banged on his door twice. "Open up."

It cracked open and, what the motherfucking hell, why didn't he have a shirt on? Did he just wander around half-dressed all the time, ready to be ogled?

"Beth?"

"For God's sake. Where's your shirt?"

He laughed, not all that friendly. "Wasn't expecting company." His gaze slid over her. "Where are your shoes?"

She shoved him with both hands planted against his chest, and his warm flesh set her body on fire. *Screw him.* "Where are they?"

"Your shoes?" He chuckled.

"Tell me." She pushed into the suite's foyer.

His head tilted. "Wanna come in and hang out?"

"No!"

"Then why are you here? You could always *go for a swim.*"

"Ahh!" She hit his chest again, but he didn't move from the open door. "I know you have people here—"

His hand clamped over her mouth. His other arm wrapped around her body. He spun her. Pressing her against the wall, his lips touched her ears. Pinned, Beth cursed her betraying body and arched against his hold.

"Be very careful of what you say." His tongue wicked across the shell of her ear, until finally, his mouth sucked the lobe. Just for a second. Just long enough that she was instantly, overwhelming wet for him. "You know better than that."

Condescending prick. She jabbed her elbow into the wall of muscle then lifted her arms over her head, grabbing his hair and yanking.

"Stronger than you look, Beth." He growled against her neck, half-kissing, half-biting.

God, enough of him. She spun but only because he'd loosened his hold. "You don't get to do whatever you want to do."

He slammed his mouth to hers, probing with his tongue, kissing as she pulled his hair. When he let her mouth go, she was gasping for more.

"But I can sure as fuck try, pretty girl."

She moved to duck out of his arms, but he rushed her back against the wall. His swollen erection pushed from behind his pants, and she cursed their clothing and her out-of-control want.

"Stop with the nickname."

"No way." He smiled as he bit her lip. He whispered into her mouth, "No fuckin' way."

She struggled against him, mostly as a bad excuse to feel more.

Roman's eyes were piercing. "You are too much fun."

"I am *not* fun." Her legs hiked up his, and she found some of the friction. But seriously, nowhere near enough.

"Bull." His hands ducked under her skirt and panties, squeezing her ass cheeks until they stung. "So much."

"What do you want from me?"

"To fuck you hard till I've got nothing left."

His words almost had her spasming, almost coming from a promise. She nodded, whimpering. "Do it."

"Bossy, wanting little Beth." With her skirt hiked around her hips, he held her against the wall with one arm supporting her ass. Legs around him, she was already spread for him, wet for him. He wasted no time, as his fingers found her and did their worst—or best.

"Roman," she moaned, biting his shoulder. "More."

Their bodies tangled, and under the onslaught of his hand, she desperately clawed between them, fighting for his belt and receiving zero help.

She closed her eyes, giving up. The pad of his thumb tortured her clit while his fingers speared her to a dizzying edge. God… her climax ripped her apart. He was a miracle worker. Her muscles clenched, spasmed. She squeezed her eyes tighter, gasping.

When she opened them again, predatory satisfaction glared at her, making her almost come again.

"Hot. But not why you stormed my door. What do you need, baby?"

What did she need? Him inside her. Him in her face, in her memories. Just him.

"Tell me," he crooned into her ear.

"Please just fuck me. Do it until you've got nothing left." She tried for his buckle again. "I need it."

"You need *me*. Not it," he growled. "Say it, baby."

"You. I need *you*." Everything about him, she needed. "Please."

Still holding her with an arm under her ass, he reached for his wallet.

"No condom," she whispered. "*I need* you. Want to feel you. Just you." She didn't even know where that came from. She needed to remember the hot sear of him pushing inside her. "I'm fine. Protected. Promise. If you say you're fine, I trust you."

His eyes narrowed. "I'm fine…"

Slowly, he abandoned his condom-reach. Beth wrapped her hands around his neck and hung onto him while he unbuckled his pants and kicked them away.

His hands ran down her back, over her ass, taking her weight again. "You sure?" His bare cock rubbed against her smooth mound then pressed against her entrance.

She gulped, immediately appreciating the difference between latex and no latex. "Please."

"Goddamn," he murmured as he shifted, inching the crown of his thick shaft into her.

Perfect soreness resounded as he moved, reminding her of how he'd driven into her yesterday. Slowly thrusting, Roman went deep. Accommodating to his size was her favorite thing. And then he roughly withdrew before rocking into her again. He was stronger, surer. Then *that* became her favorite thing.

She arched against the wall. Sweat dampened between them. She couldn't breathe, moaning and gasping. "Roman, baby. Please."

"Please. What?" He punctuated each word with quick, deep moves, biting her neck and shoulder.

"Do your worst."

"Goddamn." He groaned as his body slapped against hers, forcing her to start climbing again.

"Yes—"

His mouth found hers, and he kissed her as she ran toward the edge. "Pretty. Fuckin'. Girl."

Her clit throbbed, pussy clenched. Again, Roman did this to her. Only Roman. Lightning and firecrackers—they exploded deep inside her, shooting to every limb. Her blood sizzled as he pounded her, moaning her name as he came, deep to the root of him inside her. He strained. Hot spurts of his climax reignited hers.

Their mouths tangled, biting and kissing. He was harsh and rugged, but she knew he turned soft when only she was looking.

"Beautiful," he whispered on her lips.

She slipped her legs down, and he pulled his pants up. Their foreheads touched, then he carried her from the hallway, through the living area, and into his bedroom, placing her in the middle of the bed as if she were to be handled with care.

He didn't say anything, just undressed her completely, pulled the sheets back, and gathered her in his arms. "How much time do we have?"

"Couple hours."

He kissed her temple. "I do want a part of you."

What? Why hadn't he said that earlier? Because she was a crazy bitch. That was why. Her heart melted, but then uncertainty flooded her. His words were something she didn't know how to believe. She turned away. "You'd like to be *my friend*."

"True. But that's just an expression, ya know." His lips stayed against her skin. "I'm trying to figure out how there can be more."

"More?"

"Maybe?"

Her stomach dropped, and her mind went giddy. Then she considered pulling out of his arms, administering a self-imposed penance for falling for him—because she had, in a major way. She should embrace the guilt, knowing that it wasn't fair to her past. But... the guilt wasn't there. She wasn't wincing at his words or hating herself for the change he'd built within her. And... she was okay.

"More..." he repeated.

"Yeah?" She couldn't hide her grin.

He kissed her throat. "I like you underneath me."

"You also like me against a wall."

Roman pulled back, a seriousness darkened his eyes. "I like marking you as mine."

"Yours?"

"Got a problem with that?"

"I don't know what's happening between us. You *think* there might be more. I... don't know what's happening."

"Fuck me, neither do I. But make no mistake, woman. I've got you as mine. Whether it's now or later."

"Now or later?" Her jaw fell open. "Doesn't work that way."

"It does, party girl, if you're falling for the woman that one day you're gonna love."

CHAPTER 32

LYING IN AN ABU DHABI bed with a naked Beth must've made him stupid. The crap that had come out of his mouth? A halfway confession to falling in love? What the actual fuck?

He didn't need to say it to get laid. Didn't need to say it to stop a fight.

And... what he'd said was almost true.

Not like it was something he could plan for in the future, but falling for the girl was something that was happening *now* without his permission.

He would've cringed, except he didn't want to. If he'd thought it out, he would've waited until he was in love with the girl. But for whatever reason, realizing that love would happen *had happened* just then, no matter what plans to close his heart he'd made. Beth was flesh and blood, heart and soul. Practical rules didn't apply.

"I don't know what to say to that," she whispered.

"I don't either, babe. Just is what it is." He left the bed, shed his pants, and climbed under the covers with her. "Next few hours, just you and me in here. No job. No drama. Got it?"

She nodded.

He wrapped her hair around his fingers then committed to spending the time pressed together, as close as he could make them. He kissed her, owning every sigh, every moan as he spread her legs and took her again. And when he'd exhausted himself, wondering how they'd ever make it out of bed and to the auction where they both had to work, he closed his eyes and appreciated how much he enjoyed working with her. Even if he hated the circumstances.

Beth lay across his chest, fingers locked with his, as the hands on an ornate clock turned. It chimed.

Never before had he ignored a job. "Up and at 'em, baby."

She groaned. "Maybe he wouldn't notice if I didn't show up."

Roman shifted them up. "Right. Dude has a hard-on for you and needs you tell him how to spend his piles of money."

She tugged the sheet around her. "Why do you think the Agency has me on this?"

"Don't know."

"I think there's something more to it."

"You think?" he asked.

"I do."

"Gut instinct is usually right."

"So what am I missing?"

He shrugged. "Maybe you're not missing anything. Maybe it's who he meets, what he says. See where he goes afterward, who he talks to privately."

She fidgeted. "Don't get mad."

That was never a good opener. "Alright. Not mad."

"Technically, I have a date later."

"Definitely not mad. But..." Roman's eyebrows rose as his irritation started on a slow burn. He'd heard the whole conversation go down earlier, but that didn't mean he was ready to hear about it now. "Don't like it."

She groaned. "You know I have to spend time with him."

"You're leading him on?"

"Maybe. But obviously nothing more. And..."

His gut twisted. "Yeah?"

"He specifically said I didn't need my security detail."

Already knew that... "To which you replied that you did."

She shook her head, bedhead curls tossing over her shoulders. "I didn't say that."

The muscles in his shoulders bunched again, even though he already knew and had been pissed off before she'd shown up. "Seriously, Beth?"

"What was I supposed to do? I can be alone with the guy. He's not dangerous. If anything, he's borderline too polite, and honestly, I know the CIA says he's a thousand kinds of a bad guy, but I don't see it."

Tension turned into anger. "He's a bad guy, Beth. Act like he is. Got me?"

"Roman." She put her hand on his shoulder. "Are you mad at me?"

"Not mad. Just don't fall for his pansy-ass charm."

She rolled her eyes. "I'm not letting my guard down. I'm just saying—"

"You are. I hear it in your voice."

"No, Roman. I'm not. Whatever you're hearing, it's filtered through your overprotective, always-looking-for-a-bad-seed point of view."

He bit back his words, not wanting to upset her before the auction. Whether he agreed with that or not—which he didn't—she wouldn't be on her game if she were distracted. And she certainly didn't need to be aggravated at him when she left for a little one-on-one time with Naydenov. "Fine. I'll dial it back."

Beth smiled, but it was fake. "Thank you."

He threaded a hand into her thick hair and pulled her to him. "Go get dressed. Everything will go smoothly."

Then he kissed her as if he believed his own words, which he didn't. Time apart, specifically without security, was his definition of going off plan. Mission-critical decisions had been made without his input. A fuckin' date? Not cool.

At least he had eyes all over this hotel and a few friends on Titan's payroll that could keep eyes on her off site. If the guy made a bold move, Roman would have him hanging by the balls before the douchebag could say Abu Dhabi.

Beth savored Roman's scent on her as she cleaned up and redressed. She wandered around his hotel room, looking for her shoes, before remembering that she'd not worn any when she banged on his door. Classy. But that actually meant something. One layer of her picture-perfect shield had been peeled off.

Beth glanced over her shoulder. "Do I look okay?" She spun for him after pulling her unyielding curls into a makeshift knot.

"Perfect." His voice rumbled, and she hated leaving.

"Except the shoes." A quick toe curl into the carpet, and she had no options but to go barefoot.

He tilted his head. "Guess you should've thought about that before you barnstormed the room."

"It's a serious problem."

Roman laughed, lounging in bed with the sheet barely covering him. "Alright. Explain."

"Greg is the kind of guy you don't take your shoes off around." She looked at her toes, painted but still very bare.

"What does that mean?"

"He's just... proper."

"Dude's an asswipe."

She leaned over him as he stretched out on the mattress. "Kiss for good luck."

"How about a kiss to remind me not to kill the fucker?"

"Don't go after him, or I will be furious."

His lips twitched, and he grabbed her around the waist, pulling her into the covers. "A kiss 'cause I want your mouth on mine."

God, she loved the taste of him. "Pushy."

She untangled herself from him, and he swatted her bottom. "Get it, Tourne."

"Always do, Hart."

As she headed out, she could again feel his stare, and it made her blush. She was ready for tonight.

CHAPTER 33

WITH ANOTHER QUICK LOOK, BETH waved goodbye and braved a run to her room. She opened the door, managing not to get caught, and ambled into her hotel room. The phone—*phones*, because her suite was big enough for several—were ringing. She grabbed the closest one. "Hello?"

"Beth." It was Greg.

"Yes, hi."

"Are you okay?"

She swallowed hard, noting the high pitch in his voice. "Yes. Why?"

"I've been trying to get a hold of you."

Shit. "I'm sorry." She grabbed her cell phone and saw the missed calls. "I took a bath." She scrolled through all the timestamps. "A very long bath. My neck hurt after the flight."

"Sorry to hear that."

She kept from blowing out a sigh of relief. "Did you need something?"

"Not anymore."

"So… you called because?"

"You didn't answer. I was worried."

Shit, again. "I'm really sorry, Greg."

"No worries." He paused. "You'll be ready in thirty minutes?"

She had no choice. "Yes."

"Great. I'll knock on your door."

Beth glanced around her torn-up room. Sheets and pillows were everywhere; the furniture had been moved. A chair sat underneath a ceiling-level air vent. He couldn't see this, and she didn't have enough time to clean it up. "No, could I…?" She made her voice coy. "Maybe, could I stop by your room?"

"Of course." He took what she offered exactly the way she wanted him to.

"See you." She hung up and pulled out her clothes. There was no time for a shower. Closing her eyes, she stopped to appreciate her day. Roman was all over her skin, *still inside her,* even after she'd spent some time in his bathroom. She couldn't bear to wash him away. At least for the moment.

After a cool ten minutes of forcing her hair and makeup to look presentable, she used the remaining time unpacking, ironing, and dressing as quickly as she could.

She buzzed Roman's room. "Hey," she said.

"Hey."

"I'm headed to Greg's room. Give me a thirty-second lead before you knock on the door."

"That wasn't the plan." He grumbled and hung up.

Beth hurried out her door, knowing Roman wouldn't give her thirty seconds. She walked to Greg's suite and knocked.

The door opened, and there he was, dressed to the nines, holding a glass of champagne. "Beth, you look stunning."

"Thanks."

He handed her the crystal flute. "I figured we could toast to our planned acquisition."

Something about him was off as she took the glass. "Cheers."

He sniffed then cocked his head to the side. "Every time I see you, you look more... full of life."

She stifled a response, because it was Roman who had made her that way. "And you? You seem excited for this."

"Beyond words."

"Wow. Art does that to you?"

"I had a semi-related work project come in, paying very, very handsomely in the near future."

"Good for you." She tucked that tidbit in her memory to pass along to the Agency, then fake-smiled. For the first time, her gut screamed that his work projects were not on the up-and-up. An evil glint sparkled in his eyes, and the eeriness made her take a step back. A knock at the door interrupted his response.

Greg glared then walked toward the door. Before answering, he turned to her. "Have you ever been spoiled by someone? Spoiled beyond anything you could imagine?"

Oh, boy. "Someone, like a man?"

He nodded.

"No," she lied, because Roman had just finished doing that to her in bed. More than once.

Greg smiled sweetly with his crooked grin, but it didn't mask the hint of darkness. "Then prepare yourself, Beth Tourne, for the kind of spoiling women dream of. After the auction, I think you will be happily surprised."

"I'm not a surprises kind of girl." But she remembered what Roman had said about falling for her, maybe loving her. That had been a surprise. That had been epic. Maybe she liked surprises, just only with Roman.

Her fake smile seemed to charm Greg. "I'll change your mind."

"It'd have to be a one-in-a-million surprise, the kind you remember forever. That's the only type of surprise I might like."

Knock. Knock. Roman wasn't fooling around anymore.

"Think we should let him in? My bulldog is liable to tear that off its hinges."

Greg scowled but opened the door. Roman barged in, ignoring Greg and letting his gaze rake over her. She could feel his heat, but by the time Greg stepped around him, Roman had gone cold, masking the energy between them with the look of a disinterested bodyguard.

Clearing his throat, Greg asked, "Ready?"

"Yes." She stepped toward the door, out of Greg's arm's reach. As they walked down the hall, Roman took the lead, calling the elevator, then watched her and Greg approach. His resolve was steely—a hardened jaw, tight eyes. He swept the hall, on the constant lookout for trouble when they both knew trouble was walking *next* to her.

Greg turned to Roman. "We won't need your services after the auction. Thank you."

His jaw flexed. "I go where she goes. That's what I was hired to do."

The elevator opened, and they walked in.

"Miss Tourne and I have plans to celebrate."

Roman's eyes slid to Beth's. She couldn't disagree, and Roman was aware of the date.

So she smiled and said, "We have plans."

His lips went flat. "Let me know where. I'll be out of sight."

"That's not necessary," Greg replied as the elevator doors opened again.

"It's nonnegotiable." Roman took a step out of the car.

Beth weighed the pros and cons of interceding, knowing very well she could handle herself in many bad situations. Roman should know that too. "I am curious where we're going."

"It's a surprise," Greg said smartly.

Roman led them to the small meeting room on the second floor, moving through the invitation-only process of check-in and then past armed guards and behind closed doors.

Greg's excitement was palpable. Entering the room, he was given a marker to flag bids, along with a small catalog of the day's items. Five only. One was the Sun Bowl, but all were of major historic value.

A man in a dark suit approached. "Mr. Naydenov? Thank you for coming. The items are available for your review."

Greg accepted, and their threesome followed the suited man. They walked through a side door and down a hall, and there were the items for the day's auction.

He moved straight for the Sun Bowl, beaming over it. "Ms. Tourne? Please be my guest."

She stepped forward, inspecting without touching, searching for everything she knew to positively identify the piece and confirm its integrity and quality. After several minutes, she stepped away from it and tilted her head. "Authentic. The starting price is well placed. Good luck."

He scooted around her, and her stomach plummeted when Greg picked the ancient artifact up, turning it over. "Excellent—"

"Greg!"

He should've known better, and both she and the security agents were about to tell him that.

"Sorry. Sorry." He set it down carefully. "Won't happen again. Until I own it." He laughed. "Absolutely beautiful." His eyes went wide. His tongue licked his lips, and his gaze followed someone over her shoulder. Abruptly, he pushed away. "Excuse me. I'll be back in a few minutes."

CHAPTER 34

POWER AND MONEY—NO, NOT just money, *wealth*—gave him a spectacular high. But Greg couldn't help himself when he saw her across the room. He held his breath, appreciating the rush that was soon coming, the rush that was better than the Sun Bowl and its microscopic hidden file. He'd touched it, confirmed it. His blood had raced. But nothing like it was now.

"Greg?" Beth called after him as he took off.

He glanced back. She eyed him warily, as though ready to scold a toddler for touching someone else's toys. For the first time, she didn't push his buttons. The worry pinching her face slowed his adrenaline rush. Screw her and the brooding bulldog who was never far from her side.

What he wanted was the slender brunette walking across the far side of the room. Greg knew her. Well.

His mouth watered. She was a semi-regular fixture on the high-end antiquities market. She was also an extraordinarily high-priced call girl who'd given him the goods many times for free. Greg passed through the crowd, ignoring chit-chat and competitive hellos, and followed her down the back hall.

He made quick work of getting to her, because better than her semi-decent dick-sucking skills, she was likely to have blow in her purse. Dirty fucking whore. Exactly what he needed. Screw Beth Tourne and the good-girl routine.

How many times had he had this coke-whore? Still, not even a guess of a name came to mind. Maybe he wasn't anywhere near ready for retirement.

Searching room to room, he found locked doors but not her. Where did she go? His pulse thumped in his neck, his body shivered, craving—a hand touched his shoulder, and he spun.

"Looking for me, are you?"

He felt beads of sweat spring on his brow, in his armpits, and under his pressed shirt. He was seconds away from her nose candy, and the jittery need almost choked him. "Let's go."

She laughed. She probably thought it was her he wanted. Maybe in a second. But first...

He ducked into a small broom closet, yanking her in behind him. "Open your purse. Let's go."

Her laughter cackled. "Greedy, are you?"

"Open your goddamn purse." His need pounded in his neck. Salivating, he could taste the coke. Flashbacks of a million different snorts made him hover over her. "Now."

"Greedy man." But she dug into her tiny purse and retrieved a bumper. She handed it to him.

Once. Twice. White lightning burned his nose. Set his mind on fire, easing his rabid tension. Finally. She took it from him, hit both of her nostrils, then offered him one more. *Yes.* That was what he needed. It'd been too long.

In that beautifully high moment, he knew he wasn't walking away from this life. Not from the mega millions he made selling to the highest bidder and cleaning their money. What had he been thinking? Drugs. Sex. Money. That was him.

"On your knees." He kept the small vial, pocketing her coke, and pressed a hand on her shoulder. Greg leaned against the wall as she unbuckled his pants and sucked him deep down her throat.

Perfect. A cocksucker and cocaine. He rubbed his nose as she tugged on his sac. A professional blowjob was far handier than a woman who enjoyed archeology. Next time his brain made decisions about the future, he'd run it by his dick and nose first.

Wherever Greg had disappeared to, it'd been perfect timing. Beth scoured the auction, memorizing faces and registering who wanted what, who seemed interested in whom. It would have been much easier had the CIA told her what they wanted to know in addition to her simply accompanying Greg on this trip, but apparently, that was too much to ask for.

Twenty minutes later, Greg reappeared in the crowd. He clapped backs, smiled, and talked to others. He was evidently energized and in a decidedly better mood. She hoped he would tone down the flirtations in front of Roman.

He approached with flushed cheeks, and if she hadn't known better, she'd think he'd downed a few glasses of bubbly when she wasn't looking, along with a Red Bull or two. "Beth." He sniffed. Once. Twice. Then beamed again. "I love a good auction!"

Her stomach churned. Something was in play. Her intuition promised it, but her eyes couldn't find the missing piece. She glanced at Roman, and his stance stated his agreement.

"Ready?" Greg asked.

"Guess so…" she replied, but he'd already disappeared again.

Roman trailed behind her as she followed Greg to the bidding room. Moments later, they were in the front row of an auction, surrounded by the world's most elite ancient-art fiends. Two she recognized from Interpol's most-wanted list, and she added that to her mental list for Evan. Her handler should be happy with the intel; then he could finally move her to a decent project.

"Thank you, distinguished guests," the man at the lectern announced. Beth hadn't seen anyone distinguished so much as illicit. "Wire transfers are to be made immediately at the close of bidding. Confirmations of funds should be presented afterward. And let the night begin."

The auctioneer took off with an impressive start. Hands went up and down. Millions were thrown around. The first four pieces went without much fanfare, just simple multimillion-dollar deals with minimal excitement and polite applause. But the mood in the room shifted as the Sun Bowl was brought out. The air tingled with anticipation. Beth glanced at Roman. Again, it was evident he'd sensed the shift as well. While the relic was rare, there shouldn't have been this kind of tension in the room.

The bidding started at a decent one million. Every bidder in the room raised a hand. Her stomach dropped. Something wasn't right.

One million went directly to five. She looked at Greg, and he hadn't so much as balked. His hand easily shot up, signaling the auctioneer.

Five. Ten. Fifteen *million* dollars. A few bidders fell off. Some grumbled, and a few laughed knowingly. What was happening?

She cleared her throat, trying to catch Greg's eye, and then she did. He was on a high, wide eyed and hungry. That was absolute confirmation that she didn't know what the hell was happening. She shook her head almost imperceptibly, and Greg's crooked smile beamed as he tossed his hand up again.

Twenty million. Twenty-five.

Finally, it was just Greg and one of the Interpol men. Beth took another moment to study everything in the room. The people. The faces, their mannerisms and accents, and the way they stood. She committed to memory the auctioneer, the armed guards. The art. Hell, the carpet, walls, and chairs. Everything. Because someone would need all the details she could manage to help stop whatever was happening.

The bidding continued back and forth until it was just Greg. Greg smiled like a maniac, like he was king of the world. His winning bid was a cool thirty-five million dollars dumped on an ancient gold bowl that was worth a couple of million, max.

He turned to the man he had been bidding against and acknowledging an apparent relationship already there. Ignoring Beth, he pulled out his phone, presumably to make that absurd transfer.

"Greg?"

He waved her off as the small crowd began to move.

Roman leaned next to her. "What the fuck just happened here?"

She shook her head, trying to act as if she wasn't terrified of what they'd missed. "Something very bad. We have to keep an eye on him."

"Agreed." Roman kept his eyes moving. "Sending out a heads-up?"

Pivoting on her heel, she shifted her gaze. "Yup."

He tilted his head. "Here comes your boy. Does he get into a little—"

Greg's speed walk was faster than either expected. "That was great." He greeted Roman with a slap to his arm, and Beth's eyes almost fell out of her head. Greg was practically delirious. "Ready?"

She remained quiet.

Greg stepped closer. "Beth?" His eyes bounced around the room.

"You pushed far past what my appraisal was."

His eyes twinkled. "Wasn't it phenomenal? I haven't been in a bidding war like that in ages." He looked at Roman. "Will you see that Ms. Tourne makes it to her room safely? I have business to take care of."

"Greg—"

"Don't worry. Our date is still on. It will be a celebration."

She didn't want to leave Greg's side. Whatever business was about to happen, she wanted in. "Congratulations. This is all spectacular. I'd love to stay and—"

"No." The unexpected stern tone of his voice shut her down. The swing in moods was wild.

"But—"

"No." He nodded at Roman. "Escort her, please."

Greg's true colors were showing.

"Of course."

As Roman led her out, she ran through everything she knew about this job, making her irritation at Evan and Jasper grow. They'd known this was more than an art auction. They *had* to. And she'd gone in blind. *Again.* If this was a test, then screw them. And if this wasn't a test, then the Agency had big, unknown problems.

CHAPTER 35

ROMAN HAD ONE ARM OUT, leading Beth toward the elevators. He wanted no one around her until they knew exactly what had happened and who else was in the hotel. Parker could help with that. Titan had eyes everywhere, especially in this hotel.

Whatever had just sold, it wasn't an ancient piece of pottery. But what the fuck was it, and how unnerved should they be that Gregori Naydenov was now the proud owner?

As soon as the elevator doors closed, he pulled her close. "What do you think?"

She shook her head. "Still no idea."

"I'll get Parker to pull surveillance and try to place some of those faces."

"Okay." As the elevator climbed to their floor, she leaned against him. "I have a bad feeling."

She stepped away, and he missed her against him, as if she were his to hold, to take on her weight and worries. More than just feeling her, he knew their interactions had changed. It worked for him.

Beth took the lead down the hall, and his eyes trailed to her tight ass swaying. Sky-high legs, right-left, right-left, were walking him to the edge.

His phone buzzed with an alert he had set for her room. With a fifteen-second head start, someone had entered Beth's room around the corner. "Wait."

Pulled out of his trance, he tucked her behind him and thought about what to do with her. He could stash her in his room, but she wouldn't stay. He could hole her up in the stairwell, give her a weapon and permission to blast anyone she didn't recognize, but his overprotective nature made him want to take care of her safety himself. So Beth was with him. Not the best option.

He pulled out his sidearm and walked them to her room. "Keycard, sweetheart."

She handed him the card. He slipped it into the reader then opened the door with a hard kick, his gun pointed ahead. A man screamed. Like *screamed*.

"Hands in the air!" Roman stepped forward aggressively, finger on the trigger. He did a visual sweep of the room. "Shut your mouth."

The whimpering man did as told.

"Beth, honey, Glock in my back holster."

She slipped her hands under his suit jacket and removed the weapon.

"He moves, you shoot."

She nodded.

Roman sidestepped to the bathroom and checked behind the door and shower curtain. He moved through the rooms, clearing each as he went. No one else. He returned to see his girl handling the man like a pro, which made his chest swell. But he'd deal with that later.

He turned his attention to the squirming man. "Any weapons?"

"Weapons?" the man asked in a thick accent. "No."

Roman checked him anyway. Dude wasn't lying. Good. "Name."

"Abdul," he squeaked.

"Abdul." Roman scanned the room. "Sit."

The man dropped onto the closest couch. "I... I... I'm—"

"Explain."

"Mr. Nay-den-ovv." Abdul's voice cracked.

Of course this had to do with motherfuckin' Gregori Naydenov. "What about him?"

"Hired me. Th-th-the dress." He pointed toward the bedroom.

"Beth. Bedroom. Check for a dress." Had he seen a dress? No idea. He hadn't been searching for fashion.

She hurried into the bedroom. Beads of sweat formed on Abdul's forehead as they waited. Seconds later, she returned with a frown.

"What is it? A dress?"

Beth nodded. "An evening gown. Shoes and jewelry."

"What?" Roman lowered the weapon slightly. He turned back to Abdul. "Explain."

"I'm a wardrobe consultant. Mr. Naydenov had the concierge hire me with the instructions to provide a woman with an outfit and accessories."

Beth's head dropped. "My stupid date."

Roman holstered his weapon and rubbed his temples. "Out, Abdul."

The dude jumped up and ran for the door. It slammed behind him.

"Are you fucking kidding me?" *A dress? Shit that goes with a dress? What kind of douche did that?* As if any of that would impress Beth or not make the guy seem like a gigantic shit.

She shrugged sheepishly. "Sorry."

"Don't apologize to me." This was getting ridiculous. Where was Naydenov-the-asshole now? He pictured Naydenov running around the room, hopping from—*hopping?* The guy was totally hopped up. "What's his file say about drug use?"

Her face tightened. Maybe a light was dawning for both of them, causing some of Naydenov's actions make more sense. A banging on the door stole Roman's attention. What was up with this day? The banging continued.

"Beth?" Naydenov's voice was high-strung and high-pitched.

"Are you kidding me?" Roman turned to her. "That's your boy Naydenov?"

She stared at the door. "I guess…"

"Sounds off."

"Sounds… yeah."

More banging. Every plan today had crapped out. Nothing major, but enough deviations that Roman's overcautious-self hesitated. He put his hand up. "Babe. Stay here for a minute."

Gun resting at her side, she moved to the couch and tucked his Glock in an easy-to-reach nook.

Roman approached the door, finger near his trigger, and opened it a couple of inches, gun and Beth hidden from Naydenov's beady eyes. "What do you want?"

"Roman?"

"That's right." He blocked Naydenov's entrance. "What's with banging on the door?"

Naydenov rubbed his nose with a jittery hand. "I need to see her. Talk to her." His words ran too quick. Droplets of sweat shone on his well-clipped sideburns, and his forehead glistened.

Roman scowled. "You been drinking?"

Naydenov's bloodshot eyes darted around. "Excuse me?"

"Are you fucked up?"

He tried to push around Roman. "Move."

"Like hell."

The guy used the back of a jittery hand to scratch his nose again. This wasn't the classy, stick-up-his-ass Gregori Naydenov. This was a dude who'd fallen face first into more coke than he could handle. Naydenov was a coke head? This day was getting more complicated by the minute. Beth should've been read into the guy's drug use. "Stay."

Naydenov glared but stayed, shifting. Roman shut the door and turned back to Beth.

"What's going on?" she asked.

"Dude have a nose-candy problem?"

Her brow furrowed. "Not that I know of. But…"

"But?"

"I wouldn't put it past him."

Roman looked at the closed door, thinking about the eyes, the nose, the twitches. Maybe a post-victory snort? "He's all kinds of hopped up."

"You want to bring him in here? See if he'll give us anything?"

"Your call, babe. But if he comes in here, high as a fuckin' kite and running his mouth, I'm gonna shut him down."

She bit her lip.

"Do you have what you need, Beth? Mission objective met?"

"Yes, and then some."

"Then fuck it. Let's go home. Job's done. He's whacked. Something else is going on. I don't like it, and we can't figure it out."

"I don't either." She stood. "Alright."

"Alright? We go home?"

She nodded. "I trust you. You have a bad feeling. I have a bad feeling. Let's roll."

"I'll deal with Naydenov."

She laughed. "I bet you will."

But when Roman opened the door, the guy was gone. One less headache to deal with. They could get their own ride back to the US. He pulled out his phone and called Parker, wanting to know every move Naydenov made and needing headshots of each person at the auction. Maybe if she had enough intel for the CIA, they could get her off this asshole's job and be done with it, even after she got back to the States.

Roman was watching Beth kick off her shoes when his boy picked up. "Hey, Parker—"

"Was just calling you," Parker said. "Boss man's got something big. Something near your part of the world."

"Fine. But tell Jared we need a ride home. Now. This Naydenov guy is on the move with something hot, and we need out."

"Okay…" He said something off the phone. "You might need to stay put."

"Say again?"

"Get a hold of Jared," Parker muttered.

"Fine. But until I have orders saying otherwise, I'm bringing Beth home. Help me out, man."

"Just saying, job might not be as done as you think it is," Parker said. "But give me a couple hours, and you'll have a jet waiting for you."

"Thanks. Alright." Roman motioned for Beth to grab her shit. When she was out of earshot, he went back to Parker. "Look, something's going down here. I don't know who or what, but there are players here. We don't have backup. She's been fed a crock from her handler. We are flappin' in the fuckin' wind, and I have no idea which way the storm's coming from. Hell, I don't even know what kind of storm it is. But it's here, and I want her safe. Got me?"

"Reading ya, man. But I'm telling you, you need to talk to Jared."

"Fine," Roman grumbled. "Will do. Can you find out who's here and everything else that comes with that?"

"Already on it."

Already on it? Roman pinched the bridge of his nose. Shit was a-brewin'. "What else is happening?"

"Rocco's better. Nicola's sick. You need a jet in the Middle East, like now, and Jared and a few of the boys have gone off the grid. Easy part of my day is finding you the closest Titan jet and skipping you two back home. If that's what happens. So that's what I know is going on."

"What aren't you telling me?"

"If I knew, I'd say. But something is. I think Boss Man is working something out."

"Great. Thanks, dude. Catch ya later." Roman hung up and rubbed his head. Then went in search of Beth. "Titan's sending us a ride home."

"Good. Anything else?"

Yeah, but he didn't know what. "Nic still has the flu. So stay clear."

Her lips went flat. "Flu. That sucks."

"Something's working with a Titan job. I'll probably hit the road soon as we're wheels down."

Beth sighed. "Talking to Evan's gonna suck. I'll have to explain ditching Naydenov." She gnawed on her bottom lip. "But you know what? The guy likes to impress people. If he thinks I'm completely unimpressed with a coke problem—which I am—he'll spend some time kissing ass."

"Maybe." Roman rubbed his chin. "Give the dude some room. Not joking when I say something's not right."

"Except for today, didn't Greg almost seem kind of... normal?"

"Hell no." Roman shook his head. "No one who does what he does can ever be normal, even if that's what they want."

"You think he wants normal?" Beth asked.

"*Naydenov?*"

"Yeah. I get this vibe, this turn-over-a-new-leaf desire from him. Like maybe I stand for something different in life he wants but doesn't know how to get."

"Well, he can go to hell." That was about all Roman could offer. Naydenov wanted Beth in his life? Along with a normal life? Too fuckin' bad. Normal didn't exist. Beth was Roman's, and that dude didn't deserve anything with a happy ending. End of story.

CHAPTER 36

BETH FINISHED PACKING THEN WATCHED Roman pace in front of the expansive windows, checking his watch every few steps. She wouldn't call it nerves, but he was seriously uncomfortable with their lack of intelligence. He'd put the kibosh on asking Evan for more information, then he had reached out to Jared with no response.

"You okay?"

He pivoted, a line etched on his forehead and no sign of the sweet dimple in his chin. "Yeah."

"You're stressed?"

His eyes narrowed. "Not a chance, sweetheart." But he resumed pacing. Whatever his concerns, he wasn't sharing.

She didn't like him holding anything back. "I think you are."

"Think again."

"Roman—"

"Beth, not now."

She approached, wanting to touch him, to know his concerns. "If not stressed, then what?"

Fidgeting as though he had energy to burn, he locked eyes with her. "In this room, we're safe from just about anything. Know that."

"Okay." Though she didn't know why, she believed him.

"But there's a difference from knowing there are eyes watching our entrances, security lining these walls, and monitors that could alert me within a second of anything I don't like. There are weapons hidden around this room. This hotel. This is my comfort zone. The world doesn't know that. But I know it. Titan knows it. Now you know it."

Confirmation. She was right. This was a covert, albeit unimaginable, safe house of sorts. Titan owned the skyscraper? Sure, why the hell not? "Understood."

"But..."

"But?" she asked.

"I don't like what I don't know, because it puts you in harm's way."

"Roman—"

"No." He shook his head. "You get me. I know you do. And you know that you've inched yourself into my world. And now that you're there, I'm—" He shook his head again, lips flat and brow furrowed. "You can take care of yourself. I get that. But I don't like it."

"You don't like… it?"

"The job. CIA playing their games. You in the field, lacking intel." His glare was deadly cold. "The idea that I have you and could lose you."

"You're not going to lose me, Roman."

He turned to the window. "Shit happens."

Beth closed the distance and cupped his cheeks in her hands. "*I'm* not going to lose *you*. How about that?"

"Sweetheart, we say all kinds of things. That doesn't mean we can control the world."

She bit her lip, wishing he weren't struggling with the unknown. Her hands ran down his chest, and God, it was cut perfection. He was worked up over her safety, and her heart tripped over that. Beth's hands paused on his belt, then before she thought better of it, she began undoing the buckle.

He stilled. "Whoa! Working now."

"Shut up, Roman."

"Beth—"

"Roman." She unzipped his pants and released him. "I might not be able to control the world, but I can control this."

He shifted, understanding washing over his face, and she dropped to her knees.

"Beth, honey." His voice softened.

He was aroused. The weight of him hardened in her hand, then she took him deep in her mouth, while locking eyes with him. Roman focused on her. Not focused on protecting her, but just *her*.

Using her tongue, teeth, and hands, she loved how he reacted. Roman groaned. His lips parted when she teased the thick ridge of his crown, and he swayed when she flicked her tongue over his slit.

"Hands off, baby," he whispered.

Her palms moved to his muscled ass, fingernails digging in when he started to pump.

Roman found her hair, his fingers threading into it and tugging. "Baby, baby, baby…"

She loved how he sounded, how he whispered so quietly. She loved making him feel better, loved having him inside her. Really, she just loved him.

"Beth." Her name sounded ragged, and he fisted her hair, holding her head in place. She closed her eyes when he came, knowing wherever his thoughts had been before, his mind was calm now.

"C'mere." His hands had dropped to her shoulders as he shifted back. "My girl." As she stood, he adjusted himself, never taking his eyes off her. "You're good to me."

"You're good to me," she gave him back.

"This works. You and me."

"I know."

He wove his fingers into hers. "I was keyed up."

A grin she couldn't hide blossomed on her face. "But not anymore."

He chuckled low, pulling her tightly against him. "But not anymore."

"You better now?"

"Yeah, baby. I am." He kissed her lips then her forehead.

A knock sounded from the door.

He sighed and checked his watch. "Bellboy. Right on time."

Roman gave her one long look then took his 9mm and answered the door. The bellboy entered, greeted Roman, and started loading Beth's bags onto a cart. He completely ignored the gun. Roman snaked his hand around hers and pulled her out the door behind her luggage.

"What about Greg?" she asked. "Should I drop a note? Say bye?"

"Screw him."

"Roman..."

He squeezed her hand. "Tell him you're banging the help."

She would've said something, but another bellboy down the hall caught her eye. Roman's luggage was packed and on a cart. The guy spoke to Roman, and then both sets of luggage, with their accompanying staff members, were headed toward a service elevator. Talk about service. They'd packed Roman... while he was being *serviced*. Beth cheeks heated.

Roman looked at her as the elevator doors opened. "What's up?"

Lord, she wasn't telling him that. But then again, why not? She giggled and waited until the doors were closed. It was just them—well, and probably someone watching from a surveillance room—so she went on her toes and whispered in his ear, "Just thinking about taking you in my mouth."

He groaned.

"And how your mouth feels on me."

He pulled her closer to him. "Keep going."

"And how you make me come."

His chin touched the top of her head. "Only me."

"No one else does what you do."

"Got that right."

"No one else can touch my body. Not for the job. Not otherwise."

He stilled. Tightened. Then he dipped down to her ear. "Good. Glad you know what I know."

The doors opened to the lobby.

"You ready?" Roman asked, game face immediately back on. "Move your sweet ass, Beth."

She turned as they passed the concierge and walked backward. "When you put it like that..."

"Like what?"

"All bossy and growly."

"Keep going. Get in our ride."

She raised her eyebrows. "Are you trying to get me all worked up before we get into that car?"

"The car? No. The jet? Hell, yes. Besides, I think you already are."

No kidding. She turned on the balls of her feet and booked it for the car. He didn't chase. She knew he wouldn't. It wouldn't have fit his bodyguard role, but it also upped her anticipation. His rough hands would be all over her soon enough. She got in the waiting sedan and watched Roman stalk out of the hotel. He stopped and pulled out his phone. Looking down at the screen, he raised one finger at her. He put the phone to his ear, spoke briefly, then hung up, and continued toward her. Once Roman slid into the backseat, the driver shut the door.

"Who was that?" she asked. "Greg come down from his high and ask where we are?"

"Nope. Worse." He pulled her under his arm. "Jared wants to talk to *you*. Know anything about that?"

Her stomach soured as she wracked her brain. "Am I in trouble for stealing you away for a few days?"

"Doubt it." Roman held her close, and he smelled sigh-worthy. "He likes you. The phone cut out, though. Should hear back from him soon."

"Yay..." She mocked disinterest. Jared was a badass, and she liked him... when he wasn't scaring her.

The driver pulled out of the lot and merged into traffic.

Still holding her under his arm, Roman stared out the window, distant, until, slowly, he shifted. "Would you come to Titan if he offered you a job?"

She pulled back in surprise. "What? Why would he do that?"

Roman shrugged. "Why does he want to talk to you?"

"I don't know, but it's not that." Because that would be insane. She wasn't looking outside the Agency, and he wasn't hiring. Well, actually, no one knew what Jared did, but she hadn't heard whispers about intelligence openings.

"He stole Nic from the CIA."

"Nic willingly went," Beth pointed out.

"And you wouldn't?"

"The Agency is the only thing I know. It's how I've coped with stuff."

"Stuff? Don't pretend with me. If that's how you handled your ex—"

"He wasn't my ex," she snipped. "He was my husband. A *dead* husband, but nothing ex about him." Her eyes cut to Roman. "That came out wrong."

He shrugged.

She lowered her voice. "Yes, that's how I handled it. I was lucky they drowned me in work."

He rubbed his forehead. "One day, you'll have to tell me the ground rules about mentioning your past. You don't have to go on the defensive every time."

She cleared her throat, feeling like a bitch. "Back to Jared. He's not going to offer me a job."

"But if he did, would you take it?"

"No."

Surprise marred his chiseled face. "Why not? It's Titan."

And Titan was about as good as it got. "Honestly?"

"Yeah."

Her nerves raced. "Because of you."

"Me?" He stared at her as if she'd lost her mind. "Beth, what the hell?"

"We crossed a line. Whatever this is…" She flipped a hand between them. "This means something to me, whether it should or not. Whether there's more for us in the future or not. If it ends, fine. But it would make working together miserable. You love your job. I love what I do, sort of. So, no, I couldn't take a job with Titan. It'd mess too much up."

Working his jaw back and forth, Roman stared out the window. "Smart."

"Yup." She watched him. "And practical."

He chuckled sarcastically, slowly shaking his head.

"What?"

"Ha. All very logical."

"You just scoffed at me."

Roman nodded. "Yeah, I did."

"Why?"

His eyes held her, even though he'd stopped actually holding her, and she felt him to her core.

"Because, sweetheart, until this conversation, nothing about us was built on an ending."

"An ending?" Her stomach bottomed out. Why were they so complicated when they really weren't. "Roman, I was just—"

"Forget the logic and the smart moves and whatever I may've said and you may've thought. Tell me what you want."

Simple. You. From the bottom of her heart, to the tips of her toes, she wanted him in every sense of the word, all of him, even if it killed off her memories, even if it would be her death. "I want—"

His phone rang. "This is not over," he growled.

"M-kay."

Roman glanced at the screen. "Jared," he told her then answered the call. "Boss Man."

The conversation was mostly one sided with Roman agreeing before he hung up.

"What's going on?" she asked.

"Turns out we're not going home. Titan's coming here, and Naydenov's checked out." He leaned forward to get the driver's attention. "Turn us around, buddy."

"Okay..." Beth said. "Look, Roman. I—"

He turned back to her. Pure, tactile seriousness colored his features. His eyes flamed deep, dark brown. His jaw flexed. He grabbed her hand. "Ever look at someone and realize everything you know about the future was wrong?"

Her heart stopped.

"Answer me, Beth."

"I'm..." Her voice shook. "I'm too scared to answer that question."

Hard and fast, he pulled her onto his chest. "Funny shit. Beth Tourne has exactly one fear, and it's me."

CHAPTER 37

THEY WERE A BLOCK FROM the hotel when three monster SUVs with blacked-out windows passed them. Each screeched into the hotel's driveway and slammed to a stop. Bellboys came running toward the massive vehicles parked inches apart as if they'd choreographed the whole scene.

Beth watched out her window. "Who is...?"

The doors opened, and several large men got out, all the size of Roman, all dressed in dark clothes.

Titan. Whoa. Talk about making an entrance.

There were guys she didn't recognize, but several she did. And they were filing into the hotel as though they owned the place. Well, maybe because they did.

"Guess they failed to mention they were wheels down already." Roman opened the door. "For the sake of your cover, just in case, we'll hang back. Don't say hello. We don't know them."

She nodded, and he led her through the doors after asking a nearby bellboy to get their luggage. Roman didn't seem concerned at the lack of a reservation, and the bellboy didn't act like it was a big deal.

"How often do you come here?"

Roman winked. "Often enough that Jamil knows which room I want."

Oh...

They followed Titan at a close distance. Jared led the pack, then Colby, Cash, Brock, and the ones she didn't know. Nearby, several luggage carts were loaded with large black boxes and Titan go-bags. Those went down a different hallway. That was some serious trust for Jared to let his property out of his sight.

Jared and the group bypassed the reservation desk, heading toward the elevators. She and Roman had caught up, but no one acknowledged them. She followed Roman's lead and didn't say a word. The elevator came, and half the group left them. Another elevator dinged. Same deal. Then she and Roman were the only ones left.

She glanced behind her and noticed that several people had been staring. A few looked as though they needed the elevator but were waiting out the group of deadly-looking men. Probably a smart move.

Their elevator arrived. Her heart tripped when Roman guided her on board. He pressed the button for the twenty-first floor and the little circle lit up, apparently scanning his fingerprint. Print accepted, they started moving.

"You guys are an intimidating bunch."

Roman gave her a curt nod. When he was in business mode—even though he *was* holding her hand—it was impossible not to want him. Something about that I'm-ready-to-die-for-you vibe made her shiver.

The doors opened to an industrial hallway, nothing like the opulent, gold-gilded decorations downstairs. A few feet from the elevator was a secure door. Roman punched several digits on a keypad. A panel lifted, and he placed his hand on the scanner. A light blinked around his palm, then the door clicked open. They moved into a room the size of a closet. He shut the last door and faced an opposite one. Roman blinked into a retina scan then entered another round of codes on a pad that appeared from a secret panel.

That was CIA-level security, maybe even more complex. They walked in, and the metal door locked behind them. Roman guided her down a dark hallway with tiny running lights on the floor then through a door into a working ops center that was alive and buzzing. Computer monitors, flat screens, and more people filled the room. Weapons were available within arm's reach everywhere she looked.

"What is this place?"

"Titan's Abu Dhabi HQ."

"Oh." Because they *had* an Abu Dhabi headquarters.

Roman curled his hand around her neck, guiding her through the room. They went down another long hallway, and he opened a door at the end. It looked like a typical war room. Jared stood at the front, and the team was around a table. Roman nodded. Jared nodded back. Beth nodded because it seemed like the thing to do. Hellos apparently said, Roman continued with her down the hall to another room. He opened the door, and there was Sugar. *That* was unexpected. Boxes of ammo and parts were on the table, some piled, some in pieces, all very much in what had to be an order that Beth couldn't make sense of.

"Hey, girl. What's up with you?" Sugar kept her eyes on her work. "I want the dirty details on Roman later."

Roman laughed. Beth groaned, feeling a sudden shyness. Sugar was the most to-the-point person Beth had ever met. There was nothing Sugar wouldn't ask if it piqued her curiosity, inappropriate or not.

Finally, Sugar looked up. "Alrighty, stud. You can have her back later. Beth and I have to get to work."

At the word *stud*, Beth had to have turned as red as Sugar's lipstick. And that was cherry red.

Roman leaned close, letting his lips touch the top of her ear. "Have fun."

Then he kissed her goodbye. In front of Sugar. Which might as well have been in front of the team because it was *Sugar*, and she knew no boundaries.

Sugar waved a hand. "Get a move on, CIA girl. Finish lip-locking your man, because I need your hands."

A tiny part of Beth wanted to crawl into Roman's arms just to hide from the inquisition she knew was coming. Roman swatted Beth's butt—making her yip. He left, and when she looked up, Sugar's bright-red lips were pressed together. The woman was trying to smother a laugh.

"I saw that," Sugar sing-songed.

"He wasn't hiding it." Beth sat across from Sugar. "So what are we doing?"

Sugar's eyes pointedly went to the door Roman had just exited before coming back to Beth. "Weaponizing these babies."

Beth picked up what looked like shoebox-sized white airplanes. There were a handful of them. "Drones?"

"*Baby* drones. A Parker creation. Because the boys can't be everywhere they need to be, we're going to give them a little firepower and some agility at a fraction of the cost and on very short notice." Sugar winked. "Parker's a genius. And I ain't too bad, either."

After a five-minute tutorial on how to turn what looked like a model-airplane kit into a killing, spying machine, Beth had her tasks down, and they worked in near silence, except for the occasional click-click-click of Sugar's nails drumming on the table.

"Am I going too slow?" Beth warily asked.

"Nope."

A few more click-clicks followed.

"Alright, Sugar. Say whatever you have to say. And be nice about it."

Sugar's smile stretched across her face. "It's about damn time, you and Roman."

Beth shrugged. "Maybe. Or maybe it's a huge mistake. Who knows."

"Nah. But if you could've held out for another two months, I would've appreciated it."

Beth's jaw dropped. "Excuse me?"

"Had a little bet going with my husband as to when this was going to happen."

"You did not."

"Oh, we so did. And now because Roman couldn't keep it in his pants, I owe Jared a custom-made rocket launcher that, forever more, will be dubbed *The Jared*." Sugar smirked. "That won't deflate my man's ego anytime soon."

Beth snort-laughed. "The Jared?"

"Do you think he'd name a weapon like that anything but The Jared? *Pffsh*."

"Well, glad to see we were a topic of conversation."

"You're playing it down. A topic of conversation?" Sugar shook her head, clucking, and placed a weaponized baby drone next to her row of finished killers. "The only thing that slowed that gossip-fest down was Rocco and Cat getting pregnant. But if you remember, even at their whatever-you-want-to-call-it shower, there were a lot of eyes watching you two ignore each other."

"I don't remember it like that."

Sugar gave her a sidelong look. "So you two are together?"

Beth dropped her head back. "I guess."

"Sounds super serious." Sarcasm dripped from her words.

"What if it is?" Beth asked, crazy aware that she was asking Sugar for relationship advice when her history of stable relationships was nonexistent. Other than Jared. Beth studied the gorgeous, sexed-up woman in front of her. "Did you ever sleep with someone for the job?"

"Yup." There wasn't a hint of remorse or embarrassment in Sugar's voice. "But you and I are two different types. Sex was just a means to an end. Maybe I shouldn't have in some folks' eyes, but before I met Jared, it didn't matter at all. I was safe. It was enjoyable. End of story."

Beth mulled that over. "I think we aren't that different."

"How's that?" Sugar picked up the baby drone that Beth had moved over.

"I was married before."

"Fun fact I didn't know about you. Where is he? Cheated? Loser? Gay?"

Beth shook her head. "Dead. Killed himself."

Sugar put the plane down. "I'm sorry."

"His name was Logan, and after he died, I shut off. The only time I ever let a man touch me was when I wanted to reinforce how I felt for Logan. Because anyone else was just physical companionship. I was lonely, and they were filling a void. Logan had been my life. I was... blissfully numb to anyone else. I didn't want to be lonely, and I loved the confirmation that Logan was the only person for me."

"And now you have Roman?"

Beth nodded.

Sugar inclined her head. "I'm very protective of these boys. You have to know that."

"I know."

"And with Roman, there's more than whatever you were just blabbing about? Filling a void, that crap?"

Beth scowled. "Yup."

"How?"

"He gives me butterflies."

Sugar arched a penciled brow. "Those are good."

"And a lot more."

She raised the other eyebrow. "Those are better."

Beth blushed. "Yup."

"So what's with your hesitation? He's a solid guy. About as good as they come. Hot as hell, though he knows that far, *far* too well."

"I don't know if I can fall for someone who could die, like every single day on the job."

"Yes, you can." Sugar's certainty was concise.

Beth wasn't sold. "Plus, he's scarred for life after Nicola disappeared on him."

"Ain't that the truth."

Beth bit her lip.

Sugar continued, "So you two should just agree you're fucked. Have some great sex. And call it quits."

Beth's mouth fell open. "Really?"

"No. Are you stupid?"

Beth shut her mouth. She'd walked into that one. "Why are we friends again?"

"I'm not very good at being friends with anyone. Though I'm working on it." Sugar picked up the baby drone and adjusted a barrel protruding from its belly. "We can call Mia. She always knows the right thing to say. Or we can call Nic. Where is she anyway?"

Beth averted her gaze. "Flu."

"Huh."

"Heard Rocco's doing better."

"Yeah, he kicked influenza's ass. Staying away from Cat almost killed him. And man, that woman, all pregnant and Spanish-cursing, worrying about her man? If I didn't love her, I would've hated her. All that angsty, *Was I too mean? Should he come home?* pregnancy crap." Sugar shook her head. "Nothing but craziness."

Nicola and Caterina were going to be crazy-pregnant together. Beth had seen how Rocco acted, and Cash was going to be the same way—over the top and overprotective. That would be a show.

The door flew open. Beth jumped. Sugar didn't flinch.

Jared bore down on them. "Beth, let's go."

Her stomach twisted. Jared always made her so damn nervous. "M-kay."

She scooted her work toward Sugar and followed Jared down to another room. The lights flipped on when they entered. It was cooler than the other rooms, and everything was gray. Gray table, walls, carpet, ceiling. A little claustrophobic.

He sat and pushed a rolling chair out for Beth to join him. "Princess has the flu." It sounded like a statement, but his face said it was a question.

She said nothing.

He crossed his arms. "I need you to fill in for her."

"Doing?"

"For the past few days, we've been building the profile of a woman who can authenticate weapons codes. There's a buy going down. Those codes will lead us to an ancient, probably unstable nuke that's hot on the market right now."

Beth's eyebrows rose. "There's a stolen nuke out there?"

He dipped his chin. "And the codes. We had a failed intercept before. Now several parties are scrambling very quickly to make purchases. Think shark-infested feeding frenzy."

"And your plan is?" she asked.

"Authenticate the codes and follow them to the bomb."

"Holy shit." That was about as risky as plans could get.

Jared read her mind. "I'll scorch the earth before we fail this job again. It's go-big-or-go-home time. Nic was supposed to authenticate the codes. Word has it there's a former KGB seller and an Albanian buyer. Pretty sure the bomb's still in transit. I'm thinking there's a Syrian involved, but I'm not sure. The Albanian we know with decent certainty. We follow the Albanian; we get the bomb. You follow?"

More or less. "Yes."

"The Albanian hired Nicola. Still following?"

"Maybe."

Jared nodded. "First, you have to wrap up this CIA job. Go home, act like nothing's happened. We'll stay here, set up the groundwork. Just need to know you're game. Titan will bring you back out here. You do Nic's job. You game?"

She nodded. "Okay."

"Now." He leaned back. "About you and Roman…"

Shit. Her mind went a thousand places.

"He'll head back with you, keeping your cover up." Jared studied her with an intensity that would make a seasoned CIA spook quiver. "He'll also go wherever the meet-up is, with you, when we know."

"Sounds like a plan."

"Right." He cracked his knuckles. "Alright, woman, I'm going to try this again. About you and Roman…"

Beth kept a straight face and said nothing. Jared hadn't asked anything, and she wasn't volunteering.

"Compartmentalize whatever the hell is going on there. Do your job. Do it well. I will tell him the exact same thing. You understand?"

Her cheeks heated. "Yes, understood."

He smiled slowly, but it was as big as Sugar's smile earlier. "Ah, confirmation." He stood and slapped the table. "The Jared. Nice."

"You placed a bet on my life. Nice." He still scared her, but when he did things like joke about winning The Jared at her expense, she at least wasn't shaking in her stilettos.

"Harmless fun."

"What was she going to get if she'd won?"

He shook his head, smile still there.

"Come on. Unless it's something kinky."

"Not kinky."

"Good. 'Cause then I wouldn't want to know." Though the guy was smokin' hot in a killer-scary badass kind of way, a little kink wouldn't be nightmarish. "It was my love life you were betting on. Not even a hint?"

He shook his head, his scowl back. "She'll still get it. But tell her that, and you'll wish you hadn't."

"M-kay."

"Say it, Beth."

"I won't tell her."

"Good girl." Another hint of a smile before it disappeared. "Get back to work."

What the hell was *that* all about? And why did big, bad Jared Westin suddenly have a trying-to-hide-it grin?

CHAPTER 38

THE JET HAD TOUCHED DOWN, and Beth was whisked to Langley. She met up with Evan and told him everything she could think of, though he seemed to care a lot less than before her trip. She also confessed to *losing* Greg after *ignoring* him and that she hadn't heard from or seen him since the auction.

Again, Evan's reaction was less than expected, and his attitude confirmed one thing. This job had been nothing more than a public-relations move so that the government could say they were making good on trying to return looted art to the Iraqi museum. Or even more pathetically, this was a test to see what she would do and how far she would go when the Agency called upon her for a mission.

After landing, she should've checked on Nicola after she debriefed with Evan. But instead, Beth had returned to Roman's side, even though she'd just spent the better part of a long flight snuggled into him. But he'd offered to cook. After surviving a long minute of actual shock, she'd said, "Cool." And he wasn't kidding about cooking. While she'd been chatting with Evan, Roman had gone to a grocery store. The guy made a killer roast.

She hadn't known he could cook. She would've bet against him. Actually, no. Beth would never bet against him. He could do no wrong. He was one of those guys who always got it right when he tried. She could hate him for it, but it worked to her benefit.

The second night, since neither of them had been called up by the CIA or Titan, they got drunk and went to bed. And they stayed in bed and got wild. It was a rush. Fun. Lots and lots of screaming orgasms. God, the man knew how to make her body do things it had *never* done.

The third night, they went back to his bed and got naked again. He wasn't a sight she was going to get used to, but for some crazy reason—or not so crazy given the recent time-zone changes, the days of scorching sex, the night's big meal, and the genuine life upheaval—they lay under his roof, in his fabulous sheets, surrounded by all the warmth he'd put into his house, and just slept.

And now it was three days later, and she still hadn't caught up with Nicola. That made her a bad friend. It also confirmed that she was, without a single doubt, digging her time with Roman. But Beth was also out of clean clothes, and she refused to wash her laundry at his place. A girl could only shack up for so long before she felt a little clingy. So she went home and did laundry. She showered, using her own shampoo, not his or travel bottles. She lounged in fresh clothes and watched her phone, still waiting for the CIA or Titan to say go.

They didn't. Time just ticked by.

Beth picked at her cuticle. She hadn't been without Roman for more than a few hours in the last week. Now she was alone with her thoughts. But the time did her good. She made at least a couple decisions. First, if he didn't know, she needed to tell him how much he mattered to her. She also wanted to say that she couldn't close her eyes without thinking about how he warmed her from the inside out.

Beth searched her heart and soul for pangs of guilt. Nothing, which was good because that meant another day moving forward, courtesy of Roman. She sent him a message telling him to come over, then she put a bottle of wine out to breathe and called her local pizza joint.

Thirty minutes later, her phone buzzed. *I'm here. Let me up.*

Her man had arrived, and she felt the excitement rush through her. It hadn't been *that* long since she'd seen him. Really, that was pathetic. But she loved it—the excitement, the unknown, the comfortableness, all wrapped into one hard, hot body that couldn't keep his hands off her. Okay, there may've been a small guilty heart twinge. But it was minor.

Roman knocked on her door, and out of habit, she checked the peephole before she let him in. As wide and tall as the door, when he entered the room, he became her sole focus.

"Pretty girl." With a quick kiss on her cheek as if it had become their normal greeting, he breezed by. "I'm starving. Order in and a movie?"

She followed him to her couch. "Already ordered pizza. Half with pineapple." She made a gagging face. "And there's a bottle of wine screaming for us to drink it."

"Pineapple. Nicely done."

"Thank you."

"But the wine?" He shook his head. "Guess it'll have to work."

Five minutes later, they were on the couch, delivered pizza and red wine in hand. Like a date, except for more integrated and cozy.

On her second large glass of vino, while her hand grazed up and down Roman's chest, Beth startled when her phone buzzed. CIA or Titan? A little fuzzy; she maybe should've opted for the smaller wine glasses. She leaned forward to check the caller ID.

Fuck.

Her blood turned cold as everything stopped. Then her stomach lurched. She shoved away from Roman like the world could have seen his arm thrown around her and her bare feet tucked under her legs as if she'd found comfort, as if she'd found *herself*, with him.

No, no, no! Teresa Tourne.

The name. The picture. They stared at Beth, accusing her of being a whore. Her hands began to tremble, slowly at first, then they quaked, her muscles violently chattering as if she'd stepped from his warm embrace straight into an arctic freeze.

"Beth?"

"The date. Roman, what's the date?"

"October fifteenth. Why?"

Oh, fuck. Fuck. Fuck. Fuck.

She tried to swallow, but her throat wouldn't unlock. How had she been so stupid? So dumb? To think that she could just... ugh. Where had her mind gone? Selfish and shallow. She *knew* what she'd forgotten. She *knew* better. But damn her, she was too caught up in Roman to even think straight. *Traitorous bitch. Selfish, shallow whore.*

"Hey." Roman touched her back, but she couldn't face him. "What's the matter?"

She backed away from the couch as if he were a pariah. But really, it was her. She turned, staring at her still-ringing phone, then looked back at him.

"Beth?" He leaned forward, eyes narrowed, concern marring his chiseled face. "Who's—"

She forced her eyes from him and back to the phone. She accepted the call. "Hello?" Her tone sounded guilty to her ears. "Teresa?"

"Hey, sweetie. I was just checking on you. You survive okay?"

Beth's head dropped. She averted her gaze from Roman and walked toward her bedroom, then she couldn't go in. Roman had been in there with her. "I'm fine," she whispered. Her voice cracked, just like she was cracking up.

"You don't sound fine. Honey, are you—"

"I—" Her voice broke. "Teresa, I'm..." A whore. An embarrassment. A Tourne impostor. "I... have to tell you something."

"You're scaring me, honey. Do you want me to come over? I can be there in, um, two hours."

"No!"

"Okay. What's going on?"

"Oh God..." Tears stung Beth's eyes. "See... I don't know where to start."

"Try the beginning."

She sniffled, praying Roman would leave. She couldn't face him now. "I know you're my sister-in-law——"

"Oh, we're going back to the very beginning." Teresa's voice held a smile. "Gotcha."

"But you've always been more like a sister."

"Same here, honey. You know I love you, so no matter what you say, it'll be okay."

"I forgot." And then Beth lost it. Her tears ran hot and free. Every year, Teresa called the day after the anniversary of Logan's death. She always said she wanted to make sure Beth made it through okay.

"Oh, God. Beth. Honey..."

"I can't believe... I'm——" It would be both brutal and cathartic to just pour her guts out. But Teresa wasn't the one to share it with, to burden with her guilt. "Thank you for calling me."

"It's okay, you know, sweetie," Teresa whispered.

"No, it's not." Beth's eyes burned.

She was already forgetting everything. She was letting her guard down and falling in—no—being distracted by Roman. Because she couldn't fall for anyone, ever, especially if she was careless enough to forget about that date.

"Beth? Beth, honey? You there? I'm telling you, it's okay. *It's okay, honey*. Listen to me. It's life, and life happens."

Beth shook her head. "No. Not like this it doesn't."

"It's been years. You have to——"

"I should have remembered." She backed against the wall in her hallway, dropping her head, then remembered how Roman had her begging for his touch in that very spot. She jumped away from the wall as though it were the gates of hell.

"One day you'll forgive yourself," Teresa went on. "I've had to, and I'm better for it. None of it was your fault."

Beth stayed silent, staring at the wall.

"He'd want you to move on."

"No." She shook her head.

"One of these days, you'll——"

"Teresa, why are you saying that? Stop it!" Beth looked down the hall, and Roman stood there. She wanted to run from him, to him. Kick him, push him, scream that it was his fault she'd forgotten. Instead, she waved him away then closed her eyes.

Her memory was vividly clear. Logan hung, spinning slowly in half-circles, dangling in their garage. She remembered how she'd seen his feet first as the garage door went up. And how, when she'd eventually returned to their home days later, she'd had to throw out the bags of groceries. They'd spoiled in her trunk.

Why had he done that to her? She'd only been gone an hour. *One damn hour.* Just long enough to go to the supermarket. She'd kissed his cheek on the way out, and he'd said, "Bye, darlin'." That was it. He left her, and all he could say was "Bye, darlin'."

Tears obscured her vision.

"We'll never understand, but we will survive," Teresa said, just as she'd said so many times before.

"I… please don't hate me."

"Beth, sweetie. We'll always love you, and that's why I'm telling you this is okay."

"You don't understand…" She cried silently into the phone. "There's something else."

Teresa sighed. "Honey, is there someone there with you?"

The guilt was strangling her. Tears streamed down. "Mm-hmm."

"Good. Remember, that's alright. It was bound to happen one day."

Beth shook her head, anger, guilt, sadness all warring to take top billing.

"Is he a friend?"

She nodded. "Um-hmm."

"Maybe more than a friend?"

"Yes," Beth whispered, her voice choked.

"Good. That's good, sweetie. It's going to be okay."

Beth wiped her eyes. "You don't hate me?"

"No. Never."

"Promise?"

"I could never hate you. You'll always be my sister."

Fresh tears sprang up. "I really do love you, Teresa."

"I know you do, and I love you too. Don't you ever forget that."

"M-kay."

"If you're okay, maybe find your more-than-a-friend and ask for a hug." Teresa paused. "I'm going to jump off. Call me whenever, but definitely by next week, okay?"

"M-kay," Beth whispered.

"I love ya, Beth. Don't you ever forget it." And the line went dead.

Beth stared at her phone then scrolled to the calendar. Yeah, she'd missed it. She never marked it on the calendar because it was a date she would never forget. But she had.

Sadness and guilt stepped aside for fury. She stormed back to the couch and grabbed her wine.

"What is going on?" Roman, propped against the wall, watched her warily. "You okay?"

"Nothing. Doesn't matter to you."

His brow furrowed. "Excuse me?"

She ignored him, slugging back a gulp of wine. He stalked toward her while she glared. Of course she'd fall for him. How stupid could she be to think she wouldn't? That was why she was supposed to stay away. She knew better. Damn it. She had known better than to let him touch her. But God, it felt too good when he did. Maybe he could right now. Maybe he could make her forget it all.

No! What was her problem? Sex with Roman wasn't a cure-all.

But it wasn't a half-bad idea. Some people had alcohol, others drugs—*cocaine*. She had Roman. That was it. He was nothing more than a lay. And anything else she'd cooked in her brain about a relationship was… stupid. Just stupid. Nothing else.

Her heart hurt at that lie. But wouldn't it be easier if it were true? If Roman meant nothing more than incredible sex?

She scrubbed her face clean of tear streaks, gulped her wine again, and headed toward her bedroom. "Let's go fuck."

He didn't move. She turned.

A darkness colored his expression. "Excuse me?"

"Come on." She stormed around the room, trying to think where the best place to do this was. Here on the floor, just until she couldn't think. "Let's go."

His lip hitched, an angry, annoyed hurt on his face. "I'm not sure—"

"God." She raised her wine glass. "Wait, hold on. I need this first."

Roman strode over, stilling her arm, the glass inches from her lips. "What the hell is going on with you?"

"I was wrong about everything. If we could kick this thing between us back to hot, heavy, and meaningless, that would be awesome."

"Who was on the phone?" he growled.

"It doesn't matter."

"It does if you've gone crazy-bitch in a matter of seconds."

She pulled her arm away, splashing red wine everywhere, and took a long sip from what was left in the glass. "Fuck me and leave me, baby. It's all I want from you."

"Would you shut up, Beth."

"No. Let's go. Drop your pants. I'll even suck you off."

"Stop running your goddamn mouth. I swear to—"

"You swear what, Roman? I mean, really."

"Watch yourself. Go sleep it off. Whatever the fuck your problem is." His dark eyes grabbed hers and held on. "Don't act like you're a lay and I'm a cock and that's all this is. Because newsflash, sweetheart, you're wrong."

"No!"

He stepped back, snarling. "*Suck me off?* Are you out of your goddamn mind? Who was on the phone?"

"No one!" She circled the room again.

"Get over here," he ordered.

"I hate you! Hate!"

He smiled. He fucking *smiled* then crossed his arms. "Which apparently sucks for you, since you also love me."

"Bastard!" Beth threw her wine glass at the wall. More wine splattered. She stared as streams of red ran down to the pile of shattered crystal. "If you don't want me, then get out."

He threw his head back and laughed, deep and wounding.

She ran at him, slamming him in the chest with both hands. "Get out."

When he looked down, her fingers tightened, clawing into his shirt, his muscled chest. He was as intense as she was.

He nodded to the wine streaming down her walls. "Finally, you get some color on the walls."

"Go away!" She tried to shake him. He didn't budge, so she pushed. "Get out of my place."

"Not a chance, pretty girl." His voice was gritty and gruff. "If I'm going to fuck you on the floor, it's because I want to take you on the floor, make you scream on the floor, listen to you fuckin' moan while I slide my dick inside you on the fuckin' floor. Not because you get some phone call that makes you go berserk."

Her fingers flexed, pinching him. Her nails dug in, and the man didn't flinch. She wanted to run but couldn't let go. "I *hate* you."

The skin around Roman's dark eyes crinkled. "You have five seconds to figure your shit out, woman."

"I said I hate you." Because that had to be what burned in her soul for him. White. Hot. Hatred. Anything else was unforgivable. Had she seriously forgotten the anniversary of Logan's death? Stupid, stupid, pathetic traitor.

"Four, three—"

"You're the biggest, cockiest son of a bitch I've ever—"

"Beth." He stepped closer, shaking his head. Her fingers tightened, and still he didn't acknowledge her clinging to him. "I love you, babe."

Her mouth fell open. She was suddenly angrier than she'd ever been in her life. "You're a liar. You awful person, how dare you do that to me? Love? *Liar!* You are lying!" Hands twisted in his shirt, she threw her weight against him, wanting to shake him until it hurt both of them.

Roman didn't budge. "I'm a lot of things. Maybe a liar. Definitely an asshole. But in control of how I feel about you? Not at all."

Damn him! Her anger quadrupled until it was all-consuming, completely debilitating.

"There's nothing between us but sex," she lied, trying to make herself believe it.

"Wish that were true. You're a pain in my ass."

The veins in her neck pounded. Blood rushed in her ears. She could barely gasp out, "What do you want from me?"

Roman closed the inches between them, placing his hands on her wrists and holding them against his chest. "Everything."

CHAPTER 39

ROMAN WATCHED HER FACE CONTORT. He'd laid it out there, and Beth fought it, though there was no point. It was the truth, and he didn't have a single doubt that she loved him, too. All she had to do was work through it in her head and move forward. "Take a breath, pretty girl."

Her mouth flapped. She tried to back up, but her knees gave out. She would've crashed hard, except his hold on her forearms slowed the descent.

Her eyes rose to his, and she whispered, "Fuck you."

"Let it go, Beth. It hurts. I get it, babe. But you have to stop making yourself crazy."

"Nothing to let go." She sobbed.

"He's gone," Roman whispered. "And it wasn't your fault."

She curled into a ball on the floor. Roman watched the pain pour out of her, wishing he could wipe it clean, while knowing if he did that for her, they'd be back to the same spot all over again. He didn't know the psychology behind it all. But he knew he wasn't competing with a dead man or a memory.

"Nothing says living your life means you forget your past."

"But I did forget…" Her hands pressed to her chest, her knotted fingers digging into her breastbone. "I'm dying. Everything aches. All over again."

Roman kneeled in front of her and shook his head. "Baby, you have to forgive yourself for whatever you're holding onto, not for whatever you think you did."

"I'm just… dying," she choked out. "My heart's breaking. I'm…" Another gasp. "And you… I can't do this."

Sitting on the floor, he gathered her limp body into his arms and held her to his chest. Her fingers grabbed onto him.

Big, fat, sobbing tears poured out as she curled into him and shook. "You're strong. I'm... shattered."

"Take a breath."

She opened her eyes and hiccupped. "I can't."

"It'll be okay. Just breathe it out."

Beth sucked in a short gasp, then a longer one. Eventually, the tears stopped. "I forgot the anniversary of his death. *Forgot.*" She sniffled. "Because I was busy with you."

Ah shit... "It's going to be okay."

"That was his sister calling to check on me."

Even worse. "Don't know what to say to that."

"I forgot the worst day of my life because I was too busy making up best days instead."

Best days of her life? With him. He nodded then stood and carried her down the hall, kicked open her bedroom door and lay on the bed with her. Roman let Beth burrow into him. He didn't look at the alarm clock, didn't wonder if he could hear their phones in case their go-call came in. He just smoothed her hair and waited.

Minutes later, she wiped at her eyes with the back of her hand and peeked up at him. "Hi."

His lips quirked. "Pretty girl."

"I feel better. I think. I need to go wash my face." She got up and went into the bathroom.

When she returned, he held her tighter.

"Say something so this isn't awkward," she whispered to his chest.

"So..." He shifted her even closer, his lips brushing against her temple. "One of these days, you're going to have to get into a fight with me about *me.*"

She laughed quietly, then she locked her pinky finger around his. "I said a lot, and most of it was mean and ugly. Maybe all of it."

He shrugged. "Shit happens. Not sure you meant any of it."

"I didn't."

"See? There you go." He squeezed her finger.

"I'm sorry."

He took her chin in his hand and kissed her lips. "I know."

Beth smiled. "What now?"

"Whatever we want."

CHAPTER 40

A BRIGHT, SHINY, POST-FIGHT MORNING interrupted Beth's lazy sleep. *Go away, morning.* She had no plans to leave the warm confines of her bed and Roman's naked hold.

"Beth?" the morning whispered.

That was concerning. Times of day shouldn't talk. Still, Beth ignored whatever was tugging her awake, relaxing into slumber again as Roman's heavily draped arm snuggled her deeper into the bed. God, Roman smelled like heaven after the hell of last night.

"Beth?" morning whispered, more urgently, a little louder.

Seriously. Go away, morning.

"Beth! Are you okay?"

Her eyes shot open as the bedroom door bounced against the wall. Nicola stood there, looking ready to kill. "Nic, wh—"

"Beth!" she shout-hissed.

Was this still a dream? Nope. There was Nicola.

"Oh, my God. What happened out there? There's broken glass and a red stain on the wall—" Nicola's mouth twisted as she stopped abruptly, covering her face. "Please tell me that's not my brother's naked ass cheek facing up from your bed."

Without acknowledging he was awake, Roman tugged the covers over his butt.

Beth's face heated to the level of might-die-on-the-spot. "Oh, my God."

"You should call first," Roman grumbled from beneath the pillow.

"I did. No one answered."

"So you just come over?" he asked, face still buried, which was helpful because Beth was having a hard time putting words into sentences and explaining... everything.

Nicola raised her eyebrows, pointing to her stomach. It all came rushing back. They needed to talk. "It's what we do, Roman. If you don't mind, I need to talk to my girl."

"Nothing to talk about," he said.

"Not everything revolves around you, buddy." Nicola made a face and beckoned Beth out of the room.

Beth wrapped the bedspread around her chest. "Give me two minutes."

"Fine," Nicola said, leaving the bedroom. "I'll just clean up out here. Gives me something to do to rid my mind of that"—she made a gagging noise—"*image*."

Beth rubbed her eyes and stared at Roman's perfect body, which he hadn't done a very good job of covering. "Should we tell people?"

He turned over, and good Lord, his mussed hair and sleepy grin might be her death. "About us? Talk if you want. I don't care. Not going to change what I do or say. But you might as well before they tell each other, if that's your concern." He bunched his pillow, readjusted his frame, then looked at the door. "I thought she had the flu."

Beth's stomach jumped. "She does." That sounded way too high and fast.

His eyes had closed anyway, as if he had dozed off in the half-second it took for her to answer. Her lying ability was pathetically questionable around him. That didn't say much for her CIA training.

"I'll be back in a few." Beth slid toward the edge of bed, but his strong, rough hand caught her wrist.

Roman tugged her toward him, wrapping a thick arm around her. "Come back to bed. ASAP."

"We have to catch up."

"Then catch up fast, and come back. Fast."

Beth crawled over him. "And why should I do that?"

He turned over, anchoring his hands on her hips as she straddled him. "Should I count the reasons?"

She nodded, giggling. "Please."

"One. You're too beautiful to be running around when I wake up hard as a rock. Two, you're a fantastic fuckin' lay. That'd help with my hard-as-a-rock problem."

She shook her head but smiled even bigger. "Selfish. All men think about is—"

"And three, I want to watch your face while I make you come."

Her jaw dropped. As fast as she'd lost her ability to speak, he flipped her on her back, hovering above her, then kissed her deeply. He wasn't kidding. The man was rock hard and rubbing between her legs.

He rolled her to the edge of the bed. "Talk fast. I'll be here."

She untangled herself from his arms, and he patted her bottom. She jumped with a yip and giggled. "Roman!"

She threw on some sweats. With a quick glance in the mirror, she decided she didn't look too sex-crazed and went to down the hall. Nicola was dumping the shattered wine glass in the trash.

"So…" Nicola's brows arched, and her smile was one hundred percent interested in gossip. "You and Roman."

Beth tilted her head, looking anywhere but at Nicola's face. "Me and Roman."

"Are we talking wedding bells?"

Beth's eyes snapped forward. "Christ, Nic. Not everyone believes in happy endings. It's just…" She twirled her hand in the air. "A thing." It was so not just a thing. He'd professed love. She'd had two major mental breakdowns. It was messy and complicated, and she couldn't imagine not going back to him the second Nicola left.

Nicola turned and rummaged through Beth's pantry. "Got any crackers?"

"You're acting like Cash, going through my cabinets."

"He eats non-stop because he burns it off. I need to eat right now, or I'm liable to dry heave on your perfect floor. Speaking of perfect, let's talk about your wine-covered wall. You do that? Damage your perfectly made-up condo? I'm shocked."

"I threw a glass of wine at him." Beth shrugged, downplaying it.

"Shit." Nicola threw her head back, laughing. "I would have paid to see that."

When Nicola finally calmed down, Beth leveled her a serious gaze. "Do you think there's any of me in this condo?"

"Nope."

Beth's brow pinched. "That was fast."

"Well, no kidding. Easy question gets an easy answer."

"Why?"

"Well…" Nicola pulled out a sleeve of saltines and waved them over her head. "Success."

"I have no idea how old those are."

She opened the plastic and took a bite of one. "Doesn't matter. Stale is fine. So long as it's tasteless."

"Right. So let's talk about what's important here." Beth pointed at Nicola's stomach. "Big news to drop via text message, by the way."

"I had to tell someone, and Cash was out on a job. Anyway, hold on. I want to answer your question."

"What question?"

"The condo one. No. There's none of you in here. You are fun and wild and sweet. You have flaws and imperfections that make you beautiful."

Beth shook her head. "Those don't make someone beautiful. I'm... chaotic and confusing. No one wants that. They want... I don't know."

"What I know is you'd rather hang with me at a dive bar than deal with all that hoity-toity who's-who bullshit you go to for work. That you'd never, ever live in some place that's white from floor to ceiling. So the job lets you hide the real you and live in a place like this. It's a gorgeous, swanky, super-blinged-out art museum, and nothing like you."

"I think you're right." Beth sighed. "Actually, I know you're right."

"I'm a mother-to-be. I spout wisdom and shit now." Nicola giggled, covering her mouth and looking over Beth's shoulder. "Roman can't know before Cash."

"No kidding."

"So what's the look on your face? I thought when you and Roman finally happened, it'd be... okay. You'd... I don't know... be good with it."

"I am good with it. But having feelings for Roman doesn't change the past."

"Neither does living in the past." Nicola nibbled on a cracker. "I don't know. Maybe it's not the past you live in, but like, a desensitized moment in the present that lets you ignore the future."

"What's that supposed to mean?"

"You keep a perfectly polished world, just like the CIA wants you to."

"I do my job."

"But you never let go."

"That's what they pay me to do. It's called a cover, hello."

Nicola sighed. "Yeah. I know. It's just... you aren't using your cover to keep you safe, you're using it to avoid dealing with Logan."

"Please don't say his name." She'd thought about him enough last night.

Nicola shrugged. "Okay."

"Feelings, all this, whatever it is—"

"Emotion."

Beth rolled her eyes. "*Emotion.* Feelings. Crap. It's... it's a burden."

"That could be a song." Nicola's eyes danced.

"What?"

Nicola held her sleeve of crackers like a microphone. "Love is a burden!"

"Did you just sing that to "Life is a Highway"?"

"Maybe." She shrugged and went back to munching. "At least own up to it and say you love Roman."

"I cannot believe you just said that. Bitch." Beth glared. "*Bitch.*"

Nicola laughed, crunching into another cracker. "I call it like I see it."

Beth stepped closer, whispering, "He said he loves me."

"Because you two *are* in love. You just have to stop fighting it." Nicola's eyes bounced toward the hall. "Incoming."

Roman walked in, wearing jeans slung low on his hips. "Morning."

Nicola made a face. "Put some clothes on."

"How'd you get in here anyway?" Roman threw back.

"I have a key. *I* can show up whenever I want, thank you very much."

He shook his head. "I'm making eggs. Who wants—"

Nicola covered her mouth, gagging.

"Dude." Roman shook his head. "Swallow down the pukes."

"'Kay. Gimme a sec." She shuffled toward the bathroom.

"Man." He scrunched up his face. "She needs to give Rocco hell for getting her sick."

Beth bit her lip. Men were dense about these things, she decided.

"What?" he asked.

How funny would it be if she could say something like, "Oh, it wasn't *Rocco* who got her sick." But Roman still probably wouldn't get it, and Nicola would kill her. "I should go check on her."

He turned to the fridge then back to Beth. "What'd she say?"

"About?"

"Us."

Beth laughed. "You sound like a girl wanting in on the gossip."

"Just curious, babe."

"She thinks it's groundbreaking that I have red wine on my wall."

"I do, too." He went back to the fridge, his back to her. "Epic, really."

She watched him. Everything about their time together was epic, even if she'd rather die than subject herself to losing someone she cared about again. But she was already there. Love was an epic *burden*. But it wasn't a death sentence.

Maybe she had needed permission from Teresa to move on, maybe she'd needed Nicola to make light of their relationship, or maybe Beth had needed to realize how damn wrong she'd been. Moving forward was a possibility. All she needed was to accept the inevitable—that she was in love with Roman Hart.

He backed away from the fridge with his hands full of eggs, butter, and cheese. "What's with that face?" His brow pinched. "Don't tell me you have the flu, too."

Ha. "Nope. Not even close."

"Good." He moved to the stove.

Watching him was so… normal. Roman rifled through her cabinets, grabbing bowls and clanking them on the counter. He turned on her gas range and put a week's worth of butter into a skillet.

Nicola walked back into the kitchen as the smell of melting butter rose. She looked green.

Roman turned from the stove, spatula in hand. "You dying?"

Nicola nodded. "I have to go."

She blew him a kiss, grabbed her purse, and hustled out the door. He put the spatula down, and one huge hand rubbed his tattooed bicep.

Beth thought back. Every time there was an opportunity to worry over Nicola, he kneaded that tattoo. The realization stole her heart, and Beth almost tripped over herself to hug him. When she wrapped her arms around his bare chest, she squeezed her eyes closed, not daring to let another tear fall in front of him. "You're such a good guy."

"I know." He laughed and kissed the top of her head. "What's up?"

How many times had she seen him worry about Nicola like that? They had far more in common when it came to loss than she ever gave him credit for. Beth perched her chin on his chest. "I want a tattoo."

CHAPTER 41

THE FRONT DOOR FLEW BACK open again. Nicola rushed in, bypassed them without so much as a wave, and ran toward the bathroom. "Don't mind me," she called before shutting the door.

Roman tossed the spatula down and turned the gas off on the stove top. "A tattoo?"

"Yes."

He picked Beth up, set her on the countertop, and stepped between her legs. "What do you want?"

"I don't know. Something that means something." Beth cupped his cheeks then ran her fingers through his hair. "Something that makes me want to touch it when I'm happy or scared."

"That's a lot for a tattoo."

She tilted her head at his arm.

It took him a few long seconds to get the hint. "Ten-four, pretty girl."

"Look, I didn't realize until just now how patient you've been with me. I mean, I've been a mess, and you've been cool. God's honest truth, I was stuck in my own head, and you let me take my time."

He'd wondered how much last night would change her head space, but he wasn't ready to push it. Hell, he was barely hanging on to the idea of caring about her the way he did. "Good."

"I'm serious, Roman. I appreciate how you've handled me. I'm the living, breathing definition of baggage."

"You aren't the only one."

She bit her lip. "I know."

"So we work. Balance each other out." He stroked her back. "My sister's puking in your bathroom. You're distracting me from my eggs that are gonna burn sitting in that skillet. This isn't how I pictured our day going."

She smiled, leaning against him. "How did you?"

He dropped his gaze to her sinful body still sitting on the counter. "Already gave you a list."

She stopped, remembering. "A very good list."

"Hell yeah, it is." He wrapped her legs around him and carried her to the table, where he scooted her into a chair then took in the view. Wayward curls and unhidden freckles, two of his favorite things about her. Then his eyes swept over the table, landing on the fancy embroidered placemats. "You like those?"

"The placemats?"

"Yeah," he said. Because he hated them. They looked like expensive, rectangular doilies that his grandma would go ape shit over.

"They're hand-stitched from—"

"Do. You. Like. Them."

Beth giggled, shaking her head. "Not at all."

"You and Sugar are going to have a field day redecorating." He grabbed them all and looked at the trashcan but then thought better of it. They probably cost more than his truck. He tucked them into a cabinet.

"Those, too." She pointed at the matching cloth napkins on the breakfast bar. "Please."

"Done." He shelved them with the mats.

Nicola walked out, looking a bit worse for the wear.

He narrowed his eyes. "You should see a doctor, Nic. Seriously, what were you thinking, getting out of bed?"

She gave him a thumbs up. "Doctor, got it. Thanks."

He made a mental note to see if Beth had some Lysol. He certainly didn't want whatever had Nicola barfing all the time.

Beth smiled. "When Sugar's back in town, we're going shopping. Wanna help?"

"Of course. For what?"

"I'm redecorating."

"Yeah?" Nicola's eyebrows rose, then she looked at Roman. "What? Are you moving in with her?"

"No," he and Beth said in unison.

Nicola laughed, but she still looked queasy. "Jeez. Calm down. I was just kidding. Kinda."

Beth's eyes bounced around the room. Roman shifted, and his chest felt tight. It was less of a reaction to Nicola's question and more of an irritation that Beth had jumped that fast to say no. Just like him.

"Besides," Nicola continued, "CIA would never let you."

"Never," Beth agreed. "Wait. Never let me what?"

Moving behind Beth, he leaned against her back. "Cut it out, Nic.

No one's breaking major, life-changing news here. Just having breakfast and getting rid of some doily shit no one likes."

Nicola's eyes widened for a second. "Right. Nothing life changing to announce. Got it. Well, I have to go. For real this time."

He waved and watched her go. The uncomfortable air didn't follow her. Roman pulled a chair over and sat, facing Beth. "That wasn't awkward."

"Ha. Nope."

"You okay?"

Beth nodded. "Of course."

"Good. Because one crazy idea spewing out of Nic's mouth shouldn't ruin the morning. Though the eggs are probably a lost cause."

"Totally crazy idea…"

"Not logical at all." His mind raced at the thought of waking next to Beth's warm, naked body every morning. He pulled her off her chair and onto his lap. "Fuck, you smell good."

Beth sighed, making his dick jump. Her arms crossed behind his neck. "Normal people don't just move in together."

"We're not normal." He flexed his hips, rubbing against her. "Don't use that as an argument."

"Well, then…" She arched her back, making the friction work so damn well. "People know each other longer before they move in together."

"I've known you for years." His hands ducked under her shirt, sliding across her smooth back.

"Are you trying to make an argument *for* us…?"

"Nope, just listening to your faulty reasoning." His lips landed on hers, kissing her, feeling her mouth melt against his. *Screw breakfast.* He stood with her wrapped around him and headed toward her bedroom. "You could always leave this museum as it is and spend the nights with me."

Because that wasn't moving in together. That was sleeping with his girl.

"Maybe."

Wrong answer. He didn't like the hesitation. "Why not?"

"Why should I?"

"'Cause I want you there." He settled her on the bed. "I want the real you, living in your real space. Not some stupid CIA condo." That sounded a whole lot like he wanted her to move in with him. Because… he did. Yeah, he did. No question. "Look, Beth…"

Her eyes were large, but her mouth remained sealed shut.

"Maybe I do want you with me. Want us together."

"We are together," she whispered.

The woman was just coming around to the idea of him. And now he was springing this on her? But he wanted what he wanted. "Maybe I'm not patient."

Tugging off her shirt, his hands covered her body. He massaged her breasts and grew hard, watching her enjoy it. She grabbed his jeans, tugging them down then wrapping her hand around his cock. Beth stroked his shaft, teasing the crown with her thumb. He stepped out of his pants then tugged her sweatpants free, letting his hands run wild.

Heart in his throat, dick in her hand, Roman settled between her spread legs. "I want to wake up with you."

Her breath hitched when he pressed to her hot center.

"Baby," she whispered, mouth gaping as he rocked, grabbing her hips for a better angle.

"I want to be with you."

"You are…"

"I want this—" He thrust to the hilt, groaning into her mouth. "Whenever I want it. Under the same roof. In the same bed."

"Yes."

He withdrew and slid deep. Again and again. "Tell me."

She nodded, moaning and climbing toward climax.

"Say the words, Beth."

"Same roof. Same bed." She tumbled into an orgasm, clinging to him.

Their gasps were rapid fire, their kisses deep. Somewhere his phone rang, then her phone rang. But he didn't care and didn't stop until they both fell back onto the bed, completely sated. Limbs loose, he tucked her against him.

She turned her head. "Both phones were ringing. *I think.*"

His fingertips traced over her curves. "Yeah, you know what that means."

"We're a go."

He leaned over and kissed her. "Easy in and out."

"Nothing's ever as easy as it seems."

CHAPTER 42

AFTER A WHIRLWIND TRIP BACK to the other side of the world, Beth needed more sleep than she'd had the chance for recently. Kosovo was pretty, except when it wasn't. And the part of the little town they were in wasn't. At all.

Everything looked red and brown, made of clay and rock and dirt. The dusty, dirty town was impoverished and run down. Rusted-out cars shared the same road with mules and donkeys. Old walls were bullet ridden. Ragged children sat on the streets and broke Beth's heart.

She headed toward the mortar-wracked building that Titan had had eyes on. As an unaccompanied, obviously Western woman—despite her headscarf—Beth felt the stares as she walked to a building with a reputation for welcoming warmongers.

Beth opened the heavy, scarred door. The stench of dust and blood permeated the air. There was no telling how long ago these halls had seen violence because some odors never disappeared. She held her head high as she passed the men posted in the hallway. No one said anything because a woman dressed as she was heading into *that* building only said one thing: she was protected and powerful.

The building was a labyrinth. The hallways had low ceilings and plaster walls. The amber light flickered almost constantly. She rounded a corner and stopped abruptly as she found her marks.

"Gentlemen," she offered.

One grunted hello, but the other didn't make a sound. They turned toward the dimly lit stairs. The power flickered as they walked. The shoddy wiring surged and waned. There had to be loose wires from years of mortar attacks and rebel strikes.

"Beth, you still hear me?" Jared's voice came through crystal clear despite the thick walls. He'd been in her ear the entire walk to the building. "Cough to acknowledge."

Staying behind the men, she coughed quietly. Their tactical pants swished as they clumped up the stairs. Their weapons—and there were a lot of them—made her anxious. It wasn't her thing to be surrounded by automatic firepower when she didn't have so much as a switchblade.

"Good girl," Jared said. "Don't forget: the whole world's counting on you."

No pressure. Though she knew there were several backup plans in place and Titan was running point on this, several nations and intelligence communities were on standby if they didn't pull this off.

"Roman and Cash, read me still?" Jared continued.

"Roger that, Boss Man," Cash whispered in her earpiece.

"Here." Roman hadn't sounded okay since Beth had nodded goodbye and headed down the road unarmed. She had no vest, weapon, or close-by backup. He'd had a fit, but while she wasn't comfortable, there was no way to have any safety measures. But the risk was worth it.

Beth couldn't let a little thing like nerves compromise her cover: a code authenticator assisting two terrorists with brokering a deal. The man who'd hired her—Aleksei Polzin— would bring her in and say a few words, then the codes would be confirmed, and money would be exchanged with phone calls to the appropriate bankers. She would get out, Titan would get in, grab the codes and the nuke, and everyone would go home, safe and sound.

Jared cut into her thoughts. "Time to hide your earpiece, Beth. We'll try to keep eyes on you best we can."

Those baby drones were coming in handy. She coughed to acknowledge, then slid the piece out and slipped it into a hidden pocket inside her jacket.

Aleksei Polzin stood at the top landing. Clad in a khaki suit, he had a hard face with pale-brown eyes and a deep, ugly scar on his chin. Generic yet dangerous. He could blend into a crowd but, oh, the sins that man must've had under his collar.

"You come very highly recommended." Polzin's Russian accent was thick, and his smile was as frigid as a Moscow winter's day.

She smiled just as coldly. "I do a good job."

"You're virtually unheard of."

"Discretion is just one of the many reasons I do so well."

Polzin regarded her, his drab eyes assessing to see if he could really trust her with his mega millions and what would essentially become a terror strike.

She ignored his once-over and let her expression say that she didn't appreciate the second guessing. "You have my services for thirty minutes. Any more time wasted, I start charging additional percentages."

He chuckled, his clipped, former-KGB nature apparently appreciating her demands. "Very well. If all goes well, I hope we can continue business in the future."

Her smile never wavered, though her pulse quickened. "Once we have a partnership, it's nearly unbreakable."

Polzin smiled. "Excellent."

"Are we a go?"

"Yes," he said. "How long will the authentication take?"

"Less than two minutes."

"Perfect. As soon as I have your confirmation, the funds will transfer, as will your fee. Immediately."

Her cover story came with a tale of a client gone wrong, one who had not transferred her money as expected and had been left alive for the sole purpose of suffering. "Then let's do this."

He pushed through another door. Polzin's muscle followed, and even though she knew they were Team Bad Guy, she liked having two men with assault rifles with her as they entered an unknown room, kind of like a shitty security blanket.

On the other side of the door, the same type of men, guns, and arrangements likely waited. She wasn't one hundred percent sure. Titan had maintained eyes on the building for more than a day and saw only a few men connected to the deal enter. The drones had several shots of various rooms, but no one knew exactly where the negotiations would occur. The building was a strategic nightmare, making Roman and Cash's job of keeping eyes on her hard. Polzin led them down another dingy hallway, and her heels clicked on the broken, stained tile floor.

He stopped in front of a marred door and eyed her then his two men. "Ready?"

Everyone signaled affirmative, and he knocked then opened the door. Adrenaline pulsed through her. She swallowed her nerves and straightened her spine.

They entered a makeshift suite that was furnished and not nearly as dirty as the rest of the building. The walls were painted. The couches and tables were heavy, ornate, and as professional as one could expect in this building.

One man sat on a couch arranged behind a table holding a dirty silver coffee pot. Behind him, two mercenary types were dressed like Polzin's Rambos. The large room was awkwardly shaped, and voices floated from the back, while another guard milled along the wall. A small briefcase lay next to the coffee service, and Beth broke out in a cold sweat, knowing how close all these men were to nuclear power.

Polzin confidently strode into the large room. Attitude was everything, and it boded well for their safety. He was a major player, experienced and respected.

"We meet in person," he said as his counterpart rose from the couch. They each exchanged pleasantries. The Rambos took their positions. Beth stood awkwardly to the side.

Polzin motioned to her. "Let's start."

Beth stepped forward. The fragrant smell of coffee permeated the air, and cups clinked on saucers from the same direction as the voices, whose owners she couldn't see. The Rambos shifted their gazes, tracking all the occupants in the room, as the air sizzled with tension.

"She's the one?"

Polzin nodded again, accepted an envelope from the other man, and handed it to her. Beth's mind was calm, her resolve steady. This would be fine. She would just do her part and let Titan handle the rest.

"What…?" A voice surprised her from a far corner. "Is that *Beth*?"

Her throat went dry as her stomach plummeted. *Shit.* Beth dropped her scarfed head, knowing she was dead. Gregori Naydenov was in the room.

Polzin's counterpart turned. "Is there a problem?"

"No—" Beth shook her head.

Glancing up, she saw Greg *and* Evan. Evan, with a cell phone pressed to his ear, jumped back, grabbing a gun from his waistband. Greg was faster. He fired a bullet point blank at her CIA handler. Blood splattered as Evan collapsed, the gunshot echoing dully in the room. The lighting in the suite shook and flickered. Beth screamed, ducking behind the heavy wooden hutch.

Both sets of Rambos flew into strategic, operational positions, dragging couches and chairs into barrier lines and readying to fire. Shouts in native tongues flew. The armed guards barricaded and protected their assets. Everyone was in an armed position, except for Beth, who was tucked down and nowhere near a weapon.

"Stand up," Greg ordered. "Now!" His voice strained and cracked, anger rolling off him. "Beth. Stand."

Fuck. Slowly, she rose from her crouch, standing in no man's land between the buyers, the sellers, and Greg. She put her hands up in the air. "It's not what you think."

"I think Evan Nathaniel introduced me to you."

"Yes, but—"

"He said you were an art collector. An expert."

"I am—"

"He lied. Now he's dead because I know him. I've done business with him. I know who he is, and if he lied, there was a reason."

"Greg—"

"*What* is that reason?"

She bit her lip. "Please don't do this."

He took a step forward. His gun dangled by his side, and a wash of emotions rolled over his face: anger, confusion, hurt, and heartbreak. "What are you doing here, Beth?"

She had nothing. What was *he* doing here? Evan, too? Since when did money launderers *show up* at meets for the money exchange? Never. Did the CIA not see this coming? Or was the CIA involved? Maybe Evan was in on it with no backing from the CIA? Because Agency powers-that-be knew she was here. But Evan did not. Jasper did not. Evan was... a traitor. *Shit.*

Greg began to shake. Veins protruded in his neck as his face went red. And all the while, she couldn't keep an eye on Polzin or the other team.

Greg looked over her shoulder and told the men, "Get out of here. Go. Now." Then he turned his angry glare back to her. "Now tell me who the fuck you are."

Out of the corner of her eye, she saw the tactical men encircle their charges and leave the room. Her heart pounded in her ears, sweat dampening her body. She was all alone, just her and Greg. There was no way out of this one.

Titan could hear her. They were probably scrambling for a backup plan, trying to get visuals, maybe trying to get a man inside the building. But that would take too long. Besides, Titan had more important things to consider, like tracking down a nuke. Their priority was the weapon. As it should be.

She closed her eyes and accepted her fate. She should have told Roman she loved him.

CHAPTER 43

THE ECHO OF A GUNSHOT echoed through Roman's earpiece, but that wasn't what made his blood turn to ice. "Did someone say *Beth*?" he roared into his comm piece.

"Who's got eyes? Who the fuck has eyes? Goddamn it!" Jared bellowed. "Parker, what's going on in there?"

"Workin' it."

"Parker. Now," Jared growled.

Seconds ticked by. They all knew how many dirty windows were in that shitty building, how they had nothing in terms of decent surveillance. Roman peered from his position, checking every angle he could with binoculars. Nothing.

Who the fuck had said *Beth*? "Cash?" he asked, even though he knew his buddy would've already called a visual if he had it.

"Roman," Cash whispered with a serious level of calm-the-hell-down in his voice. "Give it a sec, buddy."

Roman scanned the perimeter, ignoring the team in his earpiece as everyone turned up a lack of intel. There wasn't much between Roman and the building. He and Cash were the closest by far, but they weren't anywhere close to being in a strategic position to enter the building.

"Stay put," Cash said, apparently reading Roman's mind. "Don't move till we know more."

This was a total game changer. With scattered thoughts, Roman mapped out the path to the building with the most coverage. He could duck out of his current spot and be there in maybe two minutes. It wouldn't be easy. There were—he scanned again—one, two possible alcoves in nearby storefronts that could shelter him, plus a few cars and street vendor carts along his best route. But nothing that would hide him in tactical gear, rushing a building surrounded by foot traffic. His heart pounded in his chest.

230 | CRISTIN HARBER

"Roman!" Jared barked. "We don't know. Hang tight."

Muttered whispers came from Beth's comm piece, but Roman couldn't tell what was said or even who was speaking. Fuck, he couldn't tell if she was alive.

"Speak up!" a man's voice boomed.

Scratchy noise echoed through her mic, then the sound became clearer.

"It's not what you think," Beth said.

Roman's heart leapt into his throat. Beth, alive, but clearly in danger. Sweat dripped down his spine as he rose into a crouch.

"I need an explanation," a man barked. "You and Evan working me over?"

"You didn't have to kill him."

Him? Evan? Her handler? And who was that? The voice sounded familiar. Then, it came to him—Gregori Naydenov.

"Parker's got a hit," Jared said.

"Naydenov." Roman was already on his feet and moving toward the stairs. "We've got problems."

"Affirmative." Jared cursed in the background. "Voice recognition matched. What do we got on him? Any history—"

"She was working a CIA job with him."

"Goddamn it," Jared growled.

Roman jumped down a flight of stairs, racing down another.

"You moving already? Roman?"

"Abso-fuckin'-lutely."

Boss Man cursed. "Christ. Cash, catch up with him. Reposition. We need eyes in there. Parker, get me better ears, and I want to see that whole damn room. Every fuckin' angle."

"Ten-four," Parker muttered.

Roman ran across the street, weaving between wide-eyed people. "I'm going in. Cash, find me."

"The fuck you are!" Jared yelled. "Heads up. Buyer, seller exiting the building. Parker, drones stay with those vehicles. Team one, you're a go to intercept."

"Roger that," Brock responded. "Move out."

Roman bit back his response to those orders. They were the right ones for the greater good: neutralize any future potential nuclear attacks. But that didn't make him any less sick over the team splitting up to follow two vehicles, leaving Beth with a serious lack of help. *Fuck it.* It was fine by him. It would be better for him to go one-on-one with Naydenov. He was going to kill that motherfucker.

"Damn it." Cash sounded as though he was packing his gear on the quick. "If he goes in, I'm right there with him."

"Stand down, Roman," Jared ordered.

Naydenov's angry words crackled in the earpiece. "Who do you work for?"

"No one." Her voice was stronger. His girl was back on her game. "Freelance."

Naydenov laughed. The sound was louder. They were standing close to each other. Roman would tear him apart, limb by limb, if a curl on her head was touched.

"My Beth," Naydenov continued, "was a DC princess who could recite textbook art history facts. Not a woman with her hands on nuclear codes."

His Beth? Roman's teeth ground together.

"They were not *my* codes. Like I said, I'm freelance. And I could ask the same of you. Why's an investment banker here?"

"Lying bitch."

"I know why I'm here." Her confidence scared Roman to death. "The ones who don't make sense are *you* and *Evan.*"

The sound of a slap had Roman on the move again. He closed in on the door.

"You've been working me over," Naydenov snarled. "Whore."

She grunted. Rustling noises followed.

"Get your hands off me."

"Who do you work for?"

"Go to hell." She let out a loud *Oomph*, making Roman think she was thrown to the floor or hit.

"CIA?" Naydenov's voice was farther away. "I've had my suspicions about Evan. Maybe you were too good to be true. Though"—feedback drowned out a few words—"you and Evan to be here."

Another slapping noise followed by another grunt from Beth made Roman's mind race. But if he went in there and Naydenov had a weapon pointed at her, a sloppy trigger finger could end her—and him, because he'd be ruined. He decided to go in but hang back until the scene was scoped.

Gun in hand, Roman entered the building, rounded a corner, and fired two shots, taking out two armed, unsuspecting guards. Slowly, Roman crept up the stairs, still listening to the showdown.

"If not CIA, then who?"

"Freelance, you asshole." More struggling noises. "Get off my—"

"Drone's got eyes," Parker called. "Hand to hand. No one else visible."

"Wait for Cash, then you're a go, Roman."

"Just behind you," Cash whispered. "Thirty seconds."

"Something's going down," Parker said. "He's patting her down or copping a feel. I don't know which."

"What's this?" Naydenov's voice was suddenly crystal clear. "A comm piece? This to your bulldog?" Greg laughed loudly into the receiver. "Who do we have on the other end?"

Roman heard more grunts, feminine and masculine. She was giving as good as she was taking. Glass shattered. Furniture broke. Both were yelling. Cash appeared in the hallway.

"And..." Naydenov's panting said Beth had been holding her own. "Here's the mic."

"Fuck you!" she screeched.

Skin slapped skin, and Naydenov shouted, "Not interested anymore!"

"Ass—"

Parker cut in. "Choke hold."

Naydenov growled into the mic, "I have your Beth. What are we going to do about it?"

All of Titan stayed radio silent. Roman looked at Cash and then at the door. Cash nodded.

Roman said, "Naydenov. Let's talk."

Naydenov's harsh laugh cackled through the earpiece. "Of course. You've come to save your girl."

"Something like that. Let's deal."

"Not interested in deals."

Roman tried again. "But you will be interested in information."

"You have ten seconds to convince me. Otherwise, she's dead."

Roman's heart froze. "She wasn't lying. She's freelance. We both are." He prayed then and gambled. "I'm coming in with my associate. You let her go. The three of us talk business. You clean money; we do the dirty work. I have buckets of loot that you can wash. Name your percentage."

"Beth stays."

Roman grimaced, readying to knock the door down. "Beth goes, and we tack on a new-friends bonus. I'll hand you a million dollars. Unmarked, untraceable cash." Roman's hand balled and loosened then clenched again. "We're outside the door. Let's do this."

Silence.

"Open the door, Naydenov."

Long seconds ticked by. No response. Cash looked at Roman, shaking his head.

Roman ground his molars. "Look, I'll even throw in an 'I'm a dick, you win' clause. I'm the dick. The asshole. Whatever you want to call it. You want the girl, you get the girl, but after we do business. Let's talk shop."

"No!" Beth screamed.

"Move!" Parker yelled at the same time.

Roman's reflexes were on it. Muscles tensed and tightened, he was ready to jump, run, dive. He turned, then the world exploded around them. Smoke, fire, and wood slapped his face, and he was thrown against the wall. His ears squealed. Blood coated his tongue. His eyes burned. He couldn't see. His lungs tried. Failed. Hot embers bit his face. His eyes tried to focus. Small flames danced on the walls. Cash was next to Roman, mouth moving, but Roman couldn't hear.

Chunks of thick, heavy walls crumbled on top of them. His mind froze. Gasping for breath, Roman fought... against the pull...

Darkness.

CHAPTER 44

BETH'S VISION WENT IN AND out as Greg dragged her around the room, arm clenched around her neck. He loosened his hold enough to grab a gun. Her eyes couldn't focus, but her mind processed that that gun had explosive power.

When Greg raised his arm and aimed at the door, she'd bucked and screamed. He pulled the trigger. The door exploded, and she and Greg fell, him landing on top of her. The blast had been strong, its aftereffects stronger. He must've fired a breaching round—not as strong as a hand grenade, but shot that close in proximity…

"Roman!" The wall caught fire quickly. Smoke billowed. Her ears shrieked from the blast. "Roman!"

She ducked out from under Greg. If the blast had thrown her that hard, then what had happened to Roman? She pushed onto her hands and knees, heading for the fiery, gaping space where the door had been. Black smoke filled the room. The building was made of tinder and sticks, bad place for a fire. Sweat coated her body, and sooty, hot air burned her nose.

"Roman," she gasped, and the acrid, burning air seared her throat. Beth sputtered and coughed, crawling toward the door. "Please."

"No." Greg's hand clasped her ankle and yanked.

Caught off guard, Beth went down, face planting into the floor, too weak and oxygen deprived to fight. *Don't stop.* She kicked her free foot, catching him with her heel.

She wasn't sure what she hit—his head? Shoulder? Didn't matter. She surged forward, crawling through the fiery haze. "Roman."

Greg jumped on her, slamming her to the ground. He wrapped his arms around her chest and squeezed.

Face smashed into the tile, she tried to blink away the stars exploding in her head. The lightheadedness was consuming. But on the other side of that blast zone was Roman. "Get off me!"

Greg shoved a gun under her chin. "Who are you?"

She rolled. He rolled with her. Her weak knee to his groin missed its crotch shot. Beth's muscles quivered from exertion and lack of oxygen. Everything felt fuzzy. Then the bastard drew back and pistol-whipped her temple. Splitting, screaming pain ripped through her head. Greg fell on top of her.

She tried to push him off her. Roman appeared out of nowhere and dove over her, taking Greg with him. Coughing and hacking, Beth rolled behind the hutch.

The two men fought hard. Greg's gun was gone. Fists flew. Greg slammed Roman into a wall then searched the floor, while Roman dropped, sputtering and gasping.

Greg straightened, holding a gun. He moved the weapon constantly, trying to stay on Roman while scanning the room. "Who are you?"

The air was too hot. Another crash came behind them. Part of the wall came down. Roman rose to his knees and spotted her. He skittered to cover but kept his eyes on her. His mouth was moving, but her ringing ears didn't allow any sound to come through. Was he saying *Cash?*

Greg continued his inquisition. Who did they work for? Why were they there? He probably wanted to know what loose ends needed tying after he killed them.

Roman threw a flashbang blast in the far corner. Greg shot blindly toward the bright explosion. Roman abandoned his cover, crawling toward the crumbling wall. Beth kept an eye on Greg as the man faced the wrong direction. Roman returned quickly, pulling an unconscious Cash behind him and leaving him behind a piece of furniture.

Greg spun and fired again at the opposite wall, and Roman lunged for Beth. He grabbed her and held her close to his chest.

He sounded ragged and wheezy. Fire spread along another wall. Roman unholstered a gun from his thigh and popped a couple rounds into the ceiling.

"We have to go," Beth urged.

"Hang tight. Fuck, it's hot."

"It's getting worse." She pulled her scarf up over her face.

Greg thumped some rounds into the hutch.

Roman looked at her. "Gotta get you out of here."

She shook her head. "Cash first."

"I know. Shit—"

More shots hit the hutch. Greg's aim—or guesswork—was getting better, and he must've reloaded.

The air was too smoky, and Beth's skin burned from the nearby fire.

Would opening the windows help? Or would the fresh oxygen fuel the fire? Shit! She didn't know what to do.

Roman popped up then dropped down. "Where is that fucker?"

"You have to get Cash out."

"You too, babe. Where... is that... fucker?" Roman mumbled. He leaned back, blood seeping from his forehead, and pinched the bridge of his nose.

They needed help. She didn't think Titan was coming anytime soon. Those that had been near had no doubt gone after the nuke.

"Roman, listen to me. We have to get Cash out."

"Know, babe. Gotta keep you alive, too. Where the fuck is Naydenov?"

Had the smoke gotten Greg? Roman needed to hurry.

"Roman, you have to know. Nicola. She's—"

"Kinda busy right now."

"Roman. Listen to me." She sputtered and coughed. "Cash is going to be a daddy. You—" She coughed again, not able to stop. "An uncle."

His eyes widened. "What?"

Sleep and heat were pulling her into the dark. Her mouth was dry, and her nostrils burned.

"Beth..." His voice seemed to come from far away.

"Nic's pregnant," she managed.

Roman pushed up on one arm, looking at where he'd hidden Cash. But Beth couldn't keep her eyes open anymore.

A roar echoed in her ears. She knew without seeing that Roman had left her, charging off to find Greg and save Cash. More gunfire rang out. An explosion and the sound of shattering glass jolted her awake. The smoldering fires exploded into violent red and orange flames. Smoke swirled rapidly.

Feeling far, far away, she spotted Roman standing in the inferno. He was moving Cash toward the windows. Men on ropes flew through the openings. They had Cash out before she could process that Titan had finally arrived. Then Roman was above her, around her. His strong arms lifted her to his chest and he carried her to a window.

Three floors up, they couldn't jump. And she didn't know where the rappelling men had gone. Her skin sizzled. The air burned her lungs. Rough hands jostled her. They propped up her body, manhandled her head. Something wrapped around her head and—

Air.

She gasped. *Air.* Opening her eyes, she realized someone had put a mask over her face. In front of her, Roman wore one as well. They huddled on the floor, against the wall. Her throat burned, and he pulled her tighter, his grip weak but strong enough. Beth could barely hold her head up, so she stopped trying and curled into him.

What felt like years passed, then Roman stood, pulling her up with him. He staggered to the broken window and hooked his legs outside the sill. The thump, thump, thump of a nearby chopper registered over the dull ringing in her ears.

Roman lifted her then laid her down. *Tied her down?* Confusion clouded her mind.

Roman gave a thumbs up, and she was jerked up. *To the chopper.* In a basket.

It made more sense as she got her bearings. But Roman needed out more than she did. His injuries seemed worse. She tried to reach for him but her hand was restrained.

Her mind drifted again, then she was in the chopper, out of the basket, and surrounded by familiar faces. An explosion ripped in the background, and her headache screamed.

Beth licked her lips, trying to find the words to save the man she loved. "Please help him."

CHAPTER 45

ROMAN HAD JUMPED FOR A line right before the fire hit a mother lode of weapons. It was a miracle they'd gotten out alive from a building that had gone down in flames. Now, he perched in the cramped quarters of the chopper as they flew low and fast. They would have a while until they landed, transfered to a plane, and got back in the air before a pack of armed, missile-launching rebels in a bad mood showed up to complicate their swift exit. So they were hauling ass.

Beth had lunged at him the second he was on board, and Brock had had to peel her off to do a once-over. As soon as that was done, she'd stayed tucked against him. Other than the occasional raised eyebrow from the guys, no one said a word. Everyone's focus was primarily on Cash, who was worse off than Roman wanted to admit.

Jared barked orders to the team that tracked the codes and weapons. Brock hovered over Cash, complaining about his vitals and cursing when nothing changed. Roman belted Beth into a seat then moved to perch near the door.

Every few minutes, her eyes would flit over to Cash then Roman. Tears would brim, and she would look away. They were feet apart in the chopper's belly, but it might have well been miles. She was shutting down.

Screw that. They would be fine. Cash wasn't going anywhere. As sure as this day had sucked, Cash wasn't leaving Nicola single and alone with a baby on the way. Roman's stomach twisted. A baby... that was heavy enough to take in, but the idea that Cash didn't know, that he wouldn't know...

"Needs an MRI," Brock announced.

Jared scowled. "What are we dealing with?"

"Hell if I know. After recently sustaining a brain trauma? This again? Lack of oxygen? No telling. We need a—"

"No telling *what?*" Roman growled at Brock.

"We're pushing thirty minutes."

"What does that matter?"

Brock looked from Cash to Jared then back to Roman. "Get him to a hospital 'cause I don't know what the shit we're dealing with. Swelling, bleeding, localized, widespread? No idea."

"Fuck!" Roman slammed his hand on the floor.

Beth's face scrunched, and tears flowed down her face. "I'm sorry," she whispered.

He couldn't hear her voice, but he knew what she'd said. It was written all over her face.

Roman crawled around Jared and bent next to Brock, who was hovering over Cash. "I need a minute."

Brock nodded and stepped back.

Roman bent and spoke low to Cash. "We've been through too much hell for this shit to take you out." Roman dropped his head back, staring at the panel above their heads. Then he pulled his headset off. "Cash. So help me God if you leave her, I'll—"

"Roman, man. Don't touch him." Brock said.

Roman looked down, not realizing that he had gripped Cash's chest.

"If he's in there," Brock said, "he might hear you."

If he's in there? "Fuck you, Brock. He's in there."

"I get it." Brock's hands went up. "Just don't move him."

Roman looked over at Beth. She had her head turned, but he could see the tears rolling down her cheeks.

Roman bent over Cash again. "Fight it, dude. You're a fighter. Too strong for shit like this to bring you down."

He could've sworn Cash's jaw flexed. Or maybe the chopper had shifted. Roman needed Cash to be okay, needed to save him for Nicola, the sister he couldn't save when she'd abandoned him years ago. This was one of those full-circle moments, and Roman had to make it okay.

Jared gave a thumbs-up to Brock. "We've got a while, but we're okay to head to Landstuhl."

Roman went back to Cash. "I know you're in there. I lost Nic once. I'm not losing my second Garrison." If Nicola counted as a first. "She's pregnant, buddy. You're—" His voice broke. "Fight for your baby, for your woman."

Roman waited, sure Cash's eyes would fly open. Nothing happened, and Roman's world began to gray. He shifted so Brock could return to Cash's side. Roman slipped his headset back on and looked at Beth. She was zoned out. The people he cared about were falling apart, and there was nothing he could do to stop it. Nothing.

Jared put a hand on his shoulder. "Roman."

He shrugged it off. "Back off."

"Easy there. Calm your—"

Roman ignored him. He had to fix this. He bent, took the rage building inside him, and threw it at Cash. "Do not leave her, goddamn you!"

Cash's eyelashes fluttered.

"Did you see that?" Brock asked.

"Keep him going," Jared ordered.

Roman couldn't swallow past the knot in his throat. He dropped next to Cash. "Wake up and go home to your girl. You're having a baby." Nothing happened. No more rustling eyelids. Nothing. "You're going to be a dad, man."

Cash's closed eyes pinched. Then nothing.

"What'd you say?" Brock asked. "Whatever it was, do it again."

"Roman?" Beth's small voice almost killed him. "Did you tell him?"

Roman nodded, holding her eyes. He needed Cash to be okay for Beth, too. He had to fix this for all of them.

"Tell him again. Wait." She looked at Jared. "Get Nicola to tell him."

Jared frowned. "What?"

Roman glanced at Cash then said, "Nic's pregnant."

No one said a word, and Roman felt long, sad thumps of his heart. God, getting Nicola on the line was going to be awful.

Jared switched channels on his radio, covering his mouth while he spoke. Brock nodded, then Boss Man switched back. "Get her on the line."

Minutes passed. Finally, Jared pointed to his headset, then to Roman, and held up two fingers. Roman switched to channel two, and his gut sank.

"What the hell is going on?" Nicola asked. "Parker? Jared? Who the hell is on the line?"

"Nicola." He swallowed. "Nic—"

"Roman?" She gasped. "Where's Cash?"

"Nic—"

"No, no, no. Where's Cash? Tell me! Where's Cash?"

"He's fine. It'll be okay, just listen to me."

"What is going on, Roman?"

"Calm down, sweetheart."

"Roman! Don't you dare tell me—"

"I know you're pregnant."

"Oh God! No! Where's Cash?"

"He's with me. He's sleeping, hon, and he needs to hear your voice."

"Oh, God." She moaned. "Roman, no. Please."

"He's okay, Nic. And he's going to be better when he hears your voice." Roman swallowed the ache in his throat. "You've got to do this for him. Got me?"

Forever ticked by through one long sob. Then Nicola cleared her throat and said, "Put the headset on him, and get off this channel."

"Alright."

"Roman?"

"Yeah?"

"You're okay?" she asked.

"Yeah."

"Good. Please. Don't let me lose him."

He nodded, even though she couldn't see. "Give me a three count, and he's all yours. You talk to him until we land. Three…" Roman slipped off the headset.

All around him, everyone switched channels as Jared held up four fingers. Roman put the headset on Cash's head, and then they went silent. Minus the rotor blades, there wasn't a sound.

Roman settled next to Beth and put a hand on her knee. She rested hers on top of his, and when he looked up, her sweet face looked tortured.

Beth squeezed Roman's hand and mouthed, "I love you like that."

CHAPTER 46

BETH HAD A SMOKE-SCENTED ARM draped over her face when she heard boots walk in. The night before, Jared had been in and out of her room. The rest of the boys had said their hellos and goodbyes last night or that morning. All except Roman.

Today, she'd washed up in her bathroom sink because taking a shower seemed like too much work. Then, she put together a plan to go find Roman and say… a lot of things. Mostly because the last thing that she'd said to him was something akin to her undying love. He hadn't responded, hadn't said a damn word, just kept his hand on her knee and squeezed.

Really, she shouldn't be nervous. Hell, he'd said he loved her. But never, not once, did he compare anything to Cash and Nicola. They were kinda the rock stars of love. Sappy, happy, sexy, lovestruck. And now, having a baby. *That* was quite the comparison. And it was *exactly* how she felt.

So when she heard boots, her heart sped up. Slowly, she pulled her arm down. Roman. And wow, was he a man. Even after the hell they'd been through, he walked in looking tougher than hell and hotter than the devil. Beth bit her lip because she still rocked the hospital gown and had used commercial-grade paper towels to give herself a soldier shower from a sink.

"Hey, pretty girl." He sat on the edge of the bed. "You okay?"

She nodded. "You?"

"Exhausted. Feel like shit"

"Me too."

His dark-brown eyes ran over her. "Make room, babe."

Scooting to the side, she sighed when he lay down next to her. His arm went around her shoulders, and she burrowed into him.

"Where's your hospital gown?" she asked.

He chuckled. "I opted out of that look once the doc said I wasn't dying."

"You check on Cash?"

"Yeah." His jaw flexed.

"And... what'd they say?"

"The bump on his head from the accident didn't help the bump from yesterday. The smoke inhalation... his brain needs rest. Or some shit like that. Nic's on her way out. Jared's making arrangements to get him home."

"This is all my fault."

Roman shook his head. "No."

"If—"

"Beth, babe. We made a decision to work these jobs long ago. And Cash and I made a decision to work this job in particular, even though we weren't cleared to go."

"What!" She jerked back, letting guilt make room for anger. "You weren't... why?"

Roman shrugged.

She slugged him in the chest. "You assholes."

"What?"

"You could've gotten yourself killed. Cash is in bad shape. All because—"

"Because there was a fuckin' nuclear weapon out there, and I didn't trust it to anyone else but Titan. I *am* Titan. So that's how that works."

She tried to inch out of his iron hold. "Suicide mentality. If you don't kill yourself now, you'll kill yourself later. *This* is why I stayed away from you."

"Stop it, Beth."

Her chest felt tight. Why did she have to love him so damn much? "Can you just go away? I need to sleep."

"Fuck, no, babe," he growled into her temple.

"Roman—"

"Everyone dies. Facts of life."

"Not soon, they don't. Not by their own hand or because they're too stupid to walk away when they should."

He turned in the bed, squared her to him, and narrowed his eyes. "I'm not *him*. You realize that, right? Say you get that."

Balling her hand into a fist, Beth nailed him in the chest. It hurt her sore muscles more than anything else, frustrating her to no end. "You're all the same."

"Nah."

"Condescending, cavalier asshole." She pushed back until she couldn't get any farther because the bed railings fenced her in. If she could scream and run away, she'd feel better. She could—

"Beth. Chill out."

She could never see him again. That would fix everything. Just like she should've done in the beginning. God, she was wrong not to have learned her lesson from Logan. "I hate you all."

"You can hate him all you want."

"I didn't say *just* him. You, too."

"You don't hate me." He laughed, antagonizing her to the point of madness.

"What the hell is your problem? Get out of my bed. Get... get out of my life already. I'm done."

Roman put two very strong hands on her shoulders and held her still. "Eyes up here."

"Go away."

"Eyes."

She huffed and glared at him. "What?"

"Love sucks, pretty girl. Love sucks whether it's family or friends or *you*. It fuckin' hurts. But—"

"I don't need some psycho-babble from a lunatic."

"But when you've got it, you own it. So even with you being all crazy woman right now, you're worth the headache, the ups and downs. Figure out who you really are. Not who the CIA wants you to be or what you're dying to avoid. Figure out you, then you're supposed to be with me. Simple." He got out of the bed. "Hell, you already know the answer. You already *said* the answer."

"Said what?"

His face darkened, something playing there that she couldn't name. "You looked at a dying man whose woman was doing whatever she could to keep him alive *via a headset*. Her heart was bleeding. Fuck, *my* heart was bleeding, and I saw your tears. You want to talk desperation? You want to see, to hear, to fear? That was them. And you, Beth Tourne, said you loved me *like that*. So don't think I don't know what's going on with you and me. Don't think I don't know where your head's at or where we're going. I know. It's you who has to figure your shit out."

She stared at him. Hundreds of thoughts ran through her mind as she replayed his words and let the truth of them soak in. Beth bit her lip. "You have your shit figured out?"

He chuckled, shaking his head. "Yeah, babe. I do." He stepped forward and kissed her cheek. "But you don't. So think on it. Realize what you know."

"Realize what I know…" she repeated.

He nodded. "I'm headed over to check on Cash and see what the plan is to get home."

"Um…" But Beth lost her thought when his fingertips traced her jaw. He pushed her hair behind her ear, drifting his touch over her cheeks. What did she know? Starting small, working her way up—that seemed like a plan. "I hate my condo."

"I would too." He sat back on her bed. "But you've already told me that. We already know what we're doing about that."

Yeah… yeah, they did. She was moving in with him. If he didn't toss her aside for being nuts and having some kind of PTSD reaction to him risking his life. "I'm sorry that I'm all over the place. It's just—"

The door flew open. Mr. Jasper stood there, red faced and narrowed eyes. He came toward her as if he were planning to tear her hospital-gown-clad ass out of bed and drag her straight to Langley. "Miss Tourne."

"Whoa! Hey, buddy." Roman jumped up and moved between Jasper and Beth when the door flew open again.

Jared this time. "Jasper," he growled, "you and me, in the hall. Now."

"Go away, Westin."

"Try the fuck again," Jared snapped.

Jasper glared at her. "Everyone out. I need a word with Miss Tourne."

"Out?" Roman's hostility was nearly palpable. "Recalibrate your approach, asshole."

Jasper tried to step around Roman. "Excuse me."

What a mistake that was. Roman caught the man by the shoulder, fingers flexing into Jasper's pressure point. "Tone it down, or you're out."

Jared stepped next to Roman, creating a two-person-wide fence of muscle. "You already know how I feel about bureaucratic, pencil-pushing wannabe spooks, Jasper. She's on my clock. She's my girl, so you take it up with me."

Roman let go, and Jasper rolled his newly released shoulder.

Beth swung her legs off the side of the bed. "What is going on?"

Roman barely turned his head. "Nothing now."

Exasperated and exhausted, she tried again. "Then what *was* going on?"

"I lost a good man," Jasper said.

"No, asshole." Roman's face twisted. "You lost a bad handler who left serious questions you need to be looking into."

"The Agency will deal with its own business," Jasper said. "Beth, you're with me. Get dressed."

"The hell she will." Roman puffed out his chest.

She got to her feet and put her hands on her hips. "You—"

Jasper cut her off. "We've been through your role, Miss Tourne. Pretty, partying, piece of ass. Get dressed—"

Roman's fist flew, catching Jasper's jaw, before she could tell the man to go to hell.

Jasper rebounded, snarling at Jared with his perfect white teeth. "Get your bulldog on a leash."

Bulldog? Greg had said that, Evan had said that, now Jasper. She found it curious, for such a specific term.

Boss Man shrugged. "More like a pit bull, but I see nothing wrong."

Beth stepped forward. "Excuse me." Jared moved aside, and she was face to face with Jasper. "You never got me from day one."

"Doesn't matter. You have a job. You do your job."

"I deserve respect."

He chuckled. "You drink cocktails and suck dick for foreign secrets. I'm not sure where you—"

She slapped Jasper. "Try again."

"Bitch." Jasper's retaliatory hand went up but stopped. He eyed Roman and Jared. "When you get back to Langley, report to the mail room."

"You're a chauvinistic waste of space. Put me in the mail room, and I'm done."

"Not much of a market for socialite intelligence officers."

"I'm done. My resignation letter will be delivered." She pointed at the door. "Get out of my hospital room."

Jasper cackled. "You're a joke is what you are. Unskilled—"

"I'm off the charts in every testable spectrum and then some. *You* lost out."

"She does have a hell of a resume," Jared added.

Jasper stood his ground. "You don't just leave the Agency, Miss Tourne."

"She does when there's a job offer." Jared walked toward the door. "Beth, I think you have this handled. I'll touch base with you later."

She turned back to Jasper. "No matter what my next move is, I know it's not with you. Get out of my room."

"You'll regret this."

"I already regret too much in life to give a flip. Out." She jabbed her finger at the door again.

The veins in Jasper's neck protruded, his face reddening. "This won't be the last word on this incident."

"Out!"

He turned and left. As soon as the door shut, she sank back on the bed.

Roman clapped slowly. An I'll-be-damned smiled played on his face. "Nicely done. And I think you just got a job offer from Titan."

Flopping back on the pillow, she stared at the ceiling. "Maybe a temporary thing while Nic's out."

"You okay?"

She looked up at him. "I didn't do anything like that for the job."

"I know." Roman plopped down beside her on the bed, kicking his legs up. "Scoot over."

She did then ducked under his arm and let him hold her. "Do you want to start over? Just... start everything over?"

He leaned over to kiss the top of her head. "You mean like, 'hi my name is... nice to meet you' bullshit?"

"Yeah." Because if they started over, if he could forget about how she'd cried over Logan, cried over the future, over them... if he could just see her as a normal woman with a normal job who had fallen for her hero, then maybe they'd have a real future.

"Nah."

Confused, she tried to read his face. "Why? This has been... messy."

"It's been fun." He tilted his head, running his hand over her arm.

"Fun?"

"I jump out of planes and kill bad guys for a living. You think I wanted a paint-by-numbers kind of girl?"

"I think the problem is I *was* that kind of girl."

"Not a chance. You were deep cover and let it get too far for the wrong reasons. I think we've both peeled back the layers and found you. Maybe found me, too."

She looked away. "Maybe..." She loved him. He loved her. She was willing to risk it all again. "You still want to move in together? That was one of those in-the-moment ideas. Rushed? Impractical?"

Roman smiled in a way that made the dimple on his chin deepen. "When you know, you know. That's far from impractical."

"And you know? Like *know*-know?"

He nodded.

"How?"

"It's pretty simple. I just know."

"I just know, too."

"Wild, right?" He squeezed her again. "I'm going to marry you one day. Just you wait."

Her eyes went wide. She'd already had the whole white-dress, walk-down-the-aisle thing, and she didn't want that again. But... she did want him. Forever.

Roman added, "But I'll take it one step at a time."

"I... could do that." The idea worked its way around in her head. The more she thought about it, the more she liked it. "What if..."

"What if what?"

"We really did one day?"

"Already know it's going to happen."

Oh? Maybe she did too, and what was the point of waiting for waiting's sake? "I don't want a ring. Or an engagement. Or anything. Just you." She held her breath. "When you know, you know. So...?"

His eyes narrowed. "So? Like *now* so?"

She nodded.

"Nope. Nuh-uh." He shook his head, letting out a harsh laugh that nearly made her panic. "No way did you just ask me to marry you. I'm a bit more of a traditionalist than that."

"So... you think I'm nuts?"

"I think you're perfect." He pulled her against his chest. "But I don't think you're going to get to do that. Fuckin' trying to propose to me. Shit."

"So you do it." She nudged him.

"Are you kidding me?"

Beth shook her head. "You've been right about us. About everything."

"Right now?"

She nodded.

"Fuckin' serious?"

"Totally."

Roman stood then dropped to one knee. "Beth Tourne—"

"Holy. Shit." She'd almost died today. And now this? She couldn't wrap her head around her life. God, she loved him, in a major, bleeding heart kinda way.

He laughed. "Love your crazy and your freckles. Love how you taste, how you kiss. How you drive me to the edge of sanity. Life's wild with you. *Wild.* And I love it, like I love you. I want my ring on your finger, my name on your name. Marry me, babe."

"Oh, God…" That was quite possibly the most perfect, most Roman thing she'd ever heard.

"That's not a yes or no."

"Baby." She smiled, feeling it all the way to her heart.

"Already know the answer, but say it anyway, pretty girl."

"Yes!" She grabbed him, pulling him up and into a kiss.

His mouth found hers; her tongue touched his. Her body sighed into him as Roman laid her down, holding her to him.

The door clicked open. "Oh!" Nicola said. "Oh, okay. I'll come back. You two are… busy."

Beth looked over Roman's shoulder, whispering in his ear, "Our secret? Until everyone's okay and on their feet?"

He kissed her neck. "Sounds good."

"Wait, Nic." Beth giggled as his scruff scratched her face. "Sorry. We're good. He's just… moving. What's up?"

Roman grumbled in her ear, "Not sure about your definition of good."

"Seriously, Roman. I can hear you." Nicola groaned. "Anyway, Cash is awake."

"Yeah?" Roman sat up, then hopped off the bed, and nodded at Nicola's stomach. "He knows?"

"Funny about that. He knew before I told him today." Nicola crossed the room and hugged him. Tears were in her eyes. "Thank you for saving him… saving us."

Roman's arms slowly wrapped his sister. "Us?"

Nicola hugged him then stepped back. "Without him, I'm nothing."

Roman hand went halfway to his bicep, his Nicola tat, but he stopped and cracked his knuckles instead. "Job well done then." He turned back to Beth and held out his hand. "So, if everyone's on their feet, want to go say hi to Cash?"

She took his hand. "What's the fun of a secret if you can't share?"

CHAPTER 47

DEEP IN THE HEART OF Langley, the utilitarian room was cold, completely devoid of life or personality. A large contraption that reminded Beth of a dentist's chair sat next to a table with machines, computers, sensors... the works. God, Beth hated this. Even though she had nothing to hide, she *hated* submitting to a polygraph. It wasn't the piece of cake folks saw on TV. This was a spy-worthy one, meant to get into her head by reading her body.

The poly technicians came in as she wondered who was on the other side of the one-way mirror.

A man approached. He didn't smile, no small talk, just a nod for her to stand next to the chair. "Shoes off, sit down, lie back."

She knew the drill and stepped out of her shoes and into the wannabe dentist chair. Then he went to work. Oxygen monitor on her finger. Sensors to catch her perspirations and pulse. Every time she shifted in the chair, it was noted. Straps went around her chest, a hat on her head, and a patch over her eye to monitor her pupils. The CIA was nothing if not thorough.

Actually, no. That wasn't the case, because if they had been as thorough as they should've been, then she might not have been here to begin with.

Once she was hooked up, another man came over to administer her questions, while the first man took his place at the table.

"State your name."

"Beth Tourne."

"State your full name."

"Elizabeth Catherine Tourne."

"Eye color?"

"Green," she replied, knowing they were going to walk her through a few rapid-fire baseline questions.

"Right or left handed?"

"Right."

"Single, married, or widowed?"

Ah, now they were getting to the good stuff. She had expected them to jump right into Roman to gauge her reactions, but this worked for shock value, too. "Widowed."

"When did you first meet Evan Nathaniel?"

"Minutes before the first lady's birthday event."

"And how long after that did you begin to work with Gregori Naydenov?"

"Approximately fifteen minutes."

"What is the extent of your relationship with Joseph Jasper?"

"He offered me the Naydenov assignment."

"And when did you accept?"

"Never. They put me in play, and I went with it."

"When did you sleep with Naydenov?" he asked without missing a beat.

"Never."

"When did you have sexual intercourse with Naydenov?"

"Never."

"When did you have oral sex with Naydenov?"

Her frustration grew. "Never."

"When did you sleep with Evan Nathaniel?"

She rolled her eyes. Jasper must have put some lies in his report. "I didn't sleep with either of them."

"But you did sleep with Roman Hart?"

And there it was. That was an expected question, but it still caught her off guard. "Yes."

"Did you question Naydenov's guilt?"

"Yes."

"Did you have feelings for Naydenov?"

"No."

"When did you decide to work with Nathaniel to sell government information and technology to Naydenov?"

"I didn't."

"When did you realize Nathaniel and Naydenov were working together?"

"I didn't. I still don't know what happened there." But she had a few guesses.

"Evan Nathaniel and Gregori Naydenov were moving money and stolen intelligence. When did you begin to assist?"

"Never."

"And how much did you personally benefit from that relationship, financially?"

She stopped her eye roll. "None."

"Explain your offshore account with multiple recent deposits."

She frowned. *That*, she didn't know. So Evan and Greg had been playing her, setting her up to take the fall if the need ever arose. "I didn't know about them."

"Explain why you struck the senior officer on the Naydenov project."

She raised her eyebrows and looked at her interrogator. "Jasper?"

"Eyes straight ahead. Why did you strike Jasper?"

"Because some assholes deserve it." Ignoring the request not to, she glanced at the man. There was the slightest uptick in his non-smile.

"Thank you for your time, Ms. Tourne."

The man at the table came over and unhooked her from the polygraph equipment. It could've gone worse. Hell, they could've waterboarded her. So Evan and Greg had been in bed together. That was as much of a confirmation as she'd ever get.

Beth stepped into her shoes and left the deep, dark hole where they'd gone relatively easy on her. As she rounded the corner, she saw Jasper huffing his way from the mouth of the hallway. Now *that* was interesting.

They passed each other without a word. Then, seconds later, she heard a muffled, "Bitch."

Whatever. She'd given her notice and set her terms. Beth would work some CIA projects. She'd accepted the opportunity to work on some Titan projects, but mostly she planned to spend the next few weeks sorting out her life. Seeing what she really wanted. Seeing what was really her and not what had been expected of her.

She walked past her desk, waved to some coworkers, and kept going until she was at her car. She had turned in the Lexus with a polite thank-you, along with the keys to her condo. That same afternoon, she'd jumped into Roman's truck, and they'd gone to a car dealership, where he haggled until she got a new Jeep. It was exactly what she wanted.

Her phone buzzed as she pulled out of the complex and hit the highway. Roman's name was on the display. She answered, "Hey, you."

"You headed home?"

"Yup. Soon as I knock out some errands" Her stomach fluttered because, even though they'd made the jump and moved her into his place, it was only just now sinking in that his home was her home. That felt pretty nice. It wasn't his place anymore. It was *their* place, with lots of pictures and color and millions of new memories in the making.

"I'm thinking pizza and TV."

"As long as it involves a glass of wine, I don't care what we do."

"Sounds good, babe."

A couple of hours later, she was on the couch with Roman. His long-neck beer, her glass of wine, and a pizza sat on the coffee table. Food was nice, but nuzzling against him while he surfed the channels was better.

Something caught her attention. "Wait. Go back."

He flipped the channel, and she saw a headshot of Jasper. The screen flashed to the local news coverage of a deadly accident.

"Another spook bites the dust," Roman mumbled. He grabbed his beer and went back to flipping the channels. "You'd think the fuckers would learn you always get caught."

She bit her lip, nodding.

"You okay?"

"Yeah." The CIA cleaned up their messes in permanent ways. "Just hits close to home."

He put his beer down and took her chin in his hand. "What's up?"

"You just never know who you work with. What their agenda is. Of the four people on that project, I'm the only one still alive."

"You're the only one that wasn't a piece of shit. Naydenov, piece of shit. Nathaniel, piece of shit. Jasper, piece of shit. See?"

"I guess."

He tilted his head. "No one knew, babe. But when they did, the Agency took care of business."

"True."

"Honestly, I'd be stoked as shit if you never took another CIA job."

"Why?"

He shrugged. "With Titan, you know what you get. You know Boss Man and the team have your back. Those Farm boys? Nothing's a guarantee."

"Titan's a guarantee?"

"I'm a guarantee."

Roman was her guarantee. She sighed happily. "I like that."

"Good." He picked up his beer. "Besides, if we're going to get married one day and have babies, you think I trust the CIA's ass to watch my woman?" He shook his head. "That'd be a no. Titan, yes. Me, absolutely. Them, no."

He'd just laid it out there, making her throat close up. "You want to have babies with me?"

Roman let out a deep chuckle. "O' course. I'm signing up for the package deal. House. Wife. Kids. Whatever else comes with it. All the trimmings, good or bad."

If her throat had been closing up before, it didn't matter, because her lungs had just given up. Her teary eyes burned, but she didn't want the waterworks to start. She wanted all of the emotion that was choking her to marinate inside her, just in case she ever forgot what amazing felt like.

"I also want you naked and in bed. So finish up your pizza, pretty girl, and move your ass." He leaned over and kissed her, bringing her back to life.

One giant gulp of wine later, she hopped off the couch and hauled ass to their room. He was hot on her tail, and that was exactly the way she needed to top off her night.

EPILOGUE

THE SPARKLING LIGHTS DANGLED, CRISSCROSSING the living room. The Christmas tree was decked out in dazzling reds and golds from top to bottom.

Beth kicked back on the couch with a bottle of water. "I'm done!"

"That's the third time you've said that," Roman said, walking into the living room. He eyed her final decorations. "Looks good."

"Well." She grabbed the remote and turned on music. "White Christmas" flooded the room with classic holiday crooning. "For real this time."

He wandered the room she'd spent too much time decorating, perhaps appreciating that she'd spent way too much time doing it. His lips upturned as if he were trying to hide a smile. "Glad you're done. People will be here any minute."

Maybe she'd gone overboard. "They'll either love it, or they won't. All that matters is I do." She patted the couch. "Hang out with me for a minute."

"You ready?" He dropped down, and she locked her pinky around his.

"Does it look like I am?" Her cranberry-colored dress was frillier than her normal, but it matched how she felt about the room. A fire roared, the tree sparkled, and poinsettias manned the corners. Perfect.

He tilted his head, letting his gaze stroke over her. "Maybe?"

She laughed, kicked off her shoes, and curled into him. "It even smells like Christmas in here."

Her phone buzzed. Text message from Nicola: *Almost there!*

Beth tossed her phone down. "Nic's excited."

"She's easily excitable." He shook his head, smiling. "My folks said they were running late."

"Mine are always late."

"Okay, considering… everything." He waved his hand around the room. "I have a present for you."

She straightened, grinning because she had known he would, and she'd been keeping an eye out so she could shut that down. "No! We said no presents."

"Sometimes things don't go like you plan, party girl," he said, which was funny because nothing ever went like she planned. He reached under the couch. When he sat up, wrapped box in hand, he couldn't have looked more confident. "Here."

She tore the ribbon off, trashed the paper, and was stunned. "Oh wow…"

The picture he'd snapped with his phone after telling her to be the real her, right before they'd first gone to bed. He'd had it framed. Their faces stared in different directions as she half-scowled, half-laughed, and Beth remembered the day vividly. Not only because she'd slept with Roman, but because he'd called her out for hiding from her past. How true that was, and now, here she was, completely found and alive.

He nodded at the picture. "I figured that was the only chance I'd ever have to get you in a white dress."

She laughed, play-slapping his chest. "It was cream."

"Looks white, babe."

He knew she'd done the white-dress thing before and wanted something different, something vibrant and colorful and exactly her. Well, exactly them. The doorbell rang.

He stood, pulling her up. "Show time."

"I love it. I really, really love it. Thank you." Beth popped onto her toes to give him a kiss. Then she slipped on her heels and walked with him to the door.

Jared, Sugar, and their daughter, Asal, stood outside. Asal was holding a box half her size with a lot of help from Sugar.

Beth scowled at Jared. "No presents, Boss Man."

"Hell, like Sugar wasn't buying you something. Call it a housewarming gift; I don't care."

Asal and Sugar headed toward the kitchen as Sugar called, "We brought disposable cameras, too. Kids will love 'em."

Jared hung back, a somehow caring scowl on his face. "You guys good?"

Better than good, but Roman just grumbled. Jared took that as an affirmative and went after Sugar. The door stayed open, and everyone started to pour in: Cash and Nicola, Rocco and Caterina. Both women had that unmistakable pregnancy glow.

Colby and Mia arrived with their kids, then Brock and Sarah with theirs. Parker showed up in a Santa hat, and then a couple of the Delta guys Roman had been working with while Cash was benched. At least Parker found some bachelor buddies in the Delta boys.

Beth's parents came in, then Roman's. There was family that would always be family from Logan's side, who were beyond thrilled to ring in the new chapter in Beth's life with holiday cheer. And there were friends from the Agency, friends from the real world. A couple of them also wore Santa hats. It was the who's who of everyone they loved.

The living room was filled to capacity, humming with Christmas cheer. Beth wandered to the end table where the picture of her and Roman at Nicola and Cash's wedding stood. She picked it up, rubbing her thumb over the glass, then went and found the framed picture Roman just gave her and placed the two pictures side by side.

Nicola walked over with cranberry juice in hand. "You look cute. Nice decorations."

"Looks good, right?" Beth bit her lip, loving how everything had turned out. Bright and vibrant, exactly how she felt. "Everything's perfect."

Jared walked to the center of the room and cleared his throat. Doing as Boss Man did, he became the center of attention with ease, and everyone dropped their conversations and turned to him. His grin didn't appear often, but there it was.

Nicola put her hands over her baby bump. "There goes Boss Man."

Oh God. Beth's heart jumped in her chest like she was about to swan dive into eternity. Well, she was. Her pulse quickened when Roman caught her eye from across the room and beckoned for her to come his way.

"You good?" Nicola asked.

"Hell, yes," Beth whispered.

Nicola patted her on the shoulder and followed Beth toward Roman, who was chatting with Cash. Cash winked.

"Alright," Jared said, "quiet down. It's not a party until I've had something to say."

A few laughs and cheers went up. The beer and the wine had started flowing almost immediately. The kids were two-handing Christmas cookies, Santa hats now on their heads. Everyone was relaxed, hanging out, and totally unprepared.

"Let's do this." He cracked his knuckles. "Titan. Delta. Friends and families."

If Beth thought the din had died down, she'd been wrong. The room went very quiet, very quickly. Beth could feel the wide eyes on her back, maybe even felt their jaws dropping. God, she loved a good surprise party. Roman took her hand and gave it a squeeze.

Jared's rare smile stayed in place. "We are gathered here tonight to celebrate Roman and Beth, two people who'd lay down their lives for you and each other. Hell, two people who were destined to be here today, getting married."

A couple of folks gasped. Colby gave a "Hooyah." Rocco and Brock did their versions of the same. All the kids started cheering for no other reason than the adults did, and Beth let Roman pull her into his thick arms. Some women wanted to stare at the man they were about to marry, but that wasn't her. She wanted to be held, wrapped tight and surrounded by him. Leaning back, she tilted her head when his cheek pressed against her temple. She sighed when his lips brushed the top of her ear.

"Luckiest guy here," he whispered.

Jared did his version of a ceremony. They recited the short vows, and then Jared crossed his arms, and announced to the hollering, clapping room, "Congratulations, Roman and Beth. Time to kiss your bride."

"Love you, Roman," Beth whispered.

Roman turned her, kissed her, dipped her back, and kissed her again as if there wasn't a soul in the room other than the pair of them. Long, hard, deep, and wet. She wrapped her arms tight and kept kissing him until the kids, and maybe some of the guys, screamed, "Ew!"

"Love you too." His lips traced against hers.

Finally, when she was standing on her own two feet again, the rounds of congratulations started.

"Thought this was a Christmas party." Rocco laughed. "Cat's gonna go into labor she's so damn excited."

Parker and Roman did some back slapping.

Parker gave an accusatory eye to Cash and Nicola. "You two knew?"

"Yup." Nicola bounced her little pregnant body up and down. "So we can get something by Parker."

"Not bad, huh?" Jared came up behind them. "Princess, looks like you've gained a few pounds."

Nicola punched him in the shoulder and laughed. "Funny. I'd hit you harder, but I'm hungry." She pecked Cash on the cheek and headed toward the kitchen. She returned seconds later with a slice of cake.

Cake? Beth frowned. "Where'd…?"

Sugar walked by, carrying two plates. "Like there could be wedding without cake."

Caterina followed with two cranberry juices. They met Nicola on the couch. Sugar sat in the middle, and Beth laughed at the three of them. She walked over, Jared following close behind.

"Drinking juice in solidarity with the girls?" Beth nodded to Sugar. "Very Christmassy."

Both Caterina and Nicola's heads turned toward the center of the couch. Nothing about Sugar was very Christmassy, and Beth knew it the second she said the words.

Jared leaned over and whispered into Beth's ear, "Told you she'd get what she wanted."

Sugar wanted... a baby? Sitting pretty in the middle of the couch, Sugar raised an eyebrow *and* her juice. "Cheers."

Beth's jaw fell along with Nicola's and Caterina's. All the kids ran around the room with disposable cameras, flashes going off along with the twinkle lights in the room.

Jared clapped Beth on the back. "Congratulations. You got a good one."

Beth shut her mouth, still trying to get her thoughts in order. "You too."

Roman came over and hugged her from behind. "Mrs. Hart."

Shivers raced down her back as she turned to face him. "You will never guess what I just found out."

A flash went off in their faces. "Say cheese!" Clara yelled a few seconds too late.

Beth saw floating lights for a second, then continued, "Our *officiant* is having a baby."

"Oh yeah?" He looked at Sugar, then hugged Beth close. "Lucky them."

"Say cheese!" another kiddo shouted at them.

"Cheese." Roman took Beth under his arm. He kissed her ear as the kid ran off. "We'll get you on that couch one day. Just like that."

Her stomach fluttered. Roman was going to make an amazing daddy.

"My turn," she said.

"For?"

"Presents."

He mocked playfully. "We said no presents."

"Lots of good making up that little rule did."

"Alright." He let her lean back in his embrace. "Where's my present?"

She pulled him toward the kitchen. They passed their friends, took a couple high fives, and chatted along the way about their surprise nuptials before they made it.

"Ready?" she asked as she opened a drawer and extracted an envelope. With a smile, she handed it to him. "Lucky *us*."

He turned the pink and blue envelope over in his hand. His eyes went wide then narrowed. When his face came up, he stepped closer to her. If she thought she'd ever seen Roman smile to his fullest before, she was wrong. He radiated. "Yeah?"

"Apparently, there's something in the water."

"Beth..." He looked at her sideways then opened the envelope and pulled out a black-and-white sonogram. "That's our baby?"

She nodded, eyes watering as she watched him stare at their child.

He circled his arms around her, pressing his lips to hers. "Package deal, all the trimmings."

THE END

I hope you enjoyed Hart Attack. To ensure you don't miss the next Titan book, text TITAN to 66866 to sign up for exclusive emails.

ACKNOWLEDGMENTS

Thank you to my family for supporting my passion. My dreams have come true because of your help.

Thanks to the readers and Team Titan. I promise you will never know how much you mean to me. I hope that I can return that joy and happiness. Romance readers are a special group. We believe in happily ever after and overcoming dark moments. Every day, every hardship, a good romance novel can help.

A shout out and thank you to my critique partners, JB Salsbury, Claudia Connor, Sharon Kay, and Racquel Reck. I continue to learn every day from you and am blessed to have the opportunity to work with you. Thanks also to Toshia Slade who has acted as eyes and ears on this book and Titan audio books.

Thank you to Rihaneh O-R, Kame Book Reviews, and Straight Shootin' Book Reviews for always showing Titan love. From the very start, they've shared a no-name author's work, and for that I am grateful.

A huge hug to JB Salsbury. She is one of a kind, and I'm lucky to say we share a brain. Not a single decision gets made without her heavy input. I simply love and adore her.

Hugs and thanks also to Claudia Connor. I'm so happy to see our books selling together. I can't love her any more than I do.

The Red Adept editorial team rocks! Thank you Lynn McNamee for jumping hurdles with me and helping Roman and Beth shine. Once again, Hot Damn Designs, did a spectacular job on the cover. Thanks to my retailer teams that stay behind the scenes and make magic happen.

Thank you to Tara Gonzalez and KP Simmon at InkSlinger for the help reaching new readers and for holding my hand when I panic. A huge shout out to Amy Atwell at Author E.M.S. for handling all the books, all my hiccups, and for doing so with a smile. The Titan production team is incredible.

Above all, thank you. Love with all my heart. XO.

ABOUT THE AUTHOR

Cristin Harber is a *New York Times* and *USA Today* bestselling romance author. She writes sexy, steamy romantic suspense and military romance. Fans voted her onto Amazon's Top Picks for Debut Romance Authors in 2013, and her debut Titan series was both a #1 romantic suspense and #1 military romance bestseller.

CPSIA information can be obtained
at www.ICGtesting.com
Printed in the USA
LVOW01s0925270316

480956LV00017B/793/P